Resurrected Trouble

by

Braxton DeGarmo

Christen Haus Publishing

COPYRIGHT

Cover design by Rocking Book Covers
For more information, go to **www.braxtondegarmo.com**

DEDICATION

This book is dedicated to all of those families who have lost loved ones under unusual circumstances. May God's peace be with you.

ACKNOWLEDGMENTS

As always, I again want to acknowledge and thank my dear wife, Paula, for her valuable proofreading skills, help and encouragement.

Many thanks as well to Lenda Selph for her expert proofreading.

Plus, a big thank you to my editor, Patrick LoBrutto, His feedback always makes my stories better.

And finally, my sincerest compliments to Adrijus Guscia for his incredible covers throughout the series.

ONE

As the sun rose for the seventh day, its scorching heat seemed to evaporate away even more of his strength. He was a man comfortable with the sea, but now, with no land in sight, perhaps it would be best to simply let the sea claim him. All he needed to do was let go.

Had he really survived a full week adrift?

The fools. He had told the boat's captain and crew to cooperate. He told them to ditch the fast boat, leaving a GPS locator aboard so they could find it later. He had a suitable and impossible-to-find hiding spot aboard the fishing vessel. Even infrared detection equipment wouldn't find his location surrounded by ice and their plentiful catch. Their paperwork was in order, and their excuse that engine problems had prompted their heading for the nearest port in Mexico was easily backed up. A special governor on the engine could duplicate the problem time and time again, as often as they needed to authenticate their claim to any intervening authority.

He stepped outside the bridge in time to see the drone coming their way. He screamed to the captain to release and move away from the fast boat on their port davit, but the man was attached to his expensive toy, despite the fact that its presence screamed "smugglers." The man's hesitation gave the drone time to come close enough that its markings as U.S. Coast Guard were clearly seen, close enough to see the fast boat. Maybe even close enough to see him.

As he rushed to the access of his hiding place, he heard the crew begin to shoot. The men had a death wish, something Abdullah did not share with his countrymen. As he secured his spot, he heard the splintering of wood as return fire from the Coast Guard began to shred the cabin and bridge of their vessel. Then came the whoosh of an RPG launch. He knew at that moment, should he survive the next ten minutes, he would not be celebrating with the captain and crew. And if he didn't, he would see them in Paradise.

Inside his waterproof cache, surrounded by the metal bins filled with ice and fish, he felt more than heard the boat explode around him. Allah protected him. The bins withstood the attack, and he believed he now floated free of the debris along with those containers. Yet, he couldn't leave his space just yet. The Coast Guard would be searching for survivors. He felt confident that there would be no others, but only by Allah's good will would the sailors not think to inspect the fish holding bins more closely.

He lost track of time inside the dark space where he lay supine. That claustrophobic world began to become more turbulent. The ice had no doubt melted, and the water it left behind began to toss and heave with every swell. With one sudden lurch he found himself upside down and his face planted against what had previously been the top of his hiding space.

Floating with the swells and cursing the sun, he now

recalled the sense of panic that had rushed through him at that moment. Panic was a foreign emotion to him. The fish bins no longer acted like their own little boat, displacing the sea and staying afloat. Whether upside down or sideways, they would begin to take on enough water to sink. In fact, it had felt as if they already were. The panic came from the thought of being dragged to a deep watery grave in a metal coffin of his own design.

In another instant, amid creaking and groaning of metal rubbing metal, he sensed his "casket" shooting upward and beginning to bob up and down. The image of a simple cork fishing bobber undulating in the wake of a boat replaced the panic.

But only for a second.

He found himself standing on his head in the rectangular cubicle. That meant the door was underwater. To open it now would flood the space with water. Or would it? Again, Allah's hand had intervened. If he could keep the container in its current position, he could escape, shut the door behind him, and keep the air trapped inside. What might have been his coffin became his flotation device.

Today, on day seven—or was it eight? —of his ordeal, he reconsidered the decisions he had made then. Sinking deep into cold water, he would become hypothermic before succumbing to a lack of oxygen in the chamber. It would have been a peaceful way to die. Of course, the cubicle's breaking away from the fish bins robbed him of that option.

Now, he barely had the strength to hold onto his bobber. His lips were chapped to the point of bleeding, and he had sores and scabs covering his scalp and shoulders.

When using his shirt to cover his head, his shoulders burned, and vice versa. Water surrounded him, but he was dying of thirst.

He closed his eyes and focused on saying his *dua*, his prayer to Allah to reach home safely. "*Alw bham a wbaa llrbhanwa tdwhb ab lsha yyghaadr 'llnyana ḥw bwal h alnḥ mld whww 'l a kll shyw'r qd yrsh aybṭwnn twamb wnḍ 'abnd wnr sajadrwny lḥr bmnaa ḥramdwn ṣndqa allahl w'khdyhr whndhṣhr 'bdh w hzm alaahḥlzhab wnḥ'dwh bk mn shrha wshr ahlha wshr ma fyha.*" I have come back, I have come back, I seek forgiveness from Allah with such a repentance that leaves me with no sin.

TWO

Through the fog of her breath, Summer Stanton watched the moving van with all of her belongings as it eased away from the snowy drive to her home in northern Virginia. Her time there at the Washington bureau had ended. In fact, her time as a mainstream media journalist had ended.

She felt a tinge of regret as the truck moved past the house that Richard Nichols had purchased . . . and died in, at her hand. The house remained unsold after his death. Of course, a questionable suicide, followed by the murder of the next owner would tend to trump "location, location, location" for any real estate deal.

She had grown fond of Richard, but he had come to learn too much about her. Of course, the whole Chappaquiddick story—that of seeking revenge for what had happened to her grandparents and father—had been only the beginning of the story. Richard had learned too much of her plan and became a tool, a way of dealing with Maggie Walther, as well as a way to gain favor with the Director, who had asked her to deal with him directly. A task that Maggie had balked at completing.

After the truck left her view, she returned to the house. She had a couple of things to do before leaving for New York City. First, the beginning of a makeover. She glanced at her phone for the time. The woman would arrive at any moment.

True to form, the doorbell rang moments later, and she greeted her longtime stylist, Erin, at the door. The woman, bundled up against the February cold, walked into the foyer, unzipped her parka, and stood, gazing at the empty space.

"Wow. This place is sooo empty." She then looked at Summer. "I still can't believe you're leaving us. You were really going places at the network."

Summer shrugged. "Sometimes life calls you toward a different direction. I'm tired of the rat race and want some time off. Who knows, maybe I'll write a tell-all memoir."

Erin's eyes widened. "Oooo, that sounds juicy."

"Not really," Summer replied, while thinking, *If you only knew.*

"Okay, so what do you want? The usual? Thin it and trim the split ends?"

Summer shook her head. "Nope. Lop it off, just off the shoulder."

She had expected the stunned look Erin now radiated her way. Her lustrous red hair, reaching to her lower back, had become something of a trademark for her, a branding she would no longer need. In fact, the long hair could become a vulnerability for her. She had at one point considered a complete buzz, going for a punk rocker look, but that would make her stand out when she would be required to blend in.

"Come on. Up to my old master bath. The styling chair is going with the house, so it's still there." Erin remained silent, and her feet seemed cemented to the imported terrazzo floor as Summer moved toward the main stairs. "Come on. Consider it a gift for charity. You can donate the hair to Locks of Love or something." She began to climb the steps, and Erin now followed.

With the first cut, Summer followed their progress in the mirror and noted tears welling up in the stylist's eyes. If the woman only knew what was coming, she might have balked altogether at the job.

"Such beautiful hair. Th-this seems almost criminal."

Summer held no such sentiment. Like so many things, her hair had been a tool to get where she wanted to be. Losing that hair aided her along the new path she now embarked upon.

Within ten minutes, those locks amounted to little more than a mountain on the floor. Eric took time to gather it up and place it into a bag.

"Let me even it up and then we'll wash it out."

Summer nodded. "Then, I want you to add some curl."

The woman smiled. The idea of adding some style appeared to appeal to her. "Yes, I think I know exactly the look to go for."

Thirty minutes later, Erin proclaimed, "Ta-daaa. What do you think?"

Summer inspected her new look in the large mirror, patting the curls to watch them spring. That was a new experience for her. Except for the occasional French braid, her long, straight hair had remained just that . . . long and straight. She really liked how she appeared, softer and much more feminine.

"I love it. Thank you, Erin. That wasn't so bad, now was

it?"

The stylist shrugged and, after giving Summer instruction on how to maintain the curls, collected her tools of the trade. Summer then led her back to the front door, producing five crisp $100 bills and handing them to the woman as Erin donned her winter garb.

Erin frowned. "Oh no. This is way too much. I've been honored to work with you over the years. Consider this one on the house." She tried to hand the money back.

Summer refused. "Nonsense. I happen to know you've had some car troubles lately and could use the extra cash."

Erin gave her a strange look, as if saying, *"How did you know..."*

"Hey, I'm not totally out of touch with mutual friends."

Erin smiled. "Thank you. It really will help." She turned to leave, but stopped. "Hey, if you're ever back in the area and need a cut or something, look me up. *That* one will be on me."

Summer nodded. "I'll keep that in mind. Drive safely." She watched the woman walk to her car and waved as she began to back out of the drive.

Summer returned to the master bath and gazed at her new style in the mirror. Yep, she really liked the look, but it, like her, would have to disappear. The high payment had more than one goal. Should she ever be asked, Erin would not forget just how Summer looked at this point.

She went to the linen closet and pulled out the items she had purchased the day before. After rereading the instructions—because this, too, was new to her—she began the process.

Stepping out of the shower half an hour later, she combed and dried her now ink black, nearly straight hair. She gave off more of a *La Femme Nikita* vibe now, although her hair was longer than that of the actress in that '90s show. The style would work. The right clothes and she became a librarian, or store clerk, or doctor. She would blend in.

She finished cleaning up and packing, taking everything remaining in the house that would fit in her car with her. She stopped for gas and ditched her garbage into the can at the pump. Her next stop—the penthouse of the CitySpire building in New York City. Francois and the Director expected her to arrive for a late dinner, and she did not wish to disappoint.

THREE

Although their flight home had been hassle-free, particularly in comparison to his ordeal getting to Cambodia, Lynch Cully was ready to kiss the ground when they landed in Houston. They had an "easy" six-hour flight from Phnom Penh to Narita International Airport in Tokyo, but the five-hour layover from predawn to midmorning had offered little convenience. The transit hotel offered sleeping cubicles that looked like some kind of Sci-Fi rendition of a suspended animation pod for interstellar travel. He was afraid he'd wake up acting like some anime character if he tried sleeping there.

Plan B had been coffee. Lots of coffee, but none of the restaurants were open yet.

So, Lynch Cully and Amy Gibbs spent their time in Tokyo staring at closed storefronts in the airport, walking laps around the international concourse, and avoiding the obvious mammoth in the room, her engagement to Richard Nichols and his subsequent murder. Curiously, talking about her father, who had been killed in Abdullah Said Abdi's first attempt on Amy's life, posed no problems. Her father's affection for Lynch seemed to make it easier for her to talk with Lynch about him.

The 13-hour flight from Narita to Houston had been pleasant despite its length. Al Nippon, as well the other international air carriers they'd flown, flew rings around the U.S. domestic carriers in terms of food, service, and amenities. Yet, by the end of that flight, Lynch had had enough. Turbulence over the Pacific had kept them in their seats, and his feet and ankles looked the size of small melons from the edema that sitting for too long had produced.

As they stood awaiting their turn to deplane, Amy asked, "Did you get any sleep at all?"

He felt surprised that she would ask. She knew he disliked flying and couldn't sleep on an airplane. She, on the other hand, was a talented amateur pilot with her own Cessna. He noted that she'd had no problem sleeping through half the trip.

"Not a wink. Every jolt of turbulence had me on edge."

She laughed. "Yeah, I guess *you* would have called those little bumps turbulence." She poked him in the arm, but then surprised him by taking his hand as they hit the concourse and headed toward their connection to St. Louis.

"Hey, the airline must have considered it turbulence, too. They had the seatbelt sign on almost the entire trip." He gently squeezed her hand in acknowledgment. They hadn't held hands in years, thanks to his earlier stupidity. The affectionate move on her part buoyed his spirit beyond all lack of sleep.

Lynch stopped at the first Starbucks they encountered after clearing customs. "Want anything?" She shook her head. He recognized it as culturally "inappropriate" but ordered a simple black coffee. He needed a jolt, not the sugars of caramel, or dense cream, or pumpkin spice. After paying their exorbitant price, he realized he might have been better off finding a can of Monster Energy or Red Bull.

He also realized he'd made a dumb move by buying the

drink. Now, she had no hand of his to hold.

"So, I know we started this conversation earlier, but we got distracted. What's the first thing you want to do when we get home to St. Louis?" They would arrive at Lambert International shortly after noon, which still amazed him. Thanks to a strong tailwind and time zone changes, they had arrived in Houston at 8:10 a.m., having left Japan at 9:50 a.m. And they said time travel wasn't possible.

Amy smiled. "First thing I want is for you to take me to lunch at La Bonne Bouchée."

He had no problem with that. Besides, the restaurant was only 17 minutes from the airport, and he was hungry.

"And what's the first thing *you* want to do?"

He grinned. "Clearly, it's to take you to lunch at La Bonne Bouchée."

Amy laughed. "There's our gate." She pointed farther down the concourse to the left.

Lynch glanced ahead and saw two serious-looking men watching the concourse. With their black suits and white shirts, all they needed were sunglasses, and maybe two additional arms, to look like extras in the next *Men in Black* sequel. And they stood just outside the gate where he and Amy headed. Feds? Something else? His right hand instinctively moved to his hip to confirm the presence of his gun, until he realized he had no weapon . . . much less authority to carry one in a major metropolitan airport. He hated walking into the unknown, unprepared.

Now twenty feet away, both men looked directly at him, and one nodded to the other. The men started walking toward them. At this moment, even Amy noticed.

A few steps away, the two men broke into smiles, and the older extended his hand.

"Lynch Cully, I'm Special Officer Sloane with the Secret Service. This is Special Agent Harper." Both men extended their creds toward the couple.

Lynch hesitantly extended his hand. "Um, nice to meet you. This is my friend Amy Gibbs."

Both men nodded. "Yes, we know. Nice to meet you, Ms. Gibbs."

"We'll cut to the chase. We don't have much time. The President wants to see you ASAP, and the plane is waiting. As soon as we collect your bags, we can take off."

"It's important," added SA Harper.

Lynch had no doubt of that, just by the fact that President Graham had dispatched these men to intercept him on their way home. He felt no hesitation in honoring the President's call. In fact, he felt duty-bound to do so. He simply wished the timing had been different.

"Can you give us a minute?" Lynch took Amy by the elbow and led her ten feet away. "Hey, I sure didn't expect this, but I can't see Graham sending agents to claim me on a lark."

"I have to agree. You need to go. I can certainly make it to St. Louis by myself, and I'll call Macy. She'll come get me. I'll be staying with her anyway, since my brother sold my house."

"I'm sorry. I'd really like to finish this trip, but I promise, the first thing I'm going to do when I get home is take you out to eat." She smiled.

They returned to the agents. "Okay. I'm ready to go, but

I'll need to talk with the gate agent about claiming my bag. It should have been routed to this flight."

The two men looked at each other.

Agent Sloane spoke. "I'm sorry. I wasn't clear. He asks to see you both. An agent is getting your bags right now. You both had just one checked bag each, correct?"

Abdullah tried opening his eyes, but they remained crusted and difficult to open. Something had changed. He still felt as if he was bobbing up and down, but differently somehow. He couldn't quite figure it out.

"*Esta el vivo?*"

"*Si no, tíralo de vuelta al océano. Recuperar un cadáver nos causará demasiados problemas.*"

Abdullah thought he'd heard someone whispering. He tried to raise his hand, but it cooperated less with his brain than his eyes did. But that's when he realized his hands were no longer lashed to his makeshift floater. He had tied them to the container to prevent his slipping off of it should he lose consciousness or fall asleep. Was he aboard a boat? Had someone found him?

"*Agua,*" he whispered. With a voice so coarse that he wondered if he was intelligible, he repeated his request, "*Agua, por favor.*"

He heard something drop and hit a floor.

"*Madre de Dios, él está vivo. ¿Que hacemos ahora?*"

"*Quizás valga algo de dinero. Dale un poco de agua y tal vez algo de fruta.*"

He recognized the words for money, water, and fruit. Yes, yes. If they would take care of him and get him to Los

Mochis, he would pay them well. He had friends in Sinaloa.

He felt the lip of a metal cup touch his lower lip. Eagerly, he fumbled at the cup with his mouth, taking in as much water as he could.

"*Beber lentamente, un poco a la vez. Tu intestino no está preparado.*"

Abdullah wanted more. He didn't understand his Mexican benefactor. "*Inglés?*"

Was the man shaking his head? He couldn't see clearly.

"My mate, he say to drink slowly. You are not ready for much water." This voice came from the man across the cabin.

Abdullah nodded. The man was right. He took a sip and swished it around his mouth. The parched tissues appeared to appreciate that. He took another sip and repeated the action. Then he felt and tasted a piece of orange at his lips. He accepted it with hesitation into his mouth because the acid stung his chapped lips. He must have grimaced or something because the man spoke again.

"My apology. That must burn. We will stick with the water first."

Abdullah nodded. "*Gracias.*" He next took an entire mouthful of water, but held it in his mouth. The moisture made it easier to talk, to move his tongue and lips. He swallowed it bit by bit. He felt a wet rag cover his face, primarily over his eyes and sunburned nose. It felt wonderful.

"Where am I?"

"You are aboard my fishing boat."

"Thank you, for finding me."

"Pure luck. The metal tank you were tied to got caught in my nets."

"Damage?" He understood the life of a fishermen and its problems.

"Nothing bad."

"And where is your fishing boat? Could you take me to Los Mochis? I will pay you, and pay you well."

"*Madre de Dios.* Los Mochis?" This voice came from the man giving him water.

"*Calma, Herme.*"

There was silence other than the thrum of the engine and the sounds of the ocean outside. After a moment the captain spoke.

"First, I must know. Are you connected to a Sinaloa gang? I do not want trouble. We are honest and simple fishermen."

Abdullah was not sure how to answer. Only a week or so earlier, his ruthless self would have answered no and had no qualms about double-crossing this poor rube. But Allah had brought them into his path to find him in the water. They would need a reward. Besides, if they sensed that he was lying, they could toss him back into the water, and he was in no condition to fight back.

"Yes, I have connections. And a healthy bank account there. But I am not a member of the cartel. I said I would pay you well, and my friends will not get involved."

Again, silence for a moment.

"*Deberíamos devolverlo con el pescado.*"

"*No, Herme. Mira este bote. ¿Cuánto mejor podríamos hacer con uno nuevo?*"

Abdullah heard footsteps climbing a ladder, followed by voices outside. Besides the owner, he heard three, maybe four, separate voices. That would give this vessel a crew of five or six. The footsteps descended on the ladder.

"My friend," the captain said, "my crew thinks we should save ourselves any trouble and just throw you back. That goes against all I believe in. However, you must realize that we are two hundred miles from Los Mochis."

"Two hundred?" That made no sense to Abdullah. "When my boat exploded, I was just 20 miles off Ensenada. How could I now be hundreds of miles away?"

"You were caught in the California Current. That's 20 nautical miles a day. Two, three more days, and you would have started drifting west in North Pacific Current."

"What is it you want?"

"A new fishing boat."

"That is all?" The man nodded. "You will have it, plus the cost of the petrol to get me there and get you home."

Abdullah's eyes were fully open now. He saw a calendar hanging on the cabin wall, its days crossed off. It had been a full ten days since his run-in with the U.S. Coast Guard. He must have lost consciousness and missed counting several days. He also saw that he had been dealing with an experienced fish monger, someone who knew how to get his best price.

FOUR

Amy felt buzzed. Meeting the President! Well, she already knew the President, but as Brad Graham, not as *President* Graham. This was exciting. It was like a movie, being called to the Oval Office on a matter of national security. Okay, maybe nothing national, or even security-wise was involved. Yet, clearly, he had been aware of their itinerary. What did he know and when did he know it? More importantly, what did *she* know and when? What was this all about? It was the uncertainty that had her adrenaline juiced.

Accompanied by a TSA agent, they had left the seating area through the "authorized personnel only" doors, descended down some stairs to the ground level, and out onto the blacktop. Amy felt a sudden shiver. She anticipated being greeted by the cold upon arriving in St. Louis, but did not realize the cold front extended so far south. Compared to Cambodia, the mid-forties in Houston seemed arctic.

On the tarmac an official TSA car awaited them, along with another special agent who had two suitcases waiting. She could sense the people watching them through the huge picture windows. She felt like a celebrity.

SA Watt acknowledged them and pointed to the suitcases. "Just want to make sure these are the correct bags."

Both Lynch and Amy nodded. "That they are, Agent Watt," responded Lynch. He helped the man load the two bags into the trunk, as well as their carry-ons, before joining Amy in the backseat.

The TSA agent took the wheel, while SA Watt took shotgun. SO Sloane and SA Harper climbed into a second vehicle and led the party away from the gate. Amy glanced at Lynch sitting in the back of the dark sedan as they crossed the tarmac, the airline gate diminishing in size as they moved farther away. This time he was the one to appear so calm, as if he'd been called in by the President on special tasks on multiple occasions. Well, kind of. Lynch had been called into service by then-candidate Graham, and President-elect Graham, but had been in Cambodia when the inauguration took place just a month earlier. This would be his first time meeting their friend as the leader of the free world.

He glanced at her. "I saw you watching the people at the gate watching us from the windows."

Was he going to chastise her for feeling special?

"You do realize they were all expecting us to be handcuffed at any moment." He started to laugh.

She sighed. He was probably correct.

Addressing the special agent, she asked, "So, are we headed to a private plane? Maybe one of the government's Gulfstreams?"

She noticed Lynch chuckling and rolling his eyes. She poked him in the ribs. "What?"

"Oh, nothing."

"I'm asking because I'm a pilot, too, and I always like

new flying experiences."

SA Watt shot a glance her way. "Well, then, I'm sure this will be one of them."

The driver entered a secure area of the airport and rounded the corner of one of the business jet hangers. SA Watt pointed to their right. Amy's mouth dropped open.

"No way!"

SA Watt and Lynch both laughed and answered, "Way."

Amy slowly shook her head in amazement. "We're meeting him on Air Force One?"

SA Watt replied, "I was told we're doing even one better than that. His next stop is St. Louis to attend to some family matters overnight. You'll be joining him on the flight."

Amy felt like a kid given ten dollars and let loose in the candy aisle of the grocery store. She was about to fly on Air Force One. Wow!

As they pulled to a stop at the base of the portable stairs leading to the main hatch, SO Sloane and SA Harper were already out on the tarmac and their car was pulling away. They jumped into action to retrieve the couple's luggage from the back of the TSA sedan. SA Watt joined them. Amy watched their luggage go through a portable scanner. They asked to do the same with her personal bag.

"All clear. Please watch your step. The President is already on board."

They were greeted by yet another agent at the top of the stairs. He carried a scanning wand, which he appeared ready to use on them.

"Nonsense, Tim. I trust these two with my life, and they've been through at least two screenings so far today.

Let 'em aboard. It's cold out there."

Amy would recognize that voice anywhere. She turned to see Brad Graham, *President* Bradley Graham, welcoming her onto Air Force One. She wasn't sure how to respond.

Lynch joined her and extended his hand to the man. "Mr. President, nice to see you again. This is an unexpected surprise." Amy heard the subtle emphasis on the word "President."

Graham offered a subtle frown. "What's with the Mr. President stuff in private? Amy? What, no hug? It is a huge relief to see you in one piece. Cara and I were so happy this guy found you in time. That was quite a mess in Cambodia. We're still trying to soothe ruffled feathers there."

Amy hugged him with her customary "church hug," as she had a dozen or more times before his election. Why did it feel so strange this time? Had she truly just hugged the President? This whole afternoon was becoming surreal.

"I'm sure you've been briefed, but it was a multinational effort in Cambodia. I'm just glad—"

"Mr. President, it's time." SO Sloane had entered the private area.

Graham nodded. "Please have a seat and buckle in. Time to leave, and we don't have to wait in line."

"Gotta love *that* perk," said Amy. How many minutes of her life had she waited her turn to take off or land?

As they taxied and took off, Amy and Lynch offered Graham their inside take on the events in Cambodia. His questions proved to be insightful. Amy hoped her answers were enlightening.

Upon leveling off, she noticed a young, female Air Force

sergeant had joined them.

"Something to eat or drink?" asked Graham. "We offer a whole lot more than peanuts, chips, or cookies. You two are probably hungry after what, 13 hours in the air."

The sergeant offered all three a menu.

"The pasta fagioli is outstanding, but after nearly two months in southeast Asia, you might just want a real cheeseburger." The President laughed. "I'll have the pasta and iced tea. Thank you, Susan."

"Yes, sir, Mr. President."

Amy and Lynch looked at each other. She could tell that he was thinking the same thing—a meal now, and they wouldn't be hungry for La Bonne Bouchée.

"Amy, want to split the pasta?"

Perfect, she thought. "That would work for me. Sure. We'll split a pasta fagioli, Sergeant."

Graham looked incredulous. "Man, this is the best airline food you'll ever eat. Actually, it'll compete with most of the restaurants you'll ever visit, and the price is right."

Lynch shrugged. "Sir, I have no doubt you're right, but we promised each other that the first thing we're gonna do is go to La Bonne Bouchée together. We don't want to spoil that meal by filling up now."

Amy unbuckled her belt. "Um, sir, does this plane have a restroom? What am I saying? Of course, there are restrooms. Um, where?"

The President pointed her in the right direction. The food was waiting upon her return. After a couple of bites, Amy had to agree with Graham. She'd had no better at any fine dining establishment in St. Louis. Still, it wasn't La

Bonne Bouchée.

Graham finished his meal and moved to a seat at the front where he picked up a remote. With a click of a button, a large screen monitor appeared. "Now that the meal is over, it's time for the show." He pressed another button and a dark, grainy photo displayed.

Lynch and Amy joined him in the front row.

"That looks like Summer Stanton," said Amy. She would never forget that woman.

"Where is that?"

"The home next to Richard Nichols' house. The homeowner had been out of the country on business and pleasure. When he got home, he started to erase the recordings, but something stopped him. He began to review the tapes and discovered this. Note the time stamp."

"The day and hour of Richard's murder," replied Lynch. "Are you thinking . . ."

Tears welled up in Amy's eyes. Did this woman have . . . she had never liked that slick, fake news journalist.

"I'm told the forensics against Maggie Walther never added up. If this woman played a role in his murder, even just a supportive one, it might make sense. She was interviewed as a neighbor, but not otherwise."

"Where is she now?"

"I asked the Capitol Police to check with the local departments. We discovered that she's resigned her position with the network and sold that house. In fact, moved out as of this morning. The locals tracked down the moving company, but everything is to be moved into storage, prepaid for a year. They have no contact information."

"Isn't that curious in itself?" asked Amy. "Seems incriminating to me."

Graham nodded. "I agree, which is why I'd like you, Lynch, to investigate it."

FIVE

The traffic between Washington and New York had been its usual heavy volume, slowed even further by the weather. At least the predicted snow had been delayed. Summer now understood why so many relied upon the trains to make the trip. Although she doubted she would have much use for her car once she settled in at her new condo in the CitySpire building, that dwelling came with its own private parking, and she planned to take advantage of the perk.

She emerged from the Lincoln Tunnel and slid, literally, onto the exit to Dyer Avenue and toward the Theater District. If traffic cooperated, she would arrive at her new home within 15 minutes.

"Siri, dial Francois."

"Dialing Francois now."

She loved the Car Play features linking her iPhone to her Roadster. Its travel directions using Google Maps had been flawless for her trip.

"Good evening, Ms. Stanton. I take it you are nearby, *oui*?"

"Good evening, Francois. Yes. I've just turned onto 8th Avenue and am about a mile away. "

"Very good. I will direct the parking attendant to show you to your personal parking spot, and I can meet you there."

"Thank you. I look forward to seeing you again."

"*Moi aussi, chéri.*"

Almost 20 minutes later, as she neared her designated spot, she saw the Director's right-hand man standing next to the opening and waiting for her. In his late sixties, Francois had served at the bidding of the Assembly through six directors that Summer knew of. Perhaps more. And with his perhaps less-than-minor role in the "suicide" of Karolus Karling, three directors previously, he had become known for his loyalty to the organization, more than its directors. No longer seen as "the butler," his opinions were respected and often sought out. To some, he was the man behind the throne.

Such had been the case for Summer. She had quickly seen how influential the man had become. In fact, had he not turned down the opportunity, he might have become the newest director himself. Summer played right into this, and now she had attained the first female position among The Three.

Ironically taken from the Bible, a book they disdained, The Three had been modeled after King David's mighty men. As noted in 2 Samuel 23, these incredible warriors consisted of Josheb-basshebeth, a Tahchemonite, as chief of the three, Eleazar the son of Dodo, son of Ahohi, and Shammah, the son of Agee the Hararite. These three had found themselves first among the warriors, and were also noteworthy for breaking through Philistine lines to retrieve a drink of water for David from the well next to the gate of Bethlehem.

She would be their equal in daring and dedication to the

Director and the Executive Committee. Of course, the one thing she would never reveal was the real reason for attaining such a high rank within the organization. If reaching that goal required becoming the Director, she would plan on adding that notch into her belt of firsts, too. No member of The Three had ever been promoted to that top position, although one nearly did. Nor had a woman ever achieved that level. If needed, she would, but she was in no hurry.

She emerged from her car and walked straight to Francois, returning his traditional kiss on each cheek, as well as giving him a hug. Despite having risen to The Three, she refused to see the hug as a sign of weakness, whether in private, as they now were, or in public. In fact, as a woman, she saw it as an invaluable tool—intimate, disarming, and potentially deadly at close quarters. Richard Nichols had discovered how deadly.

"The Director waits for you in the dining room. What do you require tonight?"

Summer retrieved her briefcase, with its important papers, and replied, "This is it, other than my carry-on bag with clothes and toiletries. The rest can be moved into the condo tomorrow morning." She then pulled the small luggage piece from her trunk, extended its handle, and pulled it behind her as Francois led her to the private elevator. Her condo was part of the penthouse complex of the top three floors, and they had their own personal access.

The elevator door opened immediately. Francois ushered her inside first. As they ascended, she noticed him giving her a visual inspection and then a nod of approval upon its completion.

"Yes. The look serves you well. I am glad you took my advice about the hair and makeup. The Director will like it as well."

"Thank you, Francois."

The door opened, and they entered the penthouse foyer.

"Please join the Director in the dining room. I'll take these to your condo . . . unless you need something in them."

"I do not. *Merci.* The dining room is ahead and to the right, if I recall correctly." She had been here only once before to present herself to a selection committee.

"That is correct. I will join you shortly."

Summer moved ahead as the elevator door closed. She soon heard soft music, a Bach concerto, coming from the area she assumed to hold the dining room. Bingo. She found it.

"Director. It's nice to see you again. Thank you for inviting me to dinner."

Arieh Arikhan turned from the large picture windows overlooking Central Park. He appeared 15 years younger than his stated 55 years of age, trim, athletic, with but a hint of silver in the hair of his temples. He had classic Mediterranean features, but his shorter stature belied his Kazakhi Middle Eastern roots. They made for a confusing blend, yet one that made him quite attractive.

"Welcome. I hope the trip went smoothly." He walked toward a small dry bar. "Wine?"

She walked toward him. "It did, and yes, please. What you're holding is perfect."

"As I was sure it would be."

She had forgotten that he probably knew her as well as she did.

They made small talk about the view, her trip, and the wine. Each seemed hesitant to broach more important matters.

"Sir, Ms., dinner is ready." Francois held Summer's seat for her, as she would have expected of a gentleman such as he.

The dining table for 20 seemed barren, or perhaps it was the two of them alone at one end who appeared out of place. Either way, the dinner of fresh salmon, a hearty grain medley, and seasonal vegetables al dente seemed simpler fare than she had anticipated. Word was that every five-star restaurant in the city had wooed the chef here to join them, but to no avail. She had expected, what? Something more extravagant? It was simply a midweek meal. Excellently prepared, but still a routine weekday dinner. Growing up she could expect leftover meatloaf most Thursdays.

The dinner conversation became a bit livelier, focusing on world politics and current events. By the time dessert— an exquisite crème brûlée—came their way, the Director had vivisected all but one G8 nation leader—and his or her main political rival—and examined their weaknesses under the Assembly's microscope. Bradley Graham had been the sole exception. Summer found it all fascinating. His take on China and its leaders proved more insightful than anything she'd ever heard while a journalist. Of course, none of this was to leave the building.

The Director stood. "Let's move to the main room. We

can finish off this wine, enjoy the city lights, and discuss one more item."

Summer stood and followed. Francois had already alerted her to the additional "item." In fact, he was there waiting for them. On the coffee table sat an array of passports from several nationalities, along with accompanying identity papers—drivers licenses, birth certificates, health cards, and more.

The Director sat on the couch behind the table and picked up one passport, scrutinized it, and laid it down. He did the same with a second one, both of U.S. origin. He swept his hand over the display.

"These are all yours, to use as required. You will, however, need to pick one as a primary identity. Beginning tomorrow, Summer Stanton is dead."

She had expected the multitude of false identities, but not that she, herself, would be required to "die." That threw her for a second. She had few close friends, but she had anticipated being able to keep in touch with them on occasion. Now, they would mourn her.

"*Chéri*, I took the liberty of unpacking the few remaining things from your car and moving everything to your quarters. However, I will need your phone and purse. Sometime after midnight your car and these belongings will be discovered having crashed off the turnpike into the Delaware River near Wilmington. Your body will be missing, but your death will be officially declared, based on these personal items found in the wreckage."

Summer knew better than to show any sign of sentimentality, but she *really* liked her Tesla Roadster. She had purchased it three months earlier, after a nearly two-year wait to get that specific model and color. Such a waste of a quarter million-dollar car. The Fendi purse, too, was her favorite, although its $10,000 price tag placed it in the low end of the Fendi collection. Still, both were expendable.

The music playlist on her phone, on the other hand, presented years of collection. This switch was looking to be more emotionally painful than she had expected.

She grabbed her bag and opened it. She looked inside debating as to what she might need.

"Please leave everything as is," said the Director. "It must be convincing and realistic."

Summer, or whatever her name was to become, nodded. She retrieved two USB drives and her phone. "I ask only that my photos and music be copied from both of these before they become casualties of the accident." She held up the phone and one of the flash drives. "*This* drive should never be found among the wreckage." She curled her hand around that one. "Too personal. Oh, and Francois, you are in my contacts list on the phone. That might need to be deleted."

Francois smiled, but gave her a different vibe, one of intense curiosity, with his eyes. "But of course." He took both gadgets and her purse and proceeded to leave the room.

"Oh, and Francois . . ."

The man turned at the doorway. "*Oui, chéri?*"

"The things you unpacked from the car? If we're going to make this convincing, you may as well return them to the car. I'll just need to go shopping tomorrow."

Francois again smiled.

"Very good," said the Director. "New identity, new look. You can purchase whatever you like and require . . . as long as it doesn't draw attention to your new identity. Your life now is in the shadows."

SIX

Their previous afternoon's plans had been scuttled almost completely upon arriving in St. Louis. Their discussion with President Graham had continued for a good thirty minutes after landing. Details of Lynch's "appointment" to Homeland Security had to be finagled and cleared with all involved agencies and department secretaries, of which the Secretary of Homeland Security proved particularly abrasive. DHS had plenty of excellent investigators. Why did they need Lynch Cully brought on board as a special investigator?

Graham had to use his best diplomatic skills for that one. No mention of not trusting the DHS folks. Nor of the suspected leaks from DHS on two different cases. And he certainly couldn't mention his suspicions about the Assembly. Its Deep State bureaucrats littered the halls of not just the DHS, but also Congress, the Pentagon, and every other federal agency, committee, office water cooler clique, and janitorial closet. While his Republican competitor had campaigned on "draining the swamp," Graham had campaigned on the less descriptive cliché of "cleaning house." After only a month in office, he'd expressed his realization that the competitor's analysis was more appropriate.

Ultimately, they had missed the time window during

which Macy could pick them up and deliver them to their respective destinations. She needed to get to her shift in the ER at Mercy. So, Lynch asked a favor of the Secret Service, with the President's approval, to transport both to Lynch's parents' new home where his car had been parked. From there, Lynch drove Amy to Macy's place. By that point, their exhaustion overwhelmed their hunger.

But that had been yesterday. Today was a new day.

Lynch glanced at his phone. Precisely nine a.m. He let a minute slide by and then rang Macy's doorbell. If they couldn't do dinner at La Bonne Bouchée, brunch would be the next best thing.

The door opened, and Macy gave him a leery eye. She was one of his biggest detractors after he had "dumped" Amy years earlier and then tried to return to her life. That was the "old" Lynch. He had changed. She didn't believe it. He recalled her last comments from their encounter prior to his leaving for Cambodia. She would consider giving him her approval if he kept Amy safe and brought her home without trouble.

Two for three wasn't bad . . . and the trouble they'd encountered was the result of Amy's doings. Again. Surely, she couldn't hold him accountable for that.

"Well, well, it's Mister Secret Agent Man himself." She wrapped her arms around her torso against the cold, but didn't immediately ask him inside.

"G'morning, Macy. She's filled you in about yesterday, I see."

"Are you kidding? That's all she's talked about since she woke up this morning. Nothing about riding an elephant, visiting ancient ruins, saving kidnapped kids, or anything else about Cambodia. All she could talk about was riding on Air Force One, watching the President ask you to become some sort of secret agent, and riding on Air Force One some more. But if you're supposed to be a secret agent, why did she tell me? Lord knows *I* can't keep a secret."

Lynch strained at restraining himself. Even for Macy, that was an understatement.

"Well, I'm not a *secret* agent. More like being a detective for the federal government. Homeland Security to be specific." He watched her closely. She seemed different. "So, is she ready for brunch?"

"Uh-uh. Still in the shower." She paused and took a deep breath. "Look, I . . ." She glanced over his shoulder, past him. "Lynch, I . . ." She turned her gaze toward her feet. "Um . . ."

Lynch smiled, but didn't want to presume anything. "Gee, Macy. Lost for words? Are pigs flying and palm trees growing in Greenland? Wait, let me get my cell phone to document this one-in-a-million occurrence."

She punched him in the arm. "Don't you go harassing me. I, uh, . . ."

"Spit it out, Macy."

Again, she turned her gaze over his shoulder, refusing eye-to-eye contact. "Okay, already. You did it. You kept my girl safe and brought her home. I owe you my apologies."

"I think you said I'd gain your approval if I did that."

"Uh-uh. I said I'd *consider* giving you my approval. I've got the body cam footage to prove it."

Lynch laughed. "Well, thank you for considering it. I have changed, as I keep telling you."

Macy finally looked him in the eye. "That's what she's telling me, too. Don't you go and break her heart again. I'll find myself booked on first-degree murder if you do that again."

Lynch shook his head. "Never again."

Macy actually smiled at him. "Well, then, I guess I can let you inside. C'mon."

Lynch had a sudden thought. Time to recruit Macy's help.

"Actually, while we're out here alone, can I get your help on something?"

She shrugged. "I guess so."

"I want to find a special way to propo—"

The door flew open. "So, here you two are. What, Macy, you wouldn't let him in? It's cold out there." Amy stood there, looking fabulous in Lynch's mind.

Lynch looked at Macy, hoping Amy hadn't heard his last sentence. Macy stood there, wide-eyed for a second, but quickly recovering.

"We were having a heart-to-heart, you might say."

"Amy, you missed a once-in-a-lifetime event. Macy here was actually speechless. It was, well, it was extraordinary. I'm still not over it."

Macy punched his arm again, but harder.

*   *   *

Watching her old network that morning was surreal. To see her obituary being "written" by ex-coworkers was bad enough. Seeing the tears flow from dear friends she could no longer contact almost broke her heart. Almost.

The headline news at the top of the hour once again led with her "story."

"It is with heavy hearts that we once again report tragic news that broke early this morning. Our longtime colleague and dear friend, Summer Stanton, has died in a traffic accident on her way from Washington D.C. to New York City, with her car reportedly going off the Delaware Memorial Bridge leading to the New Jersey Turnpike and into the Delaware River. Police speculate that she fell asleep at the wheel and lost control.

"Summer was with . . ."

From there they continued with a long list of accolades for her work, including her George F. Peabody Award for her coverage of the Bradley Graham campaign in the last election. She had never been one to work for awards. Her motivation lay elsewhere. Yet, according to these journalists, she had accumulated an impressive list, some of which she didn't recognize and was pretty sure she'd never been awarded. Someone in the Assembly's news arm had been quite creative.

She turned off the television. The repetition seemed numbing, and the lack of real news was telling. For years she had been part of that cycle of telling the public only what the Assembly wanted it to hear. Part of that process was the repetition, designed to drum it into the heads of those watching. Social media, however, now threatened that cycle, and new controls had to be found.

None of that mattered to Hannah Wilson, her new persona. The powers-that-be had given her few choices, all dictated by the identity papers they had already drawn up for her. Bridget McNamara was a name better suited to her natural red hair. Since the red was gone, that identity didn't seem appropriate except for short-term use. Claudia Roberts was another option, but when she "tried on" that name and looked into the mirror, she didn't see a Claudia. Such had been the case with Elizabeth "Becka" Longstreet, too.

In the end, Hannah appeared the best fit for her. Common, in a girl-next-door sort of way. It would allow her to blend into any American neighborhood.

Her phone buzzed with a text. The Director requested her presence.

She grabbed her new driver's license, inserted it into a new wallet, and slid both into a knock-off DKNY bag. Clothed in jeans and a stylish, but inexpensive top fitting of the LuLaRoe line, she was ready to shop for a complete wardrobe makeover. Make that three wardrobe makeovers—working class, middle class, and chic high end. This morning's plan was to work the middle-class role of Hannah. The others would come into play as she assumed different identities for their distinct purposes.

Francois greeted her at the door to the Director's penthouse.

"*Bonjour, chéri.* To whom am I introducing the Director today?"

"Francois, you are looking at Hannah Wilson, the widow of a small business owner who left her financially secure but not extravagantly so."

He smiled—a bit more widely that she had expected. They found the Director in the main living room where he sat reading the *Wall Street Journal*. He stood upon their entering the room.

"Sir, may I introduce you to Hannah Wilson."

Arikhan gave Francois a dour look, shook his head, and grabbed what appeared to be a $100 bill from his pocket, which he handed to Francois. Francois smiled and whispered to Hannah. "We had a small wager on which name you would pick."

"I should have learned a long time ago not to wager against Francois. He rarely loses." Arikhan led Hannah to the seating area where he had been sitting upon their arrival and motioned for her to have a seat. He scrutinized her from head to toe and then smiled. "Yes, the Hannah Wilson personae suits you well. For the record, my money was on the Elizabeth Longstreet character."

"My second choice, sir."

He laughed. "I doubt it, but thank you. Now that you've made your choice, additional papers will be drawn up today to back your identity and additional computer databases will be dealt with to backstop your life story. Along with that identity comes a two-year-old Audi, an A5 Cabriolet if my memory serves me correctly. I'm sorry it doesn't match up to your Tesla."

She shrugged. "Perhaps I will have access to one again in a different, higher class role."

Arikhan nodded. "That can be arranged. So, Francois told me your plan for the day was to shop, to fill out your new look."

She nodded. "I'm afraid I have to do some shopping today, or I won't have much to wear after tomorrow."

"Yes, we do understand that. However, you may have to do some or all of that shopping at your destination. We have your first assignment in your new role."

"No way! Macy, can we turn up the volume on the TV?"

Lynch looked for the remote, but did not see it right away.

"What's up?" asked Amy.

He pointed to the television. A photo of Summer Stanton, with '1985-2017' captioned underneath as if she had died, filled the screen. Macy retrieved the remote from the kitchen and increased the volume.

"It's believed that Summer Stanton was on her way from Washington, DC, to New York City and fell asleep at the wheel early this morning. According to a trucker following her Tesla Roadster on I-295, just before the New Jersey Turnpike, he had been admiring the car when it swerved only once, over-corrected, and hit the barrier at an angle that launched it airborne and sent it into the Delaware River below. State Police spokesperson, Lieutenant Angie Bellows, had this to say earlier."

The image changed to one of a makeshift press conference. The officer repeated what they had already heard and continued.

"The identity of the driver was confirmed through the car's registration and personal items found by divers within the car. These items included her cell phone, intact wallet and purse, and a flash drive of personal photos. These items, along with other personal effects in the car, made it obvious that she was traveling and alone. Divers will continue to search the river for her body. We will update you as the day continues."

"No way," Lynch said again.

"Just yesterday on Air Force One, we were—"

Lynch cut Amy off with a look. They weren't supposed to talk about that with anyone else, and Macy was definitely one to keep in the dark. He hoped she hadn't noticed his non-verbal cue for Amy to stop talking.

"You were talking about Summer Stanton with the President?" Clearly, Macy had caught on that something was weird here.

"Um, we were, um . . . " Amy stumbled with her words.

"We were talking about weird deaths . . . like that pedophile Jeffery Epstein—"

Macy cut him off this time. "No way he committed suicide for sure. I heard he made his billions blackmailing people like Clinton and Prince Andrew. Would not shock me at all to see that proven. I have a cousin who's a corrections officer who has a friend in corrections at that New York jail. That guy says an unscheduled prison transport van showed up in the sally port just minutes before that so-called suicide. Some guy in green fatigues climbed out and disappeared into the jail. Fifteen minutes later, the guy and the van were gone, and they never logged in or out. All transports are supposed to occur during daylight hours, and all are required to log in whatever time of day it is. This one broke two rules. Miiiighty suspicious if you ask me." She took a quick breath. "And then there's that private pathologist guy who says the injuries are more consistent with strangulation and homicide. Somebody, or somebodies, didn't want Epstein to live and tell all. Telling me to believe he committed suicide is like telling me vaccines are safe." She looked at Amy. "By the way, you convinced me on that last point, girlfriend. I'll choose wearing a mask at work over the flu jab from now on."

Lynch smiled at Amy. He knew if he threw Macy a bone of diversion that she would take it and run. Now he had to keep the diversion going.

"Hey, look at the time. Amy, if we delay any longer, we'll be having to order lunch, not brunch."

She nodded. "Well, I'm definitely looking forward to brunch, so we need to get going."

Lynch looked at Macy. "You know, Macy, the invitation to join us is still open." He was being polite and didn't believe for a second that she would take him up on it.

"Lynch, thank you. That sounds . . . really . . . um, nice. I haven't eaten yet either."

He watched Macy watching Amy, whose eyes were begging Macy to say no.

"But, hey, you two, um, have just gotten home and, um, I know this was, um, supposed to be a private date. So, I'll let you off the hook this time. But I expect you to make good on the offer soon."

Amy jumped to her feet, and Lynch followed. He didn't want to give Macy a chance to rethink her decision and felt sure Amy saw it the same way. Following quick good-byes, they were out the door and speeding away in Lynch's car.

Amy stared at Lynch as he drove. "Is that uncanny or what? Yesterday, you were asked to investigate Summer Stanton and her possible role in Richard's death, and today she's dead in the Delaware River. Did she know something that Epstein knew? Did she have something on the Clintons and end up being their 49th suspicious death?"

Lynch shook his head. "Did you catch that last fact mentioned by the officer? There is no body yet. If they find one, then we can speculate like that. That's a 'what if' game even I won't take part in. There would never be a resolution to it. However, I suspect they'll never find one, a body that is, and that Summer Stanton is dead only on paper."

His task had become logarithmically more difficult. Who would be motivated to help him investigate a dead woman? So what if she'd played a role in Richard Nichols' death. She had now met her fate. What was the point of the investigation?

And yet, he was sure of his suspicions. There was no such thing as coincidence, and the convenience of this accident was not happenstance. Which also begged the question. Did they know that the President had the info he had shown Lynch, or that he had tasked Lynch with finding more details? If so, how? And who was the mole?

SEVEN

The drive from New York to western North Carolina had taken just over 15 hours. Summer could have done it under 12 in her Roadster with normal road conditions, but "she" had died in a nasty crash. Hannah continued to pay attention to the newscasts about her "demise," and remained satisfied that their original story had gained traction in the news cycle. No one appeared to question her death despite the absence of a body.

The Blue Ridge Mountain range began to light up as dawn brought relief to the night. The eastern sky sparkled in varying shades of red, orange, yellow, and violet. She drove to a nearby scenic outlook, near the crest of a mountain opposite Chimney Rock and overlooking Lake Lure, and took in the glory of the sunrise. A new day dawned just as Hannah began a new life. She was free to soak in the beauty . . . in irony to the tragedies she would produce.

Before winding down the mountain, she took time to once again review the dossier on the man she had to find. If the man held to his usual routines, her task would be completed in short order. His vacation home wasn't far away, sitting on the rocky Broad River where he spent time fishing.

She put her Audi into gear and headed down the mountain toward a little burg called Bat Cave, just northwest of Chimney Rock. While Chimney Rock held the burgeoning population of 113, unincorporated Bat Cave's only claim was its own post office, no doubt set up to capitalize on tourists wanting to post cards and letters from the unusually named town. She had been surprised that not one of the handful of resorts in the area had been named Wayne Manor.

More to her liking, and her need for anonymity, surrounding both communities were scores of cabins for rent. She had secured one for a week in an isolated valley not far from her target, and yet secluded enough that she would encounter no one to hinder her plan or later identify her. Of course, that risk was diminished by the season as well. There were few tourists to be seen. For additional insurance, the rental fee had been prepaid by one of her alter egos.

After unloading her bag into the cabin, she debated taking a short nap. She had, after all, driven all night to get there, and mistakes were more easily made when fatigued. Of course, this day would be only one of scouting out the area and locating her target—Dr. Christopher Renton.

He was rumored to have arrived at his vacation home after his clinic in Georgia had been raided by the FDA and Georgia Drugs and Narcotics Agency two days earlier. In fact, the effort against the man had begun much earlier. Scripts had been written for the media regarding his "fraudulent" and "perhaps criminal" activities, as well as calling his medical treatments those of a quack or scam artist. These "facts" were already being fed into the news stream, but the bulk of the misinformation awaited his "undisputed suicide."

The kind doctor had been too successful. His work with both autistic patients and cancer victims had shown positive results in over 80% of those receiving his NiMAF compound. Ten percent had shown complete recovery. Of course, the media would focus only on the 15% who had shown no improvement at all. Such numbers supported the anti-vaxx claim that vaccines caused autism and posed a threat to the profits of every pharmaceutical company in the world that dealt with vaccines or cancer. The Assembly had too much at risk when Big Pharma was under attack.

The Director, however, still had one big question they had not been able to answer. Who had funded the man's research? Big Pharma controlled the funding of almost all medical research, whether directly or through the government. And it had 100% control of the prestigious journals, which would go under without the advertising and support of the pharmaceutical industry. As such, the Assembly could be sure that Renton's work would never find itself published in any peer-reviewed journal, but the source of his funding needed to be shut down. Its mere existence showed that someone was willing to go up against them.

After reviewing the dossier fully, Hannah felt a second wind. She could sleep later. It was time to grab a bite to eat and scope out the area. Back in her Audi, she drove the few miles into Chimney Rock and found the Rocky Broad's Coffee Shop just opening. She ordered a large cup of their signature blend and decided to splurge on the calories of an apple fritter.

The barista stopped back at her table. "Can I get you anything else, hon?"

"Can you top this off to go?" It had been hot enough that she'd only managed to sip about a quarter of the contents while enjoying the fritter.

"Sure can, hon. Be right back. I'll get you a lid, too."

Hannah wondered if the middle-aged woman was also the Rocky Broad herself, the owner. She saw no one else working the shop at the time. But then, she was one of only two customers to enter the place since it opened. Perhaps business was better during peak tourist season. The woman came right back to the table.

"Good coffee, by the way. And the fritter."

The woman nodded in acknowledgment. "Might not be the West Coast, but I know coffee. Thanks."

"Hey, I'm looking for an address on Gerton Highway. Where is that? I'm supposed to meet up with some old girlfriends from college."

"You're on it, hon. 'Round here it goes by Lake Lure Highway. Go north a few miles, and right after Chimney Rock Road goes off to the west, it's called Gerton Highway. But it's still Highway 74. Got the address? Maybe I can help."

Hannah knew the address but didn't want to draw attention to it. "It's out in the car. Thanks, though. If I have trouble finding it, I might come on back."

Hannah grabbed her coffee and returned to her car. She headed back toward Bat Cave, and true to the woman's word, found a sign calling the main road Gerton Highway. Within a few minutes, she found the address she wanted, too. It ended up being less than a mile from where she had bunked down.

Brunch at La Bonne Bouchée had been nice, but both he and Amy had been distracted. The news of Summer Stanton's death had affected them each in different ways. More importantly, putting that together with the photo President Graham had shown them raised more questions than answers.

A call from the President early that afternoon had put Lynch's plans on a new trajectory. He now sat with Delaware State Police officers in their makeshift command center in Buttonwood, Delaware, along the Delaware River. Divers continued to comb the river, taking into account its currents and tidal flows from Delaware Bay.

"So, this is it?" asked Lynch.

Lieutenant Sorbello headed the investigation and spoke. "Yes, sir. What you see here in the warehouse is what we've retrieved so far. We're thinking now maybe she hit some ice on the bridge rather than falling asleep at the wheel. Several drivers we've talked with mentioned icy conditions last night, and the DOT salt trucks didn't come through that area until 30 minutes later."

"But no body . . ."

"Correct. But I think we can come to the conclusion Summer Stanton was driving."

Lynch walked around the totaled Tesla Roadster. The windshield damage was consistent with a body being launched through it from the inside. No blood was evident; however, the water of the river would have washed that glass, and everything else, clean.

"Fingerprints?"

The officer nodded. "The only ones we've found were a preliminary match with Stanton's. Nothing else."

Lynch walked over to two eight-foot tables holding the contents of the car. Evidence bags held the woman's purse, its contents, her phone, the flash drive he'd heard about, and the contents of the small amount of luggage that could fit into the Roadster. Everything about it pointed to Summer being in the car, traveling to New York City. His past training and experience would lead Lynch to agree with the State Police's conclusions.

It was his more recent experiences that put him at odds with those conclusions. Specifically, his experiences with the Assembly. That global group was expert in hiding itself from the public whose thoughts it helped mold, and yet there was a growing grassroots movement to unveil its secrets and remove its tentacles from the government. That was one of President Graham's goals, as difficult as that would be with so many of its bureaucrats entrenched within the federal organization. They were the chief opponents of the President's agenda.

Lynch's previous encounter with Summer Stanton in Kansas City had raised his suspicions of her allegiance. She had cooperated with them to save her own skin. But now? Had she evoked the ire of someone higher up and found herself their victim? Or was this a convenient ploy to fake her death for other nefarious reasons? Had he not seen the photo of her outside next to Richard's home at the time of his murder, he would have been comfortable acknowledging the former. Having seen that image, he favored the latter. Giving her a new identity posed no problem for the Assembly.

So, unless a body was found and confirmed to be her, he would work on the premise that this accident had been staged. He wouldn't hold his breath waiting for a body.

He regrouped with the State Police cadre nearby.

"Lieutenant, you have my contact info. If you find a body and confirm it to be her, please let me know."

The man nodded. "Certainly will, sir. However, I have my doubts we'll find a body. It could be washed out to sea by now."

Lynch shrugged. "Perhaps. Thanks." He almost added that he doubted her body was even in that car when it went into the water, but he didn't want to add more mud to the river.

As he walked to his rental car, another issue came to mind—Abdullah Said Abdi. USCG Captain Will Chase had informed him that the terrorist was dead, but at that time, the Coast Guard was still surveying the wreckage of the fishing vessel for bodies. Had they found Abdi's body? The hair on his arms stood on end at the thought that yet another body was unaccounted for.

He pulled out his phone and through connections in Washington got two numbers for Chase—his office phone and his personal cell. He would use the latter only if necessary.

"Captain William Chase's office, Yeoman Walsh speaking."

"Good morning, Yeoman." Lynch went on to identify himself and his need to talk with the captain with some urgency.

"Yes, sir. You just missed him. The captain is en route to the Bertholf as we speak. They're refueling and restocking. I can contact him and have him call you."

"Thank you." Lynch provided the yeoman with his cell number. "You can let him know I'm calling about the Somali fishing vessel they encountered."

"Yes, sir. Will do. I do know they retrieved six bodies from the wreckage, but that's all I have right now. Those casualty reports go through a different office. I'll have him call you ASAP."

The man was true to his word. Two minutes later, Lynch's cell phone rang. He recognized the number as that of Chase's cell.

"Will, thanks for calling so quickly."

"Hey, Lynch. This is twice in less than two weeks that we've talked. We're definitely going to have to catch up over drinks, if our schedules ever sync up." The man chuckled. "So, you're following up on the Somalis."

"That's right. I'm looking into a case right now where no body has turned up, and I had this sudden feeling that I needed to confirm that Abdullah Abdi's body was found."

There was a moment of silence on the other end. "Lynch, I don't think it was. I mean, we recovered six bodies, and most were pretty torn up. The investigative services here are doing their forensics and DNA thing, but I looked at them all myself, and personally, I don't think Abdi was among them. No one survived, so if Abdi isn't among them, he either wasn't on that ship, or he became fish food."

"But you said you identified him on the drone video

feed."

"I did, but maybe I was wrong. Sorry, man."

That didn't sit well with Lynch. "Look, can you send me a clip of the drone video? The segment where you thought it was him."

"Sure. Now that you're with DHS, I can get that cleared. But it might take a couple of days. My crew's on shore leave, and the specialist I need to put that together won't report back until 0800 on Monday. If I can find someone else to do it, I'll try to get it to you sooner. Where should I send it?"

The two men chatted a bit longer before disconnecting. Lynch sat in his car and pondered how the day had gone so far. Too many questions. Far too few answers, which in reality, only two confirmed bodies would answer.

Yet, the ramifications of those two bodies being missing were huge. If Abdi wasn't on that boat, or had somehow escaped, then Amy remained in danger. And Summer Stanton? If she had been involved in Richard's murder, did that imply that her role in the Assembly was far from what it appeared? Was being a hack journalist simply a cover for a more notorious activity? Perhaps it would be worthwhile to track her assignments against unsolved or suspicious deaths, particularly of a political nature.

The captain's estimate of their distance from Los Mochis proved correct. Abdi was no mathematical genius, but he didn't need to be. Two hundred nautical miles at a speed of ten knots came to a travel time of roughly 20 hours. With one brief delay due to an engine issue, they had made it to the port in 22 hours.

Abdi had found his way to "friends," who in turn took him to their "private clinic." After several liters of intravenous fluids, he had become like a new man. Dinner and drinks that night had been on him.

He awoke the following morning to find companions in his bed. One of the prostitutes rolled over and purred into his ear, as she traced his facial scar softly with a fingertip. *"Buenos días, el gato de muchas vidas."* He sat up in bed, stirring the second woman from her sleep as well. This morning he had no need of their seductions.

"Más tarde. Dejame solo ahora." Both young women pouted at being told to leave him, but they had been well compensated.

As he dressed, he reflected upon the call girl's nickname for him, *"el gato de muchas vidas,"* the cat with many lives. Yes, he felt as if he been resurrected from the dead, like a cat with nine lives. *El gato* in Spanish was *bisadda* in his native Somali. Maybe he would take on the name *Bisadda Weyn*, the great cat. No, make that *Libaaxa Soomaaliya*, the Lion of Somalia.

He enjoyed a leisurely breakfast overlooking the water and made his way to the harbor. He met up with Carlos. The man might be an infidel, but he had saved Abdi's life. The debt would be repaid.

"You look much better, *Señor* Abdi."

Abdi nodded. "I *am* much better. I feel reborn." He glanced around the harbor. There were several boats with '*a la venta por el propietario,*'—for sale by owner—signs on them. "Have you found a boat you would like?"

The man nodded. *"Si."* He pointed to a vessel a hundred

yards in the distance, moored to a buoy offshore. It looked marginally larger than the man's current boat.

"It looks no bigger."

"It is. Enough bigger for us. And it come with bonus— the owner wants smaller boat and will take mine as part of the price." He smiled as if this was the deal of deals.

"So, what is the best price?"

"Ten thousand dollar, US."

"Plus your boat."

The man nodded again. "*Si*. Plus my boat."

"And everything works?" The man nodded. Abdi assumed as much, as the man had proven himself quite knowledgeable of boats en route to the harbor. "And where is the owner? Does he speak English?"

Carlos pointed to a man waiting nearby. "His English I do not know. I will come with you."

Abdi brushed him off. He didn't think he would need a translator. He walked over to the seller and found the man's English lacking. He pointed to Carlos, and then both boats. "*Cuánto cuesta?*"

The man wrote a number on a piece of paper: $10,000. He added "U.S." to reinforce the currency of the exchange.

Abdi leaned toward the man and whispered a name. The seller became noticeably anxious. Abdi grabbed the paper and pencil and wrote: $5,000 US. The seller nodded and smiled with such animated fear, Abdi wondered if he had also soiled his pants.

"*Bueno*," said Abdi. He waved for Carlos to join them. When Carlos arrived, he said, "Do the paperwork, the titles. I will be back in ten minutes with the cash."

When he returned, both men stared at him, the seller in fear while Carlos appeared disgusted. The cash was given and keys and papers exchanged. Carlos said something to the seller and walked away.

Abdi rushed to join him. "We are now even. I have made good my debt."

Carlos glared at him. "$10,000US was a fair price. Your threat might have saved you money, but it cost me reputation. I will not be welcome in this port in future days."

Abdi shrugged. "That is not my concern. I promised you only a new boat, and you have it."

With that, he turned away and headed toward the villa where he resided temporarily. He now had more important matters to attend to—returning to the U.S. and finding that woman. She had not only escaped his hand, she had cost him a boat and its crew, and now, another $5,000.

EIGHT

Amy awoke later than she expected, but then, she was unemployed, homeless, and had no need to wake up at a certain hour. Well, she was about to be homeless. Her brother had sold her St. Peter's home in less than a month while she was in Cambodia, and the closing was just two days away. Be that as it may, all her stuff was in storage and not easily accessible. She planned on staying with Macy for a while. At least until her friend drove her crazy. As close as they were, they were not really compatible roommates.

As she steeped a cup of tea and smeared cream cheese on the bagel she'd just toasted, she scanned the cable channels for anything new on Summer Stanton. The headline news of the journalist's old network had already moved their report on her death to a point after the 15-minute mark—a sure sign of a dying story, more likely continued only out of respect for an old colleague. At that last report, no body had yet been found, but police were sure that she was in the car at the time of the accident and had died.

Why didn't she accept that?

Another call from the President had Lynch flying to Washington with him so that Lynch could then drive to and consult with the Delaware State Police on the Stanton accident. At least they'd had time for brunch together. Amy felt positive that Lynch was already in Delaware, at the scene, and wondered what he might have uncovered, if anything.

So far, her first two days home were disappointing. The alleged death of Summer Stanton dredged up bad memories, but the lack of time with Lynch threw her a bigger curve. The man *had* changed. She saw that firsthand in Southeast Asia. That time together, working hand-in-hand for the children and Pastor Jim's mission work melted her resistance to Lynch and made the memory of his leaving her, years earlier, without so much as a note, wane. Amy expected the special time together in Cambodia to continue at home, and yet, somehow, Summer Stanton interrupted that, just as the woman had played a role in Amy's breakup with Richard . . . and perhaps was involved in his murder.

She hoped they would find her body and confirm her death.

At the same time, Amy felt some remorse. She shouldn't be wishing anybody's death.

She grabbed her tea, turned off the small television, and moved from the kitchen to the main living area where her laptop sat next to the couch. She had other major life decisions to make, getting back to her being unemployed and almost homeless. MedAir would take her back in the time it took a helicopter rotor to make one revolution. But did she want to go back to that? She started two new Word documents—a list of pros and cons about returning to MedAir and a list of what she really wanted in a new position. Her work in Cambodia had given her a new perspective on life. Maybe it was time to teach. Or if Lynch .

. . well, if he proposed, maybe she'd prefer being a stay-at-home mom. She often thought of her childhood as it was before her mom passed away.

She thought, too, about new living quarters. Her job decision would affect that. But so would another major life change. Was Lynch going to propose? Every molecule in her body seemed to affirm that he would. That would affect job choices as well as housing decisions.

She finally decided not to decide. She needed to let life play out with Lynch, at least for the next week or so. If he procrastinated beyond that then she would need to get serious about making her own decisions. Also by then, living with Macy would be making her crazy.

Her cell phone rang in the kitchen where she'd left it. She dashed to get it and saw caller ID proclaiming Lynch on the other end. His calling would brighten her sour mood.

"Hey there. How's it going in Delaware?"

"Pretty much like what you've heard on the news. Still no body. The ex-policeman in me would agree with the police here. Everything points to her being the driver and getting ejected through the windshield in the accident. Her seatbelt clearly wasn't in use, but I don't know how careful she was about using it. If she buckled up out of habit every time she got in a car, then why not the other night? It's a puzzle that will likely end in best guesses."

Amy knew Lynch well enough to hear between the lines. There was a hesitancy in his words, an uncertainty.

"Am I hearing a 'but' in what you're saying?"

"A big one. I can't shake the feeling that this was all staged, that she's out there under a new identity working for the Assembly."

Amy didn't like that thought.

"Amy, we need to talk."

That sparked her interest. Maybe this conversation would end on a high note after all.

"About what, Lynch?" she asked, trying not to sound too coy.

"I guess the easiest way is to just come out and say it."

"Yes, Lynch?"

"I'd prefer telling you this in person, but the timing for that to happen isn't going to work out. So, I'm stuck with doing this by phone. I don't think Abdi is dead either."

She wasn't sure which dropped the quickest, her jaw or her spirits.

"Abdi? N-not dead? I-I, uh . . ." She began to weep at the thought that her father's murderer still lived and might once again come after her.

"Hey, I'm sorry to upset you. I debated telling you now but figured you need to be alert and prepared. Look, it's not what I hoped for upon returning home, but I won't be back to St. Louis for a while. I need to go to Florida to investigate two other suspicious deaths. The media is calling one a suicide and the other natural causes, but the families of both victims claim they were murdered."

"What's that have to do with Summer Stanton? I thought you were investigating her."

"I am, but my task is broader than that. In the past year over a dozen suspicious deaths have occurred. They have some common threads. All were quickly ruled out as one cause or another without any real investigation, and the families all protested, asking for full inquiries. They also all involved doctors or naturopaths who practiced holistic medicine. All of them were involved in curing major illnesses using simple treatments. And . . ." He paused. ". . . what really caught my attention is the excessive amount of media focus in calling them all quacks or frauds, and labeling all their supporters as conspiracy theorists."

Amy could see how that would raise Lynch's antennae. Their dealings with the Assembly had shown them how labeling people as conspiracy theorists, quacks, frauds, or charlatans was a "3rd and ten" Hail Mary play from the Assembly playbook. The Assembly's propaganda arm always went out of its way to discredit those who got in their way. Their methods were almost always overkill. "Where there's smoke, there's fire" was what Lynch always told her.

"A-are you going to be looking into *all* of them? You could be gone for weeks." That was the last thing she wanted at the moment. She had grown confident in Lynch having her back, and if Abdi was alive . . .

"That's not my plan at the moment. I hate to say it, but it's all up in the air. We know how intertwined Big Pharma and Big Agriculture are with the Assembly, not to mention a lot of influential politicians. We saw what they did in Cambodia. If these doctors threatened profits, I could see them being targeted. And if Stanton had a role in Richard's murder, where was she when these other deaths went down? I've got my job cut out for me."

That was an understatement, one that added to her concern.

"Lynch, *please* be careful. I, uh, we, um . . ."

"I know. I promised you life would be different, and here I am looking into questionable deaths that some very powerful people might be behind. It could put a target on my back, too."

Amy had avoided the L-word in Cambodia. But now she recognized her feelings for Lynch had come full circle. She did not like the predicament the President had put them in. Maybe it wasn't fair to blame Graham. He had a job to do as well, and protecting the public from such powerful people came with it. Still, the man had multiple federal agencies he could call on and instead had chosen Lynch.

"Lynch, I love you. Our lives have just gotten back in sync, and I . . ." She forced back the tears with every ounce of resolve in her. She was not going to add to his stress by breaking down now.

Abdi looked out over the harbor from the villa where he now sat with a top lieutenant of the Sinaloa cartel. Abdi's "taxi" company in St. Louis still played a major role in distributing their drugs throughout the Midwest. As such, he had enjoyed the assistance, cooperation, and respect of the cartel in the past. He now sought to gain one more favor from them.

"*Señor* Abdi, what you ask is much harder now. And you still owe us for the technology we lost helping you to leave the country."

That took Abdi by surprise. He hadn't expected to pay for that equipment. But then, they hadn't anticipated its loss.

"I will cover that cost before nightfall."

The man nodded and took a sip of his beer. Abdi,

seeking Allah's favor as well, refrained from the alcohol.

"*Gracias.*" The man took another drink before continuing. "As for getting you back into the U.S., it is more difficult. You are a wanted man still. If they think you died on the boat, they have not yet taken your name off the "Most Wanted" list. And new border fencing in our old crossover territories has forced us to move our products through remote, more rugged areas. Our expenses have increased."

"I came out by small airplane. Is that not still an option?"

"Perhaps. That, too, has become more difficult. New detection technologies have made flying under the radar, as they say, well, *arriesgado,* hazardous, risky. They watch not only from the ground but from the sky as well. We have an idea as to when windows in the satellite coverage occur, but those can change. We have lost two planes and their contents recently due to miscalculations on our part."

Abdi did not like what he heard. Leaving the U.S. had been like walking in a park. Should it not be the same to get in? He'd had no trouble bringing in men and drugs in the past. Of course, he relied on the cartel to move both across the border itself.

"Expense, as you know, is no problem. What do you suggest?"

"Do you want most comfortable or most successful?"

Abdi laughed. "I just spent ten days floating in the ocean. Do I look like I need comfort?"

His counterpart offered a toothy grin. "After ten days at sea I would *want* some comfort. And not just from two whores on a one-night stand. *Si?*"

The man's comment was to remind Abdi that nothing he did there went unnoticed.

"I need to get back into the States. I want success."

The man nodded. "It will be rugged and not without danger. The weak often fall in the desert."

Abdi nodded. "I am from Somalia. I know the desert as well as the sea."

"Ah, *si*. I had forgotten. We have developed a small landing strip and base northeast of here in Coahuila, fifteen miles southwest of Langtry, Texas. The trek from there to the Rio Grande is rugged and barren. The team moves only at night, and the river crossing is also at night. Very dangerous, but we have great success there. Once across the river, you are right on Highway 90 and three and a half hours from San Antonio."

"How much will this cost me, and when can it happen?"

The man thought for a moment before replying. "I can offer you a deal. If you agree to being a mule, carrying a 70-pound pack on your back, and being part of the team, we will charge you nothing. If not, then we ask for $25,000, up front."

Twenty-five thousand? Was that the going rate for smuggling someone into the U.S.? He thought he had a good relationship with the cartel. Clearly, he would have to re-assess their relationship once he returned to St. Louis. There were other suppliers, several of which had previously approached him. Plus, he had just spent $5,000 toward another man's boat and had promised to cover the $10,000 cost of a lost, seaworthy drone.

"I will carry a pack. Again I ask, when?"

The man gave him a curious look. "We fly there once a week. Tonight is the night, or you will have to wait until next week. Are you up to this so soon after your ordeal?"

Abdi didn't want to wait. It would have to be tonight. "I will leave tonight. Time and place?"

"Fifteen hundred hours at the same airfield you used when leaving the country. Do not be late."

NINE

As Hannah parked her car back at the cabin, she realized she shouldn't have eaten that apple fritter. The sugar load was sapping her second wind rather than energizing it. She pushed herself to work through it, and grabbing her digital SLR camera, she began walking toward the river to take pictures. The brisk temperatures helped her stay alert.

Few cars passed by. She noted even fewer pedestrians, thanks to the weather. Actually, make that zero other walkers. While she didn't mind the cold and had come prepared for it, her presence was made more obvious by it. Perhaps she had overestimated her level of anonymity.

She found a trail leading to and then following the river. It appeared potentially slippery, but she decided to take it. A true photographer would do so, seeking the best perspectives for a wintry river image. Plus, it took her off the main drag where she remained visible.

As she followed the water, she recognized there were some beautiful images to capture. She had taken a photography class in journalism school, part of the training for those who would become videographers and photojournalists. She knew the basics of the camera provided to her, but realized she needed to hone that skill if that part of her backstory—enjoying photography as a major hobby—was to become believable. She made some adjustments on the camera, clicked a couple of shots, checked the images in the LCD screen, and adjusted the device again.

She deleted the previous images and tried again. Repeating the process twice more, she finally saw images that she actually liked. Plus, she gained a better understanding of the SLR's capabilities.

She continued with caution along the trail. At least the dirt remained hard and frozen, not muddy and slick. She stopped every 50 feet or so and scrutinized her surroundings. Occasionally, she took pictures and reviewed the images on the camera's screen. *I'm getting the hang of this*, she thought. There were a few photos that she looked forward to inspecting on a larger screen because they actually appeared pretty nice on the small screen. Perhaps photography would become something she really enjoyed.

Half an hour later, she realized she had gotten caught up in her "new hobby" and had no real idea where she was. She retrieved the phone from inside her heavy coat and pulled up a map app that offered data only the Assembly could provide. With the phone's satellite linkage, she didn't have to worry about commercial cell service and how many bars of signal strength she had. She suspected that otherwise she might have poor coverage within the deep valleys she now traversed.

The doctor's cabin wasn't much farther along the trail, although on the opposite side of the river. She continued her trek until she stood opposite the man's property. She took several photos of it and its adjacent neighbors. Someone clearly occupied the doctor's cabin, as evidenced by the vapor being exhausted by a working heating system. As such, the reports of his coming to the cabin appeared valid.

She found a rock to sit on and continued to observe all three properties across the river. Was she in luck? Neither of the cabins on each side of the doctor's appeared occupied. There appeared no sign of their being actively heated. No lights. No vehicles. Had an occupant simply turned down the heat while at work, the system would still kick on periodically. She saw no signs of that and surmised that each cabin had been winterized for the prolonged seasonal absence of its owners.

She was about to leave her perch when she saw an SUV pull into the drive of the Renton property. She took a photo, followed by one of the driver and sole occupant of the vehicle. Enlarging them on the camera screen, she made a positive ID of the man's vehicle as well as the doctor himself. With confirmation that he was there, she required only one other thing—to confirm that he was alone. For that she needed to be much closer.

Abdi had no desire to wait another week, and made sure he arrived at the airfield early. With only the clothes on his back and a new burner phone in his pocket, he watched as the taxi drove away. Once it left his view, he turned to scan the airfield. He saw no planes or activity of any kind. Even the small hangar where the cartel kept its private jet appeared abandoned. Had he been duped?

He glanced at his phone. He had been there a full ten minutes already and had another ten until the appointed time. His anger began to mount. He did not like being played for a fool.

And yet, he was playing on the cartel's home field. Its leaders were not men to upset. He needed their favor for a while longer and venting his ire would not play into that. He knew what it was like to be the kingpin. In his homeland, he had the power to make someone disappear, permanently, never to be seen again. Even in St. Louis, he had that ability, although it required much more planning and caution. But here? The leaders whose help he sought could make him the one to vanish.

He would remain patient. Five more minutes.

He again walked around the hangar and peeked inside its windows. Nothing.

At 1500 hours, he heard an engine. No, two engines. From the entrance to the airfield, a truck sped toward the hangar, spewing dust in its wake. From the opposite direction a small plane suddenly dipped out of the clouds and made a direct descent toward the runway.

The truck arrived at the hangar first, and five men emerged from the back. One of them pointed at him.

"Abdi?"

Abdi nodded.

"Grab pack. Quick."

He pointed to the back of the truck. The other men had already retrieved the packs they were to carry. Abdi hurried to do the same. It felt heavier than the seventy pounds he had been told he would carry. Perhaps the cartel lieutenant had been correct. Had his ordeal at sea taken more out of him than he thought?

He joined the others as the plane pulled up next to the hangar. The door opened, and two steps flipped outward to give them access to the plane. The men hurried aboard, with Abdi being last, following their lead. As he entered, he handed his pack to a man in front of him. The pack was stowed in the aft of the compartment and secured in place with the others. He looked around and counted ten seats, five on each side of a central aisle. He took a seat behind the last man.

The man who had taken his pack frowned. "No, no." He pointed to the seat on the opposite side of the aisle. Abdi switched, and the man nodded. He placed his hands, palms down and thumbs next to each other, in front of him, and moved them up and down in a partially rotating manner.

He glanced about again and saw that the others sat on alternate sides of the plane. Abdi then understood. Balance.

No sooner had they retrieved the steps and closed the door, the pilot taxied in haste to the end of the runway. The truck was nowhere to be seen. Seconds later, they were in the air.

With the absence of neighbors, Hannah saw no reason to delay her task. Yes, she acknowledged her fatigue, but this was going to be an easy score . . . once she confirmed that the man was alone. If he wasn't, then additional observation and planning would be needed.

Having returned to the rented cabin, she confirmed that the items she needed to complete her plan were in the trunk of the car. With that she climbed behind the wheel and headed toward the man's cabin. Finding the correct road proved a bit difficult in the waning light. Dark came earlier in the deep valley of the river, but that was what she wanted.

As she neared the first neighboring cabin, she pulled to the side of the road and observed the cabin. Still no sign of occupation. She grabbed a device from the passenger seat and scanned the cabin. The infrared scanner noted no heat sources, mechanical or human.

She passed by the doctor's cabin and repeated the process with the other neighbor's cabin. Satisfied that it, too, was unoccupied, she walked a short distance to what she assumed to be the property line and found a spot where she got an unobstructed view of the target. Scanning that structure confirmed a mechanical heat source. She noted no smoke arising from the stone chimney, and the scanner confirmed no heat at its base.

Perfect, she thought. *Who builds a cozy fire to commit suicide?*

She scanned the building twice more. Only one other heat signature. It appeared to be moving from the middle of the structure to the area looking out to the river.

She hurried back to the car and pulled right into the man's drive. She then boldly walked up to the front door and rang the bell. A moment later, a light at the door flashed on and the door slowly opened.

"Sir, I am so, so, so sorry for disturbing you. My name's Susan, and I think I'm lost. No, I *am* lost. It's getting dark, and I'm getting no cell service here. Your place was the only sign of life." She paused. "Again, I am so sorry to bother you." She hoped she wasn't laying it on too thick.

"Um, what road are you looking for?"

"Southside Drive. I know it goes along this side of the river, but . . ."

The doctor smiled. "You really are lost. That's just south of the town of Chimney Rock, right after the road to the state park. It's about three miles from here."

"So, I leave here, turn right onto the highway, and . . ."

The man nodded. "That's correct. It'll be the right turn just after the state park turnoff."

"Oh, thank you. Um, my husband will be worried sick, and my phone isn't getting any signal. Could I impose on you to use your phone? It will just take a minute."

He frowned and scanned the surroundings behind her. But, after a moment, he nodded. "Sure, come in. My cell coverage is limited here, too, so I understand. We have a landline here for that very reason. The phone's in the main room. This way." The main room overlooked the river.

She walked into the space and stood looking out the large picture windows. "Wow, what a view. I bet that's absolutely gorgeous in the snow, or in the summer."

"Actually, fall is the best," he said from behind her. "The phone's right here." He pointed to it with his left hand.

She approached him and the phone and, upon reaching a suitable range, pointed the 9mm handgun she had retrieved from her coat directly at his chest, and fired. Just close enough to concentrate the gunshot residue near the entry wound, and just once, no one committing suicide would fire twice.

Surprisingly, there was no exit wound. That hole was always larger than the entry wound. The medical examiner would no doubt find the bullet lodged in his spine. That was fortuitous for her, as she didn't have to avoid any blood splatter on the floor and furnishings as she would have had to do if the bullet had exited the body. She could work more quickly.

The man looked at her with disbelief in his eyes before crumbling to the floor. She stood next to him and observed. "Nothing personal," she said before the light in his eyes extinguished.

Satisfied that he no longer lived, she took his hand and placed it around the gun in order to put his fingerprints on the weapon. She let it fall naturally with his hand, so it wouldn't appear staged. She also retrieved a small spray bottle from her coat, which she used to spray a solution on his hand. Once dry, it would test positive for powder residue. Finally, she searched the home and found what appeared to be a study. The desk drawers were locked, but easily picked. She placed a receipt for the handgun, from a gun show that had taken place not far from his home in Georgia, inside the top drawer with other papers. She closed and relocked the drawers.

She inspected the front room and realized the shell casing was out of place for the angle of the gun had he used it on himself. She placed it in a more appropriate location. Looking around one more time, she was satisfied that all looked convincingly as if he'd shot himself.

She turned off the doorway light as she exited the cabin. She then relocked the dead bolt using her lock-picking tools in reverse. That always seemed strange to her, to lock a door with tools meant to unlock it.

As she turned toward her car, she heard a cell phone

ring from inside. She thought that odd at first, but then remembered she had been places with spotty service where calls came in okay, but she couldn't dial out. The ringtone stopped after four rings. She assumed the call went to voicemail. A moment later, the landline rang. Someone was trying to contact the man. How long would it take before the caller became concerned enough to contact the local sheriff?

She wasn't interested in finding out. She backed out of the drive onto the asphalt. Using her headlights for illumination, she stopped long enough to inspect the gravel drive for tread marks. Like the trail across the river, the earth and gravel were frozen and no tire tracks were noticeable.

Before continuing back to the rental, she used her phone to text Francois. "Task accomplished," was all she wrote. He would initiate the next phase as soon as the doctor's death was announced by local authorities.

But for now, she was exhausted. The cabin awaited, as did a good night's sleep. Perhaps when she awoke in the morning, she would be greeted by the news of a shooting nearby. Perhaps that news would break later in the morning. Either way, it wouldn't take long to be ruled a suicide. Case closed.

TEN

"*Paramos aquí por el día*," said the team leader as he held up his fist like some military squad commander.

The men carrying their packs did not hesitate to stop, peel off the heavy packs, and sit in the shade of a sturdy lean-to-like structure they had come to. Several took advantage of the break to drink water from the gallon jugs tied to their packs.

Abdi also welcomed the break. It hadn't taken him long to realize that the pack's 70 pounds—that he'd been told he must carry—consisted only of the drugs. Food and water added to that weight, and he was expected to carry the same rations as the others even though he would not be making the return trip to the airfield. Hiking the rugged terrain with nearly 90 pounds on his back had taken a toll on him. He did not want to imagine what the trek would have been like during the scorching heat of the day. To rest during the heat made sense.

He glanced about. As with the plane, the group filled but half of the space they now sat in. Someone had spent considerable time to construct the shelter from local rock and timbers. Abdi had not perceived the structure as they approached it; it blended into the landscape that well.

Unlike the cartel lieutenant he dealt with, the leader of this squad spoke no English. Abdi's limited Spanish held no benefit, so he simply played follow-the-leader. So far that had worked. As the others broke out some rations, he did the same. When others stopped for water, he did, too. Now, the team settled in and used their packs as backrests. Two of the men had already fallen asleep.

Abdi would attempt to sleep now as well, but he doubted he would get much rest. The anticipation of reaching the border the next night and swimming the river to gain entry into the U.S. kept him awake. He had men who would greet him on the other side. With Allah's blessing, he would return to St. Louis within 36 hours.

For the past two weeks, he'd had men at the airport on the alert for the woman's return. All commercial flights into St. Louis were covered, and he knew where she lived. He would not miss this time.

Hannah surprised herself. She rarely slept past six a.m., but this morning she awoke soon after eight. The cabin was cozy, but she had little to do while there. She had rented it for a week because of the uncertainty of her timetable. Now that her task had been completed in a day, she mentally debated what to do.

She couldn't head back to New York so quickly. Contrary to her original thinking that being off-season was to her advantage, she now realized that might seem suspicious to some. It was, she recognized, a small rural area, and despite being a tourist mecca in the summer, folks there were likely to take note of strangers in the off-season. Particularly which cabins were in use and which weren't. And a visitor leaving one day into a week's rental might catch a local resident's attention. Certainly the owner would notice. She couldn't always rely upon the influence of the Assembly to divert an investigation away from her. She needed to blend into the background.

She recalled the Director's comments when he tasked her with this assignment—that she would have to do her shopping at her destination. And that's what she would do. She had only three outfits to Hannah's name, and Asheville sat less than an hour away. The city was also home to the Biltmore Estate. She had been there once before for a story and saw much of the behind-the-scenes action. But, in reality, she hadn't seen that much at all. That could consume an additional day.

She dressed quickly and realized she hadn't considered food. She hadn't so much as dry cereal or bread to toast for a breakfast. She would need to decide how long to stay to work her cover story. Maybe that would require some supplies at the cabin. Maybe not.

Yet, that would work to her advantage. News there likely traveled faster by mouth than by media. If anyone had heard of the doctor's death, the Rocky Broad would have.

The place was half full this morning, but then it was later in the day, and the place had been open for over an hour. Hannah found a seat near the fireplace.

"G'mornin', hon. Another one of those apple fritters?" The barista smiled.

"You remember me." Hannah wasn't sure if that was positive or not, under the circumstances.

"Of course. Folks around here remember strangers, at least till the next one shows up." She laughed. "What'll it be?"

"Do you have anything more substantial than pastries?

Like, breakfast breakfast?"

"No breakfast like you'd find at Denny's, hon, but I make a mean breakfast sandwich. One egg, choice of meat—ham, Canadian bacon, pork sausage, or bacon, choice of cheese—cheddar, smoked cheddar, smoked Gouda, American, or swiss, all on a brioche roll. Or you can go open-faced with double the toppings, and with or without Hollandaise sauce."

Hannah was hungry enough for the double, but questioned the quality. Would she regret it in an hour? Still, she *had* enjoyed the coffee and pastry the previous morning. She decided to gamble and ordered her double, with the sauce. And another signature blend, grande.

A short while later, the woman returned with her food. "So, didja find the place you were looking for?"

Hannah nodded as she sipped her coffee. "No problem, once I knew what Gerton Highway was. It was supposed to be a girls' getaway with some old friends from college, but I got stood up." She shrugged. "It's that time of year. One friend's kid got sick with some stomach bug. Another got stranded by that snowstorm that hit the upper Midwest. The third had her time off canceled because so many people in her office are sick. Nothing like cold and flu season to upset plans. So, it's just me and my camera." She took another sip.

The woman appeared to soak it all in.

"Pretty quiet in this area this time of year. Not much excitement."

Well, that settled it for Hannah. The doctor's body had yet to be discovered, or she'd be getting an earful right now. As for her trip there, the seeds were planted for her to leave early. Three days. Shopping, Biltmore, and a day with her camera. Not necessarily in that order, depending on the weather.

She tucked into her breakfast and sat there amazed. The woman not only knew coffee, she crafted an outstanding, gourmet Hollandaise sauce.

ELEVEN

Lynch scanned the numbers along the street in the upper middle-class neighborhood outside Orlando. His call from the previous day had been welcomed, and in fact, he would be meeting members of both doctors' families today. They had arranged to join him at one home.

There! He'd arrived. The house was a large two-story in a Mediterranean style that reflected the status and financial state of the man who'd lived there prior to his death. His widow and older teenage children still resided there. The man's body had been discovered almost a year earlier on the golf course of the country club they belonged to. A handgun had been found next to him, along with his golf bag. Agreeing with the family, it seemed odd to Lynch that the man would feign playing 18 holes just to commit suicide on the back nine. But that's how it had been ruled by the local authorities.

Joining them would be the brother and son of a female doctor who had been found murdered in her home just six months earlier. That incident had been ruled a home invasion gone bad, but the family continued to insist that there had to be something more.

Lynch noticed three cars in the driveway. The group must have already assembled to meet him. The clock on the car showed that he was ten minutes early. He pulled out his cell phone and dialed Amy.

"Good morning, sunshine. Did you sleep well?"

She was as much a morning person as he was. Years of early shifts at work did that to one's biorhythms. Yet, when he'd called her the afternoon before, she seemed agitated. Twice in that conversation she had asked if there was any intel on Abdi.

"Not really. Took me a while to get to sleep, but after that it was okay. Macy kept reminding me that no one except you and my brothers know I'm staying at her place, and they don't even know where she lives."

Lynch gave Macy credit for that one. "Well, she's right. You're off the radar at this point. As it ends up, we didn't even arrive by commercial air service, so no one else could possibly know we're back except those we contact. You're safe there."

"Okay, but I still can't help . . . well, you know." She paused. "Hey, I appreciate your giving me something to do. It helps keep my mind occupied."

After discussing some options with the President, Lynch had decided that Amy was his best choice as a research assistant. She had the computer and search skills, and she already knew what they were looking into. Using her avoided bringing yet one more person into the loop on this investigation.

"So, have you found anything?"

"Maybe. On the date you gave me for the male doctor's alleged suicide, our friend was in Miami on a special report assignment. That's only four hours by car from Orlando. Less if the Assembly provided her a helicopter or other air transportation. I can't find anything to actually place her in the Miami metro area the whole time of the assignment. But I also can't find anything that suggests she might have gone to Orlando. As for the female doctor, our friend was in New York, so that's not a likely connection."

"Okay, I can work with that. Thanks."

"I'll keep digging. If you want, I can make a few calls."

Lynch did not think that to be a good idea. "No, no calls. First, you have no official authority to make inquiries, and that could raise red flags on several levels. Plus, you'd have to use a name. Anonymous inquiries don't go very far. What name would you use? A fake one makes the information you gain useless in court. Using your real name is problematic on many levels."

He could almost hear relief in her silence.

"Got it. Didn't really want to do that anyway."

"Hey, it's time for me to meet these families. Text me if you discover anything crucial. Oh, I hope to be back in the Lou tomorrow. I'll keep you posted."

They exchanged their affections, and he pocketed his phone. A moment later, the front door opened before he could ring the bell.

"Agent Cully?"

Lynch nodded and produced his temporary credentials. "Good morning."

"Come in, please. I'm Laura Holden, Bruce Holden's widow."

Inside the foyer, a small group of people had assembled to greet him. Introductions were made.

"Let's move to the family room where we have plenty

of seats for everyone," said Mrs. Holden.

Lynch began the discussion. "I've read the police and medical examiner reports on both cases."

One of the older Holden boys frowned and shook his head as he expressed some dismay.

"Michael, please." His mother gave him a stern look.

Lynch wanted to understand his frustration. "Michael, is there something wrong?"

The young man shook his head. "My dad was not *a case*. His name was Bruce. This is starting just like all the other talks we've had with the authorities."

"Let me start by saying that if this was just like all the other interviews or talks, I wouldn't even be here. As far as the local authorities are concerned these investigations are closed. I've read some of your disagreements with the police findings, but why don't you tell me about your dad?"

The teen appeared placated and began to describe his father. His siblings joined in. They painted a picture of a man content with life and loving his family. They had family plans for a special vacation a month after his death, plans that the doctor had been integral in making and had looked forward to. Their mother added to the story as she thought necessary. Lynch's gut "confirmed" that this was a man who had been murdered, not one who took his own life.

"What about the handgun?" Lynch asked.

Laura Holden looked perplexed. "We'd never seen it before. None of us. He never talked about getting a gun, although some friends suggested it because of threats he'd received."

Threats? thought Lynch. He recalled no mention of

threats in the police reports. But he had another question before moving to that topic.

"As I recall, the detectives found a receipt for the gun."

"That's what they told us. I never saw it, and to my knowledge, Bruce had never been to a gun show."

"You mentioned threats. What threats? Did you relay this to the detectives? I saw nothing about this in their reports."

"Yes, we did, and they just brushed it off. The threats were about some work he was doing. In fact, Doreen, um, Dr. Hagen, was involved in the same research. We weren't aware of that until after the fact."

Lynch looked at Doreen Hagen's brother and son, and asked similar questions of them. Dr. Hagen's ex lived on the West Coast and had been ruled out. She, too, sounded like a pillar of the community—active in her son's life and school, on the board of two local charities, and loved by her patients. Many of them credited their lives to her work.

Which brought Lynch back to that topic. "What was this work they were involved in?"

Mrs. Holden pointed to Sam Simmons, Dr. Hagen's brother. "Even though we've talked about this many times, Sam can explain it better than I can."

Sam nodded. "Both of them believed strongly in holistic medicine, and as such, did not shy away from what some folks label alternative medicine. Now, when I say alternative medicine, I don't mean weird stuff. They both had science degrees before med school, and were open-minded about various ideas. They didn't just jump on the latest pharmaceutical to come out, and they believed the body had the ability to heal itself most of the time.

"Both, in their own way, had stumbled across some research on an enzyme called nagalase. It's an enzyme the body produces, and in the early stages of cancer, it's been found to increase in the blood. What it does, in a nutshell, is suppress the immune system and support cancer cell growth."

"Yeah, it blocks a type of white blood cell called a macrophage, which normally would attack the cancer cells," added Michael. "I've been reading my dad's papers."

"That's right," said Sam. "The research they both came across talked about blocking the nagalase, which in turn, allows the macrophages to do their job and fight the cancer. With that and proper nutrition, my sister was actually able to help some of her patients beat their early stage cancer without chemotherapy, radiation, or surgery."

Lynch's interest was piqued. A cure for cancer? That would surely rankle Big Pharma and the profits they drove with cancer treatments. And any enemy of Big Pharma would be an enemy of the Assembly.

"You say 'with that and proper nutrition.' Was there some kind of drug they came across?"

Sam shook his head. "Let me start with the nutrition part. Doreen always saw the standard American diet as pathetic, with its added chemicals, dyes, preservatives, and such. Even most raw foods are now contaminated with glyphosate, the chemical in Roundup™, and other nasty poisons they absorb from the ground water. She insisted that her patients drink only filtered water and focus on organic foods. Many of them greatly improved their health just by making these changes alone."

Lynch saw the handwriting on the wall. Now these doctors were also taking on Big Agriculture, too. A double whammy. Targets on their chests *and* backs. One for Big Pharma and the other for Big Ag.

"So, did they find some drug to help?"

Mrs. Holden spoke. "No, it was a naturally occurring compound."

Sam nodded again. "Yes, a protein called GcMAF. That stands for Globulin component Macrophage Activating Factor. It's the protein that stimulates the macrophages into action, and nagalase blocks it from working. A Japanese doctor by the name of Yamamoto had published two or three papers on it, and a doctor by the name of James Jeffrey Bradstreet had picked up on it. He had discovered that nagalase was also elevated in autism patients. Bradstreet found a group in the U.K. that was promoting GcMAF, which they produced in a plant in Switzerland, and started using it to treat his autism patients. He had mixed results. Some patients improved dramatically. Some not at all, and these latter families began calling it a scam. The families of the 15% of patients who were almost cured of autism called it a wonder drug."

"My husband and Sam's sister saw the potential of GcMAF for treating cancer and began their own informal, off-label trials. They also tried it in some of their autistic patients, but weren't as successful with them." Mrs. Holden looked tense.

"So, what happened? I would think that the discovery of a natural cure for cancer and maybe autism, too, would be great news." Lynch already suspected what happened but wanted to hear it from the families.

"Well, Dr. Bradstreet made the mistake of going public and broadcasting just that. *THE* cure. He went on television and promoted his results, and called on Big Pharma to fund more research in the area," said Laura Holden.

Sam nodded. "Sadly, yes. He should have quietly continued his work. Within a month, the press was full of reports about his scam, of being a quack doctor. The U.K. company was raided by their authorities and all their records taken. The Swiss authorities closed down the production plant with reports of it being rat-infested, and worse. My sister had toured that facility and called it state-of-the-art. So, clearly a full court press against GcMAF had been launched. Six weeks later, Dr. Bradstreet was found by a fisherman, dead in a North Carolina river. A gunshot wound in his chest and a handgun in the water next to him. It was ruled a suicide because he was so distraught about being investigated and having his reputation and career ruined."

"Just like they did to Bruce." Laura Holden began to cry. Her younger son put his arm around her shoulders to console her.

TWELVE

Amy got off the phone to Lynch with her new marching orders. She was to find everything she could about something called nagalase and a protein called GcMAF. From what Lynch said, these held the answer to a natural cure for cancer. Yet, as a nurse, she'd never heard of any of that. Of course, she hadn't been taught the truth about vaccines either.

She brewed a cup of coffee and sat down with her laptop to begin her search. *Wow!* She thought. *There's more to nagalase than I ever imagined.* Its chemical structure and physiological function. How it suppressed the macrophages by inhibiting GcMAF. Even a named disease—Schindler Disease—for those whose nagalase didn't work properly because of a genetic mutation. Those with Type I Schindler Disease didn't live past early childhood. Autism and seizures were seen in those with Type III. How had she never heard of a disease significant enough to have three "types?"

But that was just about low or malfunctioning nagalase. The protein was elevated in not just cancer and autism, but also with flu, HIV, and other viral infections; lupus; and alcoholism. That partially explained the immune deficiencies in these patient populations.

She began her search for information on GcMAF when her stomach began to grumble. She headed out to the kitchen and prepared a salad with mixed greens, walnuts, apple, and cheese, over which she drizzled her favorite apple cider vinaigrette. She had so missed eating salads in Cambodia. Over there she had to refrain from eating anything washed and raw, such as lettuce and tomatoes, as well as anything raw that might be chopped or cut with a knife. You never knew what kind of water was being used to wash the food and utensils.

Her mind drifted to Lynch. He'd be back home in less than 24 hours. Maybe then they could get their lives back on track. She hoped that would mean following the route together.

She turned on Macy's small kitchen television and began to surf the channels for something to watch while she ate. After a moment, she wondered why she bothered scanning the airwaves, or were they "cable waves" these days? Whichever. Invariably, she would end up on some news channel or another.

She watched several Democrat congressmen grumbling about the President's conservatism and how his business-like approach to running the government was ruining their American ideal. Graham hadn't even been in office over a month. Why didn't they give it some time to see if his approach worked better than their failed, decades-old methods?

As the top of the hour approached, the camera zoomed in on the news anchor. "We have a developing story in western North Carolina. A doctor whose clinic was raided several days ago by the FDA has been found dead in his North Carolina vacation home. We will have more on this as it develops."

She stopped eating mid-bite. She needed to call Lynch. This story was all too familiar to the one he had told her earlier. Part of her didn't want him to know because that meant he wouldn't be coming home as expected. Yet, the sooner he knew, the sooner he could check it out and then come home.

Her call went right to voicemail. "Hey, it's me. Call me or check the news ASAP. Looks like another doctor's died. Details aren't available yet, but it sounds eerily familiar."

She retrieved her laptop and sat it on the dining table next to her. Instead of looking into GcMAF, she typed in "unusual doctor deaths" as her search parameter. What she discovered floored her. She pushed her salad aside and focused on the search results. How many? She worked her way through the news reports and articles by those questioning the official findings on the reported deaths.

Over a dozen doctors, all promoting holistic methods, had died under mysterious circumstances over just the past six or seven months. A few others had died earlier, but within the past 15 months. Two of those were the doctors whose families Lynch was meeting. Another was Dr. Nicholas Gonzalez, a holistic physician in California who fought to expose the dangers of over 100 chemotherapy drugs that had been derived from poisonous nerve gas. He was credited with helping Suzanne Somers beat her cancer, only to be found dead a month later. Autopsy findings were inconclusive.

She called Lynch again. She left a message, again.

Was there some sort of conspiracy going on here? What

was Lynch getting involved in? She'd read that the term "conspiracy theory"—and the subsequent use of "conspiracy theorist" as a derogatory label—first arose in the early 1960s with the CIA using the term to debunk those who questioned the official party line about President Kennedy's assassination. Most of those believed the CIA itself had engineered the assassination because Kennedy was about to sign an executive order returning the U.S. dollar to the gold standard. That would have stripped the Federal Reserve System of its power over the U.S. economy. Since the Federal Reserve was not a governmental agency, but a private one comprised of powerful global interests, Kennedy was, in essence, thumbing his nose at the Assembly and attempting to return control of the economy back to the government and the people.

Without knowing details about the work of these doctors, Amy suspected that they, too, had run afoul of powerful interests with their work. She also realized that she probably couldn't help Lynch much. Those same powerful interests had the ability to bury any sort of online information about these doctors and their work, if not delete it outright. Lynch's approach of interviewing family members was the only way to gain that information.

She frowned at that thought. Now he *would* be gone for weeks. She didn't like that.

Her phone rang as she worked through more references. Macy needed a printer. Bookmarking all these sites for later use was a pain. Hard copy would be so much easier. She saw caller ID announce that it was Lynch and answered.

"Hello again. Got your message. I'm at the airport."

"Yeah. Sounds like there's been another death of a doctor, in North Carolina."

"I know. I was on the phone with the President when you called. I, uh . . . sorry, but I have to go to North Carolina before I can come home."

"Lynch, I got curious and started searching doctor deaths. Did you know there have been over a dozen unusual deaths involving holistic doctors over just the past half a year?"

He didn't reply right away. Amy could hear the airport P.A. system announcing something. "Amy, yes, I did. That's what I told you just yesterday."

"You did?" Had he said that? To be honest, she'd been so upset at learning that Abdi might still be alive that she didn't recall the rest of the conversation.

"Yes. You were upset and worried I'd be gone to interview all of their families while Abdi might still be out there. Remember now?"

She hesitated. "Maybe. You aren't, are you? Going to interview every single family?"

"No, and with some luck, I might still make it home tomorrow, just late in the day."

She smiled. "That makes me feel better. I pray that all goes smoothly so you can."

"Thanks. I'll keep you posted. Now I just have to figure out how to get to a place called Bat Cave, North Carolina."

"And I'll keep digging into the information you asked for. Oh, and say 'hi' to Bruce Wayne for me."

Lynch groaned before they signed off, and Amy

returned to her salad. She had a lot to do yet, but maybe she needed to go to her storage unit and try to find her printer.

Abdi felt a nudge in his ribs. The man next to him motioned for him to eat something, and he assumed they would be leaving the protection of the shelter soon. Despite the heat, he had dozed off, and in fact, slept well. The toil of the previous night had physically drained him.

He watched the sky. The sun still shone brightly in the western sky, and the heat lingered. The rocks about them would not radiate that heat away quickly. He took a large draught of water from his gallon jug. Its warmth did not help to quench his thirst as a cold drink would, but he knew he would need that water in his system.

He followed the lead of the others and ate slowly. Dusk seemed to take forever to arrive in the arid lands of northeastern Coahuila. The previous night's trek had taken them less than half of the distance to the border, but it was the most rugged terrain. Tonight's hike would seem easier, but its openness increased the risk of detection. That had been explained by his contact back in Los Mochis.

As the sun reached the western horizon, its descent seemed to accelerate. Soon there was little more than a bright orange and yellow sunset emanating from the edge of the earth.

Their leader stirred. All of the men drank more water, and Abdi copied them. They had made this trip before. He trusted they knew what they needed.

"*Consigue tus paquetes. Es la hora,*" spoke the leader.

Abdi understood *hora* as time. *Paquetes* sounded like

packs, and sure enough, the men stood and helped each other with their loads. Abdi was last to get assistance.

A moment later, they started off in single file, as they had the night before. This, too, had a reason, he had been told. Because of the terrain, one row of men was more difficult to spot by air than a group spread out. Also, for much of the hike the cartel had cleared certain trails such that the men could traverse the terrain along several routes at random. Clearing single file trails had been the easiest.

Abdi found himself in the middle of the pack this time. He soon discovered why he'd been encouraged to drink so much. The residual heat in the rocks made the trek like walking in an oven. After an hour, he felt tempted to pick up his jug and consume more. Yet, he had resolved to follow the leader, and no one else went for their water.

However, by two a.m. they had stopped three additional times for food and water. Soon after, he noticed a glow in the sky to the northeast—the lights of Langtry, Texas. An hour later, he could see the distinct lights of the town and intermittent reflections of light on water. They were so close, he thought he could smell the water of the Rio Grande.

As a soft glow rose in the eastern sky, the leader took a sharp turn to the northwest. Within minutes they entered a long, narrow *arroyo*. The ravine widened as they progressed down its course, and vegetation grew lusher. He could hear water now. The city sat downstream. The river itself came into full view, and across the river, Abdi could see a larger canyon entering the main river valley.

They reached the edge of a large sandbar on the

Mexican side of the river and stopped. The men began to unload their burdens in the obscurity of the brush. With their packs removed and covered with scrub, the leader pointed to two of the men. The men hurried to a point upstream, where they uncovered a roll of steel cable. As the first man picked up one end of the cable and entered the river, the second man fed more cable to the first as that man waded into the river and soon began to swim across.

The team leader tapped on Abdi's shoulder. He held a short stick in his hand with which he pointed to a spot across the river. He then started to scratch the sand with the stick. Abdi watched as those scratchings evolved into a crude map. He put an 'X' at their current location. From there, he drew a line that appeared to follow the man across the river, into the gorge across from them, and north to another *arroyo* that rose to a plateau on the Texan side.

Abdi understood. That was the route they were to take.

At that point, the man with the cable reached the other side of the river and tightened and secured the cable there. With a wave of his hand, one of the other men grabbed his pack and rushed to the cable. He secured the pack on the line and then used it to move both it and himself across to the U.S. One at a time, they all did the same.

Abdi was back in the U.S. Now, he needed only to evade capture until his men picked him up along the Highway 25 Loop.

The sun eased over the horizon as they topped the final climb. At that point, the leader smiled for the first time at Abdi and helped ease the pack from his back. The man gave him two thumbs up. Abdi had proven his worth to them . . .

and he was now free of his obligation.

He used his hand to point in several directions, because he was uncertain which way to go. The man pointed toward the city lights. Abdi nodded his thanks, grabbed his water jug, and headed toward his next life . . . and his revenge.

THIRTEEN

Hannah awoke in the cabin after another restful night. Something about the total quiet around her and lack of city lights made sleeping here so much easier. She'd have to think about taking time off in the mountains more often.

She also felt at ease knowing that Hannah had a suitable wardrobe. She wouldn't have been able to get away with three outfits for long, even though in her current location, jeans everyday would not be out of place. She had spent the day in Asheville shopping, having found an aging suburban mall on the eastern side of town, just off I-70.

As she envisioned Hannah, her target shops would include places where she might find quality at a discount, as well as the occasional high-end garment for special occasions. The mall, and its surrounding development, included just such retailers.

Of course, Hannah's tastes had to be different than those of Summer, and that proved to be the most difficult task. For each and every piece she had to scrutinize it from the perspective of "Would Summer have worn this?" Color choices had to be different with her new hair color. Fabric choices had to be more mundane with an emphasis on wash-and-wear rather than "drop me off at the dry cleaner." Whereas Summer had to look runway-model sharp all the time in public, Hannah was more the girl-next-door. Several times she caught herself with a "Summer-style" item at the check-out and had to relinquish it.

In the end, she also had to buy new luggage to have something to carry her new wardrobe back to New York. She would give each piece a second look and figure out potential combinations in a little while. Her plan to visit the Biltmore Estate that afternoon would include a return trip to the mall should she need to return anything.

First, she needed something to eat. She had decided against stocking the cabin as most of that would go to waste after she left in two days. Besides, she found she really liked the Rocky Broad's food and coffee. There was more to that woman than met the eye.

"Mornin', hon. The usual coffee? The signature blend?"

Hannah shook her head. "Nope, gonna try your caramel macchiato latte this time. Oh, and just a single breakfast sandwich. With sausage and smoked Gouda. Unless you have something special today. I noticed the 'Ask about the Special' sign as I came in."

The barista-slash-owner-slash-chef smiled. "Actually, have two specials today. Folks like you been askin' about breakfast, so I'm testing those waters. Today I have Eggs Benedict, or for a southern flare, biscuits and sausage gravy. You won't find better for either of them."

This time Hannah had no doubt the woman was telling it straight. She hadn't had really good biscuits and sausage gravy in ages, but she'd already tasted the Hollandaise sauce. How could she go wrong with the Eggs Benedict? "Sooo, how's your sausage gravy?"

The Rocky Broad looked toward the other side of the

room. "Fred, Eric, she wants to know if the biscuits and gravy is good."

Two men lifted their heads and looked her way. Both smiled, nodded eagerly, and gave two thumbs up. One lifted his plate to show it almost as clean as if it had come from the dishwater.

"Fred, what'd you do, lick it clean?" She laughed and shook her head in mock disgust.

"Okay, sold on the biscuits and gravy."

The woman returned in less than ten minutes with her order. Hannah decided to test the waters by asking, "So, anything new and exciting around here?"

The woman sat down opposite her and leaned toward her, whispering. "I know I told you nothing exciting ever happens here. Well, I should modify that to say *rarely* happens around here. Sheriff's department found a dead body in a cabin, not too far from where you're staying, if the place where you're staying is off Gerton Highway, that is." She took a breath. "Haven't heard any details yet, but one deputy came through here and said it was a murder, but another got coffee and called it a suicide. I should have all the details by tomorrow. Those guys can't keep a secret from me."

Hannah nodded and offered a look of shock and surprise at the news. *Good*, she thought. *The body's been found.* Now the media spin would start.

The Rocky Broad looked up. "Oops, folks at the counter. Back to work." She patted Hannah's hand and rose to greet her new customers.

The woman's readiness to talk with Hannah told her

something else. Her girl-next-door persona was working. She obviously appeared approachable and as someone a person could confide in. She had chosen wisely, as Francois had said.

She tucked into her food and found it as good as the endorsements she had received moments earlier. The food didn't take long to finish, and she, too, was tempted to lick the plate. Instead, she sat there enjoying her latte and mentally planning her day.

She heard the door open behind her, as it had several times, and sensed a male figure walk past her and up to the counter. Something about his gait and haircut seemed familiar, but she couldn't see the face. And then he spoke, and the hair on her arms tingled as the gooseflesh rose on her skin.

Lynch Cully!

Multiple expletives flooded her mind. What in the world was he doing here? She wanted to stay and eavesdrop, but every fiber in her body told her that would not be a good idea. She had seen him at work and knew he had a sixth sense, his gut he had called it, that might expose her. As she pulled a twenty from her bag and placed it on the table, she heard him introduce himself as a Homeland Security agent. That was new, and scary for her under the current circumstance.

As normally as she could, she slid back from the table, grabbed her coat, and exited the shop. She backed out of her parking spot as anyone would, slowly with caution, but upon entering the road, she floored it. She took care not to speed excessively and risk getting pulled over, but she wanted out of that town *now*.

After his travel experience to Cambodia, Lynch had debated renting a car and driving to North Carolina. His map app had shown him a nine-and-a-half-hour drive time to Chimney Rock and Bat Cave. Ugh. Flight times? There was one that would get him to Asheville in four hours, but he'd missed that one. The next one with a short travel time was late in the afternoon and got him to Asheville only two hours faster than driving. All the rest had six- and seven-hour travel times and weren't that much faster than driving when time in the airport was also considered.

After a quick call to the White House, he discovered the airport had a federal government motor pool, and he'd been given top priority. Within 30 minutes, he watched the airport shrinking in his rearview mirror. Seven-plus hours later, as the lead foot flies, he found a motel outside Spartanburg, South Carolina. Now, after a refreshing night's sleep—much better since he'd had nothing to do with airplanes—he looked forward to the remaining hour's drive into the Blue Ridge Mountains.

About half way there the highway picked up and followed the Broad River along its valley. He crossed the river at the little town of Uree and soon had his first glimpse of Lake Lure. The road took him around the south end of the lake and back around the long, western arm of the lake fed by the Broad River.

The area reminded him of Osage Beach at Lake of the Ozarks with its variety of lodges, resort cabins, souvenir shops, and restaurants. Most were closed for the season.

Plus, it was early in the morning. The body had been found the previous afternoon, and he wanted to get there as soon as possible to see the crime scene. His biggest hopes were that the local authorities hadn't trampled the scene too badly and that they hadn't worked through the night there. With some luck, he would be able to see the place pretty much the way they found it, minus the body.

First, he needed more coffee and directions. The first place that he found open was some coffee shop called the Rocky Broad's. There were a number of cars in front. That was either a good sign or an indication that nothing else was open.

As he entered the shop, he scanned the clientele. A trio of men who appeared to be locals sat talking to one side. An elderly couple occupied another table. A woman with short, black hair sat facing the stone fireplace, her back toward him. A handful of twenty-somethings with laptops or phones sat staring at their screens at scattered tables throughout. A lone, middle-aged woman stood at the counter.

"Good mornin', hon. What'll it be?"

Lynch had always been pretty much a black coffee—strong enough to strip paint—kind of guy. Perhaps that was because he'd gotten used to such as a detective. Personally, he brewed what he called "cop coffee" to satisfy his taste. He glanced at the overhead menu.

"Biggest, blackest coffee you have. To go. Thanks."

"That'll be my signature blend. One 24-ounce Venti coming right up."

As she returned with the coffee, he flipped open his

credentials.

"I'm Agent Cully with Homeland Security. I'm here to look into a death that took place in a cabin near here. If I gave you the address, could you point me in the right direction?"

She gave him a crooked smile. "Hon, I don't need the address. Here's how you get there." She proceeded to give him turn-by-turn directions complete with mileage to the tenth of a mile between turns.

Lynch chuckled. "Don't guess you could give me all the crime details, too, could you?"

She lifted her head with proud assurance and replied, "Not 'til tomorrow morning, hon."

He nodded and pointed to the blueberry cake donuts. "How about two of those blueberry donuts, too."

She retrieved them for him and placed them in a small bag. "Anything else?"

He shook his head. "That's all. Thanks. How much do I owe you?"

She held up her hand to refuse payment. "Law enforcement's on the house."

"Well, thank you. You're too kind."

He started to turn to leave and had a thought. This woman was clearly a hub for all local news. In the summer, he wouldn't expect her to know, but in the off season, there was a good chance she'd encounter most of the visitors to town at some point. He turned back to the counter.

"There is one other thing." He pulled his phone from his coat and opened up a picture of Summer Stanton. "You wouldn't by chance have seen this woman in town?"

She scrutinized the photo. "She looks mighty familiar."

She took the phone and held it varying distances from her eyes and at a couple of different angles. "I recognize her now. She's that news lady who died when her car went into a river in, what, New Jersey maybe?"

Lynch's hope deflated. It was worth the chance, but Summer was pretty well-known and he knew he might run into her celebrity status as the source of recognition. He reached to take his phone.

"But, you know, I'm real good at faces, and her doppelgänger's right over . . . well, she was right over there at that table by the fireplace. Didn't see her leave. Anyway, could be this gal's twin sister, except for short, black hair instead of long and red."

Lynch dashed to the door and scanned the parking lot. No one. One car was missing, but he hadn't thought to take notes on the cars and license plates. He headed back to the counter.

"You wouldn't happen to have a security camera of the parking lot, would you?"

"Sorry, hon, haven't needed something like that. Why would you be asking about her here in Chimney Rock? That's mighty strange." She paused and looked reflective. "Wait a minute, that doctor's death and this so-called dead reporter . . . are they somehow related? What—"

"I can't really comment. But thanks for your help. If you see her again, please call me. Here's my card. Really, 24/7, call me." He took a sip of coffee through the hole in the lid. It was really good. "Hey, great coffee. Thanks again."

He headed out the door, convinced that the gossip lines for Chimney Rock were about to have a meltdown. He felt assured of one other thing, his gut instinct about Summer Stanton was correct.

FOURTEEN

After an afternoon and evening of frustration, Amy had had enough. She had friends who did everything digitally. Everything. Banking. Correspondence. Photos and music. They went so far as digitizing every old photograph they'd ever taken and throwing away the hard copies. They had no need for a printer, and on those rare occasions when they did, they used one at work.

But that wasn't Amy, nor Lynch. Sure, both did a lot on their computers, but when it came to reviewing research material, there was something about reading it on paper, being able to annotate it easily and highlight important facts.

She had bookmarked over four dozen websites and research papers on PubMed. Some had to do with suspicious deaths. Others with nagalase or GcMAF. A few talked about the controversy with Jeffrey Bradstreet's work. She could see why Lynch viewed so many of such articles with caution. They were over the top in their condemnations. They made her recall the Shakespearean quote, "The lady doth protest too much, methinks."

Even though she organized the work by category, it was tedious to call up the URL, wait for the ever-present ads to load, click away the ads on some of the websites, and read the paper, scrolling and clicking to read the entire thing. She could read and review them much faster on paper and knew that Lynch would prefer the same.

Her dilemma? Her printer was in one of the two storage bays she had rented. She suspected it was in the back half of the smaller space, but she could be recalling that incorrectly. It had been almost three months since she packed things away there.

Not only would she have to leave Macy's and go out in public, she might have to spend well over an hour at the storage facility trying to find the device. With Abdi unaccounted for, she didn't relish that level of exposure. She knew in her mind that she shouldn't be afraid, that the Lord doesn't give us a spirit of fear, and that fear was the antithesis of faith, but she hadn't convinced the rest of herself of that.

Her feeling of intimidation was irrational. Of that, too, her mind was convinced. In Cambodia she had stepped up to the plate and put herself in harm's way for those children. Fear had never entered her mind.

And yet, here, on her home turf, things were different. It was just her. She had no children to protect. Abdi's whereabouts were unknown. He could actually be dead for all they knew. The number of people who knew she was home could be counted on the fingers of one hand. Why the hesitation?

After bookmarking another few websites, she took a deep breath and stood up. She was being ridiculous. She needed her printer, and there should be no reason preventing her from retrieving it.

She bundled up against the cold and decided to wrap a scarf around her lower face for better anonymity. She stepped out into the cold and headed for her car. Soon, she found herself at the storage facility working her way through her smaller rental bay.

As both the day and her body heated up, the latter from working to move boxes, furniture, and other items, she began to strip away her "protection." The scarf and hood were first to go. She had trouble seeing with them getting in the way every time she turned her head. Then the coat came completely off.

An hour later, with the smaller bay completely emptied and repacked, she closed and locked the door and moved to the larger space. A third of the way through that storage area she found her printer.

She carried it to her car and stashed it on the backseat, tossing her coat on top of the box. She needed to cool down. Plus, she could adjust the heat in the car as needed. Speaking of which, her car needed gas. Thinking now only of the work she had ahead, that work required paper as well. She should probably get more ink, too, just in case. She should also contribute to the food stock at Macy's.

Lynch had suggested that she avoid any known past locations such as the MedAir offices and her old house, but like he said, only a few people knew she was back. No one would be looking for her—if Abdi was even alive. Which he wasn't, right? So, since she was out, maybe she should also check her house one last time. She still had one key she wanted to leave there. The new owners would take possession the next day. Pretty soon, she had a mental list of things to do, items to purchase, and places to go. Abdi was the last "thing" on her mind.

Abdi's return to St. Louis had gone without a hitch. Two of his men were waiting at the designated spot along US Highway 90 outside Langtry. The exhaustion of carrying that pack through the rugged terrain took more of a toll on him than he expected. Or had it been the combination of that and his previously being stranded in the ocean for over a week? He would never admit that he needed more time to recuperate after that ordeal. He was, after all, the Lion of Somalia. He slept while they drove nonstop back to the Gateway to the West.

Word had gone out that he was safe and heading back to Missouri. Along with that message, he started the task of finding the woman. Men were to watch her home and place of employment. His people at the airport were to be alert to her arrival there. Likewise with those working gas stations near her home, as well as the men driving his taxis. They were to do nothing but report back to him that she was home. He would take care of the rest.

Feeling much better upon his arrival, he had called together his lieutenants and received their reports on his business dealings. The taxi company continued as it had. They'd had opportunities to expand, but, without his agreement, his lieutenants delayed those decisions. Each new taxi expanded their drug routes and delivery capacity. Several inner-city gangs had approached them for supplies due to disruptions in their previous supply chains. They attributed those disruptions directly to new segments of the border wall being built.

Abdi told them of his own experience at the border,

embellished by his being the leader of the group, not a mule. He reassured his men that their supplies would not be easily threatened and authorized the purchase of six new vehicles to expand their territory.

The meeting was followed by a celebratory feast prepared by his own wives. They knew his favorite foods, as well as his other pleasures. He was indeed welcomed home in grand style.

As he awoke, the memories of the past two months seemed distant. The Lion of Somalia had survived the sea and the desert. He began to tell his stories of these adventures to the young men of his clan.

". . . suddenly, the U.S. Coast Guard surrounded our boat. But your people stood firm. They resisted the boarding of their boat and fought valiantly. They told me to take the fast boat and flee to fight another day. They would defend my escape. I said I would fight alongside them, but they insisted and forced me into the boat before cutting it loose. They killed many of the enemy, but in the end, the vast superiority of the military firepower overwhelmed them. They died martyrs for Allah and our cause. I, too, almost died when they shot the fast boat out from under me, but Allah gave me a vision of leading the intifada here and protected me. I floated for days, fed by the fishes themselves. Then Allah arranged for my rescue by a Mexican fishing boat, its crew honored to come to my aid."

The time neared noon and his stomach grumbled. His wives had been appalled by how skinny he'd become and were delighted to fatten him up. As he ate, one of his men approached.

"Lord Abdi, she has returned—the woman you seek. She has just been spotted in her driveway and entering her house. The back of her car is loaded with supplies."

Abdi smiled. "Tell the man to back off. I don't want him spotted and the woman alerted." The messenger nodded and left the room. Abdi rubbed his hands together. He would strike soon, now that he knew she was back in Saint Louis. She would not escape him a third time.

Amy checked the time. The closing on her house was still half an hour away, so technically she wouldn't be trespassing by going inside. Still, she hesitated opening the front door. In truth, she wanted nothing to do with entering the house, but she had one remaining key that she needed to leave behind. She slowly turned the key, unlocked the deadbolt, and opened the door.

Tears immediately welled up in her eyes. The good times here—friends gathered in her living room, nieces and nephews searching for Easter eggs or focused on presents under her Christmas tree, meals and movie nights with Lynch in the "old days" before their separation in the past, and more—haunted the front room.

But the bad times overwhelmed the good. The bullet hole in the door frame of the spare bedroom-slash-office, from the failed abduction attempt on her, was still there. Richard's memory filled the dining room where they shared a first meal after she accidentally got drunk out of nervousness over fixing him dinner for the first time. The night started well, but did not end that way.

She had memories from each room, good and bad, but

there was one room she couldn't force herself to enter. Despite so many good times happening there over her years of ownership, one negative overwhelmed them all. She would not, could not, enter the kitchen and began to sob at the memory of her father being murdered there by Abdullah Said Abdi. She envisioned his blood stains still being there on the vinyl flooring, even though from a distance, through the doorway, she could see that new flooring had been installed.

She left the key with the others on the mantel and fled through the front door, allowing it to lock itself behind her. She wanted to lock the memories inside as well, but they managed to make it out the door beside her. As she opened her car door, she stopped for one last look and noticed yet one more reminder of the evil events that had occurred inside. The postal service had changed the number of the house, as it often did for houses where a murder had taken place.

FIFTEEN

Lynch found a single sheriff's deputy at the scene of the death when he arrived. He glanced at the man's nametag as he came near.

"Deputy Morgan, good morning." He presented his DHS credentials. "I'm Agent Cully with DHS. Anyone else here today?"

The man touched the brim of his cap and nodded. "No, sir. The Forensics Services folk finished up last evening, and the body's been taken to the medical examiners at Wake Forest Baptist Medical Center. I'm expecting to release the crime scene to the family as soon as they get here."

"What can you tell me about the death?"

The deputy shrugged. "Not much to tell. Family in Georgia couldn't get ahold of the man and asked for a welfare check. Another deputy got the call, couldn't get any response at the door, and went around to the windows facing the river. That's when he saw the body, with a handgun next to it."

The case already had Lynch's "gut" tingling. Where had he heard this story before?

"Anything else?"

"I wasn't on duty yesterday, so all I have is secondhand. My buddy told me they found a single shell casing and powder residue on the man's right hand. Oh, and a recent receipt for the gun. Anything else, you'll need to ask the sheriff or Forensics Services sergeant. Sorry."

His hope to see the scene as it was without the body was gone.

Lynch nodded. "No problem. Thanks. So, where do I find the forensics folks?"

"Main headquarters. That's in the county seat, Hendersonville."

Lynch must have looked confused, and admittedly, he had no idea where that city was located.

The deputy added, "Head back out to the main road and go north, that's left. Follow US Highway 64 where it splits off to the southwest. You'll enter the city about 15 miles down the road. To find the crime lab and sheriff, turn left on N. Grove Street. You can't miss the place."

Half an hour later, Lynch did as the man said, turned left on Grove St., and found the sheriff's office building. Ten minutes after that, he saw a burly, forty-something man enter the lobby area and approach him.

"Agent Cully, I'm Sergeant Andy Reynolds, of the Forensics Services Section. Come on back."

Lynch was escorted into the secure area of the building and led to the man's office, where the sergeant offered him a seat across from his desk.

"What can I do for you?"

Lynch had prepared for such questions. He couldn't give away much about what he'd been tasked to investigate, so he kept it vague.

"We have an interest in the death yesterday of Dr. Renton. What can you tell me about it?"

The sergeant gave Lynch a curious stare. "Looks like a plain vanilla suicide. Of course, the ME will offer her official findings after the autopsy and labs." He pulled out a folder and opened it on the desk. He fanned out prints of the crime scene photos for Lynch to see.

Lynch focused on the photos of the body and weapon. The handgun clearly had been dusted for prints, as shown in later photos of it alone.

"What can you tell me about the trajectory of the bullet?"

The sergeant offered a subtle shrug. "Pretty much dead on center mass. From the location of the entry wound, it had to have shattered the sternum and entered the heart. Powder marks on the clothing and residue on the right hand. No exit wound. I don't have anything preliminary from the ME, yet."

That, too, sounded much too familiar to Lynch.

"So, why would a physician shoot himself in the chest? Seems a strange choice. He could have OD'd on any number of drugs at his disposal."

"Don't have that answer. We can only guess what went on in his mind."

Lynch nodded. "True. Just seems odd."

"Actually, it's the second one I've seen in the last, oh, five years. Another doctor did himself in farther downstream on the Broad. Fisherman found the body on the shore."

"Yeah, a Dr. Bradstreet. I've been looking into that death, too. Any connection between the two doctors? Besides coming to your county to die."

The section chief looked surprised. "I, um, don't know. I'll have to raise that question with the detective in charge."

"What about fingerprints?"

"Yep, got good full and partial prints off the weapon. Our print expert is about two weeks backlogged, but says a cursory look at them seems like a match to the victim."

"Do you have a copy? Can I see them?"

The man nodded and rifled through the file again. "Here you go?"

Lynch scrutinized the images. He had significant experience in analyzing fingerprints, although he'd never worked in a forensics lab. Something was off here.

"Do you have any enlargements, or a magnifying glass?"

The sergeant went through the file again, but didn't produce anything new. He stood up and walked to his bookcase where he retrieved an old magnifying glass. He handed it to Lynch.

"Haven't had to go 'old school' for a while, but I keep it around just in case."

Lynch returned to the fingerprint photos. There was indeed a discrepancy.

"These are accurate, right? Index finger partial on trigger, other fingers on handle and thumb partial on the opposite side."

"Sure. Just what you'd expect from someone holding a handgun."

"Exactly. So, how did he hold the gun to shoot himself dead center on the sternum?"

The man pretended to hold a gun and point it at his chest. He tried several iterations of that movement, finally contorting himself to achieve a mid-sternum entry.

"I see what you mean. He could never get that shot off with his fingers located on the gun as they are."

Lynch nodded. "That's right. The best he could do would be an angle like this." He demonstrated. "At point-blank range like that he'd have an exit wound out his left back ribcage. To get a dead center shot, it's easiest to hold the gun so the thumb pulls the trigger. That's not what you have here." Lynch let that settle in. "Oh, and I'd check the prints on the other doctor, Bradstreet, again. You might find them very similar."

Something else came to Lynch's mind.

"I heard you found a recent receipt for the gun."

The sergeant was still trying to shoot himself in the chest to match the findings. He stopped and returned to the file.

"Here it is."

Lynch looked directly at the doctor's alleged signature at the bottom.

"Have you compared the signature to other documents signed by the victim?"

"Only a preliminary one. The fingerprint tech also looks at signatures and handwriting for us. But to be honest, we hardly ever need that kind of analysis, so he doesn't have a ton of experience. If we need a real expert, we can send it to the state labs."

"Do these look the same to you?" Lynch held the gun receipt next to the real estate document given to him a moment earlier.

"Pretty close. The detective in charge thinks they're the

same."

"Look again. See the slant of the writing. The doctor's signature on the document looks like that of a left-handed man. Have your detective ask the family or friends if the victim was a lefty. I think you'll find that he was."

The implications of that did not fall on deaf ears with the sergeant. The fingerprints on the gun were not only in the wrong place; they were from the wrong hand, as was the powder residue. And that meant only one thing—the odds were that the man had been murdered.

Hannah's death grip on the wheel of her Audi didn't relax until she arrived at the rental cabin, and that was only because she had to let go to run into the place, pack, and clear out. Of all the people in the world, Lynch Cully would be last on her list to show up in Podunk, North Carolina, two days after her first hit as Hannah. And of those billions of people, he would be the *last* one she wanted to show up. Hair changes, different wardrobe, new persona—none of those would prevent him from outing her.

She had seen him at work in Missouri. She knew his reputation, as well as his doggedness. Why was he in Chimney Rock? She felt pretty sure he wasn't just passing through.

Well, she wasn't waiting to find out. Within twenty minutes she had packed and cleared her things out of the cabin. With extra caution she maneuvered onto Highway 74 and headed toward Asheville. She made note of every car, particularly those with out-of-state plates. She did not want to encounter him on the road.

Yet, on second thought, maybe she did.

She took a deep breath and allowed the ice to return flowing through her veins. Some of her previous co-workers had nicknamed her "Elsa" and a few used the term "Ice Queen"—both as pejoratives. Where she saw herself as cool and collected, focused on getting the story, they saw her as uncaring, willing to step on anyone to get what she wanted. Perhaps. She now acknowledged that trait served her well as Hannah.

And in recognizing that, she didn't like the thought that seeing Cully had rattled her so. Not one bit. However, she knew better than to make an unsanctioned hit purely for personal reasons. That would not sit well with Director Arikhan, or even with Francois.

Cully had made an enemy of the Assembly's discredited director, Karolus Karling, but the man's "suicide" had ended Cully's being on the blacklist. That needed to change. Being on "the list" would make him fair game. Francois would remember him and the trouble he had caused for the Assembly. She would enlist the man's aid in convincing Arikhan that Cully deserved to be on "the list."

In the meantime, should she encounter him on the road and his car end up in the river, well, that would spare her the effort and save them all time.

*　*　*

Leaving Hendersonville via I-25, Lynch passed Asheville to the southwest as he picked up I-40 toward St. Louis. As he neared Knoxville, Tennessee, he pulled off for gas and used that opportunity to call Amy.

"Hi. Heading your way by car. I'll be there sometime after eight tonight."

She laughed. "You do realize you're dating an amateur pilot. You won't be able to avoid airplanes."

Lynch didn't even want to think about Amy's acrobatics the last time she'd taken him up in her Cessna. Her father never let him live down the tear in the upholstery he claimed was the result of Lynch's white-knuckle grip on that flight.

"Yeah, well, they didn't really offer me an advantage time-wise, by the time I drove the car back to an airport with a federal motor pool, waited around for a flight, made a connecting flight, and so on. Besides, this gives me time to think about these cases without the distractions of airports and other passengers."

No, if he was honest with himself, it let him avoid flying. He needed to change the topic.

"So, how's your day going?"

Was that paper he heard being shuffled in the background? That definitely sounded like a stapler.

"Well, I got tired of bookmarking websites and not being able to highlight certain things I found on them. So, I ventured out to my storage units and dug around until I found my printer. While I was out, I ran some errands, mostly to get supplies for what I'm doing and food to contribute to the cause here at Macy's."

Lynch's first reaction was concern, but he'd been the one telling her there was little to be worried about, that no one knew where she was staying except him and Macy. He decided to let it go and be encouraging instead.

"Great. See? Nothing to worry about."

"Well, it took me a while to convince myself of that, but once I got out, it felt good to be back to a normal life. Well, as normal as it can be living with Macy."

She paused, and Lynch again heard noises of papers being "processed."

"Anyway, I have about a ream of paper already printed, collated, highlighted, and categorized. You wouldn't believe what I've found about nagalase and GcMAF. I even found cached copies of Dr. Yamamoto's work. I haven't had time to scrutinize them yet, but the amount of work that went into discrediting them was mind-boggling. Same with the Brits who made the GcMAF in Switzerland. You'd think that whole research track was dead in the water, but in the past year, an Israeli firm has picked up where these folks left off. They're doing some serious research, and if there's one thing I've seen about the Israelis, they don't back down."

A ream of reading awaiting him . . . Lynch knew what would be filling his next few days.

"What about the doctors?"

"Well, not as much available there, at least as far as factual reports. Of the websites and reports I've found, they either go into the conspiracy theory realm or the far extreme on the other side discrediting them." He heard her take a breath. "Yes, I know how you feel about the term 'conspiracy theory,' but I use it only to get my point across. Both ends of the spectrum are covered without anything in the middle ground."

Lynch nodded. He'd expected as much.

"But I did find one thing you're going to want to dig

deeper into."

More paper being handled. He waited for her to continue . . . and waited . . . and waited. The dead air finally got to him. "Are you going to tell me?"

"Uh, sorry, I'm trying to find the article on it. I just sorta stumbled across it by accident."

Lynch knew better. "By accident," aka coincidence, didn't exist.

"Give me the abridged paraphrase." He needed to get back on the road and wanted her to keep this as brief as possible.

"Funny. Okay, I'll keep it short. Bradstreet and Renton knew each other."

That got his attention. He wanted more info.

"And?"

"You said you wanted the abridged paraphrase. That's it."

Lynch gave his best "Amy eye-roll" imitation, although no one was around him to witness it. Yet, he'd asked for it.

"Sorry. I'm antsy to get back on the road and get home."

"Awww, I can't wait to see you, too." She paused. "So, the two of them met at a medical conference a few years ago. On a hunch, I checked real estate records, and Renton bought his place in North Carolina a couple of months after that. I bet they got together there more often than anyone knows. Anyway, the article hints at some form of collaboration that ensued, and Renton came up with a compound he called 'nagalase inhibiting, macrophage activating factor,' or NiMAF. Like GcMAF, he claimed it was a natural compound and didn't fall under FDA jurisdiction.

It sounds like he was using it on a group of patients, but no papers were ever published or results announced."

Amy had been right on target in stating he'd be interested.

"Good work. The FDA raided Renton's clinic a few days ago. I'll have to dig into what they took, but it sounds like just the thing to have a target etched on your chest by Big Pharma."

After saying goodbyes, Lynch climbed back into the car for the remaining eight-hour drive. He'd just cleared the Knoxville city limits when his phone rang—number unknown but the exchange was western North Carolina.

Without hands-free calling in the motor pool car, he preferred pulling to the side of the highway when talking on his phone. But he'd already spent so much time on the call with Amy that he didn't want to delay his trip any further.

"Lynch Cully."

"Agent Cully, this is Andy Reynolds, with the Henderson County Sheriff's office. Thought you'd like to know that the case is going to be ruled a homicide. Ends up, you were right. The man was left-handed. As for the other case, that victim was right-handed and, after reviewing the fingerprint data again, I can't say that the print pattern was questionable."

"Thanks, Sergeant. Maybe someone just got sloppy on this one, but I'd bet a year's wages these cases are related. Let your detective know the two men knew each other. It's an avenue worth exploring."

Indeed it was, but he had a different road to travel. Lynch debated giving them a heads up on his conversation with the Rocky Broad owner, but she wouldn't sound believable. The idea of a reincarnated Summer Stanton playing a role in the doctor's death was *Twilight Zone* material. And Lynch was about to enter the *Zone* at his own risk.

SIXTEEN

Hannah hadn't allowed her encounter with Lynch Cully to fully ruin her day. She had already purchased tickets for Biltmore House and decided to make use of them. The odds of Cully finding her there were infinitesimal, so why not? The 12-hour trip back to New York could wait until the next day.

Or so had been her reasoning yesterday. The Director had seen otherwise.

Francois' call had been short and to the point. She had been summoned to see Arikhan promptly at nine a.m. So, after the drive and five hours of sleep, she presented herself to Francois outside the penthouse.

"He will see you now."

Francois seemed curt, his tone no different than it had been on the phone the previous day. The look on his face was one of disappointment.

"Ah, Hannah. Thank you for returning so quickly." The Director ushered her into his study and pointed to a chair opposite his.

"I drove back as soon as I got Francois' call." As if she had any real choice.

As soon as the Director sat down, Francois appeared with coffee for both, each cup prepared to the drinker's preference. He tucked his tray under his arm and remained standing at the doorway. That in itself was significant to Hannah. Clearly, the man wanted to hear what was said. If only Hannah knew why she'd been summoned, she'd have a better understanding as to what might be about to happen.

She was about to ask how she might be of service, but thought better of that. She would speak only when spoken to.

"So, Hannah. What happened in North Carolina?"

"What happened, sir? I don't understand. The target is dead, as requested."

"Yes, but . . . tell you what, why don't you give us a detailed account of your trip."

Hannah took a deep breath and a step-by-step presentation of her actions up to leaving the cabin with Renton dead. She included everything, her trip to the coffee shop and her conversation with the owner, her taking photos along the river, and her scouting of the man's property. She left nothing out.

The Director looked at Francois. Hannah followed his gaze in time to see Francois nod. She still had no clue as to what was going on. She'd made a clean hit. Nothing could blow back on her.

"Sir? I don't understand. What's going on?"

"Are you aware of what's happened in the past 24 hours?"

She took another deep breath. "Clearly, by the fact that you're asking that, I'm not."

"The death has been ruled a homicide, not a suicide."

That was impossible. Well, not impossible, but surely improbable. She hadn't left any traces to suggest someone else in the cabin. Everything at the scene pointed to a self-inflicted gunshot. How in the world could it be ruled otherwise?

"What? I don't see how that's possible. I was careful."

Movement in the periphery of her vision caught her attention. Francois had moved from his place next to the door to the side of the desk.

"You were fatigued. You should not have completed the task as soon as you did. You were given plenty of time. You should have taken advantage of that." Francois' demeanor had softened. He now looked at her as he always did.

Arikhan nodded. "I would agree. From your account of your movements, you engaged the target too soon."

She had little to say in her defense. Her first thoughts had been to get a good night's sleep. "I-I hear what you're saying. I had planned just that, but I got a second wind and saw an open opportunity. The next day could have brought other family members, friends, or even police."

"That is true. All contingencies that would have to be worked around. But your fatigue led to an error. Our sources tell us they found fingerprints from the right hand on the weapon."

She nodded. "True. That's the hand I used."

"The man was left-handed. Now they're scrutinizing the gun show receipt and ballistics. Who knows what else?"

Hannah had to think hard. The receipt should hold up . . . unless they start digging into the gun dealer himself. Could those backwoods cops do that kind of digging?

"Sir, both of those should hold up to inspection. The county sheriff's department doesn't have the resources or experience to dig deep enough to expose the counterfeit. I'm surprised they caught the wrong hand evidence." She realized she shouldn't try to rationalize her error. "And I apologize. You are correct. I shouldn't have continued the task while tired. I wasn't as on top of my game as I should have been. In hindsight, I now recognize the target used his left hand to open and close the door, and point to the phone. I missed that. It won't happen again."

She still felt surprise that the rural county's forensics team had caught the discrepancy. And then it dawned on her. "Cully." She said it as a whisper, but Francois picked up on it right away.

"What did you say?"

"Cully. Lynch Cully. Remember him?"

"I do indeed," replied Francois. "He caused us all kinds of trouble during Karling's days."

Now Arikhan picked up on the new source of tension. "Why do I not know this name, and what about him?"

Francois spent the next five minutes briefing the Director on a once-upon-a-time St. Louis detective who became the security chief for Bradley Graham, until the Secret Service took over. He provided information that surprised even Hannah. The man's success rate in his previous occupation had been amazing. No wonder he'd been such a thorn in the Assembly's side for a brief period of time. Yet, Francois' ability to pull that information from his head at the spur of the moment astounded her even more.

When Francois finished, they both looked at her.

"I stopped into the coffee shop again yesterday

morning, and while there, Lynch Cully walked in. He didn't see me, or at least my face, and I was able to leave before he did. However, in that brief interval, I heard him mention that he was with Homeland Security. I have no idea why he was there or what he's up to, but if he was there somehow connected to Renton's death, he could have led the county sheriff's people to find the hand discrepancy. I'm positive they wouldn't have found it without help."

The two men looked contemplative. Hannah wondered what each might be thinking.

"Francois, do we have a file on this man?"

"*Oui*. It is in the database. May I?"

Arikhan nodded and scooted his chair away from the desk. Francois stepped behind it and bent over to use the keyboard and mouse. Within seconds, he stepped back and used his hand to motion to the data. The Director returned to his place and spent a few minutes reading.

Hannah had her own opinion on the topic but knew better than to offer it. This was best left to the two men in her presence.

"Francois? Your opinion?"

"*Monsieur*, this man is very talented, and persistent. If he now has Homeland Security credentials and the ear and backing of this president, he could become quite troublesome."

The Director nodded in agreement. "Indeed." He looked at Hannah. "Hannah, this was your first official case, and we are prepared to overlook your error. But mind you, we are not a three-strikes-and-you're-out organization. If you fail in your next assignment, well, I think you know what your fate will be."

She did, and she would not fail. She could not afford to.

"Yes, sir. I won't let you down."

"Good. Take out this Lynch Cully."

Abdi's thoughts smoldered with hatred toward the woman who had made a fool of him and set him running for his life—twice now. The word he received that she was home had caused him to think of nothing else. He wanted to make her death a slow and painful one, and his men had been tasked with preparing a warehouse he owned to become the perfect place for him to exact his *ciqaab*, his retribution. By noon he received notification that they were almost finished with their work.

"It is this way, lord."

The man gave a subtle bow to Abdi and led the way into the building. Abdi took a moment to think of the man's name. Ah yes, Bashiir. He had done well to accomplish this task so quickly.

Inside the larger open space of the warehouse, a smaller chamber had been constructed, its walls soundproofed. The door to the enclosure was solid steel and three locks secured it. A CCTV camera provided surveillance of the area fronting the door.

The man opened each of the three locks and finally the door itself. Inside, Abdi found a space of roughly 20 by 20 feet in which were multiple forms of torment, from a car battery and cables to a steel table accompanied by a complement of tools organized for pulling, cutting, and burning. In one corner of the room he found a three-by-five brick cell, modeled after those in Tuol Sleng, Prison S21, in Cambodia. She would understand its purpose.

What was missing was a supply of water or food, and any form of toilet. She would "live" in her own filth . . . but not for long.

SEVENTEEN

"Good afternoon. Is Macy Johnson available to talk?"

Lynch had come to the triage desk of Mercy's Emergency Department rather than ring in through the ambulance entrance. He was, after all, *not* on official business, although no one there had to know that.

When he didn't recognize the staff at the desk, though, he decided to have a bit of fun. He flashed his DHS credentials. The young woman's eyes widened.

"I, uh . . . is this . . . has she, um, is she . . ."

With all seriousness and a deadpan look, he answered, "I'm not at liberty to say. If she's not on a critical case, please get her now. If she's on a critical case, I can wait. Thanks." He pulled a pair of handcuffs from inside his coat.

The nurse's eyes went from wide to bulging. "Um, I'll check." She rushed from her station to the department's main work area.

A moment later, he could hear Macy's voice through the soundproof wall. "What? Why that . . . I'm gonna kill him!

The voice intensified as she approached the door connecting the two spaces. She burst through the door and stopped, glaring at him. "What gives you . . ."

Lynch grinned, twirling the cuffs on his right index finger. "Gotcha."

She counted to ten before folding her arms across her

chest. "Look here, Mister Secret Agent Man. I was just beginning to like you. Don't you go screwing that up now. If I tell Amy what you just did, she'd—"

"She'd laugh," he interrupted. "You know she would."

Macy's bluster deflated. "Yeah, she probably would." She shook her head and took a deep breath. "Okay, so what do you need? I can't talk for long."

Lynch pulled out a small box, opened it, and held it up for Macy and the triage nurse to see. Lynch angled his head to see the nurse's nametag. "Nurse Gittemeier, you are hereby sworn to secrecy." He turned his attention back to Macy. "Think she'll like it?"

He moved the ring about in the light to highlight its sparkle.

"OMG, Cully. What'd you rob to pay for that? It-it's beautiful. My girl's gonna have to work out at the gym to carry that on her finger for any length of time."

He nodded. "I'll make a note of that—add gym membership to gift list."

She looked ready to hit him on the arm but hesitated in front of witnesses.

"Seriously, Cully. That's what, at least two carats. Being Graham's security chief must have paid you well."

He shrugged, not willing to admit or deny that, or to confirm that it was nearly three carats of highest quality diamond, in a princess cut, set in a custom gold filigree and ring. "Actually, I made a friend of a local jeweler when I managed to recover all two million dollars' worth of gem stones and jewelry he'd been robbed of a week earlier. He got the stone for me at his cost and did the gold work for free."

She gave a low whistle and whispered, "Better not let some of the lowlifes around here see that. Want me to get security to escort you out?"

"I'll be okay. No one's looking except you two." He glanced around to make sure that was still the case. He closed the box and slid it into his pocket as a young family with two kids approached the desk. He slid down to the farthest end of the desk, and Macy followed.

"Look, I need your help. I'm struggling to find the perfect place to propose. Any ideas?"

Her face took on an instant blank stare.

"I was thinking maybe of renting out La Bonne Bouchée for just the two of us."

Macy immediately shook her head. "Nope. Not good. Richard, may he rest in peace, did that with the Bridge Tap House when he proposed."

Lynch immediately scratched that idea from his mental list. That had been his go-to plan, but with it having been used before for Amy's previous ill-fated engagement, it became a horrible idea. Unfortunately, now his mind was blank.

He felt crestfallen. He wanted the "perfect" spot. It didn't have to be elaborate, like some he'd seen on social media. It had to be special to *them*.

"Help me out here, Macy. I was so set on that idea, I don't have a plan B, or C."

She shook her head. "I'm gonna have to think on this one. Give me a few days."

"Okay. Thanks. If you come up with something, let me

know ASAP."

Amy paced restlessly around Macy's place. Lynch was supposed to pick her up for lunch at noon, and now it was half past. This was characteristic of the "old" Lynch, and her concern wrenched her thoughts in a different direction. He said he'd changed. She had seen a different, a "better" Lynch in Cambodia. Had that just been due to their environment, being out of their country? Had coming back to their old haunts initiated a reversion to old ways? Maybe old dogs really can't learn new tricks.

As her worries mounted, the doorbell rang. Upon opening the door, she discovered Lynch standing there with his phone to his ear. He kept talking as he walked into the apartment.

"Yes, Mr. President, I understand . . . Yes, sir. Actually, I just arrived. I'm with her now." He rolled his eyes and bobbed his head up and down. "Yes, sir . . . Yes, thank you . . . Yes, sir, I'll tell her . . . Again, thank you. Goodbye, sir."

He disconnected the call and sighed. "Amy, I'm so sorry. I've been in my car, in the parking lot for the last 40 minutes, but they were calls I couldn't ignore and didn't feel comfortable taking with you present."

Didn't feel comfortable with her around? She must have given him quite the look because he quickly backtracked.

"Wait. That didn't come out quite right. Look, the first call was from an analyst at Homeland Security. They, the department, don't know about your working with me with the approval of Graham, and we don't want them knowing. Remember? So, I couldn't lie to the guy and tell him I was in a secure spot, meaning alone, to talk with him if I was in here with you. And then Graham called right after I hung up on the first call. That's when I figured it was okay to head in from the car to get you."

Her worries abated, and her feathers unruffled. "Okay. I just wish you'd let me know somehow that you were out there. I was getting worried." She didn't let on as to *what* had her concerned.

"Sorry. I'll do better if it happens again."

"Well, I'm hungry. Let's go."

Instead of moving toward the door, Lynch eased off his coat and sat on the couch, patting the seat next to him. "We need to talk."

She didn't like the tone he used to say that. She hesitated but then sat next to him. He leaned forward, put his elbows on his knees, and rubbed his hands together. She had seen him do that before and braced for what was coming.

"The call from DHS was, well, about Abdi. It seems our concerns are valid. There's been chatter both in southwest Texas and here, in St. Louis, about someone calling himself the Lion of Somalia."

"But that could be anyone."

Lynch nodded. "True. But the timing is not a coincidence—less than two weeks after the Coast Guard blew that fishing boat out of the water. If he survived that, drifted at sea for a while, got picked up by someone, and worked his way back to the U.S., two weeks sounds reasonable."

Amy groaned. This was *not* what she wanted to hear.

And yet, Lynch's timetable assumption seemed sound.

"Then, just in the past day, Abdi's taxi company here ordered six new cabs. Would they have done that without his approval?"

"Well, whoever took over for him might have done that." She felt as if she was grasping at straws.

"Again, true. The bottom line is that we don't have a clear picture as to his fate. But there's a high probability that he's back in St. Louis. We've asked local authorities to keep an eye out for him. I mean, his arrest warrant is still standing, but after hearing he'd left the country, the local cops no longer focused on finding him. So, we've asked them to renew their vigilance."

Amy had to mentally regroup. She didn't like the uncertainty, the foggy picture that Lynch referred to.

"Can't the police raid his taxi company, his home?"

Lynch shook his head. "Not without a warrant, and that's going to require more proof that he's actually here. They might have gotten a warrant under our previous county prosecutor, but this new guy came out of the Ferguson riots and is on the side of the criminals, not the police. Abdi could stand outside his door, thumbing his nose at the police, and this new prosecutor—and I use that term loosely—wouldn't throw the book at him. We might have to use a federal warrant, but like I said, that will take more direct proof."

Amy felt a righteous anger rise within her. The realization that they could be facing battles on two fronts—Abdi and the Assembly—had at first seemed overwhelming. But the verses out of 2 Timothy 1—*...for God gave us a spirit* *not of fear but of power and love and self-control.*—and Romans 8—*If God is for us, who can be against us?*—came to mind and bolstered her spirit.

Along with those verses came another thought. They needed to go on the offensive, and she had an idea as to how to confront one of those two enemies using their own tactics.

EIGHTEEN

Hannah would not make the same mistake this time. Her new quarry was more than a worthy opponent. He had skills and contacts that no unsuspecting doctor or businessman would have. He also had the support of the new President and access to the resources of the Department of Homeland Security.

Yet, they had their own assets within that department. Just as the Assembly had started a quiet *#resistance* movement within the bureaucracy against this new President, they would add one Carson "Lynch" Cully to their list. His requests for information would get lost, his queries stymied, and his access to government services slowed.

In the meantime, she had full access to the Assembly's data banks, money, and media outlets. She did not expect to use the latter. After all, he had no research or other work to be discredited. He was simply a personal nemesis and threat to the organization, one who would die unexpectedly. His death would be recognized by the local media, his accomplishments touted, but nothing more. The less fanfare the better.

She did, however, take full advantage of her access to the data banks. She spent the afternoon pulling up everything she could find about Lynch Cully—his school records, his employment records, where he spent time on the Internet, although that footprint was surprisingly small. She had his home address, phone numbers, a list of family members and friends, and restaurants he frequented. There, too, however, 'frequent' was hardly the word to use. He either ate out rarely or used cash, which couldn't be tracked.

She tried to trace and cull a list of his daily, weekly, and monthly habits, but found that the man had none. He lived life in as random a fashion as one could imagine, as if he knew that routines could prove dangerous. Even his cell phone location data showed his use of varying routes between destinations, while most people became set in their ways of traveling from spot A to spot B.

She thought again about the cash aspect. To use cash, he would have to visit a bank or ATM to get it. Yet, she found no records of regular visits to one or the other. Did he print his own? She chuckled at the thought but realized this was a blind spot in the data they had collected on him. She made a mental note to get their analysts working on this shortfall.

All in all, he was going to be a challenging target. She would have to give serious thought to her plan as she drove to St. Louis the next day. Without routine travel routes or frequently visited locations, she couldn't really plan an accident along the way. As with her previous target, his home appeared to be his primary weak spot. A home invasion gone bad perhaps.

And then she discovered that he was renting his home to someone else and that his parents were out of the country. Another possible family link, his sister, lived out of state, where he was unlikely to visit. Finding him might prove more difficult than she had hoped.

Yes, she would have to think this through and plan accordingly. She could not fail this time. At least she had one advantage. Summer Stanton was dead. She had the element of surprise on her side.

All was ready. Abdi had dispatched spotters to the woman's house shortly after confirming that her final "home" was prepared. He personally would not be there to take her, as he was a wanted man and more than one of his people had informed him that they were under surveillance. He would, however, be there in the virtual sense. His men would live stream the event to him as they took her and brought her to the warehouse.

He gave the word to go. Now they had only to wait for the opportune time. Should she not come out to get her empty trash can at the curb, they would wait until dark to break into the house to get her. Abdi blessed Allah that he would see fit to make this easy by having her come to the curb.

He settled into eating his evening meal, albeit a bit earlier than usual. He wanted to be ready to "host" his guest when she arrived. He finished as dusk approached and focused his attention on the video feed. Lights had popped on inside the dwelling.

His mind drifted until a voice alerted him from the video. The garage door was opening. The woman, bundled in a coat against the cold, hurried from the opening toward the trash can. At the same time, the men in their van pulled out of the nearby cul-de-sac and drove her way. As she neared the curb, the van screeched to a stop next to her, and two of them jumped out. The woman screamed as one of them placed the hood over her head and wrapped his arms around her torso to control her arms. She began to kick, but the other man grabbed her legs, lifting her off the ground, and directed them into the van. With the woman and both men inside, the door closed and the van veered away from the house.

The video feed showed the front of the house long enough for Abdi to glimpse a man running from the front door toward the street, waving his arms and yelling. The video then showed one of the men injecting a sedative into the woman's upper arm. Within minutes, she calmed down and went limp. The men bound her wrists and ankles and the live stream stopped. He would see the woman again at the warehouse, where she would awaken and Abdi would remove the hood and watch the horror on her face as she saw her captor and realized her fate.

The plan now entered a critical phase. They could not risk being caught, so the van would first drive to the back lot of an abandoned business nearby, a location not visible from the streets. The men would switch the woman to another car, which would proceed to another rendezvous point about halfway to the warehouse where the process would be repeated.

The original van would be filled with cleaning supplies and equipment, with magnetic business signs attached to the sides of the vehicle. If stopped, there would be no sign of the woman, not even enough room within the van behind the front seats to hold a person. Every contingency was thought of, from the materials added to the van, to the paperwork of a legitimate cleaning business, to the smell of soap and wax in the cargo area. Bashiir, again, had been very thorough.

He smiled at the mental replay of what he'd just witnessed. Not only had he captured the woman, he had done so in front of the man who had helped her evade him overseas. Abdi delighted in the knowledge that the man likely now felt helpless, knowing the fate of the woman at Abdi's hands, unable to free her.

Abdi had planned on meeting the woman upon her arrival at the warehouse, but that plan had changed. The sedation, he was now told, would not wear off for at least a few hours. He gave his men orders to chain her within the three-by-five cell inside the chamber at the warehouse. He had no need to rush. The delay would increase her fear. She would awaken in the dark, chained and hooded, to contemplate her last hours on this earth.

NINETEEN

Abdi had a restless night, not out of agitation but out of eagerness to wreak his revenge. His mind had played over and over again what might happen when he ripped off the woman's hood and saw . . . saw what? Fear? Resentment? Anger? Indignation? Repulsion? A will to fight? These scenarios and more repeated in his mind.

But now, the time had come to see what this woman was made of. No. Actually, he had seen what the woman was made of in Cambodia. If only she hadn't made him look like a fool those many months ago when she disrupted his plans of terror. Had that incident not made him lose face in the eyes of his people, made him look weak, he realized he could have come to respect this woman and the strength she had shown in southeast Asia.

That water buffalo had already escaped its pen. He had to follow through on his plans or she would once again win.

Bundled up to maintain his anonymity more than against the cold, he sat in the backseat of the car as it traveled to the warehouse, contemplating what he would do first to this woman. In his mind he continued to play out various scenarios. Would she plead for mercy? Would her anger make her defiant? Would she show the weakness of all women and cry, begging for her life?

Assured they had not been followed, they finally

approached the warehouse entrance. The men inside rushed to open the vehicle door and allow the car inside, closing the door just as quickly once it was. He was greeted by the man he'd left in charge as he exited the vehicle.

"Lord, she awakened a few hours ago. Would you like to see the recording we made for you?"

Why not? he thought. They walked to a corner of the building where a variety of electronic gear was set up. His man pushed a button, and the video began to play. The woman at first began to cry, appealing to be released. She went through a litany of questions and pleas, as he had expected she might. "What have I done to deserve this? Why? Where am I? I promise not to tell anyone if you release me. PLEASE let me go!"

But then she said something he hadn't expected. "Is my husband okay? Have you hurt my children? Whatever you do to me, please leave them out of this, whatever this is."

Husband? Children? Was this a ploy for sympathy? She had no husband or children.

Abdi rushed to the chamber and went inside. He yanked the woman up from the floor of her cell by her chains. She began to whimper.

"Release the chains," he ordered his man. "Put her on that stool. In the light."

The woman sat unsteadily on the stool, her wrists and ankles still bound by cable ties. As he came near, she must have sensed him and cringed.

He ripped off the hood and screamed. "You fools! This is not the woman! Where is that woman you were to bring to me?"

In anger he backhanded the man he'd left in charge across the face. If he'd been armed the man would have died on the spot. He took several deep breaths in an effort to control his anger. His mind roiled over what to do next. This woman had seen his face.

He stormed from the chamber, trying to come up with a rational plan. This woman could identify him. She should be killed. But then, this was not her fault. Killing for Allah was one thing. Killing an innocent woman was another, even if she was an infidel. Allah had shown him mercy in the ocean, and he would show this woman mercy. So what if she'd seen his face. He was already a wanted man. What would one more charge amount to if they caught him?

He walked back into the chamber and put the hood back on the crying woman. "What were you doing at that house?" he demanded.

"W-we just m-moved in. We b-bought the house a m-month ago." She tried to back away from his voice and nearly fell off the stool.

He slapped her head, hard but only once. "If you go to the police to identify anyone you saw here, or if you try to testify against us in court, we will come back to your house, kill your husband in his sleep and make you watch as we torture and kill your children. Do you understand? That is the price for your life. The option is to die, right here, right now, and we will dump your body in the river, never to be found."

She cringed again and whispered, "I w-won't tell. I p-promise."

He turned and left the chamber without another word.

Outside, in the warehouse, he glared at his lieutenant. "I want the men responsible for this. Now!"

The lieutenant turned to his man, Bashiir, and ordered him to get the men.

Fear etched the subordinate's face and he turned to personally plead before their leader. "Lord, please be merciful to them, to us. Look, here is a photo of the woman from two days ago when she was first spotted." The man rushed to a nearby table and fetched a photo from it.

Abdi looked at it. It *was* the woman.

"Lord, how were we to know she had sold the house? Y-you ordered us to stop surveillance after she was seen. We might have seen this family moving in otherwise. A-and last night, this woman was bundled against the cold so that we had no way of knowing it was not the woman you sought. Even when we placed the hood on her, it was near dark. To show mercy on the men will speak louder about your leadership than to punish them."

Abdi looked at the man. The man had *xanjo*, gumption, to speak the truth as he saw it. The man's work and his bravery had caught Abdi's attention earlier. He now saw that his courage extended to more than just physical fighting. He would pay additional attention to this man.

"Thank you, Bashiir. You speak the truth. It has been an unfortunate mistake. Take the woman and drop her off someplace near her home, someplace without cameras."

"Yes, lord." The man offered a subtle bow, turned, and headed for the chamber.

Now Abdi faced a new dilemma. The woman no longer lived where they thought she did, she had not resumed work at the helicopter place, and he had no means of finding her quickly. There was but one avenue to explore that came to mind. She had been dropped off at the airport by a friend. That had been reported to him by one of his men working in baggage handling. How much would it cost him to access the security video footage near that terminal entrance on that particular date? A face and a license plate would give him a new starting point in his search.

TWENTY

Lynch had tossed and turned all night and didn't sleep at all between two and four. It didn't help that he was sleeping on a mattress on the floor of his parents' new home, a home they had yet to actually live in. He was surrounded by unpacked boxes and covered furniture. By eight a.m. he gave up and dragged his body into the kitchen to produce "cop coffee," as he called it. The result was more like caffeine syrup disguised with a mocha taste, the end product of a pot of regular brew sitting on the warmer all morning in a department's call room. It was an acquired taste.

Once the initial brewing finished, he boiled the coffee to remove some water and simulate its sitting on a warmer for hours, thickening and concentrating it. As this took place, he scrambled a couple of eggs and toasted two slices of bread.

He sat down at the small table in his kitchen and took his first sip. His lips puckered at the taste. It had been a long time since he'd needed a jolt of this caliber. His acquired taste must have evolved into a refined taste for better coffee. He endured a second sip and began to feel his head clear. By the end of the fourth drink, he felt ready to take on the current heavyweight boxing champion. Today's energy drinks could not compete with his "cop coffee." He thought it highly likely that the idea for current energy drinks first originated with some overworked, night-shift police sergeant.

As he ate, he mentally addressed the concern that had kept him awake: how could he keep Amy safe while trying to track down the killer he was now convinced Summer Stanton to be? Two other thoughts plagued him, though— the first about the woman at the Rocky Broad's, the one who the owner said could be Stanton's doppelgänger and who had quietly disappeared after he'd entered the shop. If that was a reborn Summer Stanton, she would have recognized him. That, in itself, would have been cause enough for her to slip out unnoticed.

And if she was the doctor's killer, and had stayed long enough to overhear him tell the Rocky Broad that he was there about the death, would she feel threatened that he was coming after her? In fact, at this point he *was* coming after her. Her death had been faked. Of that he felt confident. And the picture of her next to Richard's house at the time of his murder, along with her presence in the town where the doctor had been killed, were motives enough to find her.

Lynch had always loved playing the "what if" game in trying to solve a crime. Of late, however, he'd lost his taste for it. Now it always seemed to involve how to keep Amy safe, or for that matter, himself.

His other major concern was Abdullah Said Abdi. With nothing to corroborate his belief, he knew the man to be alive and back in St. Louis. How in the world was he going to be able to track down that man and keep Amy safe while also hunting for Stanton? He now faced enemies on two fronts. Perhaps he needed to call in reinforcements.

As he cleaned up his mess, tossing the paper plate and other refuse into a black plastic garbage bag sitting on the floor, his cell phone rang. Caller ID told him it was Amy.

"Hey there. Good morning."

"Good morning to you, too. Can you come over here this morning? Macy's at work and we can talk openly. Something's been bugging me, but I might have a way to tackle the issue."

Lynch took a deep breath and hoped whatever it was "bugging" her wasn't going to throw more gas on the fire. He didn't need another complication.

"What's been bothering you?"

"Well, seems to me we're looking to fight a battle on two fronts."

Lynch gave a subtle sigh of relief. *Great minds meet*, he thought.

"I've been thinking the same thing."

"Gee, great minds think alike, eh?"

Lynch chuckled and smiled. "Um, that they do. So you have an idea that might help?"

"I do. Come on over, and let's brainstorm."

Amy hung up the phone after Lynch's assurance that he'd be right over. Actually, she'd spent most of the early morning brainstorming her idea. Maybe Lynch would add to it, maybe not. One way or the other, she needed him there. She also had new research to share with him, but more importantly, she just wanted him with her.

The research materials were already organized for him, and he would be at least half an hour in getting there, if traffic cooperated. To kill time, she flipped on the local news. The female anchor interrupted a story on the economy and newly released jobs numbers.

"In breaking news, we move now to the police station in St. Peters for a hastily called press conference."

The images moved to a scene that Amy recalled all too well from once having been arrested and jailed there. That story had a happy ending. What she saw on the screen seemed to scream the opposite. The podium was surrounded by officers and FBI agents, as well as one distraught man about her age. The man had three young children clustered around him, holding him tightly. They appeared frightened and the older two—maybe ages six and eight—were crying. The police chief stepped up to the bank of microphones.

"We're calling on the public for help. Last night, one of our citizens, a young woman, wife and mother, was violently kidnapped from the front of her home in one of our quiet subdivisions. The attack was witnessed by the victim's husband . . ."

The image now changed to an evening shot of a home, police lights flashing and lighting up the front of the home. Amy's heart dropped into her gut, and tears flooded her eyes. The house on display was *her* house. The mailbox was *her* mailbox, with its new number. The woman taken was one of its new owners.

Amy curled up into a ball on the couch, unable to watch anymore. It didn't take the proverbial rocket scientist to realize that she, Amy, had been the intended target and to know who was behind the kidnapping. *Lynch, hurry up and get here.*

Lynch found the traffic to be lighter than usual, and he seemed to catch every light on green. As he thought about it, he *had* caught every light on green. He made it to Macy's place in record time. The idea of divine intervention came to mind.

Macy's front door flew open before he could even knock, and Amy jumped into his arms, wrapping her arms around him like a boa constrictor taking down its prey. It took only a second for him to realize that her greeting was not one of joy. He practically carried her inside and shut the door.

"Okay, okay. What's wrong? Calm down."

She squeezed him tighter. Was she going to crack a rib?

"Relax. I . . . can't . . . breathe," he whispered.

She released him and let him back away.

"He's here. He's really here, in St. Louis. He's not dead."

Lynch led her to the couch and convinced her to sit down next to him.

"I have a pretty good idea who you're talking about, but we've discussed this. We have no proof yet."

Amy shook her head. "We do now. He kidnapped the woman who bought my house. It's all over the news." She went on to explain what she'd seen on the newscast.

Lynch sat there in disbelief at first, but the clarity of what happened hit him. Abdi, having been out the country at the same time they were, had been unaware that Amy sold her house. The kidnapping had to be a case of mistaken identity. He prayed silently for protection over the woman.

"Give me a sec." Lynch stood, grabbed his phone and dialed an old friend. He paced between the kitchen and front room as he talked.

"Goodrich."

"Sam, this is Lynch Cully. I'm calling about that kidnapping last night."

"Lynch, ol' buddy. Long time no hear. I thought you were in D.C. living the high life."

"Ha. I'm with Homeland Security now. About that kidnapping—"

"Yeah, it was at your old girlfriend's house. Couple had just moved in. I had seen it up for sale. Not surprised, after what happened there and all."

"Sam, I'm back together with Amy. In fact, I'm with her right now. We think this was a case of mistaken—"

"Just a minute, Lynch. Back with you in a minute."

Lynch heard the line go mute. He'd been put on hold. Lynch paced the floor as one minute stretched into five.

"Lynch, you still there?"

"Still here, Sam."

"You're not going to believe this. The woman's been found. Dumped not far from her house. A few bruises and lots of mental stuff, but otherwise no worse for wear. Seems to have been a case of mistaken identity." There was a pause.

"Whoa. That means—"

"Yeah, we know what it means. Amy was the real target."

"Gee, just like old times. Um, sorry, shouldn't have said that."

The man had a point, as much as Lynch didn't want to

admit it.

"Do we know who took her?"

"No names, but the description is just like old times, too. Thin black male, foreign accent, and a long scar on his left cheek. Guess we need to refresh the BOLO for Abdullah Said Abdi."

"Yes, you do." Giving a condensed version, Lynch went on to inform his detective friend about what happened in Cambodia and how they thought the Coast Guard had killed Abdi along with his band of smugglers and terrorists.

TWENTY-ONE

As Hannah inched her way through the Lincoln Tunnel, she reflected on Francois' parting words, "Do not fail, *ma chérie*." It wasn't so much the words he said as how he'd said them. At the time, they'd put a slight chill in her heart.

Now, an hour later with New York City only 13 miles in her rearview mirror, her frustration level overheated every organ of her body. She'd made a point of getting a full night's sleep ahead of the nearly 1,000-mile journey to St. Louis. While rested, the downside was a late start in leaving the city . . . along with what seemed to be 10,000 fellow travelers heading west. That didn't account for the hundreds of trucks as well, all funneling into two lanes of highway where the construction zone in New Jersey began. Inching ahead in that "parking lot" made the work zone appear to go on forever. Add in the cold rain and windy conditions and she was convinced that whoever had authorized this road work in mid-February needed to be committed.

She had never been the patient one. A life coach she once interviewed on the air had encouraged her to develop that trait, but she wanted it to happen overnight. She had no time to learn patience. She was part of that generation of which Meryl Streep once said that instant gratification wasn't soon enough.

She focused on calming her mind. Fuming about her

lack of progress wasn't going to change anything. In fact, as she thought about it, that life coach had been right. Patience held a crucial role in her new line of work. She had learned that lesson with the last assignment, and now, she had to succeed, or else.

Amy felt relief in learning that the woman who'd purchased her home had been released without significant injury. Her encounter with Abdi could have fared much, much worse. She wondered how soon the house would be back on the market and hated the idea that her once cherished home could soon be considered cursed. Not that *she* believed in such things.

"Sam said they'd reissue the BOLO for Abdi and seek a warrant to raid his workplace and home. Since this incident involved a kidnapping, which gets the FBI involved, they can go through a federal judge and bypass a bunch of red tape. That should get the ball rolling."

Amy nodded. Yet, she understood that's all it would do—get the search started. The odds of finding Abdi at either place were slim. The man wasn't a fool.

"You okay?" Lynch looked concerned.

"Actually, yeah. As soon as you arrived, I felt as if the peace of God covered me like warm oil flowing over me from head to toe."

Lynch nodded. "I know the feeling. Suddenly I felt that things were going to take a bizarre twist, and this was the first turn. To paraphrase Habakkuk 1:5, look around and watch, wonder and be astounded, for I am going to do a work in your days that you wouldn't believe if someone told you it was about to happen."

Amy pondered that and tried to put it into perspective with the idea she'd had. The time had come for Lynch's input.

"Want something to drink?"

"Water would be great, thanks." Lynch followed her to the kitchen, and back to the front room where they both sat down on the couch. He took a drink and turned his full attention to her. "So, what's this idea you had?"

She gave a single nod of her head, clasped her hands together, fingers intertwined, and took a deep breath. This was unusual for her. Usually it seemed that Lynch was the one with all the ideas.

"Well, we both were thinking about fighting battles on two fronts. It's now confirmed that Abdi is alive and a continued threat. We suspect that Summer is alive, too. How much of a threat she might be is still unknown."

Lynch nodded. "If she's doing hits for the Assembly now, she could pose a serious threat because that means she's been trained. She's more of a problem than Abdi because we have local police and the feds working to find Abdi. Nobody's looking for her."

"My thinking exactly." She grinned. "See, great minds really do think alike."

Lynch downed another swig of water.

"So, we need to turn the tables on her, as our primary target."

"Target?"

"Yeah. We've been on the defense ever since, well . . . ever since Richard was murdered. We need to take the game to them. What's your pet peeve about attacks on honest people by the liberal elites? The thing you call their hallmark tactic."

"You mean how they go so far over the top to defame someone?"

"Exactly. In the past they used the newspapers and television news. Now they use social media and the Internet with fake groups and websites all dedicated to smearing people who disagree with them."

Lynch offered a slight, knowing smile as he nodded slowly. "I think I see where you're going with this. Go ahead."

"So. What would it take to create a few websites that begin to paint a different picture of Summer Stanton? We could use #summersnotdead and #lookoutforsummer on Facebook and Twitter. What do you recall from that coffee shop?"

"Well, the woman I suspect was her had ink-black hair just off the shoulder with a slight wave to it. She was dressed like a soccer mom. I never saw her face, but otherwise she blended right in."

"Then we put out a social media BOLO of our own with a Photoshopped image of her with that hair style. There are pictures of her all over the web. Shouldn't be hard to come up with a virtual mug shot."

Lynch grinned. "I like this. She won't be living in a cave. She's got to get out and about. So, if we can get this to go viral, she won't be able to hide anywhere. I know just the guy to do the websites and photo manipulation—Mike Jurgesmeyer. And I think I know someone who would love to be first to say she saw Summer. I've learned that that little coffee shop of hers has an international following, not just a national one. Chimney Rock is a big tourist spot, and anyone and everyone who's ever stopped in there for coffee or food seems to follow her on Facebook. She's gonna love this."

"And I'll get my old co-workers to help promote it on their social media pages. We should be able to flush her out in no time."

Lynch furrowed his brow in thought. "You know, this might actually do more than flush her out." He went on to explain his thinking.

Amy hadn't thought of that consequence, but she found justice in it. She watched Lynch reach out and take her hand, kissing the back of it. An electric tingle rose up her arm.

"You know, we make a great team," he said.

TWENTY-TWO

Hannah had been happy to leave the road construction and heavy traffic behind in New Jersey, although she found the number of cars and trucks heading west to be much greater than she'd anticipated. Of course, in her previous life, she rarely had to deal with a lot of road travel. She jetted to one city or another for an assignment, had access to helicopters, and never had to drive herself. She could sit in the back of her chauffeured car and work, oblivious to vehicles around them. To get stuck in traffic became a convenience, allowing her more time on her laptop or for making phone calls.

She'd had the option to fly to St. Louis. In truth, many of her assignments in this new life would also require air transportation, most of which would be by private jet, too. Unlike with commercial flying, she could take the tools of her trade with her on one of the Assembly's aircraft. That was a necessity, not a luxury.

However, she had chosen not to fly for two reasons. First, driving would give her time to fashion a plan for dealing with Lynch Cully, and this was proving more complex than she'd expected. Second, planes, even private ones, had to file flight plans. Flight plans could be scrutinized and traced, providing anyone who might investigate his death with a lead that could cause trouble for her and the Assembly, which, in reality, meant double trouble for her.

No. Her driving to the Midwest provided more anonymity.

The clock on the car's dash showed the day nearing four o'clock as she followed the split off I-70/I-76 southeast of Pittsburgh onto I-70 west toward St. Louis. Three more hours would put her in Columbus, Ohio, where she could enjoy another full night's sleep before a relatively short six-plus hour drive to her destination.

Her cell rang, and she picked up the call on the car's Apple CarPlay interface. Fortunately, the acoustics of the convertible with its top up were pretty good.

"Good afternoon, Francois. I'm just passing to the south of Pittsburgh."

"Very good, *chérie*. I have the information you requested."

Hannah had come to realize that a direct approach on Cully would not work. He would recognize her in an instant. He also had no regular haunts or habits she could capitalize upon. Then it hit her. His Achilles Heel, if she was correct.

"Your memory serves you well. Yes, it appears that Lynch Cully and Amy Gibbs go way back and were a couple at one time."

Those memories dated back a year with that debacle in Kansas City during the campaign and the failed assassination attempt on the Prince of Wales at Westminster College—a failure that ultimately led to the opening among The Three that she now held. Amy Gibbs had been with and engaged to Richard Nichols at the time. She and Summer had an antagonistic relationship, which was not surprising, given Summer's role in trying to compromise Nichols for the Assembly.

She had seen the two of them interact only briefly during that incident, but Lynch Cully's affections toward Amy Gibbs seemed obvious. She wondered if they had a past together, and Francois now confirmed it.

"In fact, not too long ago, Miss Gibbs became the target for a Somali terrorist named Abdullah Said Abdi. She inadvertently foiled the man's plan to terrorize the Midwest, for which even now she remains in his crosshairs. Abdi's bullet missed her and murdered her father instead. She left the country and went to Cambodia where Abdi followed to finish the job. Mr. Cully flew to Cambodia to warn and protect her, which he clearly succeeded in doing, as they returned together roughly one week ago."

Hannah smiled. She loved being correct. "So, I was right."

"Yes, but there's more. We learned that just last night, a woman was kidnapped from in front of Amy Gibbs' home. Well, make that her ex-home. It was sold in her absence and the new owner was taken in what is believed to be a case of mistaken identity. A BOLO for Abdi has been re-issued. As I said, Miss Gibbs is still in this man's crosshairs."

"Where can I find Amy Gibbs now?"

"Good question. We can find no new rental agreements or deeds in her name. She has two brothers in that area but does not appear to be staying with either one. We are trying to develop a list of friends. You should also know that Mr. Cully no longer has a home there. Although he still owns the house, he rented it out upon taking a position on the President's transition team. We believe he is staying at his parents' home in a suburb of St. Louis, but cannot confirm that."

She had already discovered the info about Cully's home. "Thank you, Francois. Could you please—"

"The information is already in your private access files online."

"A step ahead of me, as always. *Merci*, Francois."

"*Pas de quoi, ma chérie.* As always, I am here to serve. I will send more your way as we develop it. *Que votre chasse soit couronnée de succès.* Take care."

With Francois' help, all of her hunts will be successful. Of that she was sure.

Now she felt eager to get to Columbus where she could access her briefs from the privacy of her motel room. She had much more to work with, a tack that should prove more productive than trying to isolate the man himself.

That afternoon, Abdi learned of the new BOLO for him. The woman had given the police his description after all. He could no longer afford to move about freely, as he had been doing. The warehouse would become his new quarters. He had his men establish a reasonably comfortable living space within one corner of the structure.

By dinnertime, Abdi's roller coaster of emotions that day had gone from eager elation to despairing disappointment to open optimism, then rising rage and, finally, hope. He awoke knowing that he would get his revenge on that woman, only to discover they took the wrong person. With the recollection of the woman's friend dropping her off at the airport, he saw a new chance of finding his prey.

And yet, within an hour that expectation clashed with its price tag. $10,000! To get a copy of that day's security video at the airport? A copy. For $10,000? The man talked of the great risk he would take in making a copy and giving it away, of what would happen to him if caught. Abdi could not see what risk his request posed and only incompetents got caught. Abdi had smashed glasses, thrown furniture, and destroyed drywall at learning what it would cost just to bribe an airport employee for a copy of that video on a flash drive.

This woman was bankrupting him! It now became more than saving face and restoring his reputation among his people and those he worked with. He didn't want to tally up the financial costs, but another $10,000 was too much.

And then Bashiir offered another option. As he ate, Abdi reflected on their conversation from the early afternoon.

"Lord, perhaps there is another way."

Abdi had encouraged him to continue, content that he had not exacted any punishment on the man for the earlier mistake.

"Lord, I will take the man who saw the woman being dropped off at the airport, and we will go first to the helicopter company and watch their parking lot for this friend. If we do not succeed there, we will go to the hospital where the woman used to work. Those two places hold a good chance of finding the woman's friend."

Abdi liked the idea.

"With Allah's help, we will have a name soon. And with a name, we can find an address."

Bashiir. The man had come through again. Without hesitation in the future, he would have to consider this man for more important tasks, give him priority over some of the others.

As he completed his meal, he sat back with his hookah and relaxed. Bashiir had taken even further initiative. He purchased a large bouquet of flowers and went to the reception desk of the helicopter place. He asked for Amy Gibbs or her black friend, who he believed was either a nurse or paramedic. The flowers were for them for saving his father's life several months ago. He would have brought them sooner, but he didn't know where to come.

The receptionist appeared to accept his story. Unfortunately, she said, Amy Gibbs no longer worked there and to her knowledge they had no African-American flight nurses or paramedics in the St. Louis region. Bashiir and their man waited until the end of the day and watched the employees leave for home. The woman who dropped Amy Gibbs off at the airport did not work at the company's headquarters.

To track the employees at each helicopter base could take weeks, so Bashiir suggested they take the receptionist at her word. The hospital now held the greater chance of finding the woman they sought. He and their man would go to the medical center first thing in the morning for the shift change and watch the employee parking lot. Even that might require two or three days, maybe more, depending on schedules.

When Bashiir suggested that the friend might not work at either place, and that the airport video might still be needed, Abdi cut him off. He didn't want to hear of spending another $10,000 to find this woman.

No, he felt confident they would find the friend at one of the two places. Just as they had other Somalis as friends, nurses tended to have other nurses as their friends. They understood each other, the training they had endured, the work they did, the struggles they faced, and more. To congregate with like-minded people was common to human nature.

He sat back and smiled as he smoked. A few more days at most and he would locate that woman, that Amy Gibbs.

TWENTY-THREE

Lynch startled awake with the ringing of his cell phone. Despite so much going on, he'd fallen right to sleep and had slept soundly through the night—the result of the previous night's sleep deprivation, no doubt. He picked up the phone. Six a.m. Seeing Mike Jurgesmeyer on Caller ID roused him to being fully awake.

"Hey, Mike. What's up?"

"Are you near your computer, or have your phone with you?"

"Umm, yeah, I'm, uh, talking to you on my phone. So . . ."

"Oh, right. Sorry. Been up all night working on your request. I think you'll like the result."

The man's sleeping habits, if one could call them that, had always been a mystery to Lynch.

"This project sounded like so much fun I decided to dive right in. I did the Facebook page first. Take a look."

He gave Lynch the name of the page, which Lynch proceeded to after placing Mike on speakerphone. #summersnotdead emblazoned the cover image which held a photo of Summer Stanton's car being hoisted out of the river, water draining from every opening. Lynch scanned down to find copies of the crime scene reports, in detail. Should he even ask where those came from? Yet, what struck him the most was the graphic showing Summer before and after, long red hair to short black hair. How in the world had he done this much overnight?

"Mike, how did you get hold of the crime scene reports and photo of the car? Make that photos of the car?" Lynch had just discovered an album of crime scene photos of the car and its contents.

"I have my ways. That's all you need to know. What do you think? You can cruise over to the website, too, but it's much the same. If you approve, I'll move it to my server and make it live."

"What is it? SummersNotDead.com? I'm not finding it."

"Oh. Sorry again. I made that one LookOutForSummer.com to get two different hashtags moving. I'll create the second one with the first name, but I wanted to work on different material so they don't look the same. By this afternoon, I'll have them both up and running."

Lynch saw no reason to hold back. Amy was as likely to be as impressed as he was. He did want to run the image by the Rocky Broad, however. She was the only person he knew who could identify Summer in her new look. But that posed a problem for him, one he hadn't thought of earlier. Getting her involved in the hunt, whether by simple affirmation of the photo Mike had conjured or by actively commenting and acknowledging that she'd seen Summer personally could make her a target. He didn't want that.

And yet, he had learned that lesson before. He would let her decide.

"Go for it, Mike. I'll text Amy with the links. If she has any ideas, I'll pass them on."

"Got it. Oh, and you didn't hear this from me, but don't be surprised if this gets posted on her old network's website. It was an easy hack, and it'll take 'em at least a day to figure out how to delete it without it continuing to pop back on." He laughed. "Boy, what'd I'd give to have a camera in their webmaster's office." He laughed again, but this time it seemed more diabolical. "Hey, got work to do. I'll text you when the second site is up."

As they disconnected, Lynch sighed in relief that Mike was a friend and on his side. Lynch texted Amy, as he was pretty sure she wouldn't be awake yet. However, the Rocky Broad would be up and at 'em. He looked up her shop's website and phone number.

"The Rocky Broad's Coffee Shop."

To Lynch's best recollection, the voice was hers. "Is this the Rocky Broad herself?"

"The one and only, hon. What can I do for you?"

Lynch went on to re-introduce himself.

"Oh yeah. I remember you, good lookin'. You heard they're callin' that doctor's death murder, didn't you?"

"I did. One of the first to know."

"I figured as much."

"Does the Rocky Broad have a real name?"

"Yessiree. Merilee Hanson, at your service. You know something else? Ever since you left, I've been thinking about that woman. You know, Summer Stanton's doppelgänger? Was she involved? She sure seemed interested in what was happening around these parts without coming right out and asking."

"That I can't say, but I will tell you there's no evidence

that she was, if that helps put you at ease." Lynch decided he needed to be a bit more up front with this woman if he was going to get her involved. "What I would advise, however, is that you *not* go around promoting the idea that she was. I wouldn't want that coffee shop to be looking for a new owner who doesn't know coffee like the present owner, if you catch my drift."

"Loud and clear. Like I think I told ya, I read a lot of suspense and thrillers, so if she did it without leaving any evidence behind, she knows what she's doing. I better watch my p's and q's."

Lynch's assessment of her from that morning at the coffee shop was right on. She was a sharp one, as well as observant.

"Look, something has come to my attention this morning. Do you have Internet access handy?"

"Sure. In my office in the back."

"Are you busy right now, or could you take a look at something for me?"

"Hon, it'll be another hour before we get really busy. Let me hustle back there."

Lynch heard a door open and close, as well as footsteps.

"Okay. I'm there. Whatcha got?"

Lynch gave her the Facebook page.

"Looks like you're not the only one who questions her death." That was a true statement. He didn't have to confide that the only others questioning Summer Stanton's death were him, Amy, and the President. He let the implications of his comment stand.

"OMG, that's her. That's the woman who was here."

There was a pause. "Double OMG. Does that mean Summer Stanton is a hit man, er, woman? A paid assassin? Wow, what a book that could make."

Lynch knew it! He'd been confident that the Rocky Broad would confirm their suspicions.

Abdi paced the long, open bay of the warehouse. The abduction of the woman from St. Peters had topped the local newscasts, even before he had released her. There would be no point in attempting to make good his threats to her. She and her family had no real part in this drama.

Yet, all the attention was a benefit. Even though his name had not been mentioned, there would be those in the police who were astute enough to link the address of the kidnapping to previous events there tied to him. And the release of the woman, and her subsequent interrogation, already had confirmed to them that he was involved. They would start looking for him again in earnest. Perhaps he'd been wrong to let her live. That was water already downstream.

One of his men entered the structure and rushed toward him. Abdi recognized him as the man Bashiir had taken with him, the one who had seen the woman's friend. He offered a curt bow as he came up to Abdi. His name was Warsame, meaning "good news." Perhaps they had found the friend.

"Yes, Warsame?"

"Lord, you were right in staying here. The garage and your home have been raided by federal agents."

Abdi had guessed that might happen.

"And your visit to the hospital?"

"I'm sorry, lord. All of the women were hidden behind scarves for the cold. We could see no faces. We will try again this evening and hope that the temperature is warm enough." He again bowed.

Abdi nodded. No, the man did not bring good news, but it was news that might have been anticipated. At the least, because of the move toward 12-hour shifts at the hospital, they did not have to waste time covering three shift changes. Or did they? Perhaps the friend worked for a doctor at the medical office building there. Those workers would go home at a different hour.

"Warsame, find Bashiir and make sure you watch the parking lot when the doctors' offices close, too. We cannot assume this friend works in the hospital itself."

"Yes, lord." At that, the man left.

Bashiir's comments that the friend might not be a nurse at all came back to him. He discounted that idea. It left open too many possibilities and a great chance they'd never find the woman's friend. He could not accept that.

Hannah had slept in until almost nine. She hadn't done that since college. She enjoyed a free breakfast in the motel lobby, as she caught up on the national news. Sadly, the motel's television was turned to Fox News, not her old network. As such, she paid attention to it selectively.

Back on the road, she called Francois.

"Good morning. Do you have anything new for me?"

"*Bonjour, ma chérie.* We do. We have the parents' address. It appears they, too, have moved recently. Of more interest, perhaps, is that we have the whereabouts of Abdullah Said Abdi. The FBI raided his taxi company and home this morning, but our intel has him in seclusion inside a warehouse owned by a shell company, which the FBI has yet to uncover. I will forward that address, but be forewarned, the man is dangerous and will not take lightly to a stranger showing up on his doorstep."

"Is he aware of the Assembly?"

"Not that we know of. Tread lightly."

"*Merci*, Francois."

Tread lightly. That really meant she might have to take out his "soldiers" first. Easily done, but she preferred starting a relationship on friendlier terms.

TWENTY-FOUR

For Amy, when it came to breakfast, if she couldn't eat at her favorite French bistro and bakery, then The Shack was a close second. From the rustic interior, with its tables and walls "enhanced" by the graffiti of its customers, to its over-the-top breakfast offerings, its approach to the best meal of the day was eclectic gourmand compared to La Bonne Bouchée's traditional European fare. Her favorite was their trademarked *Love Me Now, Hate Me Later* plate, a massive breakfast burrito stuffed with scrambled eggs, hash browns, crushed Fritos and cheddar cheese nestled on a bed of beanless chili smothered with their special cheese sauce and topped with green onion. It lived up to its name . . . for several days.

With Lynch's temporary living arrangements being little different than hers, it was a place they could meet that was about halfway between them. She arrived to find that Lynch had already secured a table and ordered coffee. He stood to greet her, and they exchanged a quick kiss.

"I got your text, but didn't have time to really scrutinize the links. I thought the image of the old and new Summer was amazingly good."

Lynch nodded. "And the owner of the coffee shop in North Carolina confirms that's exactly what she looks like."

Amy smiled. Her plan appeared to be coming together

better than she could have anticipated.

"Have we seen any action on either the Facebook page or website?"

She desperately wanted this to go viral so they could catch her, and sooner would be better than later. At that moment, Lynch's phone signaled a new text message. He glanced at his phone and grinned.

"Not yet, but this might help."

As she watched, he tapped a link in the message, and his phone displayed Summer Stanton's old network's website. As its lead news item, she saw an article with the headline, "Have you seen Summer?" Their two hashtags led the story. She read it along with Lynch. His friend Mike had outdone himself. Her grin matched that on Lynch's face.

"How did he manage that?"

"He told me I couldn't ask." He laughed.

"Well, that should sure turn up the heat on her. How long do you think it will take to catch on?"

As they watched, a first comment appeared after the story.

"A second, I guess," replied Lynch.

He took a sip of coffee, and the waitress appeared to take their orders. After she left the table, they read the comment together.

"OMG. Where did this story come from? No one here will admit to posting it. We're all grieving here at the network and the thought of Summer still being alive would seem surreal except for one thing. I was her regular hair stylist, and the morning before her death, her alleged death, she paid me extremely well to cut and curl her hair. I didn't color it, but the

hairstyle in this image is exactly like the one I gave her with the curl mostly washed out. To think she might have staged her death is, well, beyond all of us here."

Lynch just slowly shook his head. "I think we've started something big."

Another comment quickly appeared.

"I can't believe it. I saw and talked with her. She was here, in my coffee shop, for breakfast three mornings in a row. She looked just like this picture. She really is alive."

Clearly, the Rocky Broad had taken his warning to heart by not mentioning the nearby murder. Her comment was perfect. And then a third comment.

"I saw her 2, yesterday afternoon gassed up her car next to me I am in east PA. We was on the turnpike heading west."

The two grinned and gave each other a fist bump. Amy's idea seemed to be taking off. When her plate arrived, she tucked into it as if she hadn't eaten in a week. She glanced over at Lynch to see him picking at his food. She'd seen that look before. His thoughts were elsewhere.

"What's wrong?"

He looked over at her. "Um, nothing. I'm sure it's just my overactive imagination."

Amy knew him better than that. "You mean your gut talking, and I don't mean your stomach growling."

He nodded his head to one side as if saying, "Eh."

"Seriously, what's on your mind?"

He didn't answer right away. After maybe a minute, he replied, "That last comment. Something about it hit me. Why would she be on the Pennsylvania Turnpike heading west?"

"Who knows? Could be any number of reasons."

Amy laid her fork down as one answer dawned on her. They had speculated about how Summer might respond to seeing Lynch in North Carolina. Was this their answer? The turnpike was I-70, and a 12, 13-hour drive west from eastern Pennsylvania led to one place . . . St. Louis.

Just outside Terre Haute, Indiana, Hannah pulled off the highway for gas, a pit stop, and a salty snack. While the hot tea "to go" from breakfast now filled her bladder, she really didn't feel hungry, despite being midafternoon. Her craving for potato chips was more from the boredom of the drive. She had a better understanding of why East Coast folks considered this fly-over country. At least there were hills. She didn't want to fathom driving across the flats of Kansas.

She filled up her tank and paid for the gas at the pump with one of her alternate credit cards. She would use cash for the snack purchase inside. She felt more anonymous that way.

She moved out of the lane and parked away from the door but in front of the building. As she neared the door, one patron at the pumps glanced at her and then appeared to do a startled double-take. Hannah did her own double-take as she opened the door. The woman appeared to be doing something, typing something, into her phone. One more time the woman looked at Hannah and resumed her typing, then she raised her phone as if to use her camera. Hannah turned away and entered the store.

A sense of unease invaded her body. Her fight or flight reaction kicked in. She needed to get out of there. She rushed to the aisle with the chips, grabbed a large bag of her favorite kettle-cooked potato chips, and on to the checkout counter. Several people lingered about—getting oversized drinks, snacks, and various sundries, and none paid the slightest attention toward her. Even the cashier looked bored as she took her cash and made change.

Hannah took a deep breath and sighed as she turned to exit. She had overreacted. The woman outside had to have been responding to something on her phone, not to Hannah. Hannah told herself to be reasonable. She had never been to Terre Haute and certainly didn't know the stranger. Why did she feel so jittery?

As she exited the store, the woman's car was still there. The woman suddenly popped up from the driver's side of her car, raised her phone toward Hannah and appeared to take a picture of her. This time it wasn't the flight reaction that Hannah felt. There could be no photos of her floating around.

A direct confrontation would stir up a crowd. Plus, the store had security cameras. Instead, Hannah acted as anyone would and strolled to her car. The woman had lingered in her car for a minute before pulling out. Traffic came to Hannah's assistance and prevented the woman from entering the street. Hannah pulled in right behind her.

The woman must have been a local, as she did not get onto the interstate but rather took to the side streets. She wound her way to a nearby grocery store, parked, and went inside. If she had any fear of being followed, she didn't show it. She hadn't glanced about or rushed inside.

The delay was ideal for Hannah, because the woman would be even less suspicious coming out of the store.

Hannah saw this as an exercise in the patience she needed to develop. She waited. Thirty minutes later the woman emerged with a cart-load of groceries, which she loaded into the trunk of her car. Hannah resumed tailing the car, looking for an opportune time and place to confront the woman.

It didn't take long. The car turned onto a road heading out of the business district toward rural homes. With no other cars around, Hannah used the first stop sign to hit the woman's rear bumper. Not enough to do damage, but enough to make the woman stop, get out, and come to the rear of her car to inspect it.

As the woman emerged from the vehicle, she looked angry. As she turned to inspect her car, Hannah got out and approached her. The woman turned and saw her. The look on her face turned to one of curiosity.

"You?"

Hannah was in striking range. "Why did you take a picture of me? Where's your phone?"

"What? It's all a hoax, right? I—"

"Where's your phone?"

"Are you really . . . are y-you Summer?" The look on her face became one of confusion.

At the mention of Summer, Hannah snapped. The blade of her knife erupted through the winter coat and into the woman's chest. Unable to see landmarks on the body, she first hit the sternum and had to back out for a second stab an inch lower. This time there was no resistance. A few quick flicks of the knife ensured maximal damage.

The woman's visage showed first pain and then the realization that death was imminent. She gasped and struggled to breathe. As she slumped to the ground, Hannah took the opportunity to retrieve the woman's purse and dump its contents on the ground next to her. She took the time to take the woman's cash and credit cards, as well as her phone. It needed to look like a robbery gone bad.

She leaned over the woman and said, "Nothing personal, but no one must know I'm still alive."

The woman whispered but Hannah had already moved toward her car. She couldn't dally at the scene. She looked about. Still no cars in sight. She made a U-turn and headed back toward town and the highway. At the first stop light, she took a look at the woman's phone. She was surprised to find it password protected. Who locks their phones like that?

As the light turned, a car passed, heading to where Hannah had been. *They will soon come across the scene, call police, and need counseling. Everybody today seems to need counseling*, she thought derisively.

In short order, she entered the ramp onto I-70 West and continued her trek. Two minutes later, as she crossed the Wabash River, she slowed as much as traffic allowed and edged as close to the left side barrier as she could. The phone, cards, and cash flew out the window. The phone made it over the barrier and, hopefully, into the river. The rest she didn't really care about. The knife was next. It, too, made it over the barrier.

She continued toward her unscheduled appointment with a terrorist. From what she'd read in Francois' report, they should make a great team, although he might need some convincing that a woman could help.

Thinking of Francois, she decided to call in. She had made an unsanctioned kill, and while she was not restricted from doing so, Francois liked to know so he could provide backup support as necessary. Often that meant burying a story in the media. On occasion, the right gift to a politician or prosecutor helped. In this case, she didn't expect any blowback. He would want to keep her identity as safe as she did.

Strange. He didn't answer. He always answered.

Yet, that got her thinking. Why did the woman suspect her to be Summer? How would one's mind leap to thinking that someone was a dead person, celebrity or not? But the woman had explicitly asked if she was Summer. Why?

Something else bothered her as she thought about it. The woman's last whispered words were, "Lord, forgive her." *Forgive me?* Hannah thought. *If there is a God, why would he or she forgive me?*

TWENTY-FIVE

Abdi sat huddled with two of his top men in a corner of the warehouse. They were not to be disturbed. Abdi wished to expand their vendors list. He had not liked how their current supplier had required payments of him. Had he not provided them with plenty of profit over the years? And they had made him a mule. Him. The *Lion* of Somalia, not a mule. There were other cartels who would love to have his distribution channels.

The key, however, was making use of multiple supply chains without each knowing about the others. They all had a rash tendency of wanting exclusivity. Abdi had an idea that he wanted his lieutenants' opinions about. These were the men who typically worked with the suppliers. Yes, *he* was the leader, but he valued their ideas, even to the point of abandoning his idea should it prove unworkable.

He saw Bashiir enter the building, turn toward them, and stand still, waiting.

"One minute. I need to speak with Bashiir," he told them. He stood and walked over to greet the man. Bashiir offered an appropriate bow of submission as Abdi neared.

"Lord, Taban actually had a heart attack. He is in the hospital."

"What?" Taban was Abdi's elderly uncle, an unassuming, pleasant man who lived up to his name's meaning, cheerful sunshine. He made Abdi laugh.

"Were you not told, lord? Warsame was told to inform you."

"No, he did not." That would have been twice that Warsame had failed to live up to *his* name. But then Abdi recalled that the man had entered the warehouse and had been prevented from approaching Abdi while he was in conference. "But I was not to be disturbed. He came here and was turned away. It is not his fault."

"When our attempt to find the friend failed this morning because of the cold weather, I thought of another approach. I knew that Taban had not been feeling well, so Warsame and I took him to the Emergency Room, pretending he was our father. We told them he was having chest pain and shortness of breath. They took us right in."

Abdi saw the smile creep onto Bashiir's mouth.

"And?"

"Allah smiled on us. The nurse was there, in the Emergency Room. She works there. From her nametag, she is called Macy Johnson. I was able to take a photo of her for others to use. We need now only to identify her car and get its license number. With that we can find an address where it is registered."

Abdi smiled as well. Perhaps Warsame should have brought this good news after all.

"Lord, the bad news is that Taban really had a heart attack. That is why he was not feeling well. They said it looks like it happened several days ago. They have kept him at the hospital for more care."

Abdi did not like that. He could not visit his uncle under

the circumstances.

"You must continue to pretend you are his son. Tell him I would visit if I could."

"Yes, lord. I already told him that, and he said he understands."

Not everyone in their Somali community knew about the drugs, not even everyone in Abdi's family. Many knew only of their taxi company. He had wondered just how much Taban knew. He might have been a modest and quiet man, but Abdi suspected his ears picked up a lot more than he let others believe.

"I will have my wives make up his favorite food, and you can take it to him."

"Yes, lord. As for the nurse friend, I have distributed her photo to a dozen others. Some will focus their taxi work around the hospital. A few will take turns watching the employee parking lot. It should not be long before we have what you want."

Abdi nodded. Yes, for $500 he could get an address from the DMV. That was much more affordable that $10,000. He remained amazed that someone would ask so much for such a small task.

"Come, Bashiir. Join us. I think it is time for you to learn more about our business."

Lynch had spent a good bit of the day with Amy as she delved into more information on nagalase and GcMAF, as well as its offshoot NiMAF, and the doctors who had touted some success with both. Lynch would review the material she found, and typically, the questions he asked pushed her into looking for more.

When they took a break, they spent the time looking at the Facebook page and websites. As expected, sightings of Summer were reported all across the country. Some were quickly discounted, such as a possible sighting of her sunbathing in southern California and on an Alaskan cruise. While remotely possible, the timelines didn't jibe. She couldn't be both places at the same time. Besides, who sailed on Alaskan cruises in February? Were they even offered in winter?

Others didn't conform with the timeline of her known whereabouts while in North Carolina. And some placed her in locations before her "make-over" and alleged death. Lynch had seen this before whenever a "tip line" was set up for a police case.

On their second afternoon break, though, they both saw one report at the same time.

"That one . . ."

"Look at this . . ."

The report was from a woman in Indiana stating she'd seen Summer at a gas station off I-70 in Terre Haute. She had also posted a photo.

"That's her. That's the Summer we're looking for," said Amy.

Lynch had to agree. The picture was nothing like those of other highly sought celebrities—Bigfoot came to mind— where the image was so grainy you wondered if it was taken through bubble wrap. This was as clear in detail as a professional wedding photo.

"Terre Haute, eh? That's only two and a half hours from

here. When was that posted?"

Both scooted closer to look at the time stamp on the post. Their heads bumped together. Lynch eased back and laughed.

"I guess that's one way for great minds to meet. Literally and physically."

Amy turned toward him. She was close enough their noses could touch. If he'd been an Eskimo, a *kunik* would follow. Before he could swoop in for a real kiss, however, she turned back to the screen.

"Two hours ago. She's almost here. Do you think she's gotten wind of this yet?"

Lynch shook his head. "If she's been driving all day, maybe not. More importantly, has the Assembly gotten wind of it? Of that, I'm sure they have. Having one of their darling propaganda networks hacked with a story about one of their own? I figure they're on full alert and their tech wizards are probably pulling out their hair trying to figure out how it happened."

Amy smiled and its radiance pulled Lynch in. He still hadn't found the ideal place or way to pop the question. He wanted to make it perfect, but they couldn't afford the distraction right now.

"How do you think they'll respond?"

Lynch had mulled over that very question for the past day. How would they respond? Or would they be more likely to *react*? The latter might not bode well for Summer. If they placed a high value on her service, they might call her back, have her "go to ground" for a month or two, and give her another makeover, maybe even plastic surgery, before releasing her on unsuspecting targets again. On the other hand, if she was dispensable, she might just be targeted for her own "suicide."

"Not well," he replied. Whether or not Summer deserved it, he didn't wish death upon her. And he didn't want to share those thoughts with Amy. How would she respond to the thought that her idea—of turning the tables on Summer—might cause Summer's death?

He needed to change the subject. "Hey, what time does Macy get back?"

"Well, the shift is from seven to seven, but she went in early to relieve someone who had to leave before seven this morning. That person is paying her back tonight, so if all goes well, and she's not tied up on a critical case, she should be home by six, six-thirty."

"Then I hope she's on an easy case. I'm starving."

Amy poked him in the belly. "Yeah, just wasting away to nothing."

Hannah tried to reach Francois two more times from her car, once while driving and again after she arrived at the motel. Each time she received the same response, none, no answer. She hoped nothing bad had happened to him. She reasoned that had something happened to him, Director Arikhan would have had his calls forwarded to someone else, himself most likely. So, the lack of an answer posed a mystery to her.

She had stopped at a fast food place for a burger just before reaching the motel. The order and purchase seemed straightforward enough, but the cashier at the window gave her a funny look. It sort of reminded her of the way the woman in Terre Haute first looked at her. As soon as she had her food, she bolted from the premises.

She preferred motels with outside entrances to the rooms—easier to escape. At the motel she'd selected, when she first went to the desk to sign in, nothing seemed out of the ordinary. She'd had her winter coat on with the hood up. But several minutes later, after she'd carried her bag and food to her room, she returned to the lobby to ask for change for the vending machines. This time, the clerk stared at her the entire three minutes she stood there at the desk. As soon as she turned back toward the hallway, the clerk jumped to her computer and frantically typed something into it.

Hannah again felt a bit unhinged. What was going on? The weird interactions with people she didn't know. Being asked about her old identity. The failures in getting hold of Francois.

She turned on her old network and unwrapped her sandwich. The first bite landed like a lead weight in her gut. There, on the screen, was a picture of her, Hannah, not Summer, with a caption that asked "Is Summer Still Alive?"

Now it all made sense . . . except for her inability to reach Francois. She hurried to open her laptop and log onto the Internet. *C'mon, c'mon*, she thought as she went through the hoops of signing into the motel's WIFI service. She surfed to the network website. The top story: Summer's Not Dead with its own hashtag and another: #lookoutforsummer.

The article, although admitting to being speculation, seemed to follow her as she transitioned from Summer to

Hannah. Of course, there was no mention of the Assembly or her mission in North Carolina, but it mentioned her being there. There were hundreds of comments. How had the network allowed this to happen? How had this gotten past the Assembly?

A second, much shorter article, presented itself as a disclaimer. The article was not the work of the network. They had no idea how it came to be posted on their website. And worse, they were unable to take it down. Every such attempt resulted in it reposting at the top of their page. Yet, they tried to assure everyone that Summer Stanton had indeed died in a fatal car accident. They offered fresh quotes from the Delaware State Police. They called for the FBI to investigate this massive hoax.

Nothing they did appeared to make a difference. In fact, the comments on the second article mocked the network and the liberal politicians it supported. "Looks like the Russians are getting back at the network for its meddling in the election." "Time to impeach the network." "Do we have to approve the death certificate to see if she's really dead?"

A deeper worry surfaced in Hannah's mind. If this was the response being seen on her old network, what were the others reporting? She scanned the rival networks and major news portals, even Facebook. She was everywhere!

Then her concern morphed into gut-wrenching fear. Francois wasn't answering because she'd been compromised. She was now expendable. In fact, her phone was now their tracking device, her laptop's camera their own video portal into her life. Could they see the fear she now felt? Was it as palpable to whoever watched her as it was to her?

She slammed shut the computer. The phone she would deal with. They already knew where she was. But first, she needed to know one more thing. She hadn't seen anything on the network's site, so she accessed Facebook on her phone and went to the Summer's Not Dead page. She scanned as quickly through those posts as she could.

What time had she filled up her car? Two-ish? She looked for posts with time stamps around then. There were dozens. And then she saw it. A photo of her exiting the convenience store. Not a problem by itself, under the circumstances. The photo of her car, however, posed a larger problem. Now the Assembly was not alone in knowing what she drove. Like her face, her car could also be used to spot her. She felt like a deer frozen in the headlights of her car.

The Director had probably already dispatched agents one and two of The Three to deal with her. Unlike her choice on this case, they would fly. At this point, they could already be on the ground in St. Louis.

Had she come this far only to fail to reach her goal? She had only one real option, and getting back into the good graces of the Director and Francois wasn't it. She needed to find Lynch Cully and deal with him.

TWENTY-SIX

The clock showed the time to be six thirty-eight when Macy finally rolled through the door. She looked more than tired.

"Hey, she's home," Lynch announced to Amy in the kitchen. He looked at Macy and said, "I'm hungry. So, change clothes, and we'll head on out."

Macy gave Lynch her evil eye. Or at least what Lynch interpreted as such. He had heard Amy describe the facial gesture Macy called her "evil eye" several times, but she'd also said it usually appeared when Lynch turned his back. He felt he was making progress with Macy, such that she'd become more transparent around him.

Macy looked at Amy as she walked into the front room and sighed. "Girlfriend, I know you guys promised to treat me to a meal and that we'd agreed on dinner tonight because I was supposed to get off early, but I'm exhausted. It was one of those days from you-know-where."

Amy looked at Lynch, who returned the glance with a subtle shrug.

"No problem from our end. You must be hungry, though. Days like that don't usually give you time to eat."

"Eat? We barely had time for potty breaks. I almost broke down and used a bedpan in the supply closet. I'm famished."

Lynch waited for Amy to poke her friend in the belly as she had done with him. Thirty seconds later, nope, wasn't going to happen.

"So, Macy, what would you like? I can go out for Chinese, Mexican, Thai. We could order some pizza. That Mediterranean place we all like has carry-out now. Your choice. Our treat."

Macy sat down on the couch, removed her shoes, and began to rub her feet. Lynch had witnessed the same action by Amy on more than one occasion in the past. She glanced up at Lynch.

"What would be fastest?"

Amy replied, "Is that what matters? Which would you prefer?"

"I'm not picky. I'm hungry. And I don't want to wait longer than necessary. My cousin Walter, he—"

"We've heard this one, Macy," answered Amy and Lynch in unison.

Macy stuck her tongue out at both of them. "Then you know what happened."

Lynch looked up from his phone where he'd been searching out restaurants on his map app. "In reality, pizza would be fastest and they deliver. A pie or two could be here in 40 minutes or less. It would take me a minimum of 45 minutes to drive to and pick up any of the others."

"Pizza it is," replied Macy. "Girlfriend, you know what I like. Go ahead and order. I need a shower." Macy headed to her bedroom.

Lynch looked at Amy. "Do we have beer?" She shook her head. "Then I'll go grab a six-pack. You know what I like, too."

"Make that two six-packs. Geesh, I guess I get to pay for it, too."

Lynch tossed her his credit card. He smiled at the thought that he'd have to get used to that once they married.

Lynch returned to find Amy and Macy in the front room. Macy already looked more refreshed. He carried his bag into the kitchen and returned with cold ones for the ladies and himself. He watched as Amy showed Macy what they'd started.

"OMG. That went viral faster than the mumps on that Navy ship in the Middle East."

"Look at some of these comments." Amy pointed out some of the funnier ones she and Lynch had discovered earlier. Some made light of the whole thing and joked about the network's being punked. Others were angry. The expected text wars broke out with people taking sides over things they clearly knew nothing about. Amy switched to Facebook and showed Macy the post with the clear picture of Summer Stanton with short black hair.

"Is that really her?"

"We think so," replied Lynch. At that moment his cell phone rang. He glanced at the Caller ID. "Sorry, gotta take this one." He stood and looked about for someplace more private to talk. "Yes, Mr. President, now's as good a time as any."

Macy's eyes widened. Lynch pretended not to notice and headed for the bathroom, where he shut the door.

"Yes, sir, I can talk now."

"Lynch, now that we've established that Abdi is back in

St. Louis, I thought you could use some help, but I figured it needed to be on the QT, without naming you. So, I asked the FBI to monitor some things and report them directly back to me. First, I asked them to check on anyone specifically asking about you, your parents, Amy or her family, and even Macy, since Amy's staying there. I expressed my concern for all of your welfares because of Abdi. They're on the search for him. At my request, they also made some calls to Amy's ex-employers and found out two black men with foreign accents had asked about Amy at MedAir. But get this, they asked about Amy's black nurse friend, too."

Lynch didn't like the implications of that. He felt it safe to assume these men had ties to Abdi. Some might call that racial profiling. He called it a common sense deduction. How did they know that Amy had such a friend? At least they had no name, and that was a good thing. Names could lead to addresses.

"That's not good, sir. If they know about Macy and get her name, then . . ."

"I know, Lynch. They're both in danger then. I'm afraid it gets worse. When they called on the medical center's Emergency Department, they learned that three black males, also with foreign accents, had come to the department. The elderly man with them actually had had a heart attack. The two younger men claimed to be sons, but they bore no resemblance to the patient or each other. They also had no IDs to prove themselves relatives."

"Well, being related is still in the realm of possibility, sir."

"I know, but one of them was spotted taking a picture

of, guess who? Macy. Lynch, if these two are with Abdi, it seems they now have her name. This could all be coincidence, but we both know there's no such thing."

"Thank you, sir, for the heads up. I can take it from here, on my end."

"Wait, Lynch, I'm afraid there's more bad news. After you informed me that Summer Stanton might be heading your way via I-70, I also asked the FBI to watch out for any unusual deaths along that corridor. The director asked why, but I didn't tell him. Oh, and he was amused by your little #summersnotdead stunt. He doesn't know you're behind that and never will, but I found his reaction interesting, in a good way. He might be someone else we can trust with this venture. Anyway, there was a murder not far from I-70 in Indiana. Seemed like a robbery gone wrong, but, again, this is no coincidence."

Lynch didn't like where this was heading either. "Where in Indiana, sir?"

"Terre Haute. The police interviewed the family, and one thing stood out, at least to me. The victim had called them to say she really saw Summer Stanton, that the news story was true and not a hoax like they all believed. She even posted photos on Facebook. I took a look myself. It's her all right, just like the photo your make-believe friend conjured up. Fifty minutes after that posting, this woman was dead."

Now Lynch felt awful. They'd been so elated that the plan seemed to be working and that it had gone viral. Now it was responsible for a woman's murder. Lynch didn't know how to respond.

"Lynch, you still there?"

"Y-yes, sir. Still here. I am so, so sorry. Her death is our fault. We never envisioned someone else getting hurt, much less killed, because of our plan."

"Lynch, don't blame yourself. You didn't kill the woman. That one's on Summer Stanton when we catch her."

Lynch shook his head. No, she was good. They'd never find any evidence to pin that murder on her. She'd been careless in North Carolina. She wouldn't be again.

"Sir, Amy must never know of this. This would hurt her tremendously."

"She won't hear of it from me. As for the FBI, the local authorities, and the family, they don't have the bigger picture that you and I have. No one else has connected those dots. They're still working this case as a robbery gone wrong."

"Thank you, sir." His heart remained heavy. His commander-in-chief was correct in saying that the murder was on Summer's hands, but they were the ones who had forced the wild beast into a corner where her only choice was to lash out. "As always, I'll keep you posted on events here, sir. Are there other deaths you want me to check into?"

"Perhaps, but right now you need to stay put and let the hunters come to you. We need to finish this chapter and get these two off the streets. Be careful and stay vigilant."

"Yes, sir."

"Goodnight, Lynch."

"Goodnight, sir."

Lynch took a few minutes to use the bathroom, but mainly to compose himself. He returned to the front room to find the ladies chowing down on pizza.

"Hey, Mister Secret Agent Man, if you want any, you better act now. Your girlfriend and me got raging appetites. It won't be around long."

He put up a hand and shook his head to decline her offer. He wasn't really hungry now. He went to the fridge, pulled out another cold beer, and returned to the room. Amy's brow furrowed. She knew he'd been hungry earlier.

"What's wrong?"

"Eat up, ladies. Then pack your bags. We need to move."

Abdi had once heard a saying in America to count to ten before reacting to bad news. He'd gone as high as 20, before picking up the closest object and throwing it against the wall of the warehouse. *Allah, give me strength*, he thought.

He labored to contain his anger. That struggle had become all too familiar to him since his first encounter with that woman. Perhaps patience was overrated.

"Tell me again! How did you fail?"

This time, too, Bashiir was not directly involved. If he had been, perhaps they would have had a better outcome. The three men standing before him were tasked to watch for and follow the black friend by name of Macy Johnson. At a minimum, they were to get her vehicle's license number for tracing. He had already paid the bribe to trace her driver's license for an address. It led to an empty apartment complex that was being torn down for redevelopment.

"Lord, we were all there half an hour before the nurses changed shifts. We watched for over an hour after the shift change. We saw dozens of black women leave work to go to their cars. She never left the building."

"Did you cover all of the parking lots?"

"Lord," a second man replied, "we covered the Emergency Room entrance, the main entrance, and the access to the main garage. That allowed us to watch the main parking areas, too."

The first man joined in. "The weather was warmer. We could see the women's faces. The woman in Bashiir's photo was not among them. Maybe she left early, or stayed late. We can watch again in the morning . . . and tomorrow evening. However long it takes to follow her."

A disturbance at a side door to the warehouse caught everyone's attention. The men rushed to take cover, and Abdi and his bodyguards pulled handguns, prepared to fight.

"That door is locked, lord. We must watch the main doors." Two of the guards rushed to cover those entries.

And then the side door opened without so much as a squeak in the hinges and a thin, mustachioed man sauntered in, his hands raised to the level of his shoulders to show them to be empty.

"How . . . ?"

Abdi was puzzled. How did this man get past his guards outside and through a locked door?

"Where are my men? Who are you? I could shoot you on the spot!"

"I don't think you would survive long enough to aim."

At that moment the red dot of a laser sight flashed onto Abdi's chest.

"Lord!" One of his men pointed to his torso. Abdi looked down, saw the dot, and lowered his weapon.

"Who are you, and what do you want?"

The man lowered his hands and approached Abdi with caution. "Who I am is unimportant. What I want is collaboration I believe we have mutual interests. You want Amy Gibbs. I want Lynch Cully. We find one, we find the other. Interested?"

Abdi motioned for his men to lower their weapons, because he suspected that they, too, would not live to take aim if they tried. Besides, yes, the proposal interested him.

"What can you do for me? How can you help? I almost have her."

The man smiled. "But you don't, do you? We have an old saying, close only counts in horseshoes and hand grenades. You are only close enough to have a name, Macy Johnson. I can tell you where she lives."

The grenade reference Abdi understood, but how did a horse's shoes come into play? He would play along as if he understood.

However, Abdi felt troubled by the presence of this man. How did this man know they hunted for Macy Johnson as their key to finding Amy Gibbs? Who was this man and who did he work for? Did they know all about *him* and his enterprises as well? Abdi had the realization that this man was not someone to take lightly.

"And in return for that information?"

"I need more manpower. Speaking of which, all of your men outside will be fine, but someone will need to cut them loose." He pointed directly to where each man had been positioned outside the warehouse walls.

Abdi nodded to one of his men, who ran to the main

door and left the building.

"I certainly wasn't going to injure men I might be counting on for assistance. As I said, I need help with manpower. I need more eyes on the ground than I have, if I want to corner Lynch Cully. He's a resourceful and formidable quarry."

Abdi furrowed his brow. "I do not know this word, quarry."

"Something being hunted."

"Ah, yes. I saw him in action in Cambodia. He is a worthy opponent."

"And he will do everything he can to protect Amy Gibbs."

Abdi nodded. He saw that in Cambodia also. Yes, this man's proposal was a good one. He waved his arm toward the table and chairs where he conferred with his lieutenants.

"Please sit. Let us talk. Would you like something to drink?"

"Your traditional Chai tea would be wonderful. *Mahadsanid.*"

That the man knew his language, even if just enough to say 'thank you,' surprised him. Abdi gave the order for tea.

"There are two of us." The man waved toward the side door where he had entered the building, and another man walked in, heading to the table. The second man placed a tin container on the table.

"We brought *halwa*, enough for everyone."

Abdi smiled. The glutinous, sweet treat made with sugar, corn flour, and ghee, and spiced with cardamom and nutmeg, was a festive offering often served at weddings and other special occasions. It was common throughout the Middle East, India, and northern Africa. He opened the tin.

"Ah, you have used slivered almonds and pistachios, as well. This was the tradition of my home town's *halwa* maker." The production of *halwa* was labor intensive and every town had its own maker of the treat. "Perhaps I should serve strong, dark coffee instead. It cuts the sweetness of this delight very well."

The man returned the smile. "But then, I would miss your special Chai tea. I understand it is quite good."

Abdi scrutinized the man again. How did he know about the Abdi family's Chai tea? This man truly presented Abdi with a dilemma. On one hand he offered Abdi a solution to his problem in finding the woman. On the other, he appeared to know much more about Abdi than he was comfortable with. Would working with this man come back to bite him?

*　*　*

Hannah's choice to drive appeared to be the correct one. Within her first hour there, she formulated a plan using the car and her location as bait for Lynch Cully. In addition, her use of the car had afforded her the ability to transport extra "goodies" that she might have left behind had she flown. The first "goodie" was what she liked to call her "door hacker."

Her first item of business—changing rooms. She wasn't as worried about the clerk posting on social media about her presence there as she was about his giving up her room number to an agent of the Assembly.

She scanned the area outside her room. Satisfied that she would not be noticed by others, she stepped outside, went to her car, and pretended to get something from the backseat. Using another "toy," she clandestinely aimed the small laser at the security cameras at both ends of the building. It had enough power to fry the electronics of the cameras. Now her movements would not be recorded until the cameras were replaced.

She walked back to the room's door and then kept close to the building—so as not to be noticed by someone looking out their room window—with the "door hacker" in hand. Using RFID technology, the device scanned through the spectrum of codes used by magnetic locks until it found the right one and unlocked the door. She used it to unlock an unoccupied room two doors away. With the device, she also permanently altered the door lock's code such that even the motel management would not be able to enter.

Within five minutes, she changed rooms.

Her next move? She used two small cameras to set up a surveillance area outside the room. The first was placed onto the top left corner of the room's window, furthest away from the door for the widest angle of viewing possible and the least amount of overlap with the next camera. The second one was placed right over the keyhole viewing port of the door. That would allow her to see anyone at the door just as if she put her eye to the portal to look out directly. That also prevented her from being targeted at the door by someone knocking, waiting for the viewing port to darken from the inside, and shooting, either through the door itself or through the viewer. Both cameras linked to a receiver she sat on the side table of the bed. As for monitoring what the cameras saw, she had an app for that.

Satisfied with her setup, she set out for step number three. She needed to regain her anonymity. That meant changing her appearance yet again. She drove to 24-hour pharmacy—not the closest one, but one a few miles away.

Inside she grabbed some hair color and a curling iron. At the checkout, she watched the clerk give her what was becoming an all-too-familiar double-take as she placed her items on the counter. She rolled her eyes and sighed.

"You, too? Everywhere I've gone today, people have been giving me strange looks. And one guy kept following me through the Galleria, taking video. They think I'm that Summer person. Have you seen it? On social media? What're they calling it? Hashtag Summersnotdead?"

The clerk smiled. "Well, you do kind of look like the photo online."

"Well, I've looked this way since college. If anyone is a doppelgänger, it's that other person, assuming she's really alive after all. And why would she do that? Who fakes their death? That's Hollywood stuff, right?"

The clerk looked sheepish and offered a subtle nod. She began to ring up Hannah's items.

"I guess you can tell that I'm tired of it. I can't any work done, so beginning tonight, I'm giving myself a new look. Always wanted to see what it was like to be blonde."

The clerk handed her the bag containing her purchase. "Good luck. Hope this solves your problem."

"Me, too. Thanks. Have a good night."

The woman went back to her work without a second

look at Hannah as she left the store. Hannah's frontal approach seemed to work.

Back at the motel, she parked in front of her assigned room. She wanted the car to be noticeable there. She walked to the door and that room and stopped. She hadn't noticed anyone looking out from their window. Again, keeping close to the building, she walked to the room two doors away and let herself in. Phase two of her plan would begin in the morning.

TWENTY-SEVEN

Lynch slept in his car outside Macy's apartment. He wanted to be close at hand in case a problem developed. His preference had been to move the women to a motel room first, and then someplace safe. He couldn't talk them into that, particularly Macy. She had two days scheduled to be off, but she had plans for those days and did not want to give them up. Amy proved to be more flexible. She understood the danger, but she also refused to leave Macy.

He glanced at his phone—eight a.m. Macy was likely up. Amy, maybe not. He'd been awake since six and already purchased donuts to entice the women, sweeten them up to his way of thinking. It was time for that surprise.

Macy answered the door on his second round of knocking. He'd kept it somewhat quiet, and had refused to use the doorbell, on the off-chance they were both still asleep.

"You're here early," she said softly. "The princess is still sleeping."

"Not surprised. Being unemployed seems to agree with her." He grinned. "Brought donuts. Ready for a sugar fix?"

"Any day of the week, Mister Secret Agent Man. You bring donuts, and you can be my special agent anytime." She opened the door wider to let him in.

They walked to the kitchen, where he placed the box on

a counter. Macy retrieved two plates from the cupboards.

"Coffee? I was just about to brew a cup, but I can make a pot."

"Sure. Thanks. We might just need a pot."

Lynch watched as Macy went through her routine for coffee. It wasn't going to be close to "cop coffee," which he wanted, no, needed at the moment to jolt him back to life after trying to sleep in his car. Yet, he knew better than to say anything.

As the coffee brewed, he thought he heard a toilet flush and water running. Was it inside the apartment or from an adjacent one? A moment later, he heard footsteps shuffling down the hall. He watched as Amy entered the kitchen.

"Lynch?"

Her eyes flew open, and she grabbed her pajama top as if it were a robe she could close in an effort to remain modest. Her hair was a wreck. She wore pink, fluffy slippers he'd never imagined on her. He grinned.

"Wh-what are you doing here?" She gave Macy a desperate look. "Be right back."

She rushed out of the room. Lynch heard a door slam.

Macy looked at him and raised a brow. "You sure that's what you want to wake up to every morning?"

He laughed. "Yep. *Every* morning."

Macy pulled three mugs out of a cabinet and began to fill one for Lynch. As she did so, Amy returned, her hair brushed, jeans and a loose top on. She gave Lynch a sheepish look.

"Good morning, sunshine."

"Uh, morning, Lynch. Um, what are you doing here so

bright and early?"

"I never left. Slept in my car out front."

At that revelation, Macy stopped and looked at him.

"That wasn't necessary. We can take care of ourselves."

Lynch took another sip of joe before commenting. "Under ordinary circumstances, I have no doubt of that. But, Macy, you don't understand whom we're dealing with here."

She took a defensive stand with her arms crossed over her chest.

"I have a pretty good idea."

Amy looked at Lynch and then at Macy. "Macy, you're my best friend, but no, you don't. I-I haven't begun to share with you some of the things that happened in Cambodia because of this man. I . . . well, I'd rather not remember some of it myself. I wish I could unsee a lot of it." Tears came to Amy's eyes. Lynch put his hand on her shoulder.

"Macy, the President called me last night to warn us. The FBI is actively looking for Abdullah Said Abdi. And their intel is saying he's looking for Amy by trying to find one person. You. Somehow, he learned that you two are friends, and Abdi believes he can get to Amy through you. They inquired about you both at MedAir two days ago, and remember the old man and his two sons in the ER yesterday? The old man had had a heart attack."

Macy nodded. "I remember them. Becca was his primary nurse, but I helped her."

"Yeah, well, the old man is Somali and the FBI believe he's part of Abdi's extended family. In talking with Becca, the agent learned that one of the so-called sons took a picture of you. I'm pretty sure he did so to give Abdi's troops a face to look for. If they can get an address for you, well, you're the leverage they need to get to Amy. They don't know Amy's staying here. At least, I don't think so. But they know that they can use you to flush her out. And when he's done with you, he won't hesitate to kill you."

Macy had nothing to say, but this time Lynch had no desire to rub it in. She did look contemplative, rather than her usual cocky self. Maybe, between Amy and him, their words were starting to soak in. She sat up straighter and sighed.

"I really looked forward to the plans I have for these next two days, but . . ." She paused and took another deep breath. ". . . I sure don't want to be the one they use to get to my friend here. What do you have in mind?"

"I think we need to get you both to a motel ASAP. Then, we have to find someplace safe, preferably out of town. I still need to work on that part. I didn't want to spend time looking for a place until I knew you were in agreement."

Amy perked up and smiled. She raised her hand up and down to shoulder level as if saying, "Choose me. Choose me."

Macy and Lynch turned together to look at her.

"I have the perfect spot. Macy, you'd love these people. They're special friends, and their place is out in the fresh air with plenty of space to roam."

Lynch smiled, while Macy frowned.

"I hadn't thought of them. That would be perfect," said Lynch.

"Not for me," Macy retorted. "Sounds like I'm gonna have to milk cows and feed chickens."

Lynch chuckled. He knew for a fact that Macy was

aware of the Bircher family farm in mid-Missouri, overlooking Stockton Lake. Amy had talked about her family's old friends often, and prior to her father's death, flew to the farm's private airstrip to visit them several times a year. Lynch had even flown with her there once or twice. Their last time there, she had produced a surprise picnic by the lake. The place was about four hours away by car and over one hour by air, but he doubted the airstrip was a feasible alternative in February.

"C'mon, Macy. You've heard me talk about them almost as often as you mention your cousins. You'd love the place. Their guest cabin has a huge wood fireplace, and we'd have separate bedrooms. We could kick back and relax. Let me call Jimmy."

Lynch had heard the stories about James Bircher Jr., too. In junior high, Amy had the biggest crush on James Jr., only to have her heart broken when he called her a skinny ol' beanpole who'd be worthless on a farm and who'd never find a boyfriend. And then, after college, when she joined her family at his wedding, he actually stuttered when they met. Usually garrulous, he was a total loss of words around her, and his bride wouldn't let him near Amy until after the wedding. She learned later that he'd been stunned to see her "all grown up." Payback, she called it, for his meanness that one summer. She told the story better than Lynch could. He was just glad Jimmy was married and settled.

Macy seemed half mollified. "Well, as long as I don't have to do any of that farm stuff, that might be nice."

Amy crossed her heart. "Honest, you won't have to do anything you don't want to do there."

"Okay, I guess. I'll need to make a couple of calls and cancel my plans." Macy deemed it late enough in the morning to bother people and headed back to her bedroom to make those calls.

Amy looked at Lynch. "We'll need to drive. Their grass airstrip might still have snow and ice on it. I'll call Jimmy right now." She went to her bedroom for the call, a move Lynch found curious but wrote off to habit.

Lynch remained in the kitchen, nursing his cup of coffee. Getting these two out of the way would greatly ease his mind and enable him to work unhindered by concern for them. But what next? He was one guy. True, he had the FBI working on their behalf to find Abdi, but he wanted to be pro-active, to continue on the offense, as Amy had put it. How should he proceed?

Hannah awoke with a start. The previous day had been emotionally and physically draining, and she felt the fatigue the previous night as she attempted to stay awake and vigilant. The Assembly knew where she was, at least where her car was and where her credit card had last registered. She worried their agents would get to her before she could get to Lynch Cully.

And yet, she must have fallen asleep. At least her surveillance system, as minimal as it was, hadn't alerted her to any threat.

She took a quick shower to help wake up, as well as freshen up, changed clothes, and brewed a cup of coffee to further jump-start her day. Before she could initiate the next phase of her plan, she needed to make sure of one thing—

that she didn't take a bullet as soon as she walked out the door. Agents one and two wouldn't worry about being up close and personal when they "retired" her. A sniper shot from an adjacent property would serve their purpose.

But she had another "goodie" in her bag of tricks. Since she was on a solo assignment, she now counted on their not anticipating her having this device. Designed for group missions, it allowed her to track her partners' locations. If they were within 50 miles, she would know they'd arrived in the city. If they were within 500 yards, she would know they were near enough to be a danger. But in that proximity, the instrument would more than alert her to the potential harm, it would tell her their precise GPS coordinates.

She clicked it on and waited for it to register with the satellites overhead. The downside was that by activating it, they could see where she was, too. By the display, she saw that they were indeed in the city, but not within striking distance. She quickly turned it off and hoped her use of the device had not been noticed.

Time for phase two.

She checked her security cameras to make sure no one was outside to see her leave that room, grabbed her bag, and walked nonchalantly to the motel's breakfast room. The reaction as she entered the room was as expected. More than half of the two-plus dozen people there did a double-take. Several tried to hide their cell phones as they took pictures. The room quieted, with only whispering to be heard.

She went to the buffet, grabbed a plate, and began to add fresh fruit and a small container of yogurt to it. To take more time, she decided to make a waffle. While waiting for it, she collected a spoon of scrambled eggs and a couple of links of sausage. Collecting the finished waffle, she grabbed a glass of juice and juggled everything as she found a place to sit smack-dab in the middle of everyone. She hid from no one. Anonymity was not her goal this morning.

She took her time eating. Checked her phone for social media posts and current news. Upon downing her last drink of OJ, and satisfied that she had gained the attention she wanted, she stood and walked casually back to her room. A few people followed her outside and she noticed them taking pictures of her car—THE car. She entered her assigned room, waited five minutes, and then checked outside again. No onlookers. She rushed to the room two doors away and dashed inside.

All she needed to do now was wait. Lynch Cully would show up. In the meantime, she had time for her makeover.

TWENTY-EIGHT

Abdi ordered that half a dozen taxis be removed from service in order to free up some men. These men, along with others he used to move his drugs, now congregated at the warehouse. They had arrived singly and at staggered times, moving through designated checkpoints where other men watched to see if they were being followed. None had been.

The two men from the previous evening, first known to Abdi as One and Two—names he thought childish—had also arrived. When asked again, they called themselves Adam and Cain. These names were not lost on Abdi. Allah had created Adam as the first man, while Adam's first son with Hawwa, Eve, was Cain, the second man. Adam was clearly the spokesman for the two.

He knew not to press these men further for their real names. Besides, if they could help him get the woman, who cared what they wished to call themselves?

They had brought a smorgasbord of Somali dishes: *sabaayad*—a favored flatbread served for breakfast with dried meats, *malawax*—the Somali version of a sweet crepe, more *halwa*, dried meat delicacies, fruits, and more. Enough for twice as many men as had appeared that morning. These two men had more than won over Abdi's men with this offering.

"Adam, you have won over my men's stomachs. How

can they assist you, specifically? We talked only generalities last evening."

Adam nodded. "First, here is what I promised you—the address of Macy Johnson. You might want to send two men to watch for her. And if you find Amy Gibbs through her, contact me on this burner cell. I am the only one you can call with this cell. Any other attempted use will simply go to dead air."

Abdi glanced at the address he'd been given, raised his hand, and snapped his fingers. "*Laba!*" At that, two men rushed to his side.

"You each have the photos of the two women we seek, yes? You must make sure you have the right women."

He was not about to bring in the wrong person again. The men nodded.

"Good. Here is the address you are to watch. Call me if either of them shows up there, and if the white woman appears, but leaves before I get there, follow her, discreetly."

"Yes, Lord Abdi." Both men bowed and hurried away.

Abdi turned back to Adam. "Now, your request."

"Here are four addresses. I need two, preferably three, men at each address. And here are photos of Lynch Cully and another woman. If either of them appears, I am to be contacted immediately."

Another woman? wondered Abdi. He already knew what Lynch Cully looked like, so he glanced at one of the copies of the woman's image. He might have been holed up at the warehouse, but he was not isolated from world events. It was the woman half the world seemed obsessed with.

"So, the reporter woman really does still live. Why do you hunt for her?"

Adam's face revealed nothing. "That is not your business."

Abdi could tell from the tone of the man's voice that he should not pursue that line of questions. For that matter, he realized he had no idea why the men hunted Lynch Cully. Other questions arose in his mind. How were this woman and Lynch Cully connected? And how had they offended these men or their employer? That they had an employer seemed clear, but who was their employer? Was this company, or entity, or whatever, someone or something that could benefit *his* operation?

These two men had subdued six of his best men the previous evening. Their weapons were several calibers above that of local police. They had access to Somali food far better than anything he had experienced in St. Louis, including the cooking of his own wives. Even the technology of the cell phone he'd been given appeared beyond that of normal, retail channels.

Yes, these men were well trained and had resources Abdi could only dream about. He would need to step up his game to impress these men, and by doing so, perhaps make an impression on their employer as well.

Amy glanced over at Macy as they drove along I-44, heading southwest toward Springfield, MO. Her friend had been uncharacteristically quiet since they'd left her apartment. In fact, her first words of the trip were, "Pull over. I gotta pee," as they approached the St. Clair Rest Area

45 minutes into the trip. Amy was happy to oblige. The coffee had worked its way through her as well.

Twenty minutes later, as they passed through the sleepy town of Sullivan, Amy had had enough.

"Okay, Macy, what gives?"

"Huh?"

"What gives? You haven't said a thing since we left. "

"Sure I have. I asked you to pull off at that rest stop."

Amy looked at her friend and frowned. "That doesn't count and you know it. Do I need to turn around, take you back to the ER, and have you fully checked out? You're not yourself. You talked more than this the last time you had the flu."

"Yeah, 'cuz it was that mandatory flu shot for work that got me sick."

She had a point. That *had* been all she'd talked about. That, and how she'd never gotten sick before until they forced the flu vaccine on everyone.

"Okay, fair enough. I can sit in silence for the rest of the trip. That's only another three hours."

She heard Macy grunt.

"What?"

"Nothin'."

Amy drove on in silence, watching the clock on the dash to see how much longer Macy could hold out. Just over three minutes later . . .

"Okay, okay. You always win our staring games, too. You wanna know what's wrong? I'm not looking forward to this. That's what's wrong. I was looking forward to lunch today with my cousin, Akeisha, and shopping with a few of the ER nurses tomorrow. Now I'm gonna end up plucking chickens or riding broncos or something."

Amy sighed. "Macy, I told you, no farm stuff, unless, of course, you want to try something. It's just going to be like a girls' get-away. There are a couple of wineries not much farther down the highway. We can stop, do a tasting, and pick up a couple of bottles of whatever you like."

"Might need four or five if I end up plucking chickens."

Amy rolled her eyes.

"Hey, I saw that."

"Yeah, and you keep it up, we're going to have to add an 'h' to the word wine."

Macy grunted again.

"Macy, there's got to be something else bothering you. I've known you too long."

Amy's quick peek at her friend saw Macy peering out the window. She wouldn't push things. Macy would tell her in due time.

"So, I still say you're going to love this place. It's quiet and beautiful, although I will admit February isn't exactly the prime time to appreciate that beauty." She paused for a moment. "And yes, they have chickens, but mainly for eggs. You won't even have to see the chicken coop. Would you like to ride horses? We could take a ride down to the lake instead of walking there."

Macy gave her the evil eye. Amy got the message.

"Sorry. I forgot. No horses."

She had forgotten about the time when several members of the nursing staff, including Amy and Macy in their first year together in the Mercy ED, joined together for a trail ride and bar-b-que luncheon at a ranch in Jefferson County, south of St. Louis. It started off well enough, until one of the horses got spooked, in turn kicking Macy's horse and sending it off at a full gallop across the field. She ended up in a patch of briers, and several of the nurses took turns after lunch picking the plentiful thorns out of Macy's backside.

"Hey, here's the exit for the wineries. Let's check 'em out."

Lynch held back as he followed Amy to the interstate and out of town. He didn't want her to see him following her, but wanted to make sure no one else did so as well. He drove as far as Six Flags and decided to head to his parents' new home not far from there in the rural community of Wildwood. To think of his parents as stereotypical rural residents seemed far-fetched with the average home in their zip code listing at half-a-million dollars on multi-acre plots.

Like Amy, most of Lynch's personal belongings occupied a storage unit. Following Bradley Graham's election as President, he had taken enough to furnish his small apartment in Washington, D.C., but that style of living had grown old quickly. With his role on the President's transition team morphing into one of being an off-the-books special investigator for the man, he hoped he might find his way home on a permanent basis. Yet, he had leased his own home to a fellow police officer who recently married and wanted out of his own apartment-based lifestyle.

Another style of living was aging even faster than apartment life—living out of his car. Of the four nights he'd actually been in St. Louis since returning from Cambodia, two had been spent sleeping in his car. He had some clothing and other items stashed at this "country house," as his mother had called it, and a shower and change of clothes would do him well.

His folks still owned the home where he'd grown up, but minor remodeling projects now consumed it as they prepared it for the market. He didn't quite understand his father's insistence on putting money into it just to sell it, but maybe they would see that expense recovered in a higher sale price. As for the new place, his folks had succeeded only in moving their belongings there in time to leave the country for a six-month teaching sabbatical in Australia. He had the option of crashing at either place, but neither seemed comfortable.

As he turned from one winding country road onto another and onto the road which led to his parents' new house, he was about to overtake an older sedan when a still, small voice inside told him to lay back. In Cambodia, he had grown to trust that voice more completely. He took his foot off the gas, slowed, and then followed the vehicle at a distance.

As they neared the long drive to his parents' home, the car slowed. He pulled off onto a wide, gravel patch and stopped. The car pulled into his parents' drive and stopped. Two men hopped out and spread out into the woods on both sides of the drive. From his vantage point he could no longer see them, but the driver of the car backed his vehicle out of the drive onto the road and moved a hundred yards or so beyond the driveway, where he pulled off to the side.

To call this activity suspicious was not an overreaction. His parents' place was unoccupied, secluded, and ripe for the picking. Yet, they had a security system, as did every other home in the area. With most everything still boxed from the move, would-be burglars would find themselves stymied to find anything of real value before police would arrive.

No. A different scenario cautioned Lynch. They were there looking for *him*.

As he reached for his phone to call in the suspicious activity, it rang. Mike Jurgesmeyer.

"Hey, Mike. What's up?"

"You remember I told you I put a flag on #summersnotdead to alert us to any place where there were more than five sightings? Well, that flag is flying straight out from the pole this morning. Over 25 postings from a motel in St. Charles. Over a dozen photos from breakfast and a few of the car. I called the motel. That car's still there."

TWENTY-NINE

Hannah watched the video feed from her cameras for maybe a quarter hour after breakfast. She found it amusing to watch others practically tiptoe towards her car, whispering and pointing. None would actually walk right up to it but stayed several yards away, as if it carried a contagious disease or was about to explode. She saw no one approaching any of the rooms, but since none of them knew her room number, that was to be expected.

However, she had things to do. With all of the activity in the breakfast room earlier, she expected a visit from the management, the police, local reporters, someone feeling the need to investigate this massive sighting of a "dead woman." She fully anticipated that someone to be Lynch Cully. She needed to be ready.

She grabbed the items she had purchased the night before and entered the bathroom. With a little good fortune, she would be prepared for his arrival.

The wine tasting side tour had been a good idea. With the equivalent of two glasses of wine downed in less than half an hour, Macy had loosened up . . . to put it mildly. Amy had kept her intake on the conservative, "I have to drive" side. Now, she watched as a young man from the winery loaded a mixed case of reds, whites, and rosés—something for every palate and food choice—into her trunk, all courtesy of Macy.

"Careful, boyfriend, I'm gonna need every one of those bottles. We're heading to a farm and this city girl don't like chickens." Macy wobbled a bit as she talked.

Amy gave the guy a wan smile and rolled her eyes. "Thanks. That was too heavy for me."

The man laughed. "No, thank *you*. You just made our day a profitable one. Enjoy." He tipped his hat and headed back into the building.

Yeah, and it's only 9:30, thought Amy. She wondered how Macy was going to react to purchasing nearly $300 worth of wine after metabolizing most of that alcohol. Well, she had tried to warn her.

"C'mon, girlfriend, let's get back on the road. We need to get there before I get thirsty. And I *will* get thirsty if I have to be on a farm for two days."

Back on the highway, Amy looked at her friend again, wondering. "Macy, I keep telling you, this isn't going to be so bad. Why do you keep harping on it?"

Macy sighed. "'Cause it's easier to complain about that than, well . . ." She paused.

"Easier than what?"

"Easier than thinkin' about someone out to kill us. I didn't grow up in some housing project or in the hood. I grew up in the suburbs and didn't live the reality of drive-bys, or gangbangers on the corner. Some of my cousins did, and I've worked in a level-one trauma center now, what, ten years? I know what people can do to others. It freaks me out to think someone wants to do something like that to *me . . .*

or you."

"We'll survive. Heck, they don't even know where to find us."

"Yeah, for two days, and then it's back home. I don't understand how you can be so calm. You can't promise we'll survive, like you jes said."

"If we can survive chickens, we'll be fine." Amy smiled.

"That's not funny." Macy paused. "Well, yeah, I guess it is, the way I been carrying on."

Amy realized she had never seen her friend feeling so vulnerable. Amy's trust was in Christ. She had leaned on Him and taken refuge in Him in Cambodia. That had built her faith. Macy shared no such faith. She rarely acknowledged the existence of God, much less any level of belief in Him. She had, in fact, rebuffed Amy's previous attempts to talk about God.

"Let me tell you about what happened in Cambodia ..."

For the next hour or so, Amy shared her experiences in southeast Asia, sparing no detail—from the faith of the parents whose children had been kidnapped to the brutality of the men using those children as medical guinea pigs. She described the makeshift graveyard at the "school," which had yielded a total of 47 young bodies when all the investigations were over. However, she stressed how God had divinely intervened and used her to expose the evil taking place there. She ended by quoting part of Psalm 91:

He who dwells in the shelter of the Most High
will abide in the shadow of the Almighty. I will say
to the LORD, 'My refuge and my fortress, my God,
in whom I trust.' For he will deliver you from the

She glanced again at Macy and saw that her friend had tears in her eyes, but she didn't push it. They would have two days together.

Amy suddenly hit the brakes. "Whoa."

"What's wrong?"

"I was so busy talking, I almost missed the turn. We're only ten minutes away."

Soon they pulled up to the main farmhouse, where a young man and woman and gaggle of children emerged to greet them. Amy and Macy exited the car and introductions were made.

As they talked, Macy jumped back. "Ack!" Then, she started laughing hysterically.

Amy looked to find two chickens pecking at the ground next to Macy's feet. She began to laugh, too. Looking at their hosts, she said, "It's an inside joke."

James Jr. smiled and handed her the key to the lake cabin. "It's all yours for as long as you need it. Why don't you join us for dinner tonight? We've got some catchin' up to do."

Amy looked at Macy, who nodded. "We'd love to. Thanks."

A few minutes later they pulled in front of the cabin. "Whaddaya think?"

Amy looked over to Macy, but Macy wasn't focused on the cabin. She was focused on her phone. She jumped out of the car and began waltzing around, raising her phone up over her head, looking for a signal on her phone. She smiled, stopped, and made a call. After disconnecting, she hurried back to the car.

"Cabin looks nice."

Amy shook her head. "What was that all about?"

"What?"

"The urgent phone call."

"Oh, nothing really urgent. I called my cousin, Mary."

Amy furrowed her brow. "Isn't she the one who watched your place when you went to Vegas for that nursing convention?"

Macy nodded. "That's her. I forgot to water my plants, so she's gonna stop by to do it for me."

"But last time she killed your fish. Are you sure they couldn't wait until you got home?"

Lynch had learned his lesson once before, about going to a potentially dangerous scene alone. He'd almost died that time. And Summer Stanton? If she truly killed Richard and that doctor in North Carolina, then she was about as sweet and innocent as a black widow after mating.

Nope. He entered the motel parking lot to find two St. Charles patrol SUVs waiting for him near the office. He knew both officers from previous work encounters, and the older of the two, Bill Peniston, held the rank of sergeant. He and Bill had had the opportunity to go fishing together once or twice. It had been a while.

After greetings and handshakes, he asked, "Bill, has anyone approached the car? Or her room?"

The sergeant replied, "No. We staged here as you requested, and there are two other officers at the other end of the building. Here's her room number." He handed Lynch a note sheet from the motel with a number scribbled on it.

"Good. Look, I think this woman is as dangerous as they come. Whether or not she's actually Summer Stanton is yet to be determined. Whoever she is, she's a suspect in two, maybe three other murders, so be careful."

"You know, if there's a possibility of shooting, we might want to clear the nearby rooms first."

Lynch thought about that. The officer had a good point, but Lynch worried they would lose their advantage of surprise.

With reluctance he said, "You're right. You two start at this end and get your guys out back to start at that end. I'll watch the room and car."

He moved into a position to observe and the officers began to go door to door. Within ten minutes, a group of over a dozen people shuffled away from the target room. There were a handful of men in suits, ties loosened and briefcases in hand, four couples, one young mom with two preschool-aged kids, a curly, blonde-haired woman with dark-rimmed glasses, a long-haired brunette who was a bit on the pudgy side, and two single guys, one of whom first came to the door wrapped in the room's bed cover. Per plan, they were urged to shelter in the front lobby.

Lynch watched as two officers, one on each end, eased back toward their cars, just in case their subject bolted to her car and managed to make a break for it. Lynch and the other two officers approached the room. Lynch stood to one side of the door, while the others positioned themselves on the other side, away from the window. Lynch leaned toward the door and pounded on it.

"Open the door. Police!

No response. He could hear no activity inside. He signaled the others and asked with his hands whether or not they discerned anything going on in the room. Both officers shook their heads.

"We need to talk with you. Please open the door."

Nada.

Lynch took the pass card to open the door and slid it across the magnetic lock. The light turned green, and he heard the latch give way. Still standing away from the opening, he used his hand to push open the door. As it opened, there was still no response.

Lynch peered around the doorframe and into the room. No lights. The bed sat undisturbed. The door to the bathroom was wide open with no light there. The two officers accompanied him into the room, and one checked the bathroom.

"Sink's dry. Towels are unused."

Lynch nodded. "Yeah. This room hasn't been used at all. I think we've been played."

He walked outside and began to inspect the car. The vehicle was licensed in New Jersey and otherwise appeared clean. There was nothing visible inside through the windows. He looked at the sergeant, who was in the process of releasing his men back to patrol. The man approached

Lynch once he finished.

"Whatcha need, Lynch?"

"Bill, can you run these plates, and did we get the search warrant for this car?"

The man nodded. "Sure. Let me get my car and bring it around."

With the warrant confirmed, Lynch gloved up and proceeded to open the car. He examined the passenger cabin, glove compartment, and area behind the dash. Clean. He popped the trunk of the Audi. Empty.

The police sergeant climbed out of his vehicle nearby. "Car's registered to a small rental agency in Jersey."

"A rental? I found no rental agreement. The car's clean."

"You sure this is the car you're looking for?"

Lynch nodded. "Well, it's the car that seems to be linked to the woman we're looking for." He paused to ponder his next move. "Look, could you have forensics dust it for prints and maybe check for any fiber evidence? If this *is* the car, I suspect it's been wiped clean of prints, but we might find something else."

"Do you think she just dumped it here to throw off the hunt? She could be anywhere."

Lynch began to nod in agreement but stopped as a thought slapped him upside the head. "Or she changed her appearance and walked right past us." The curly blonde! Different hair, but the right height and size.

"That blonde who came out of the room two doors away. Cover the front."

As the officer rushed back to his SUV, Lynch ran toward the front lobby. He scanned the room. Two of the businessmen appeared to have left, but the other three, the couples, the mom and her kids, the single guys, and the chubby brunette were there. No blonde. He rushed into the breakfast room. Empty. The pool area was clear. The small fitness room, also.

Back in the lobby, he asked, "The blonde woman who was with you. Did anyone see where she went?"

Most of them shook their heads. A few looked puzzled as if wondering, what blonde woman? The clerk pointed to the front doors.

"I think I saw a blonde go out the front door as soon as she came in here. But I didn't see where she went."

Lynch approached the desk. "Cameras? Do you have a security camera for the front door?"

"Sure. And unlike the movies, it even works." He grinned. "Back here."

Lynch followed the man to a back room, where he showed Lynch their security system. Lynch glanced at the time. "Go back 30 minutes."

As they followed the timeline forward from that point, sure enough, the curly blonde exited the building through the front door. Using other cameras, they watched her rush along the side of the buildings, opposite to where the police and Lynch were. They lost her as she moved past the tall hedge surrounding the parking lot on that side. *She could be anywhere now*, thought Lynch. He frowned.

"Thanks. Don't erase any of that. The forensics folks will stop by to make a copy."

He stepped outside where the sergeant had positioned his car near Lynch's, and informed the man of his suspicions as well as what he'd learned. As they spoke, a tow truck entered the lot, and the sergeant directed the driver to the back. Lynch joined in to watch the driver hoist up the Audi Cabriolet to take it away to the labs.

He thanked the officer and walked back to his car. He climbed into the driver's seat as he watched the truck drive past with the car on its flatbed. He waved at the sergeant, started his car, and pulled onto the street. As he joined the traffic, he felt a cold metal cylinder press against the back of his head.

Glancing into his rearview mirror, he saw only a mass of curly, blonde hair.

"Keep driving."

It was a voice he recognized. "Summer Stanton. Back from the dead."

"I don't care where you go, just make it someplace secluded and far from here."

THIRTY

Abdi paced the length of his warehouse. He didn't like being "imprisoned" within its walls. Yet, he knew he was a hunted man and that his usual haunts were very likely under surveillance.

However, there was now a new factor in his cabin fever—Adam and Cain. He couldn't explain it. The men were cordial at first and had supplied gifts not just to his men but to him as well. Despite that, there was something about the two men he couldn't quite put his finger on. As time wore on, their friendliness waned and impatience increased. They talked more among themselves, with side glances and laughter that seemed aimed at Abdi and his men.

He knew ruthless men. He knew greedy ones. He knew politicians who fit both categories. These men he couldn't read. Sinister was a trait that came to mind. It rolled ruthlessness, greed, and so much more into one word. Maybe that was it. He'd met men like that in the cartel.

Bashiir approached, his cell phone in hand. He extended it to Abdi.

"The men at the friend's apartment wish to report."

Abdi nodded and put the phone to his ear. "Yes."

"Lord, there is no sign of the woman you hunt or her friend. We have asked others living here if they have seen them, but no one will cooperate. How do you want us to continue?"

Abdi wanted to slap his forehead. Must he write it out, Step A to Step Q? He thrust the phone back at Bashiir.

"Instruct these men on how to do a stakeout."

He noticed Cain observing him. Gooseflesh prickled across his arms. He walked across the width of the floor to join the two men.

"My men are all in position."

Adam nodded. Cain asked, "Trouble?"

Abdi shook his head. "Not at all. Two of the younger men needed some additional instruction."

Adam glared at him. "Inexperience or incompetence?"

Abdi felt like saying both, but instinct told him that would be the wrong answer. "Inexperience. Until now they have been only taxi drivers."

Both men nodded. Adam muttered something under his breath and shook his head as Cain spoke. "Inexperience we can deal with. Incompetence we prefer to weed out. You might learn to do the same."

The gooseflesh returned. Abdi could only hope that by the end of this collaboration, they did not see him that way. These men had access to money and power that he wanted to share in. He would tolerate their growing insolence for a chance at that.

Bashiir approached again, but this time signaled that he wished to talk with Abdi. They stepped a few yards away, but not far enough from Cain's incessant stare. Bashiir leaned to whisper into his ear.

"The men in Wildwood have run into a bit of trouble. The police arrived and now check out the property.

Warsame was spotted parked alongside the road, and the police detained him to ask questions. He told them he had car trouble and was waiting for assistance. They asked him for more details, and then one officer reached in, turned the key, and the car started without difficulty. He was instructed to move on. Tawfiiq and Xuseen remain hidden in the wood, but the police seem to know someone is there."

Abdi frowned, but acknowledged this as a minor setback. "Have them pull back, away from the house. Perhaps they can watch from a spot across the street. After all, if someone shows up, they will do so by car, not by walking through the woods."

"Yes, lord. I told them as much already. They report that there is no sign of anyone living there."

"Very good, Bashiir. I trust you will keep them in order."

Abdi returned to his two benefactors. "There appears to be no one living at the house in Wildwood."

Adam nodded. "We know that. The man's parents moved there recently but left the country. We suspect he might use it to hide the woman or himself. Do not fail to watch it."

Abdi bristled at the man's condescending tone. Yet, he pondered that statement. How could they know that the parents had moved there, or that they had left the country? What else did they know? What did they know about *him*? He didn't dare ask.

Bashiir hurried toward him again. This time he appeared excited.

"Lord, a woman, the friend, has returned to her apartment."

"They are sure? I do not want a replay of what happened before."

Bashiir continued to hold the phone to his ear. "They are moving closer to make sure."

A few minutes later Bashiir's countenance fell. "It is not her. She has a key and let herself in, but she has left already. It was not the friend, Macy Johnson."

Abdi turned to inform Adam, but Cain was already up and walking toward him.

"We are not so unreasonable as to expect results in one day, but do not fail us, Abdullah Said Abdi. You would fare much better with the FBI than with us, should you fail to deliver. You have the phone. Keep in touch."

At that, Adam joined him, and the two men exited the warehouse.

Amy and Macy settled in, each with their own bedroom, although the bath was shared. Amy had gone outside to discover a stack of freshly split firewood on the back porch. She used this to start a fire in the large stone fireplace.

Macy exited the bathroom, coughing and sputtering.

"What'd you do, girl? Set the place on fire? What's with all this smoke?"

"Go open the front door. I'll get the back. I forgot to check the damper on the flue when I started it. It was closed, but it's open now. We just need to air the place out."

Macy stood next to the door, fanning it back and forth. Not that it helped. After about 15 minutes, the air inside was breathable again.

"Can I shut this now? It's getting cold in here."

Amy replied, "Sure. Sorry about that."

The fire began to crackle, the dry wood catching the flame readily. Macy walked over next to it, turning from front to back to front again as close to it as she dared.

"Isn't this supposed to produce heat? My hair drier does a better job."

"Hey, it's just getting started. Give it some time. Maybe you should go open one of your bottles of vino. I much prefer that wine to *your* whine." She held her nose on the last word to give it an extra-nasally twang.

Macy waggled her head back and forth in a mocking action. "You used that line already. So, why'd you forget the damper thingy on the chimney? That's not like you." She paused. "And what's for lunch? I'm hungry."

"We brought a bunch of stuff to eat, but I figured maybe we'd do cheese, crackers, hummus, and summer sausage for lunch since we're joining the family for dinner. And I think we can find something suitable to drink with that."

Macy held up a bottle of Cabernet Sauvignon and two glasses. "Got that right. I still can't believe I bought all that. Even with your help, that's enough wine for months, maybe the year if you continue that 'I have to drive' stuff."

Amy went to the fridge and an adjacent cabinet and retrieved the rest of their lunch. She placed the cheese and sausage on a small cutting board and carried it all to a table in front of the fire.

"So, you gonna answer my question?"

"What question?"

"You're the one who seems preoccupied now."

"Oh. I tried calling Lynch to let him know we arrived. I

texted him, too. I haven't heard back from him. Under the circumstances, I guess I'm a little worried. Hope he's okay."

"Mister Secret Agent Man can take care of himself. I'm sure he's fine, but didn't he tell you not to use your phone from down here?"

The phone in Abdi's pocket vibrated. He hesitated to pull it out but knew that failing to answer might not bode well for him. He took a deep breath before connecting.

"Yes."

"Your men at Macy Johnson's apartment can be called off today. Her credit card made a purchase at a winery in St. James, Missouri, a few hours ago. It was a large purchase, and the staff there remember her well. She was with another woman, a white woman, and they commented about heading west for a girls' get-away."

That was not what Abdi wanted to hear. "Did they speak of how long? Or where?"

"No. But we checked the hospital staff schedule, and she is not due back to work until Sunday afternoon. You must focus your attention on finding Lynch Cully until then. He is your priority target."

No, Abdi thought, *he is not* my *target at all.* He wondered if Adam was telling him the whole story. He sensed that the man was not.

"I am going to pull my men from one address you gave me, the house belonging to Lynch Cully. There is another family living there now. I can use—"

"No. You will keep your men there. The man living there is a friend and former co-worker who would let Cully crash there if needed. Same with the fourth address we gave you."

"Then I will pull some men from the parents' old house. They report only workmen coming and going there, no sign of Lynch Cully. I have a big—"

"My friend, you will keep the men at each assignment . . . or there will be consequences. I do not think you would like those consequences."

Abdi grew angry at the command. He was not these men's lackey and the men were *his* men, not Adam's. He had a large drug shipment arriving and needed more men to assist with it. His manpower was being wasted watching houses where their target seemed unlikely to appear. In his mind, only the Wildwood home held promise, but watching it, too, had become more complicated.

"As you wish." He would pull one man from each location, as well as the three watching the apartment, and not tell Adam of the change. They could go back to surveillance once their product had been repackaged and distributed.

"Must I remind you that finding Cully holds as much or more promise as finding Macy Johnson when it comes to getting Amy Gibbs?"

Not if that woman was off on a girls' getaway. But then, they had no confirmation that the woman with Macy Johnson at the winery was the Gibbs woman. Perhaps Adam had a point. What if the Gibbs woman was with Lynch Cully and someone else was with Macy Johnson?

"We are still committed to helping you find Lynch Cully. The Lion of Somalia does not back down or shirk on his agreements."

"The lion of . . ." The man laughed on the other end. "Right. Whatever you wish to call yourself." His voice turned gruff. "Just do your job."

Abdi felt his anger rise up within. No one laughs at him. He would let this man intimidate him no more. Adam and Cain were on *his* turf.

THIRTY-ONE

Hannah had found it easy to evade the motel's security cameras and double back to Cully's car. She had lucked out in finding it unlocked. It saved her the time she would have needed to unlock it. Yet, her biggest risk was climbing into the backseat and ducking down as far as she could into the leg well. Only a quick glance into the back windows would have revealed her. She had gambled on his preoccupation with the car in keeping her undetected . . . and had won that bet.

Her world had been turned upside down and inside out, scorched and burned, over the past 24 hours. The idea of falling out of grace with the Assembly, and of being placed on their target list, tormented her. She had no idea what to do next, where to turn, or whom to trust.

Intuitively, she sensed that Cully had somehow orchestrated this disruption of her life. In doing so, he had played his queen and moved into position for checkmate. However, what he very likely didn't fully understand was just how readily the Assembly would cheat. They were adding two new pieces to the board—two players he knew nothing about.

She knew the players involved. They would come for her, too, unless she dealt with Cully first. Yet, even if she killed Cully, there were better than 50-50 odds they'd still come for her. Would she exit a building, step out of a car or plane, or walk through a park only to be greeted by a bullet to her head? Would she end up face down in a river with a gun lying next to her? Her mind rotated from scenario to scenario of what could happen. Where did her best chance of survival lie? She'd come so close to her goal. Her trek couldn't end now.

She couldn't afford to reveal herself as long as he remained in the parking lot. They needed to be moving, and she crossed her fingers that he would not delay. She refused to believe in karma, as hers would be rewarded in ways she wouldn't like. However, something, someone, some force must have been on her side so far. She had remained undetected and now they moved into traffic and headed away from the motel.

As he sped up, she placed the end of her gun barrel against the back of his head.

"Keep driving," she said.

Lynch followed the commands of his captor and headed west on I-70. He knew that as long as he had control of the car, he had an advantage, albeit a slight one. Admittedly, the 9mm Sig in her hand could be a bigger advantage.

He decided to take the opportunity to ask some questions that had been floating through his head for days. Whether or not he would get any answers was yet to be discovered.

"So, why the faked death?"

His phone beeped for the third time since he'd gotten into the car.

"Those messages are probably from Amy. If I don't respond, she'll call in reinforcements. Folks'll start looking for me."

He looked into his mirror to see if there would be a response. The woman sat back in the seat, looking comfortable with her weapon aimed at his head. She appeared contemplative, and yet, mildly disturbed. Of course, he realized, anyone who would kill people for hire, if his assumptions were correct, was more than mildly disturbed.

She finally gazed into the mirror and met his eyes with hers.

"My question first. Whose idea was it to take to social media, the #summersnotdead gambit?"

Lynch was not about to tell her that Amy had come up with the idea. Amy faced enough of a threat from Abdi without having to add one more crazy looking for her.

"Mine. Looks like it worked. Flushed *you* out of the woodwork, didn't it?"

He glanced back into the mirror. From her countenance, he realized that he wouldn't like playing five-card draw with her.

"Who flushed whom? Who's on which end of the gun?" She paused. "Where'd you get the picture?"

He quickly debated whether to come up with a story or to tell the truth. A gentle nudge of the gun barrel against his scalp told him not to waste time creating fiction. He looked back through the mirror again.

"Purely a creation of Photoshop. I had what I thought was a reliable description of the new you. So, we took a stock photo of you, made the changes, and put it out there. Strictly a gamble."

He heard her sigh, followed by the words, "Rocky Broad" under her breath. He did not confirm or deny that comment, as he didn't want to put that woman in any more jeopardy. Her comment did, however, establish that she had been there and had seen him in the coffee shop.

He saw Summer shake her head. Her next question seemed to come out of nowhere. Why was he so calm? The answer to that was easy. His faith.

As he drove on, her comment about who flushed out whom caught his attention. She *had* played that masterfully well, using his own tactical maneuver to flank him. He had once heard that redheads were simply blondes without impulse control, but the blonde, previously a redhead, in his backseat clearly laid those stereotypes to rest.

He glanced back in his mirror again.

"You keep looking in that mirror. What do you expect to see, the cavalry coming to your rescue?"

"Habit. I'm driving and want to know what's behind and around me."

All he could see were her eyes as she leaned forward toward him. That meant she likely could see only his eyes in the mirror as well.

"Funny things, mirrors. The eyes are the mirror to the soul. Keep looking, you'll never know what you'll find."

Where did that come from? he wondered. *What did she mean?* Was she referring to herself somehow?

He drove on for another five or six minutes in silence, having no concept of where she wanted him to go, short of "someplace secluded and far away." In another few minutes they would be leaving the more developed communities along the interstate and heading into rural farm land. Did she know where she was headed?

"Where are we going?"

"Keep driving."

Lynch felt strangely calm about heading into sparsely populated areas where no police authority could respond within minutes, with a gun at his head. Most people he knew, even some cops, would be soiling their clothes about now as they recognized their demise was on the horizon with their bodies about to be dumped where they might never be found. Somehow, he sensed this would not be the case, but about what was to happen he had no clue.

"So, again, I ask, why fake your death?"

"What better way to reinvent yourself?"

Finally, she seemed willing to talk. He needed to keep her talking.

"As a hired killer?"

She didn't answer right away. "We like to think of ourselves as troubleshooters."

He grunted. "Yeah, shooting anyone the Assembly sees as trouble."

He heard another sigh. "Yeah, I guess you could see it that way. By the way, the Assembly sees you as trouble."

Lynch actually felt both surprise and honor at that statement. He couldn't think of any organization he felt more gratified in disrupting than that self-serving, greedy, power hungry, godless collection of elitists. To be considered a thorn in their side was a worthy accolade. Still, he'd had only three significant interactions with them—stopping their terrorists' plan to destabilize the economy, defeating their attempt to overthrow the British monarchy, and rescuing Bradley Graham from kidnappers trying to sway the election. As he thought about it, he could see that maybe that was enough.

It seemed obvious that she was there to shoot the troublemaker.

"Look, I know you killed Doctor Renton. The evidence is circumstantial at best, but I know you did it. Did you also kill Richard Nichols? He was a friend."

She shook her head. "A friend? Seemed to me he was competition for a certain someone's affections. I thought you'd be glad to get rid of that leg of the triangle."

"Not at all. Be honest; he didn't deserve to die. He didn't do anything against the Assembly."

She didn't answer. He checked the mirror again to see her looking at some sort of electronic device.

"What's that?"

"You'll find out soon enough."

Her focus remained on the device and something outside. She appeared to be looking for something. Lynch watched some of the roadside scenery go by. He couldn't figure out what she might be watching for.

"Hey, if you're going to kill me anyway, you could at least answer that question for me. It's not like I'll be using your confession against you."

She didn't answer but focused her attention to the road ahead. "Get off at the next exit."

The upcoming exit was for the small town of New

Florence. As he recalled, the exit held only a truck stop, a McDonald's, a mom-and-pop cafe, and a few motels strategically placed there because the state road to the south led to the state's major wine producing region. One small winery had opened just off the exit to take advantage of the Kansas City folks coming to explore the wine trail.

A couple of minutes later, he complied. His heart rate accelerated a bit. He would have to keep his head about him if he wanted to keep it.

"Turn right onto the service road."

He did. Less than half a mile later, she pointed to an abandoned building on the left.

"Over there. Pull in behind the building and park. Turn off the car."

Lynch didn't like what he saw—seclusion, in plain sight. They were close enough to the interstate he could hear the traffic inside his car, and he could probably hit the service road if he threw a rock over the old building. And yet, no one could see them from the road, and the traffic noise would cover that of a gunshot. Besides, in rural Missouri the occasional gunshot caught no one's attention.

"Okay, get out of the car. Slowly. Put your hands behind your head and interlace your fingers."

As he complied, he heard her door open in concert with his.

"Step away from the car."

He did so.

"A little farther."

He just lost his advantage of slamming her car door into her. He heard her exiting the vehicle now.

"Kneel down."

He hesitated.

"*Kneel* down!"

She knew what she was doing. She wasn't close enough for him to kick out at her. She had complete control of the situation.

Hannah struggled with her options as Cully drove west, away from the dense population areas. She had endeavored to contact Francois several more times overnight and that morning. Each attempt had failed. Each failing lessened her hope for a reconciliation.

She watched Cully closely, just as he did her. She couldn't just shoot him while he was driving at interstate speeds. While her life was likely already over, she couldn't bring herself to create a major accident on the highway that could kill many others. She had never wanted to "go out with a bang."

After a short while, he began with the questions. She had anticipated as much. He went straight to the point, but she had questions first. And she was in control.

She met his gaze in the mirror.

"My question first. Whose idea was it to take to social media, the #summersnotdead gambit?"

"Mine. Looks like it worked. Flushed *you* out of the woodwork, didn't it?"

His answer didn't surprise her. His confidence about flushing her out was misplaced. *She* held the gun, not him.

One thing really puzzled her though.

"Where'd you get the picture?"

No one had had an opportunity to take her picture, and the coffee shop in Chimney Rock had no security cameras. She had checked that the first morning she had stopped there.

"Purely a creation of Photoshop. I had what I thought was a reliable description of the new you. So, we took a stock photo of you, made the changes, and put it out there. Strictly a gamble."

She sighed and muttered, "Rocky broad." The woman had been more observant than Hannah had recognized. In hindsight, though, she should have guessed that. The woman had remembered her and what she'd eaten the days before. She made a mental note. If she survived this situation, she would not frequent the same eatery. Again, her fatigue had contributed to her failure. She had intended to remain anonymous, only to eat breakfast at the same place three mornings in a row.

She observed Lynch as they traveled. He had a sense of peace that she could not comprehend. No anxiety tainted his speech. No tension appeared in his hands as he gripped the wheel. She had a gun on him, and surely he must be thinking he's about to die. Yet, he displayed utter calm. Why? How?

She shook her head in confusion. "I don't get it. You're not stupid. You know what's coming. And yet, you remain calm."

She saw his eyes glance back at her in the mirror. "It's called faith. My life is in God's hands, not yours. If I die today, I'll enter the very presence of Christ. If you died today, where would you end up?"

She didn't want to think about that. She'd covered

stories about fallen pastors and Christian leaders—always the negative stories, not the positive ones. She knew the concept of heaven and hell, but that was fable, wasn't it? Where had God been for her family?

As they drove on, he came back to his initial question. She debated how much to tell him and decided to offer only what he already knew, or suspected he knew, that she worked for the Assembly. He might believe that she killed both the doctor and Richard Nichols, but as he stated, all he had was circumstantial evidence. Her fatigue hadn't made her *that* sloppy. They'd never find evidence directly linking her to either death . . . and she wasn't about to admit her role in them.

His question about Richard Nichols did surprise her.

"A friend? Seemed to me he was competition for a certain someone's affections. I thought you'd be glad to get rid of that leg of the triangle."

Competition was something she had learned to eliminate. Summer's rise up the journalistic ladder had been one of doing so. That had been another factor in earning her nickname, "Elsa." She didn't quite understand Cully's shock at the death of a rival.

She checked her location device off and on, checking mileage markers along the road. She needed to make sure she was out of range of the same devices possessed by the other two "troubleshooters." Satisfied that they were, she told Cully to get off at the next exit, to a town in the middle of nowhere. As they neared the exit, she spotted an abandoned building along the north service road. It would do.

"Okay, get out of the car. Slowly. Put your hands behind your head and interlace your fingers."

As he complied, she opened her door in line with his but stayed in the car. She didn't want him using the door as a weapon. There was a chance he would bolt, but he couldn't run faster than her bullet. She counted on his realizing that, along with recognizing that she was no stranger to using her gun.

"Step away from the car."

He did so.

"A little farther."

He was now beyond the range of using the door, so she exited the vehicle. She needed him in a position where he had no way out.

This was her make-or-break point. Her world was crumbling around her, and she had to make a decision. Her hand began to tremble as tears flooded her eyes. She forced her voice to remain steely.

"Kneel down."

She repeated her command more forcibly. For her plan to work, he could have no choice but to obey.

THIRTY-TWO

Amy paced outside the guest house. The skies had cleared and the air temperature was at a seasonal norm in the low 50s. Still, the fire inside felt cozy, and the flames held a mesmerizing, calming effect. Or maybe it was the single glass of wine she'd imbibed.

Perhaps her feeling of fatigue was due to the emotional strain of their situation. They had only postponed the problem by fleeing to mid-Missouri. Abdi still hunted for her. Macy was still in danger, too. Plus, she couldn't rely so heavily on Lynch. He had a job to do, and he couldn't put it on hold just to protect them.

She held her phone above her head and continued pacing. Macy had found a signal. Why was one eluding her?

"Four paces to your left. See that X scratched in the dirt? That's where I found a signal." Macy stood on the porch watching her, grinning.

"What's so funny?"

"Oh, nothing."

Amy walked to her left and found the X. She manipulated her phone over, around, and through every dimension with no success. Macy's grin seemed to gain Cheshire Cat proportions.

"Okay, what's funny?"

"Nothing really. Just watching you march around trying

to place a phone call after you telling me to chill. What goes around comes around."

Amy acknowledged that Macy had a point, but . . .

"I haven't heard anything back from Lynch. That's not like him. I'm really worried now. Something's got to be wrong. Maybe we should head back to the city."

"Whoa, girlfriend. We just got here. What happened to 'we'll have a great girls' get-away' and 'Macy, you'll love it; it'll be fun'?"

Amy glanced down at the dirt. Macy had three points now, but . . .

"I'm going to head down to the lake. Maybe I'll find a stronger signal along the way. Want to come along?"

Macy shook her head. "Naw, I'm gonna walk to the barn and see if I can find any chickens to feed."

Amy gave her a double take. "Okay, I'll come with you then."

Macy laughed. "Whoa. Just kidding. I don't want to feed any birds. I'm going back inside to sit by that fire and have another glass of wine."

Abdi hated the feeling of spinning his wheels. He had no leads on finding the woman. The friend—and maybe the woman, too—had left town for a period of time. He regretted his association with the two strangers, but was in over his head with those two. Yet, he couldn't let his growing anger with them cloud his perspective. They needed him, and he had thought that he needed them. Perhaps he no longer did.

"Bashiir!"

The man talked with two men at the far end of the warehouse. Abdi watched him give them a last command, turn, and jog toward Abdi. The man had taken on more and more responsibility and had excelled with each task assigned to him. Abdi began to see the young man as a worthy successor. Perhaps even as a son-in-law once his youngest, unmarried daughter reached womanhood. True, their Islamic tribal tradition of arranging marriages for girls who began to shed blood monthly was at odds with American law, but no one within their community would dare to expose the practice or the marriage under Islamic law. Yes, he would consider Bashiir an excellent son-in-law.

"Bashiir, I grow tired of going nowhere. We have no idea where to find the woman. These men dictate terms to us, and we are no closer to finding this Lynch Cully. I believe they are using us to do their own work. They do not tell us the whole truth."

Bashiir nodded. "I so believe, also. If we find this Cully without finding the woman first, they will not lift a finger to help you. But they have a point. Finding him might lead you to her."

"We must find a way to bring him into the open, to flush him out of the brush as we would the object of a hunt back in Somalia. I have grown to respect your ideas."

Bashiir gave Abdi a brief bow. "Thank you, lord. You are too kind. I will not disappoint you, but I do not wish to offer a suggestion without giving it much thought. I do have one idea but wish to weigh its risks before speaking of it further."

Abdi smiled. He trusted Bashiir to come through. He

would not be dissatisfied.

"Lord, with your blessing, allow me to finish with the men working on this new shipment. Then, I will turn my attention to your request."

Abdi nodded. Yes, the shipment had priority today. "Go. Finish your work."

Bradley Graham swiveled his chair away from the C&O desk, his only real choice of desk for the Oval Office since the Resolute desk used by his predecessors since 1993 now required some minor restoration.

Only six desks had ever been used in the Oval Office. Two of those now resided in the presidential libraries of the presidents who were most associated with their use. One was in use at the Vice President's office in the U.S. Senate. The only other option was the desk used by Nixon to hold his recording equipment. Its association with that Watergate Scandal was enough to steer Graham to the C&O desk. Perhaps it was time to put a call out to the nation's woodworkers to add a new member to the collection.

He gazed out across the dormant rose garden and for a moment wondered what it would look like within a few months. Being an outsider to the Washington Beltway as well as the federal bureaucracy, which had both pros and cons, he had never been to the White House prior to his inauguration. His mental images of the rose garden in bloom came only from photos and Hollywood depictions.

That thought lasted only long enough to register on his consciousness. The reason for his contemplation was his inability to reach Lynch Cully. His calls to Lynch were typically answered by the second ring.

His mental deliberations were disturbed by his secretary, Paula. She took such command of his calendar and schedule, while keeping him straight with his 'i's' dotted and "t's" crossed, she might as well put in her bid to become his chief of staff.

"Mr. President, FBI Director Renzoni is on the line. He says it's urgent."

"Thank you, Paula."

He returned to face his desk and picked up the phone. Anthony "Zio" Renzoni had been finally confirmed only a week earlier by the Senate. He, too, was a Beltway outsider who shared Graham's zeal for cleaning up Washington. His battle for confirmation had been a rough one.

"Zio! Again, congratulations on surviving the confirmation process."

The man on the other end didn't laugh.

"Thank you, Mr. President, but I'm calling directly rather than go through the acting Attorney General. It's about that topic we discussed privately."

Graham braced himself for what was about to come.

"Sir, I need to talk with you personally. Can you clear 15 minutes for me?"

"When?"

"I'm on my way there now."

"Done. See you shortly."

Part of that earlier conversation had involved Graham's desire for a "special" investigator to look into certain activities of the Assembly, although he never mentioned Lynch or the fact that he'd already put Lynch to work. He had known Zio for nearly twenty years and fully believed they shared a common distaste of the global elite's "Deep State." They knew that any attempt to bring the government back to being one "of the people, by the people, for the people" would face stiff resistance and require slow, steady work. As a believer, however, he understood that this quote, while borrowed by Lincoln for his *Gettysburg Address*, came from John Wycliffe in 1384 when he wrote in the prologue of his Bible translation that "The Bible is for the Government of the People, by the People, and for the People." The United States government needed to take that to heart. The Assembly, on the other hand, with its fingers throughout the bureaucracy, ridiculed God's Word.

He notified his secretary. "Paula, when Director Renzoni gets here, usher him right in and block all calls. Thanks."

Graham stood and returned to gaze out the windows. He wondered what could be so urgent that Zio called and requested the meeting.

It wouldn't take long to find out. In less than five minutes, the director was ushered into the Oval Office. After greetings, the pair sat down in the couches facing each other at one end of the room.

"Sir, I needed to come here personally because, despite your phone lines being secure, we both know the NSA monitors your calls. I appreciate your seeing me on short notice."

Graham nodded. He still wasn't used to thinking along those lines. The concept of constant monitoring, just like 24/7 personal protection, would take time to become accustomed to.

"Thank you, Zio. What's on your mind?"

Leaning forward in his seat with an air of grave concern on his face, the director said, "Sir, about that conversation we had, we might have picked up on some intel about recent actions by the Assembly. Have you been briefed on the #summersnotdead social media buzz?"

Graham knew all about it, even from before it went public, but it was not yet time to reveal his actions and those of Lynch to the director. That time would come, but only after Graham had totally vetted Zio to his own satisfaction.

"Yes. It's believed that Summer Stanton did not really die in that car accident, that the whole thing might have been faked for reasons we don't understand."

"That's right, sir. Well, it's caused quite a stir, and I found it curious, so I put an agent on it to see what might really be happening. It seems there was a flurry of sightings this morning in your hometown, and the car was found at a motel in St. Charles, Missouri. A name came up with the police reports—your friend Lynch Cully."

Uh-oh, thought Graham. *Where do I let this take us?* Was it time to confide in his FBI director?

"When I personally tried to find Cully, I learned two things. He now has DHS status with a very high security clearance, none of which was vetted by my agency. And, he seems to have disappeared. He hasn't been seen or heard from since working with the local police at that motel."

That confirmed Graham's inability to reach Lynch, which made it all the more concerning to him.

"I'm not sure where this is going, but I asked DHS to

take him on. As for his clearance, he was fully vetted previously by the FBI to be on my transition team. I can only assume DHS took that into consideration."

Zio let out a deep breath and sat back in his seat, but he didn't appear fully placated.

"Of course. I didn't think about that. We only looked at his DHS application. That said, sir, why would he be interested in this Summer Stanton thing?"

Graham decided to go a little further in explaining Lynch's task without mentioning the possible association to the Assembly.

"Cully was tasked with investigating a series of unusual deaths in the medical community. With Summer Stanton's prominence in the public arena, he asked if he could look into it as well. As you know, no body has ever been found."

Zio nodded. "Yes, sir." He paused and glanced toward the windows in thought. A moment later, he resumed. "Sir, I'm going to go out on a limb here, based on our earlier conversation . . . is there a link between these deaths and the Assembly? Is that really what Cully is looking into?"

Graham had always appreciated Zio's astuteness. That was one of the many traits that earned him his nomination to become the FBI Director. Graham should not have underestimated the man's ability to put two and two together.

"This doesn't leave this room, but yes, that's exactly what he was trying to discover."

"I was afraid you might say that, sir. Cully might be in trouble. One of our wiretaps picked up chatter from St. Louis. Two men are asking around about him. They're looking pretty hard because they've asked multiple agencies, using bogus federal credentials to gain access to those agencies. Those inquiries also intersected with our search for the terrorist Abdullah Said Abdi. It appears these men approached someone called the Lion of Somalia. We couldn't determine who this person was, or where he is, physically, but who else would use such a moniker? We're giving that search a bit more manpower now."

Now Graham began to worry that his friend no longer inhabited this earthly plane. Yet, deep inside he knew that God had plans for Cully, and "no weapon formed against him" stood a chance of success.

He believed it safe to assume these men were from the Assembly. How else could they have obtained the credentials they'd been using? And if Lynch's suspicion that Summer Stanton had faked her death to take a position as a "hit man" for the Assembly, that would make three trained assassins seeking his scalp. Add in a collaboration with that terrorist, Abdi, and Lynch faced what most would see as insurmountable odds.

Graham had to take stock of his own level of faith. He said a quiet prayer for both Lynch and Amy . . . and then felt complete peace about bringing his new FBI Director fully into the loop. Their assault on the Assembly might become a full-frontal attack sooner than he'd ever expected.

THIRTY-THREE

Amy spent more time than she'd thought by the lake. The sun was well past its zenith and the air began to cool. She wondered if Macy had been able to keep the fire going, although it was time to let it die. They would be heading to the main house for dinner soon.

She had discovered a good cell signal near the lake. She saw no nearby towers but speculated that the water somehow allowed the signal from a not-too-distant tower to travel across its surface rather than dissipate with distance. Much like sound that sailed across the water but did not penetrate it. However, she was not an electronics expert. Maybe she was simply in range of a tower she could not observe.

Her first attempt to contact Lynch upon arrival at the lake ended with the same result—voicemail and no response. She had given him plenty of time to reply, aimlessly watching the water and occasionally skipping a stone or two that she picked up from the shoreline. As she sat and watched nearby ducks searching for food, the occasional fishing boat navigating what anglers called structure, and the clouds flying by ahead of a high-pressure front coming from the northwest, her mind wandered across as many topics as there seemed to be clouds. And those thoughts seemed to move at about the same speed.

She stood up from the picnic table, but couldn't get her legs to start walking in the direction of the cabin. She had a signal here. She needed to try one more time. The call went once again to voicemail.

"Lynch, it's me. I know, I've called too much and used my phone too much here, against your advice. I honestly don't think they can trace it since it's a prepaid, so don't worry. Speaking of which, *I'm* worried. You haven't called back or texted. I need to know you're okay. Please? Let me know. Bye."

The air was definitely cooling down now, so she hurried back to the cabin. The walk still took every second of 15 minutes to complete. She opened the door to find the fire almost out, Macy's glass still full of Cabernet, and her friend in the chair where she'd been sitting with her chin on her chest, snoring.

Her first thought was to ease the door closed so as not to wake Macy. Yet, they needed to get ready to join Jimmy and his family for dinner, and Macy needed to wake up. She slammed the door with gusto. Better to let the noise awaken her friend than to try to arouse her directly and the woman wake up swinging.

Macy jolted upright in her chair. "Wha—? Who? Wh-what was that?" She inhaled deeply and glanced back and forth three times before her gaze settled on Amy. "Girlfriend, you're back. How was the lake?"

"Not as peaceful as I would have liked, but that wasn't the lake's fault."

Amy attempted to pour a finger's worth of wine into her glass to find the bottle empty.

"I did find a good cell signal there."

"How's Lynch? Like I said, doin' fine, right?"

Amy shook her head. "Called twice and got voicemail twice. Something has to be wrong."

"Girl, think positive. Maybe he got called to the White House on a national emergency and has been on a plane this whole time. You know, had to put his phone on airplane mode."

Amy didn't believe that to be the case, but maybe Macy was onto something. Maybe he *did* have to go offline for some reason. But something else clicked in her brain. Was thinking the worst any way to display her faith? The Bible talked of fear and worry being the antithesis of faith. She needed to get rid of her stinkin' thinkin', as her dad had always called it. She sure missed him. *He* would have been able to cheer her up.

"You're right, Macy. I need to think good thoughts."

"There you go, Tinkerbell."

Amy startled at the ringing of her phone. *Lynch?* she thought. She fumbled getting it out of her pocket and dropped it to the floor. In picking it up, she didn't recognize the number, but then she saw the Caller ID and her eyes bugged out. How in the world did this person find her on a prepaid phone?

She took a deep breath and answered the call. "This is Amy Gibbs."

"Amy, it's Brad Graham."

"Yes, Mr. President. How are you, sir?"

She saw Macy's eyes bulge wider than her own. Macy seemed more excited than she did, and began fanning herself with her hand. But Amy's excitement soured quickly as her thinkin' started stinkin' worse than a day-old filled bedpan. Was he calling to notify her that something had happened to Lynch?

"To be honest, Amy, I'm worried. Do you know where Lynch is? I can't seem to raise him by phone."

The man had been able to find her on a prepaid phone, but he couldn't find Lynch? That didn't sound right. Still, she felt a bit better. No news was good news?

"No, sir. I haven't been able to reach him either. I was hoping maybe you'd sent him off on an assignment, and he was on a plane somewhere, unable to use his phone."

"Sorry, Amy. That's not the case. Are you someplace safe?"

"Yes, sir. I'm with my friend Macy, and we're—'

"Don't tell me. Look, I've just finished meeting with my new FBI Director. I trust him and have brought him into the loop about Lynch's assignment. He's going to see what he can do without stirring up new problems."

Amy's mind blurred as he went on to describe two men looking for Lynch and teaming up with Abdi. At least, it sounded to her like they had teamed up. The odds against three evil men—four people, if Summer Stanton was really involved—seemed unbeatable.

What was that Bible verse Lynch had mentioned? Habakkuk 1:5? Something about being surprised and amazed. What was God doing?

"Amy, stay vigilant. All things work for the good of those who believe and trust in God. I fervently believe that. And Lynch quoted Habakkuk 1:5 to me on an earlier call. I'm trusting in God's Word that that is true."

Three times now. Three times her attention had been taken to that verse. Once when Lynch first mentioned it. Just now when it came to her mind without prompting. And a third time a moment later when the President mentioned it. Amy felt a surge of faith. The number three had special significance in the Bible. Something truly unexpected was about to happen.

"Thank you, sir. We'll keep our eyes open."

"Here's a number you can call to reach me. If you run into trouble, and Lynch isn't around, call me. I'll see what I can do."

"Yes, sir. Again, thank you."

She copied the number into her contact list, under "The Big Guy" and hung up. She turned back to Macy to see her just as wide-eyed as before.

"Are . . . are you some sort of secret agent now, too? I think I'm gonna start calling you double-O nine."

The sun was moving lower in the sky, and a late afternoon chill seemed to settle in the air. A front was moving in, but that's not what occupied Lynch's thoughts.

He'd been kneeling on the gravel for what seemed like eternity, and his knees began to hurt from the jagged rocks digging into his skin through his pants. What was she waiting for?

"If you're going to shoot me, go ahead and get it over with."

No response. For a moment he wondered if she was still behind him. He wiggled his fingers and started to unlace them behind his head.

"Don't move."

She was still there. So, why the delay?

"If you're waiting for some type of plea or begging, you'll be disappointed. I have no fear of death. The Bible says that to live is Christ and to die is gain. I know where I'm headed after death. Do you? You can't beat death. Well, not without Jesus."

"Shut up!"

He sensed stress in her voice. Throughout her career as a journalist, he had only witnessed confidence in her words. He rarely agreed with her liberal, globalist positions, but he never saw wishy-washy reporting. She took a stand and supported it, although he preferred facts to emotions when backing up one's position on social issues. At this moment, her emotional state could be understood simply by hearing her voice.

"You know, if you need to talk—"

"Quiet! Close your eyes!"

If she was behind him, how would she know whether or not his eyes were closed? He heard footsteps in gravel next, and within seconds she stood in front of him.

"Close your eyes."

The last thing he saw before shutting his eyelids was her directing her gun toward him.

Summer no longer saw herself as Hannah. That person had died with the onset of the #summersnotdead social media campaign. Even though she held the gun, Cully had killed Hannah Wilson with one deft move, no bullets needed.

Someone had once said that the pen was mightier than the sword. She knew it wasn't a Shakespearean quote. Some other lesser known English author had first penned it, but his name escaped her.

No matter. The power of the pen, in its modern virtual reincarnation, had put her in desperate straits. She needed to act, to find the same resolve she had possessed as a journalist and with her first two kills. But that boldness evaded her along with the name of the English author.

"If you're going to shoot me . . ."

Why did he suddenly feel a need to start talking? She needed to think. Her mind felt as if only splinters of thoughts filled it—each one jabbing and irritating, but none of them coalescing to form a complete idea.

She saw subtle movement in his fingers. Was he going to free his hands and make a move? She wasn't ready for that.

"Don't move."

Oh no, here it comes, she thought. All that Jesus stuff about being saved and escaping death. And yet, he showed no fear, just as he said. Not so much as a bead of sweat appeared on his neck or hands. She couldn't see his face. He needed to close his eyes, but how could she tell if he complied?

She forced her legs to carry her to a position facing him. Yes, his eyes were now closed, and she extended the gun toward him.

THIRTY-FOUR

"Now open your eyes."

"What? thought Lynch. *She just had me close them.*

He looked up at her to see her extending the gun to him, but grip first, its magazine released and chamber open. She was giving him the weapon. He didn't understand.

"You might as well kill me. My life is over." Tears rolled from her eyes.

Lynch cautiously stood up, watching her other hand as closely as he followed the Sig. Richard had been stabbed. Could she have a knife hidden in the other hand?

She used her free hand to wipe her eyes. No knife.

Lynch moved quickly to take the gun. As soon as he had control of it and cleared it, she fell to her knees. The sudden reversal of roles and positions amazed him. As soon as the word 'how' entered his mind, he knew how.

"Go ahead, shoot me," she cried.

"You know I won't do that. I'll take you in, and you'll go to trial."

She tried to laugh. "Trial for what? Surviving the terrible accident of my car going off the bridge? Wanting to start over, begin a new life?"

"Murder. Richard Nichols and Christopher Renton."

"Ah. And you have evidence of that?"

She had him there. What he had was circumstantial at

best—a photo of her on a home security camera and a witness placing her in North Carolina. The latter was shakier than the former. The Rocky Broad could attest to a raven-haired woman buying coffee and breakfasts, but the woman now kneeling before him was a curly blonde. No one could attest to *when* Summer had become a blonde. The customer in Chimney Rock could have just been a close look-alike.

"Well, do you? Do you have evidence that would compel a DA to charge me?"

No. Following the evidence would not indict Summer Stanton of murder.

"I can see it in your face that you don't, and even if I did kill them, I wouldn't admit it. Not that it would make any difference, I'm a dead woman walking."

"What do you mean?" Lynch hoped that by playing dumb she might admit more than she wanted to.

She didn't respond right away. Lynch could see the turmoil raging inside her. If he was in her shoes, how would he answer that? She had already admitted to being a troubleshooter for the Assembly.

"Think about it. You've dealt with the Assembly before. That's why they put you on their troublemaker list. Your little social media stunt has burned me, made me expendable. Where am I going to go and stay alive? They created this identity for me. They would find me in days, maybe hours. WITSEC would be a sham."

She had a good point. Assuming they came up with evidence linking her to either murder, she would end up dead at the first opportune time in any jail or prison they put her in. Jeffrey Epstein was a prime example. And if she remained free, where could she go that the Assembly couldn't find her? It might take a month, maybe longer, but eventually they would get to her. WITSEC, the Federal Witness Protection Program, would be worse. With the Assembly's infiltration into the U.S. Marshals Service, she'd be outed and dead within a week.

Now he understood her quandary. It had become his. He couldn't let her go, and he couldn't hold her in custody either.

Deep in thought, he cleared the handgun a second time and started to tuck it into the waistband at the back of his pants out of habit. He stopped. It wasn't his gun. His was secured in the car, but that gave him an idea.

"Who's the gun registered to?"

"Me. Well, to my new personae, Hannah Wilson."

He smiled. He had her—18 US Code 922, Section 6.

"But Hannah Wilson is a fraud. I can arrest you on federal gun charges."

She nodded and sighed in desperation.

"And we're back to the same place. Put me in jail, and I'm dead within days."

She was correct, again. He had one hope in keeping her—to get enough info on the Assembly to put a major dent in their operation. But how could he do that? How could he keep her alive long enough? *Where* could he do that? Would she even be willing to testify?

"What do you propose I do?"

"May I reach into my pocket? No weapons."

He nodded. She pulled out a flash drive.

"What I propose is that you, personally, keep me alive

until we can figure something out. In return, I'll testify on video about my dealings with the Assembly and provide you with this flash drive. It holds all the records I could download from the director's network in the brief time I had to do so. There's enough here to keep a dozen FBI agents busy for months."

He stopped himself from smiling. He couldn't let her see that. This turn of events was more than amazing; it was supernatural . . . just as God had promised him.

"So, you want me to babysit you. I'll have to take that up with my boss."

"I think President Graham would be eager to get his hands on this."

She held up the flash drive before stashing it back into her pocket. Lynch was a bit surprised that she knew he worked directly under the President. Lucky guess? Maybe. Still, he wasn't going to force the drive from her. Her cooperation was too important to alienate her now.

But that still didn't solve their dilemma.

"What else do you want in return? You said yourself that letting you go would simply end up with the Assembly chasing you down and killing you, however long that would take."

"I'd want a real identity change. Some plastic surgery. A new identity created outside of WITSEC. Relocation somewhere safe, or safer anyway. I understand there will always be a risk, but I'm willing to take it."

"Okay, but, again, someone with a higher pay grade is going to have to make that decision."

She nodded. "By the way, I don't see this as babysitting

me. I see this as a collaboration, because what you don't know is that the Assembly has sent out two assassins—well-trained and very experienced—to kill both of us."

Abdi tired of the pushing by these two men identified only by Koranic names. Do this, do that. Send this many men here, this many there. Their dissatisfaction with Abdi was starting to become evident to his men, and that could not be allowed to continue.

They had left for the day but promised to return in the morning unless Abdi's men came across Lynch Cully and this other unknown woman overnight. Then they were to be notified. More instructions, more expectations. Abdi felt convinced he was being used to do the job these men were being paid to do, without the compensation they would receive. He no longer cared to "impress" whoever funded and sent these men.

And yet, their argument that finding Lynch Cully held more promise for finding the woman as well, made sense. They had also given him a way to smoke out the man.

"Bashiir, where be Warsame, Tawfiiq, and Xuseen?"

"Lord, they have fallen back to avoid the police. Two have found locations to hide where they can watch the road to the house, while the third remains in the woods across from the driveway entrance. Between them, they should see any traffic coming or going to the house."

Abdi nodded. "They have been there all day, yes?"

"Yes, lord. They could use a break, or they might fall asleep during the night."

"Agree. And the middle of night is when I would sneak

in or out. We must not allow that."

The embryo of an idea had been forming in Abdi's head earlier. Now it became full-bodied. *Yes, that might work,* he thought, as the thought grew into a plan.

"Yes. Send more men. Awaken more of the drivers if you need to. And they will need *Bambaanooyinka Molotov. Saddex.* That should be enough. No one occupies the house, yes?"

"That is what I understand, but it is covered by a security company."

"That is not a worry. Get the men ready to watch. When ready, near midnight, we will set house on fire. The men who watch must keep eyes open for this Lynch Cully and be prepare to follow him. Make sure they all have photo, know what he look like. We will get his attention. Then, he will lead us to that woman."

Lynch had Summer sit in the passenger seat where he could watch her. He could only trust in God that she had no other weapon on her person, because he was not about to frisk her privately. Under the circumstances, that might be considered acceptable by many, even in this day of political correctness and #MeToo. For him, it would require an intimacy he did not want to incur, at least not without another woman present. He'd learned that lesson from watching Richard Nichols endure sexual accusations with this woman once before, during the campaign.

He did, however, inspect her bag. He found no other weapons, but he did discover the device he'd noticed her using earlier in the car. He held it up as they headed back onto the interstate.

"What's this?"

She didn't answer right away.

"Well?"

"I don't know if it has a formal name. It was presented to me as my FFP."

"FFP?"

"Yeah, friendly fire preventer. Basically, when two or more troubleshooters work together, they can use this to locate each other. It can zoom into a radius of about 100 meters and pinpoint any other device that's turned on. It has an expanded range up to 80 kilometers, or 50 miles, which is why I came this far on the highway. I needed to make sure they hadn't located me and weren't following us."

"Were they?"

"No. If you noticed, I would only turn it on for a brief moment. Long enough to see them and hope they didn't see me. They appeared to be stationary, together in one spot for our entire trip here."

Lynch could envision the FFP nickname. You wouldn't want to be shooting in the direction of your comrade, no matter how good your aim and skill. Beyond that, however, he saw a different utility to the device. One he could foresee using.

"Where are we going?"

He glanced at her. "Someplace even the Assembly would have a hard time finding you."

He planned to join Amy and Macy at the farm, and to take time to formulate an appropriate plan of action. He pointed to the glove compartment.

"There's a phone in there. Would you hand it to me, please? Slowly."

She reached into the compartment and retrieved a phone. "Don't worry. I'm relying on you to protect me. I'm not about to bite the hand that feeds me."

"I'm not so sure of that." He took the phone and powered it on.

Following Summer's announcement that there were two "troubleshooters" on their trail—or assassins as she called them, self-incriminating or not—he had turned off his cell phone and removed its battery. They would not be able to use that to trace him. Unfortunately, that also left him out of touch with Amy and the President, at least until he reestablished communications with them with the burner phone he'd stashed in the car, just in case. Ladies first.

"Hey, it's me. You have room for two more?"

"Lynch! Finally. I've been worried sick. Did you get my calls, my messages?"

"Sort of. It's a long story. You guys okay?"

"We're fine. We just got back from a great dinner with Jimmy and his family. Macy even had her first encounter with live chickens and survived."

Lynch heard Macy shout something in the background. He couldn't make out the words, but it sounded like a cry of victory. He chuckled.

"Well, I'm headed your way. Should be there in about two and a half hours."

"Okay. I can make up the couch for you." Amy paused. "Wait. You said *two* more. What, who . . . wait a minute. What's going on?"

This was the part Lynch dreaded. Amy's encounter with Summer Stanton in that fiasco with Richard during the campaign had not left a pleasant taste behind. There had been a few times when she would have loved to have intubated Summer and plugged the tube. And with her being implicated in Richard's murder? Well . . . now he was about to ask her to help him babysit.

"Umm, you might call it protective custody. I need your help, and . . ."

"Help with whom?"

She did not sound happy. There was no beating around the bush now.

"I have Summer Stanton with me. I'll explain—"

"You've got to be kidding me. This isn't April first, Lynch. Even if it was, that would be a cruel joke."

"Amy, I'll explain when—"

"No way, buster. I don't want anything to do with her."

He noticed Summer looking particularly attentive to his call, almost smiling . . . in a Cruella deVil sort of way. He was heading for the doghouse as it was. She didn't have to enjoy it at his expense.

"Babe, I know you feel that way, but I'm between a rock and a hard place here. I can't put her in jail. The Assembly would learn of it and kill her within days. And I can't just let her go."

He heard nothing on the other end. He'd seen Amy mad on a number of occasions. This time he envisioned her as furious.

"Okay, I guess there's no other choice. We'll find her a stall in the barn."

Dead air.

She'd hung up on him.

THIRTY-FIVE

Summer hated to admit it to herself, but she felt strangely secure in Lynch's presence. She had always been self-sufficient, relying only upon herself. Her analyst had attributed that to the many tragedies of her childhood. She preferred to think of it as common sense in a world where self-interest came first. Who else would have her best interests at heart?

And yet, in Lynch she saw someone who really did put others first. He could have simply cuffed her and taken her to some jail, leaving her there for the hand of "justice" to raise its partisan palm and swat her from existence. He had shown her that her life had value, at least to him. Furthermore, his quixotic quest against the Assembly was more than tilting at windmills. He sincerely disliked what he saw as unparalleled corruption that had infiltrated the government, big business, the media, and more and that affected the lives of thousands, not to their betterment. He was willing to put them, people he'd never meet, first.

Yes, she felt a peace next to him that she couldn't describe. And if the truth be told, she also felt a bit of jealousy toward Amy Gibbs. He had mentioned his faith. Could that be something real? Could she possibly have that, too?

The drive into rural Missouri, to a place she would

never find on a map, was a quiet one. She suspected the fireworks at the end of the journey might be fun to watch, however.

Lynch only missed one turn before finding the entrance to the Bircher family farm. He thought that quite remarkable considering he'd only flown into the place with Amy in the past, had never driven there, and that the sun had set within the first hour of the drive. The leg of the trip to and past the Lake of Ozarks was easy enough—four lane roads, lots of lights, and plenty of billboards to direct them to various attractions X miles away—then Y miles, then Z miles, to "You missed it, turn around."

He'd made enough trips "to the lake," as they'd say in St. Louis, to be able to drive that stretch blindfolded by memory. It was the part of the trip after the lake that became problematic. Weaving his way in the dark through such Missouri metropolises as Pumpkin Center, Buffalo, and Half Way became the challenge.

But he succeeded, and now the tires of his car grumbled across the gravel of the long drive to the farmstead. As he neared the main barn, he saw Amy waving at him to stop. He had alerted her to his arrival by text a few minutes earlier.

He pulled up next to her and put down his window.

"Hey, good to see you. We made it. It's cold out there. Hop in, and I'll give you a lift to the cabin."

She crossed her arms and shook her head.

"No way. We put a cot in a stall in the barn. A stall we can lock. She can stay here for the night."

He noticed Summer roll her eyes and look away. Yet,

the smirk on her face revealed that she was enjoying this.

"How do you expect me to sleep . . . with her in the cabin? I'll have one eye open all night. And I sure wouldn't want her around my friends."

Lynch sighed. "Amy, it's cold, and I don't think that barn has central heating. Seriously. You don't really expect me to lock Summer in a stall, do you?"

"Sure. That snake can hibernate in the cold and warm up in the sun tomorrow."

Lynch was wrong. He'd seen her angry. He expected her to be furious. But, nope, she'd gone ballistic.

He turned to Summer. "Give me a minute to talk with her." He climbed out of the car and approached Amy.

She kept shaking her head as he neared.

"How dare you expect me to watch over her, after all she's done. I just can't believe you'd ask that of me."

Lynch proceeded to explain his predicament, how she had willingly turned over her gun to him, and how she'd volunteered to testify against the Assembly and turn over valuable evidence if they kept her alive and gave her a new identity. Amy seemed a bit calmer.

"The answer is still right over there, in the barn."

He continued by explaining that at the moment all he had to charge her with was falsifying her identity on a gun registration. She might get five years in prison and a fine, but her cooperation might result in probation instead of hard time. He had no evidence to pursue one murder charge, let alone two. No matter what they, he and Amy, believed.

Her breathing rate had diminished. Her nostrils no longer flared. But he was out of ammo, and she continued to point toward the barn. All he had left was the big gun, the howitzer. He hated to use it, but . . .

"What would Jesus do?"

Amy looked as if she'd been hit with a bucket of ice water. She began to cry, and Lynch enveloped her with his arms. He knew where she was coming from. Richard deserved justice. Doctor Renton, too. His family deserved closure. Possibly a woman from Terre Haute. Maybe others they knew nothing about as well. However, that justice would come from a divine source.

THIRTY-SIX

Abdi had been cooped up in that warehouse too long. Yes, he had equipped it with many of the comforts of his own home, minus his wives, but it wasn't home. He had men accompanying him 24/7. Yet, that security had eliminated privacy.

However, privacy was not what he wanted this evening. He wanted freedom to breathe fresh air, to walk farther than 50 yards before having to turn around, and to see the stars—or the clouds, if that was the case. Unless it was rain beating on the metal roof, he had no idea what the weather was outside. Even night and day were evident to him only by the clock on his phone.

He needed to get out. The cover of darkness would be his ally.

"Bashiir!" He looked about but could not see his newly appointed lieutenant. He called to the men guarding the main doors. "Where is Bashiir?"

The men offered a subtle bow of their heads. The younger of the two deferred to the older.

"Lord, he has gone out. I heard him say he had to get the materials to make your plan happen tonight."

Abdi's first thought was why Bashiir could not delegate that task to someone else, but then he realized that maybe the man wanted to make sure things were done properly. He gave Bashiir ten more minutes to return before calling him.

"Bashiir, where are you?"

"Lord, my apology. You were preoccupied, and I did not wish to disturb you. I am at the garage, getting the materials we need."

Abdi nodded. They did have kerosene and all the materials to make firebombs there. But the garage was under surveillance.

"Lord, I did not trust the men to get these things without causing suspicion or leading the authorities to the warehouse. As one man, I could slip in and out without being seen. And I will make sure I am not followed."

Abdi smiled. Once again, the man was a step ahead in his thinking. Then, as if reading Abdi's mind, he added.

"I should be back at the warehouse within 20 minutes."

True to his word, Bashiir entered the warehouse 18 minutes later and walked straight to Abdi. He extended something toward Abdi in his hand. "Here, lord."

"What is that?"

Bashiir opened his hand to reveal a tactical balaclava. "For you to hide your face when we go out."

Abdi scrutinized the man. He had said nothing to him about going out with them, as much as he had planned to do so. Could this man *actually* read his mind? Although committed to Islam, Abdi had been taught the ways of the old religion of *Eebe-Waaq*, with its *ayaanli*, or messengers from *Eebe; Huur*, the messenger of death; and *Nidar*, the righter of wrongs. The *wadaad*, or priests, of the ancient temples, *xerro*, could do many supernatural things, but only *Eebe* could know the thoughts of men.

"How?"

"Lord, you pace the floor. You ask about the weather. You talk about your wives. What they call 'cabin fever' in this country is what you show by your actions. Forgive me if I was wrong to assume you would want to go on this mission. Its success is important to you."

Just when Abdi thought he knew the talents of Bashiir, the man surprised him yet again. The man was more observant than Abdi himself, with a deep insight into men's behavior. That would be another valuable asset to Abdi, and yet also something he would have to remain aware of, that the man could also "read" him.

Abdi accepted the balaclava. "Thank you, Bashiir. You are correct. Are the men ready?"

Bashiir nodded. "Yes, lord. Most are already in place. The others are on their way and will be ready by the time we get there."

As they drove, Abdi decided it would be a good time to learn more about Bashiir, the man. He would need an heir to his leadership of their "clan." And his young daughter would need a worthy husband upon becoming a woman. That thought—about giving his daughter to Bashiir to secure their relationship—had crossed his mind once before.

"Bashiir, tell me of your family."

"Lord, there is not much to tell. I am second generation Somali-American. My grandparents came from a region south of Mogadishu, Middle Juba, along the coast. He was a fisherman, much as you were, but not the leader of their clan. He also dabbled in smuggling, to help feed his family, but only when the fishing was bad. When I was young, he would tell me of his exploits."

At Abdi's prodding, he learned about what led to the grandparents coming to America, of their lives here, that of Bashiir's parents, and more. Bashiir had grown up in the Somali enclave in Minnesota, but had gained a job with Abdi's company through one of Abdi's nephews. He made a mental note to bestow a favor on that nephew for bringing Bashiir to them.

As they now drove into the rural countryside of Wildwood, Bashiir slowed and pointed to their left. "There is our first team. They will alert us to police coming from this direction."

Abdi looked toward where Bashiir pointed. "I do not see anyone."

Bashiir smiled. "Good. That is the point, is it not, lord?"

Abdi laughed, trusting Bashiir's plan. "That it is, Bashiir. Excellent."

They continued on. "Here is the driveway to the house itself. There are two men in the woods across from it. Again, you will not see them."

They drove past and soon came to another crossroad. "And we have a team here, to watch the other approach."

Abdi saw nothing here as well. "Is it just the darkness that hides them? The police might use spotlights to search."

"No, lord. We found hiding places that are suitable even in broad daylight."

Abdi smiled. If this plan succeeded, he would indeed give his daughter to Bashiir as a wife.

The man turned left at the crossroads. "About a hundred yards on, there is a utility road leading to a cell tower. Our team is assembled there. A wooded ravine and stream lead behind the properties here—the man's parents' home as well as neighbors. We can make it to the house this way without being seen."

After turning onto the gravel road, Bashiir parked, and they exited the car. Four men, each wearing his own ski mask or balaclava, joined them near the fence surrounding the base of the cell tower. Bashiir gave his key fob to one of the men and pointed to the car. Two of the men hurried to the car and retrieved two boxes from its trunk.

Bashiir donned a pair of latex gloves and gave the same to everyone there. Abdi nodded in approval. No fingerprints could be used to identify them. Bashiir also handed out lighters, testing each one before giving it to the man.

From the boxes, Bashiir gave out capped bottles and rags. He gave two to each man, but Abdi grabbed one from the nearest man.

"Do you think I want left out of the fun?" He grinned.

Bashiir grabbed a gallon can of kerosene. "Okay. You each remember what to do? We will use this kerosene to soak the rags once we get there. Then open each bottle and place a rag into it. Each man pick a window, light one rag, and throw the firebomb through the window. The second bottle is for the roof. Once you have thrown your bottles, run back to your cars." He pointed to the two drivers in succession. "You head east. You head west. Go home. Celebrate a job well done."

The roof? questioned Abdi. Typical asphalt shingles would not catch fire. That was why they were made of asphalt materials.

The men headed out, single-file toward the house. Abdi grabbed Bashiir's sleeve to detain him.

"The roof will not catch fire."

"Lord, it is made of cedar shingles, not asphalt. The plan should work."

Bashiir took off to lead the men. Abdi nodded and hurried to catch up.

Bashiir stopped behind a home. From the back, Abdi assumed it to the correct home, trusting his lieutenant.

"This is it," said Bashiir. He opened the kerosene and each man took turns dousing their rags. The smell of the kerosene was strong, but unlike gasoline, its vapors were not so volatile as to flare up simply by igniting the lighter nearby.

"Okay, go!"

Abdi led the way, throwing his bottle toward a large picture window overlooking the woods. He began to run, hearing the shatter of glass behind him. Within a moment, he heard more glass and the sound of feet running over leaves and twigs on the forest floor behind him. Within minutes, they had collected near the tower, the men entering their cars and leaving, not turning on headlights until they were on the road and driving away from the scene.

Bashiir was the last to arrive. Together they looked back and witnessed the growing flicker of fire in the distance. As they headed north, Bashiir's phone rang. He answered, listened, and said only, "Okay."

"The first observation team reports that the police and fire departments are responding."

Abdi nodded. Even if little actual damage was done,

they had accomplished their goal. The man, Lynch Cully, would eventually show up. Maybe this very night. Maybe tomorrow, or the next day. But he *would* show up. And he would be seen and followed. He would lead them to that woman.

THIRTY-SEVEN

Lynch found the couch in the cabin to be surprisingly comfortable. Of course, anything beat sleeping in the car, which he was tempted to do to avoid Amy's glares. Macy had moved into the other twin bed in Amy's room, and Summer had been given the room and bed that Macy had slept in. He, then, had the couch in the living room between the two bedrooms.

He couldn't be sure, but he figured that Amy and Macy might take turns sleeping while the other one guarded the door. No Deep State assassin was going to catch them by surprise.

Lynch, on the other hand, felt an amazing peace about the situation. He had observed Summer both yawning and stifling yawns for the last hour of their trip. Even if she'd had adequate sleep before arriving at the motel, she likely slept little the night before while at the motel. She had learned of #summersnotdead that evening, as well as of her sudden estrangement from the Assembly. The fear of being caught unprepared by her fellow "troubleshooters" could not have resulted in much sleep. Add to that the emotional fatigue of her situation, he suspected she would sleep well . . . at Amy's expense.

The emotional fatigue caught him as well. His adrenaline ran high the entire time he drove west with a gun and accomplished killer at his back. To have his life given back and to be someplace out of harm's way had resulted in the adrenaline plummeting within his body. That always led to its own form of withdrawal with its resulting fatigue.

Between feeling exhausted and having a supernatural calm that Summer would cause them no harm, he slept much better than he'd anticipated. He awoke with the dawn to find the rest of the cabin's occupants still sound asleep . . . as best he could tell. He wasn't about to tap at Amy's door and be greeted with a swinging fireplace poker.

The sleepiness still clinging to him quickly dispersed as he stepped out the front door onto the small porch. The promised warm-up had yet to appear, and the late February temperature hovered near freezing. He instinctively rubbed his arms for warmth and gathered an armload of firewood. The women would wake up to find a fire roaring in the fireplace.

As the flames began to build, he moved to the small kitchen area, found the coffee maker and coffee, and started a pot. He resisted making 'cop coffee' as he'd be the only one to appreciate it. As the brew first began to drip into the carafe, he heard a cell phone ring from Amy's shared room. The ringtone was that of Amy's phone, and she apparently caught it before the second ring. A moment later, she emerged, fully dressed in the clothing she'd worn the night before.

"No, Mr. President, it's fine. We were, uh, . . . You don't have to apologize for calling so early . . . Actually, he's right here. Let me give him the phone." She rolled her eyes as she yawned and handed Lynch the phone.

"Good morning, sir." He stepped back outside, despite the cold.

"Lynch, where the heck have you been? I've been trying to reach you for the past 18 hours."

"Sorry, sir. For reasons I'll brief you on later, I had to turn off my phone and take out the battery so it couldn't be tracked. I have a prepaid, burner phone. I didn't want to wake you overnight, so here's that number." Lynch repeated the new number and went on. "Sir, I have a lot to tell you, but the details will have to wait until we can talk in person. I—"

"Lynch, you can brief me later. I have two things you need to know. Well, three, actually. I've brought FBI Director Renzoni into our circle of confidence."

Lynch smiled at that news. He felt confident that the new director was on their side against corruption, particularly by the Deep State, the Assembly, and that he was a trustworthy man. Lynch had been on the team that vetted him for the job. And, as FBI Director, he would be privy to info that normally might not reach the President's desk.

"That's good news, sir. He'll—"

"Hold that thought, Lynch. He got intel that there are two assassins on your trail. Are you secure?"

"Yes, sir. I'm already aware of that development. We're all safe and out of harm's way."

He heard a sigh of relief from the White House. "Good. How in the world did you find out?"

Lynch decided to get straight to the point.

"I have Summer Stanton in custody, so to speak." He

waited to see if he'd get interrupted again.

"What? Sorry. Go on."

"Well, sir, as I said, I'll brief you on all the details later. It's quite a story in itself, but in a nutshell, she's been cut loose by the Assembly because of our exposing her. She believes a termination order had been issued against her. She gave herself up to me and told me two 'troubleshooters,' her term, not mine, were tracking her in order to get us both. She went to ground, and now she's here, with us."

"What? Lynch, are you sure you should have her there? She should be in jail somewhere."

Lynch went on to highlight that there was nothing but circumstantial evidence against her regarding the murders, that all he could hold her on was a gun charge, and of the predicament that produced. "Sir, she seems to trust me to protect her. In return, she'll turn state's evidence against the Assembly. Well, that and one other stipulation, but I don't see that as a problem. She wants a new identity, outside of WITSEC, so they can't find her."

There was a moment of silence on the other end.

"Yes, I agree. No problem. If she does anything to call attention to herself in that new identity, the Assembly will be all over her. I think you're right. Okay, we can cross that bridge when we get there. What about these 'troubleshooters?'"

"I have a plan, but I'll spare you the details right now. Can you let Director Renzoni know I'll need some resources in St. Louis?"

Lynch could almost envision the man nodding and jotting down a note to himself. Just between the time he officially announced his candidacy for the presidency and now, the man's handwritten notes could wallpaper the Lincoln bedroom.

"Speaking of St. Louis, that brings me to the third item. Lynch, there was an arson attempt at your parents' new home in Wildwood last night. Director Renzoni got wind of it earlier this morning."

Lynch winced. The last thing he wanted was to drag his family into this. He was glad they were out of the country. He already felt weighed down by having to protect Amy, Macy, and now Summer. To have them in personal danger would add to his burden. And yet, he felt confident that the Lord would never place more on him than he could handle and that he could do all things through Christ who strengthened him. And that scripture verse from Habakkuk came back to mind.

"Any word on damage?"

"Sorry, no details have crossed my desk, but Director Renzoni also received intel that your 'troubleshooters' may be in contact with Abdullah Said Abdi. We don't know who might be responsible for the fire, but in my mind, it seems planned to smoke you out, pardon the pun."

That thought had already crossed Lynch's mind. But the possibility that Abdi and the Assembly might be collaborating added a different dimension to the problem. He would have to ponder that.

"Got it. I'll need to get to Wildwood ASAP. We're about three hours away. The drive time will give me a chance to think through my plan."

"If anything critical comes to my attention, I know how

to contact you now. Godspeed, Lynch."

Lynch was a bit disappointed. He had started to look forward to a trail ride around the farm. He became quite comfortable with horses after riding an Idaho wilderness hunting for a kidnapped presidential candidate. That search paid off, as the man was his boss and a friend who had his back.

Lynch disconnected the call and reentered the cabin. The warmth of the now blazing fire welcomed him immediately. The stares of three women, not so much. Amy and Macy stood on one side of the room, Summer on the other.

Oh boy, he thought. *Talking about fire, did I just step into it?*

"Good morning, ladies. I hate to disrupt your morning's plans and coffee time, but we need to get back to St. Louis, pronto. I'll put out the fire and clean up out here while you pack."

All three were clothed in what they wore the evening before. Summer had her one bag at her feet, and lifted it to show that she was ready. Amy and Macy stepped into the bedroom and came back out with their bags already packed. Lynch knew it would be dangerous to smile. Macy's evil eye confirmed that.

THIRTY-EIGHT

The travel arrangements had been made easily enough. Amy refused to have Summer in her car, while Summer refused to leave Lynch's protection. So, they rode two and two in a short caravan toward St. Louis. Lynch had Amy lead the way. Her lead foot was equal to his, and it was a good thing he had taken the rear guard. Within five miles of their getting onto I-44, a state patrol officer tagged Amy with his radar, lit up his lights, and pulled her over.

Lynch pulled in behind the patrol car, which did not make the officer happy. The man exited his car, his right hand on his gun, a scowl on his face, and his left hand held up commanding the occupants of Lynch's car to stay put. Lynch could understand. These days, too many "simple" traffic stops proved fatal to the officer. Lynch lowered his window and held out his credentials.

As the man seemed to ease his stance, Lynch announced, "I'm getting out of my car." He eased open the door, keeping both hands in full view of the officer. He approached the man so he could more easily scrutinize those credentials.

"Hey, sorry about the speed. She's with me, and we need to get to St. Louis ASAP."

The officer did not seem placated. "Do you know how fast she was going?"

Lynch nodded. "Yep, because I was keeping up with her."

"I could give you both tickets."

Despite popular belief, LEOs and their family members weren't "exempt" from traffic tickets. On occasion, off-duty officers caught speeding were given just a warning, as a courtesy. That offer of grace varied from jurisdiction to jurisdiction. This time, however, they were speeding well beyond the limits of forgiveness. Lynch would have to play his ace from his sleeve if the officer got aggressive.

"You're absolutely right, but I don't think you'd really want to get into that pissing match. I'd have to call my boss. He'd call your boss. Your boss would call you and chew your butt off." Lynch didn't want to name drop, as in saying who his boss was. He hoped the man would read whatever he needed to between the lines and lay off.

The officer looked contemplative. Few patrol officers wanted to hear from the top brass unless it was for a commendation. This clearly did not sound like it would be such.

"Look, I'll tell her to tone it down. But we really are in a hurry, and I'd prefer to get back on the road, not make that phone call."

The officer did not look pleased. "Okay. Just slow it down."

Lynch nodded. "Will do. Thanks." He walked past the patrol car, passed the word on to an appreciative Amy, and returned to his car. The officer pulled out as he climbed behind the wheel. He glanced at Summer. "Wipe the smirk off your face. You enjoyed that too much."

"She's a handful, isn't she?"

Lynch didn't answer.

Forty miles later they pulled off for gas, pit stops, and a fast food breakfast. Lynch took the opportunity away from Summer to make two phone calls. One went to Sgt. Lorna Gregory, a detective with the St. Louis County Police who had assisted him during the "LA Rapist" case where Lynch had almost died. She forever felt she owed a debt to Lynch for messing up, as she put it, and he decided to call in that favor. In reality, this was his first opportunity to do so, and yet, his asking would give her closure in knowing that debt had been repaid.

The second call went to the St. Charles PD.

"Sgt. Peniston."

"Hey, Bill, it's Lynch. When your guys work that car from the motel, ask 'em to dig really deep—behind insulation, roof liners, behind the dash, you name it."

"Mornin', Lynch. They said they'd get to it today. Lookin' for something specific?"

"I am. I can't go into a lot of details right now, but I'm looking for a relatively thin-bladed knife, probably spring-loaded, four to six inches long, with a spearhead point."

"You mean the kind that comes straight out of the handle?"

"Exactly. The ME in Alexandria, Virginia, believes that type of blade killed a co-worker of mine in the Graham campaign."

"Yeah, I remember that case, the social media guy, right?"

"Yep. Good guy. Didn't deserve to die. If you find one,

make sure they tear it apart and look for blood and trace DNA inside. If they find any, check it against that case in Virginia. I think they have the wrong woman arrested, but I need evidence."

"The blonde from the motel? Summer Stanton, or whoever she turns out to be. You think she did it?"

Lynch didn't reveal that Summer was now in his "custody." His time alone was short and the story too long.

"I do, but all I have right now is circumstantial. I need something concrete."

"You got it, Lynch. Helping to solve a big, national case like that one will spur our guys on. I'll keep you posted. Is this a good number to reach you?"

"Yes. Long story, but I had to disable the phone with the number I gave you yesterday at the motel. Don't know yet how long I'll have to keep it offline."

"Got it. I'll be in touch."

Lynch checked his watch. He'd been in the bathroom too long. Amy would be fit to be tied at having to watch his charge much longer. He exited the lavatory and made his way back to their table to find the three women chatting. To his surprise, he sensed no hostility. This was twice in two days he'd been amazed at an unexpected turn of events. He made a quick, silent prayer of thanks.

Amy looked up as Lynch approached. "Did you know that Summer won an award for her exposé on human trafficking and that our case in St. Louis was featured prominently in the story? I never saw that. I was giving her an inside look."

Macy nodded, wide-eyed. "And I'm learning things

about my girl I *never* would have imagined."

Summer nodded, too. "To answer your question, I had a source in the FBI, and Darko Komarčić had been on their radar for some time. Why did he kidnap you?"

Lynch saw tears form in Amy's eyes and knew he needed to change the subject. If the conversation turned to Richard Nichols, with Amy's knowledge of their suspicion that Summer had killed him, things could get nasty really fast.

Seeing that the women were finished eating, he grabbed his now lukewarm breakfast sandwich and pointed to the door. "Let's get going. I can eat this as I drive."

Amy gave him a look he couldn't quite figure out, but then stood and hurried toward the door in silence. Macy stood to follow, but not before rolling her eyes and signaling with her body, *What got into her?*

Lynch knew precisely what had flipped that switch.

When Lynch had informed her the night before that he had Summer Stanton with him and they were headed toward the farm, she had become angrier than she'd ever been in her life. Yes, she was prepared to lock the woman up in a stall. She was even prepared to feed her hay and water like the animal Amy thought her to be.

Until Lynch pulled the Jesus card and the Holy Spirit slapped her upside the head.

She had always been a bit impetuous and emotional at times. Well, maybe more than a bit. She recognized that. Yet, she'd also been working on that character trait. One particular Bible verse had come alive to her in Cambodia. In

2 Corinthians 10:5, she read, *We destroy arguments and every lofty opinion raised against the knowledge of God, and take every thought captive to obey Christ.*

Did she do that? No, not prior to her trip overseas. There, something in her had changed. She began to focus on the negative thoughts that often plagued her, particularly those about her father's death, and to bring those thoughts into line with the Word.

She had been holding the line pretty well until Lynch went off the radar the day before. And then the idea of Summer Stanton joining them resulted in a major backslide. Richard's death affected her more than she realized. She held the woman responsible for his death, despite the lack of evidence. She just *knew* that Summer had killed him for the Assembly.

As they drove toward St. Louis, she chastised herself for allowing that stinkin' thinkin' to take control again just 24 hours earlier. Her mind, distracted by these thoughts, hadn't paid attention to her speed. Flashing lights brought her back to earth. Lynch replanted her feet in the ground with his admonition to slow down . . . after he'd spared her another ticket. If it hadn't been for time away in southeast Asia, her license could have had more points than an NBA game.

By the time they stopped for food and gas, she had managed to regain control of those thoughts. She decided she would show restraint. She wanted to be a good witness for Christ. She focused on that goal. While Lynch was in the bathroom, Summer was the one to actually break the ice.

"Did you know I did a project on human trafficking in this country? The documentary even won a News and

Documentary Emmy Award. The case against Darko Komarčić was a significant part of the report. I understand you had dealings with him."

Amy really didn't like talking about that experience, but she had come to a point where she could discuss it objectively. "It was a bit more than dealings with him. He kidnapped me and decided to put me into his personal kinky harem. The man was a psychopath."

She proceeded to talk about her stint in captivity. Her ability to discuss it seemed surreal, as if she was describing the plot of some dark Hollywood thriller rather than personal events. As she finished, she asked, "How did you know about Komarčić?"

Lynch returned and interrupted briefly with Macy.

Summer seemed to ignore the intrusion into the conversation, nodded, and replied, "To answer your question, I had a source in the FBI, and Darko Komarčić had been on their radar for some time. Why did he kidnap you?"

Tears began to well up in Amy's eyes. Why? To use Amy as leverage over Richard. The negative thoughts fought for control, and fortunately, Lynch interrupted with his decision to get back on the road. She stood up and rushed to her car . . . before the tears overwhelmed her.

THIRTY-NINE

As they climbed back into their respective cars, Lynch could only imagine what Amy felt at that moment. He knew that she still struggled with how she had broken off her engagement with Richard and with his murder not long after. The man was a ghost he'd have to deal with through compassion for Amy, not by competition with her memories.

Macy had whispered to him that Summer was the one to bring up that topic. Why? What had she hoped to gain by raising that specific topic?

Only one reason came to mind—to torment Amy. But again, why? At that point, Amy's use of a stall no longer seemed so far-fetched.

He drove on in silence, but noticed that she spent almost as much time scrutinizing him as she did watching the dull, brown, winter scenery whiz by. He didn't like the implication of that observation. He didn't want to be her white knight on a horse . . . unless it was to have her bound and roped to the horse as a prisoner walking behind him to jail.

He watched the St. Clair rest stop pass by. They weren't far from their destination now. His calculation for an ETA was interrupted by his phone. He would have used his hands-free option to answer the call, but not with Summer in the car and certainly not considering the caller. He shifted the phone to the ear away from her.

"Yes, sir."

"Where are you?"

"Just east of St. Clair, but, sir, I can't talk freely."

He noted Summer perk up at that. The comment was like an invitation for her to try harder to eavesdrop, but he felt obligated to inform the President of the situation.

"Understood. So, just listen. I thought you might want some good news in the middle of all of this. I just finished a call from someone who thinks very highly of you, Lynch. Or should I say, *Sir* Lynch?"

Lynch could feel the blush in his cheeks. He would never live that down.

"Anyway, His Majesty sends his regards and called personally to inform us of something that happened just today in the U.K."

Lynch knew that the citizens of the U.K., emboldened by the success of Brexit, had also voted in a conservative government. Their new Prime Minister held similar beliefs to President Graham when it came to supporting the people, not big business and the elitists.

"They took down a major arm of the Assembly in Britain today. He gave me a laundry list of corruption, racketeering, money laundering, drug and human smuggling charges, but you can peruse those later. That's good news, yes? But I'm calling you with that news now because it could affect you here. Be extra cautious. They're a wounded animal now."

"Yes, sir, that they are. Thanks for the good news and

the heads up. I'll report in later."

He disconnected and tucked his phone back into his coat's inner pocket. He felt Summer's stare again.

"Good news, huh."

"Well, for some of us. Maybe not for you."

She turned her gaze out the window as he glanced toward her.

"The Brits cut off the Assembly's head in the U.K. today. Sounds like some people are going to be put away for a long time."

She looked back at him. "You think so? If that operation didn't take down a good chunk of their judiciary with it, don't expect grand results. If you don't cauterize the wound, that head will grow back as two."

She had caught his reference to the Hydra of Greek mythology. She also had a good point.

She smiled. "But, keep me safe, and I'll give you all you need to keep that head from growing back." She patted her thigh where the flash drive sat in her pocket.

Lynch saw the exit they needed coming up. Highway 100 would take them to the center of Wildwood where he would leave the women behind while he went to his parents' home. He pulled ahead of Amy, and a few minutes later, he pulled up to The Wildwood Hotel, right across from the offices of the St. Louis County Police's 6th Precinct. Amy pulled in right behind him. As he parked outside the entrance, Lorna Gregory emerged from the building. He waved as he exited the car.

"Hi, Lorna. Good to see you again."

"You, too, *Agent* Cully. When did that happen?"

"A few weeks ago. You might call it a special dispensation from the President."

"Well, it certainly helped persuade my boss. You have me as long as you need me, and I even get paid for the time." She grinned. "I got two rooms, as requested. They're cleared and ready."

Lynch nodded and made introductions. The detective's brow shot up as he introduced Summer Stanton, but she quickly recovered and said nothing.

"Ladies, you're with Lorna until I get back from my parents' house."

Amy and Macy nodded in unison. Summer shook her head in protest.

"I'm under *your* protection, not hers. I'm going with you."

Amy rolled her eyes, but at least she was being civil. Maybe it would be best to separate them. Lorna hadn't signed up for stopping tigress fights. Yes, Lynch was being harsh in thinking that, but he needed to be realistic. Summer appeared to be going out of her way to antagonize Amy.

"Look, if we have men out to kill us, you need the advantage I can offer you."

"What? Men out to kill you? Lynch, what—"

Lynch struggled to keep a poker face.

"Calm down, babe. She's exaggerating."

But she was right. Summer knew the two men. She knew their techniques.

"Why can't we stay together here, Lynch? We can make plans here. It's right across the street from an entire police department." Amy's eyes pleaded with him. "What's so important at your parents' place?"

Lynch sighed. Summer was *not* making this easy. That stall looked better every hour. He had promised Amy he would never lie to her, and he had skirted that promise with his previous comment. The time had come to let everyone know where things stood, including Lorna, who had been briefed on more than Amy but not all.

"Okay, here's the deal." He went on to explain what he knew to be fact and what he saw as speculation. "So, as I see it, this is a safe spot. None of these guys are looking here. But I need to talk with the arson investigator. I need to get a read on who did this, as well as see what damage was done."

Lynch looked at each woman. Lorna shrugged. Another day on the job. Macy looked, well, totally lost and out of her element. Amy frowned, and Summer crossed her arms across her chest. She spoke first.

"Like I said, I'm under *your* protection. I go where you go or you can kiss the information I promised good-bye. I forgot to tell you that flash drive is encrypted. You need me to open it."

Lynch had anticipated as much, but Summer had no knowledge of his computer skills or those of his buddy Mike Jurgesmeyer. Or was he underestimating the skills of the Assembly's programmers? Keeping her placated and on his side would prove the easiest and most expeditious route. He looked at Amy next.

"You didn't say anything about a deal being made, but I get it. I also see something you've not mentioned. Who's covering *your* tail? It doesn't make any real difference who started the fire. They did it to get your attention and bring you out in the open. Don't you think they'll have someone follow you?"

Yes, Lynch had considered that probability. How to handle it though? He hadn't worked that out, other than being alert to other cars around him.

Summer nodded. "Actually, she raises more than a good point. One of the favorite MOs of these guys is auto accidents. The roads out here look like prime candidates for that."

Amy added, "Of course, large wooded lots are great for snipers, too."

Summer kept nodding. "Are you sure the investigator is even out there?"

This bout of brainstorming was his fault. He'd been the one to teach Amy his "what if?" approach to problem solving. Or was this some form of one-upmanship? He wasn't sure, but he noticed Lorna bouncing her gaze back and forth between the two.

"Lorna? Your thoughts?"

"All good points. And while we're discussing them, we're standing outside here, in the open, where you all can be seen. Did you ever think they might watch the police offices, expecting you to stop in for a report? I'm going inside."

Macy finally chimed in. "Me, too, sister. I shoulda stayed on the farm with the chickens. I need a drink."

Lorna and Summer gave her funny looks. Amy said, "Long story. You had to be there."

They found a small, unoccupied meeting room and sat down. Lorna took to her phone, made a couple of calls, and ended up handing the phone to Lynch.

"Your fire investigator. He's already been to the house and is back in his office."

"Oh." He took the phone. "This is Lynch Cully."

"Yes, Mr. Cully, I'm Dan Hall, an investigator with the arson team. I understand you want info on your parents' house."

"That's right. How much damage was there?"

"Surprisingly little. Actually, it baffled me for a while until we found an intact bottle below one of the large picture windows. The size of the windows required safety glass, so the firebomb didn't break the window, and for some reason, it didn't break either. We found it half full of water and half full of kerosene. The fires in the rooms with broken windows never really took hold because the water dispersed the kerosene into smaller pools that never ignited. Looks like they tried to set fire to the roof, too, but modern cedar shingles are treated with a fire retardant. Really, the main fire consumed the leaves in the back yard. That traced back to a kerosene can and probably made it look like the whole house was ablaze from a distance."

That was good news, although like the investigator, Lynch found it curious that the Molotov cocktails were made to inflict little damage. He did catch one other thing the man said.

"You said 'they.' Can you guess how many people were involved?"

"Well, there were eight separate sites involved, four on the roof, three in the house, and the one unbroken bottle. Plus the leaf fire. We found disturbed tracks of leaves consistent with people running away from the house through the woods to a utility road for a cell tower. There were at least four distinct tracks, so there were at least four people, maybe more."

Lynch thanked the detective, disconnected, and handed Lorna's phone back to her.

"Well?" asked Amy.

He looked at Summer. "Would the Assembly's men hire someone to start a fire?"

She shook her head. "Not their usual MO. They're goal is take care of troublemakers, not inflict collateral damage, even if family. The Assembly wants these things done cleanly and without casting suspicions."

Lynch started to ask another question but didn't get the first word out.

"But they might collaborate with someone with a complementary goal. You mentioned this terrorist looking for Amy. If he finds you, he finds Amy, and vice versa. My ex-colleagues might have nothing to do with the fire. It's not their style. But this terrorist might."

That made sense to Lynch. Both Lorna and Amy were nodding, too.

"The investigator said he thinks at least four people were involved. That, to me, points to Abdi getting impatient."

"Well, all I can say is that Adam and Cain—not their real names, but that's what they go by—are not going to be happy. This Abdi guy is in for some trouble."

No one spoke, but Lynch could see the mental gears grinding. He had a plan. He just wasn't sure how to implement it with his "committee" judging every move and shadowing his every step. How could he get rid of them?

Amy spoke first. "Lynch, I'm tired of this. We need to go on the offense, take the game to these guys."

He didn't like the sound of her using "we." Yet, going on the offense was just what he wanted to do. He, too, was tired of ducking and defending.

Summer dug around in her bag and produced the FFP. "This'll help you find two of the three." She turned on the device and two blips appeared. By scale they were about 20 miles away and were not together. She quickly turned it off.

Lynch had asked the FBI Director, via the President, to make some resources available, but even with that, Lynch wouldn't have the manpower to take those two down in two simultaneous incidents miles apart. He needed them together. However, he also had no legal reason to take them. Would Summer's word be enough to convince the local FBI SAC to assist? Using whatever info she might provide could take weeks to build a solid case against the men.

He looked at Summer again. "I'm curious, are they on the move or stationary?"

She flipped on the device again. "Definitely on the move. They're closer." She turned it off.

"Check again in ten minutes."

Lynch didn't like that they were heading closer. Had they spotted Summer's location during the brief seconds the device was on?

Macy raised her hand. "Folks, I'm tired. If'n you all want to follow Mister Secret Agent Man here into danger, fine, but not me. I want to take advantage of one of the rooms you mentioned and take a nap."

Lorna looked at Lynch, who nodded. "Sure. Looks like you'll be safe here."

Or so he hoped. Lorna handed a key card to Macy. "Room 211."

Everyone watched as Amy's friend grabbed her bag and headed toward the elevator. For some reason, Macy seemed the only sane one in the group.

When the wait ended, Summer used the FFP again. This time, she zoomed into their location. "Hey, looks like they've converged on one spot. It's about 15,16 miles from here."

"Let me see that." Summer handed the device to Lynch. "What am I seeing here?"

Summer pointed to the screen. "It's a lot like any map app. We're here. There's a scale for the map. Their FFPs are identified by those two icons. Tap on the building and an address will pop up."

Lynch did so and showed it to Lorna. "Can you find out who owns this?"

"Give me a few minutes. I can get that in the offices across the street." She ran out of the room, as Summer flipped off the device.

Lynch looked at Amy. "Look, I know you don't want to stay behind, but if these guys are meeting with Abdi, I . . ." He started to say 'don't want you there,' but realized he needed different wording. ". . . don't think it wise for you to be nearby. If he slips away again and finds you, he won't hesitate to, well, you know."

"But—"

"Please, Amy, this becomes a police matter. No

civilians."

"But she's going to go." She pointed to Summer.

"Only because she's the only one who can positively identify the two hit men."

"And because I only trust you to protect me."

Lynch sighed. What had he signed on for?

"Please think about it while I make this call."

He stepped to one end of the room and called the St. Louis FBI offices. The operator quickly switched him to the SAC.

"Agent Cully, I was told to expect your call."

Lynch filled him in with enough info to ask for help.

"So, we don't know for sure that Abdi is there, right? And you have no intel on these two other men, you don't even have names, right? I don't know what to tell you. Abdi remains our main target, but I don't know that I can commit men this fast based on a hunch."

"Well, sir, we might not get another opportunity like this, and I sure don't want to go it alone. We're checking ownership of the building as we speak."

There was a pause, but Lynch heard muffled speech on the other end, as if the SAC had his hand over the phone.

"Okay. Look, I was told to cooperate and that the order comes from the highest authority in the land, so I'll round up half a dozen agents to stage near that address. There's an elementary school a half mile away. It's Saturday, so no kids. Meet us there. But let me know ASAP if this doesn't pan out."

"Yes, sir. I'll find the school. I'm 25 minutes out." He disconnected and returned to the women.

"Amy?"

She nodded. "Okay, I'll stay with Macy, but you keep me in the loop." She grabbed her bag and left.

He looked at Summer. "That leaves you and me. Why don't we walk across the street and see if Lorna is making any progress."

She shook her head. "I prefer staying here. I don't want to be surprised with a jail cell across the street."

Lynch prepared to convince her when Lorna rushed into the room.

"I think we've found him—Abdi. The building is a warehouse that's registered to an import-export business with offices in Minneapolis, New York, and, get this, Mogadishu. I alerted the county tactical ops unit. They're mobilizing to meet us there."

Lynch pumped his fist once in the air. "Yes! Summer, are they still there?"

Summer turned on her FFP and nodded. "They are. They haven't moved."

"Let's roll."

FORTY

Abdi looked at Bashiir with approval. The man came through with the firebombing. From the blaze visible from their cars the night before, he held no doubt the entire structure was a smoking shell this morning. Yet, he'd not taken time to scan the local news services for any reports on the blaze.

He rewarded the four men with the day off, with pay. Bashiir, however, he told to sleep in but then meet him at their main warehouse at nine a.m. This warehouse, in the south city area, was their main staging area for drug distribution. It was held by a different shell corporation than the warehouse in Fenton where he had isolated himself.

Abdi arrived ten minutes early to find Bashiir waiting for him. Yes, the man was proving himself worthy. Abdi recommitted himself to what he was about to do.

He smiled as he approached the younger man. "Bashiir, you have impress me time and time again since you join us. Even more so these last few days since I return." He put his arm around the man's shoulders. "I have look for someone to, how do they say it here, groom for the job to take my place when I decide to retire. Not that I plan to do so soon." He paused. "I have choose you."

Bashiir's eyes widened. "W-why, thank you, lord. I am deeply honored. I will not let you down." He bowed before

Abdi.

While Bashiir was familiar with the building, there was one area which only Abdi accessed, his office. All of his men knew that place was off-limits, violation of which would be punished by death. Here he had the computers that held the accounting, the contacts, the trade maps—all of the details corresponding to the drug enterprise. He now gave the access codes to Bashiir.

"Over the next months, I will show you how I manage this. I will introduce you to my cartel contacts in Mexico, warlords in Afghanistan, and more. They will come to accept your word as mine in our business dealings. But it will take time. They are a cautious bunch."

"I don't know what to say, lord. Allah be praised."

Abdi shook his head. "No, no. You no longer need address me as lord. I am also give you my daughter, Aamiina, to be your wife. You will be a son to me."

"I-I do not know how to express my gratitude. *Mahadsanid.*"

"Call me by my given name, Abdullah, or even *aabe*, father."

Bashiir again bowed in respect.

Abdi clapped his hand on Bashiir's shoulder. "Come. Let us go the other warehouse and celebrate. Aamiina's mother is preparing a feast."

As they drove, Abdi began Bashiir's lessons. He talked of the Mexicans they dealt with, as they remained the primary conduit for their drugs. The 25-minute drive seemed to fly by, only to be interrupted by a brief call to Bashiir.

"That was Warsame. An SUV from the arson squad was at the house, but has left. No other visitors. The man, Cully, has not shown up."

"He will, he will, Bashiir. I am confident we will soon confront him. And then he will lead us to that woman who show me such disrespect."

Bashiir nodded. "Yes, *Aabe*."

Abdi smiled. He liked the sound of that from this young man.

Bashiir drove around the area to make sure they would not be spotted before driving up to the vehicle door of the warehouse. A man emerged at the edge of some shrubs, nodded, and spoke into a phone before concealing himself again. The door quickly rose up before the car, and Bashiir drove inside.

Abdi frowned as he glanced about. Something was wrong. He exited the car with caution and started to walk toward the area set up for food, with tables and chairs. His wife, Aamiina's mother, sat in one chair with fear in her eyes. No, she was bound to that chair with duct tape. Adam and Cain sat across from her.

"What is meaning of this? Let my wife go!" screamed Abdi. These men had gone too far, way too far.

Adam stood and approached Abdi. "You fool! Did you not think we would learn about the foolhardy arson attempt last night?"

Abdi's anger flared. "Your ways produce no result. Wait and watch here. Wait and watch there. Wait, wait, wait. I grow tire of wait. The fire will flush out this Lynch Cully and the woman you seek. And then I will find *my* target."

"You are an idiot, Abdullah Said Abdi. Your fire did nothing but put the police on notice. Who do you think they will blame for that fire? Teenagers? They know of your vendetta."

"Do not call me idiot!"

"We should never have called on you for help. You're a disabled Mogadishu whore! C'mon, Cain. We're done here with this *handicapyahow*."

Abdi had had enough of this man's condescension and belittling. He now added outright insults and Somali slurs. He showed greater disrespect than even the woman. Abdi pulled a handgun from his waistband and shot Adam in the chest. As he aimed for Cain, the man had pulled his own gun. Pain like he'd never experienced burned through his chest as he fired a second time.

The last thing Abdi saw was Cain falling before him.

FORTY-ONE

Lynch and Summer found the FBI team at the elementary school as arranged. Lorna joined them, along with members of the tactical ops team from the county police—their version of SWAT. Lynch made a point of not identifying Summer, as that could have led to additional delays. Lorna, gratefully, followed his lead adding only that she, Summer, could identify the other men in question.

With the tactical ops team taking point, the group converged on the warehouse. Lynch now controlled the FFP, without showing it to the FBI and others. Now was not the time to ask questions as to its origins and functions. He confirmed there were two vehicles, each on opposite sides of the warehouse. Each proved to be unoccupied.

The tactical ops team found six men outside the warehouse, each bound and gagged. Weapons were found near each. Clearly, these were outlooks, guards. Only one man, adjacent to the large roll-up vehicle door remained free to do his job. They quickly subdued him.

With the outer perimeter secured, the team prepared to breach the building. Gunshots rang out from inside. The tactical ops team rammed in the man doors and rushed the building. Gun drawn, Lynch preceded the FBI team and entered the warehouse.

Lynch had expected bedlam. What he saw was an

unexpected quiet. Three men near the door stood with hands behind their backs in the custody of tac-ops officers, the three men's eyes fixated in disbelief toward one end of the space. There, food and drink occupied tables in one area. A woman sat nearby, bound to a chair. Another man knelt on the ground, his hands with fingers interlaced behind his head, and two more tac-ops officers stood over him.

At first, everyone's gaze seemed fixated on three men on the floor, handguns lying next to them. Lynch discerned no movement there. His training kicked in, and he joined the others in fanning throughout the building. There were rooms and open stacks of pallets and crates to be checked and cleared. In one makeshift structure he found a small brick cell reminiscent of Tuol Sleng prison in Phenom Penh. He held no doubts as to whom that had been intended for.

With the building secured, he walked toward the bodies. Abdi was among them. One officer checked each for a carotid pulse and shook his head. Lynch wasn't about to rely on someone else for confirmation again. In the case with Abdi, he had done that once before, relying on the Coast Guard. He also checked each body for a pulse and checked their pupils.

Lynch felt an immense weight lift from his shoulders. Finally, the reign of terror of Abdullah Said Abdi was over. He assumed the other two men, one Caucasian and the other possibly Hispanic, to be Adam and Cain. He would get Summer to confirm that in a moment. Lorna watched her outside as the assault team entered the warehouse.

The younger man he had seen kneeling with his hands behind his head had been led to the other end of the building. An FBI agent talked with him now, but Lynch could only see the man's back. He walked over to join the conversation. Clearly, the man had seen what transpired.

As the man's face came into view, Lynch stopped and took another look. The man gave him a look that Lynch easily read. He followed that lead.

He addressed the FBI agent. "Hey, could I have a minute with this man? I'll turn him back over to you as soon as I'm done."

The agent gave Lynch a questioning look, but shrugged and nodded. As soon as the man was out of earshot, Lynch whispered.

"Aaron? Aaron Amburo? What in God's name are you doing here?"

The man furrowed his brow and whispered in reply, "Man, Lynch, don't blow my cover. I've been deep here for months. Before you went to Cambodia."

Lynch had had an opportunity to work with the DEA on a drug trafficking case on the Mississippi River. Aaron Amburo was an agent he'd worked closely with.

"What happened?"

The man feigned not wanting to talk, but under his breath muttered.

"I've been trying to get to the top of Abdi's drug operation. Finally gained his trust. Then these two guys show up from who-knows-where and start ordering Abdi around like they owned him. Today was to be, um, a celebration of sorts. We showed up. Abdi's wife was tied up and bam, that was the last straw. He took out the first guy, went by Adam, and then the second guy, Cain, and Abdi shot each other simultaneously. Push me into the chair. Look angry."

Lynch pushed him roughly into a nearby chair and scowled at his old colleague.

"What do you call yourself?"

"Bashiir Khalid. I'm trying to get the goods on the top guys bringing drugs into Abdi's chain. I'm almost there. I need to stay under cover a while longer."

Lynch made some threatening gestures.

"I do need to thank Cain for one thing, though. He saved me from marrying a thirteen-year-old."

Lynch coughed. He turned to the FBI agent nearby and said, "Says his name is Bashiir Khalid, and they shot each other. Won't say anything else." He turned back to his friend. "Was it you who made the Molotov cocktails?"

The man replied with a subtle nod.

"Thanks."

Bashiir flashed a quick smile, recovering just as the agent returned.

"He's all yours," said Lynch.

Seeing the bodies on the floor again, he remembered he needed to get an affirmative identification of the men by Summer. He headed outside and hurried toward his car, only to find Lorna standing alone next to one of the two victims' cars.

"Where's Summer?"

She looked puzzled. "What? She went into the building right after you, with the FBI agents. I thought she was with you."

They both ran into the building and split up to cover

opposite sides of the structure. Lynch met up with Lorna by the vehicle door, which was open just enough to crawl under. He opened the door further and walked outside. Nada.

By all appearances he was the one who had messed up this time and lost his charge. He mentally pummeled himself. Of course, her nemeses were now dead. Why would she need protection by Lynch any longer? She had him so convinced that she was cooperating that he'd let down his guard.

"Wasn't the other suspect vehicle parked over here?" He pointed to a spot 15 feet away.

Lorna nodded. "Looks like it's gone."

He scanned the area where a pickup once sat. On the pavement, he found a flash drive. Would he have to put Mike Jurgesmeyer to the test? Would he find it empty? She had said it was encrypted and useless without her. But then, he'd believed she was cooperating.

Lynch pulled the FFP in his possession from his coat pocket and turned it on. Sure enough. Two icons still appeared. One was just 50 meters away by the device's scale. That would be suspect car number one. The other was roughly three miles away, about to get on the nearby interstate. The scale changed as he watched it move east, join up to the outer belt, I-270, and head north. A moment later, the icon disappeared.

FORTY-TWO

Summer rushed into the building along with the FBI, right behind Lynch. Her concern was not the need for those men to protect her but one of being outside, in the open, should Adam and Cain not be in the building. She knew her colleagues were sometimes sloppy in their use of their FFPs—leaving them on and running down the batteries, relying on them as they would a map app on a phone. Yet, she could not put it past the two men to use their FFPs as bait to bring her out. Without protection, the bullet of a single rifle shot from a surrounding building could have her name on it.

As the SWAT team and federal agents fanned out within the building, she made a beeline toward three bodies on the floor. The black man had to be Abdi, based on the descriptions she had overheard. The other two men were Adam and Cain. She could not describe the sense of relief that flooded her body at that moment.

She glanced about and felt surprise that no one else hovered over the bodies. Perhaps the agents saw no need before securing the rest of the building. Three motionless bodies on the floor posed no threat.

She took the opportunity to reach into Cain's pockets. From one she retrieved his car keys. They had parked near Adam's Land Rover on the one side of the building. With the

FFP showing the two men's cars being on opposite sides of the building, she deduced that Cain's would be outside the large vehicle door at the other end.

She also grabbed his wallet, pulled the cash and credit cards from it, and threw it next to the body. It would be useless to the authorities. The ID they would find represented a ghost. The men's fingerprints, dental records, and all other potential identification methods would prove useless. Just like Hannah Wilson, they no longer existed in the real world of birth certificates, government record keeping, taxes, and obituaries. The Three were but three more heads on the Assembly hydra—mythological creatures.

As the first FBI agent approached the bodies, she said, "It's them. The men Cully spoke of."

She then backed away, only to ease toward the vehicle door as the agent knelt down to check the bodies. She opened it as quickly as she could to a height she could pass through and slipped underneath on her knees. Once outside, she glanced about and found Cain's Silverado pickup. Someone would soon catch some flak. No one guarded it.

While she felt a little sorry for playing Lynch Cully, her survival instinct had always been strong. From past and current experience with him, she saw him as a man of integrity. She held no doubt that he would live up to his word, if she lived up to hers. Yet, there were others higher up the food chain who could supersede his promise. She had no wish to play the odds that might have her end up in prison.

What a stroke of luck. The thought struck her that

Lynch might call it providential. She felt about under the seat and smiled as she found Cain's FFP stashed there. The mental debate about leaving or sticking with Lynch lasted only a second. She still had a task to fulfill, and this was her opportunity to get back on that track.

She climbed into the truck, started it up, and yet, hesitated to drive away. She had one more task to accomplish. The man she held up as a mentor had thrown her to his dogs at the first opportunity. Yet, from the material on the flash drive she had learned that he was more than that. He was the man she'd been searching for.

She pulled the flash drive from her pocket. Lynch would soon discover she'd been bluffing about encryption. Yes, the drive had password protection, but the guy was smart. He'd figure it out soon enough—hopefully, not so soon as to stop her from getting her revenge. She tossed it to the pavement near the truck, carefully backed away from the spot, and drove away.

FORTY-THREE

Lynch reentered the warehouse and headed toward the small cluster of FBI agents next to the three bodies on the floor. Out of the corner of his eye, he saw "Bashiir" being cuffed and led toward the main doors of the building. Several police cruisers had arrived to take away the occupants of the structure for processing and further questioning. Lynch hoped they hadn't blown a hole in a huge DEA operation.

"Who was supposed to watch the suspect's pickup truck outside the vehicle door?"

The agents either shook their heads or shrugged. One finally said, "I thought the county guys had it secured."

"Did any of you see the woman who was with me?"

One agent nodded. "She was here by the bodies. She confirmed to me that these two guys were the men you wanted."

"Did you see her leave?"

The agent shook his head. Recriminations would no doubt follow soon, but Lynch had no time for that game. Summer had escaped, and attempts to lay blame wouldn't change that.

Lynch felt as if he was a Vegas juggler with multiple knives and hatchets in the air. And now, someone was tossing in new balls, but those balls ended up being grenades with their pins pulled. He needed to get rid of them sooner rather than later. Yesterday would not have been too soon. Had it really been a scant 24 hours since Summer had taken him for a drive at gunpoint?

There was one knife he could drop now. He stepped back outside and called Amy.

"Hey, it's me."

"Was it him? Do you have him?"

He could hear the stress in her voice.

"It was. All three of them. Actually, they shot each other. No survivors."

"You're sure."

"I'm sure. Saw the bodies and checked for pulses myself. Pupils were fixed and dilated, as you once taught me."

He could hear the tears of relief flood from Amy as she thanked God for His protection. He whispered a prayer of thanksgiving to join hers.

"Th-thank you, Lynch. The nightmare is finally over."

"Hey, look. You're safe to head back to Macy's."

"Okay, but I don't think Macy wants to leave yet. The room's paid for, and it has a hot tub, plus room service. I think."

"And no chickens!" Lynch heard yelled in the background. The woman would never live it down . . . if he had anything to do with it.

He chuckled. "That's fine. Just let me know when you go back so I know where to find you. I need to call the President, and we had one hiccup in the operation. Summer escaped in one of the men's pickup truck."

Silence greeted that remark.

"Is . . . will . . . d-do you think she'll be coming after you again?"

"You know, I don't think so. She left her flash drive behind for me. I can't see her doing that if she still planned on targeting me. Plus, she could have stuck around and finished the job while I'm here. That device she left behind showed her several miles away and moving north before she turned off the thing in the pickup."

"You're sure?"

"Well, you know nothing is 100%, but, yeah, 95% sure. I even have an idea where she's headed. I need to call Sgt. Peniston back at the St. Charles PD."

He heard Amy groan. "No, no, no, not him. Please don't mention me."

"What?" Why would she react like that? "Do you know him? Is there something I should know?"

"He's the one who put me in jail. I still get a little embarrassed about that."

Lynch scratched his head on that one. Then it hit him. She had been arrested for harboring a fugitive mother and her disabled daughter. The daughter had been "kidnapped" by the State of Massachusetts, only for her mother to take her out of the psych unit and flee the state. The mother had been proven right, and the Assistant U.S. Attorney determined she had no winnable case against Amy for helping that mom.

"Different guy, Amy. That was Officer Jennison in St. Peters, not St. Charles."

He heard another sigh. "Oh. Right. Never mind."

"Gotta go. Lots to do. After talking with the President, I might have to leave the city. I'll let you know. Love you. Bye."

Summer drove straight to the motel in St. Charles. She had left Cain's FFP turned on until she saw that hers had also been activated. She had expected Lynch to utilize it to check on her. She could have flipped off the device right away, but she wanted to give Lynch time to try to track her. She hoped he would see her moving away from the warehouse as a sign that she would no longer be after him. Moments after she saw her icon, she turned off the FFP. She wanted to signal him, not allow him to track her cross country.

Summer's first stop: the motel. With her car gone, she doubted the place would be monitored by police. They had better things to do. In anticipation of launching her plan, she had discovered a spot to hide all of her toys. For her plan, she had only required the one handgun and her FFP.

However, now, the surveillance gear, laser, door hacker, additional firepower, and other goodies might be needed. To her advantage, she had Cain's vehicle, FFP, and any of the toys he'd left in the truck. He had once shown her the special compartment under the truck's bed where he kept his armament. She wished she'd had the time to grab the phone in his pocket. Attempts by Francois or Arikhan to track her would be foiled, finding that her car and FFP remained in St. Louis. They would only see Cain on his way back via the GPS on his truck and his credit card usage.

The trip back to New York would give her time to formulate a plan to reenter the Assembly's "fortress" atop the CitySpire building. Cain's truck would get her into the secure parking area. If they, Francois and Arikhan, didn't learn of Adam and Cain's deaths, her penetration into the quarters and offices might be easy. If they did learn of their deaths, armed resistance could be expected.

However, before heading east, she had one more task to accomplish.

FORTY-FOUR

Lynch paced outside the warehouse, trying to collect his thoughts . . . and disarm some juggled grenades. Something nagged him at the edge of his consciousness. It was like the time terrorists sought to take down the railroad bridges across the Mississippi River in their effort to disrupt the economy of the country. He had just started working for the Graham campaign as the chief of security, and something did not add up about the funding of that attack. That was his formal introduction to the Assembly. Prior to that, he had considered the Deep State as nothing more than an urban myth, much less as having an actual name.

Why would the Assembly leadership want to take out Summer, one of their own? It couldn't have been simply because the #summersnotdead campaign had outed her. Summer herself had requested a new identity, with plastic surgery to conceal her appearance. Why couldn't the Assembly have done the same? They had made an investment into her many talents. Why would they throw that away?

The only answer he could come up with was that they learned something new about Summer, something that threatened them directly. That was the only thing that really made sense. But, what?

He looked at the flash drive he'd been fondling in his

hand. Was the answer on it?

Lorna disrupted his thoughts with a tap on the shoulder.

"Hey. I'm no longer needed here, so I'm heading back to file my report. Um, should I mention Summer in it?"

Good question. Lynch thought about it for a moment.

"You know something, maybe not. I'm not so worried about having lost her. My boss will get the full details. But I don't want the wrong people learning she helped us. Something's just not kosher about this whole thing with her, but I can't put my finger on it. Let's consider her presence here as a need-to-know kind of thing."

The detective nodded. "Thanks. That makes my report about 95% shorter." She smiled. "What about the others here?"

"Yeah, I'll need to ask their cooperation, too. Good thing I didn't actually introduce her. All they can reference is some mystery woman in my company. Thanks for bringing that to my attention."

She nodded and then pointed to the nearby Land Rover. "CSU is here. See ya." She walked to her car as Lynch headed toward the white county CSU van. He recognized the detective.

"AJ, did you get lost?"

Neil 'AJ' French was assigned to the county's 1st Precinct in north St. Louis county. What was he doing at the opposite end of the county, in the 5th Precinct?

"Naw, they were short on manpower, and I volunteered to take this one when I heard you were here. I figured it would be an easy call, with little to process." He grinned.

Lynch chuckled. "Yeah, right. That car over there alone might take a few days." He pointed to Adam's car. "Belonged to a professional hit man whose body is one of three inside."

AJ nodded. "Okay. Sounding more interesting already. ME here yet?"

Lynch shook his head. "No word from them that I'm aware of."

"Well, I'll take a quick look but will probably save the inside until they have their turn with the bodies."

Lynch observed as the man took what seemed like hundreds of photos of the crime scene inside. He began to grow impatient. He needed to call the President, but he needed to touch base with Sgt. Peniston before making that call. And he wanted a look at Adam's car before he called the sergeant. He needed the first domino to fall, but he also knew there was a process to be followed.

Lynch grew optimistic when the detective returned outside. But then he began taking photos of the outside—the outside of the building, the doors, the car from a distance, the car up close, and maybe even birds in the barren trees.

"I was told there's a second vehicle."

Lynch wasn't sure how to respond. The more people who knew about Summer, the greater the risk of word getting back to the Assembly that she was on the loose, and that he still lived.

"Um, there *was* a second vehicle. It's gone."

The CSU detective looked incredulous. "It's gone?"

"Yeah, the tac ops guys thought the FBI was watching it, and the FBI thought the tac ops guys had it covered. I discovered it missing a few minutes before you arrived. No idea where it's gone."

The last part was true, although misleading by omission. He knew who had it and the direction it headed, just not where it was now. And he wasn't about to reveal his possession of the FFP. He suspected he would need that.

AJ shook his head. "Well, then, let's look at that car." He gloved up, grabbed his kit, and approached the Land Rover. "Nice set of wheels." He scrutinized the door frames, handles, and any other likely place for fingerprints. He dusted some of those places but came up clean. "This guy was a pro all right. Didn't even leave prints on his own car."

"Left it unlocked, though." AJ opened the driver's door and visually inspected the interior. "I'll process this in a moment. I want to check under the hood and in the back. Something doesn't look right through the windows back there." He popped the hood first and walked around to the front end. "Looks well maintained. Hey, look at this."

Lynch joined him near the front grill as he pointed to a silver box inside the engine compartment. "Is that what I think it is?"

"Only if you're thinking it's a commercial GPS tracking system, like trucking companies use to monitor their 18-wheelers. Whoever this guy worked for wanted to be able to track him at all times.

Lynch wondered if Summer was aware of that. Did her car have that "option?" The possibility of that began to energize him.

He followed the CSU detective to the back end of the Rover. On lifting the tailgate, first glance seemed innocent, but then he saw what AJ must have seen—the space of the cargo area was too small. A fake floor? The detective took more photos and then began to fiddle with the "floor." After a minute, the carpeted platform lifted to reveal a hidden compartment with enough armaments to equip the Tactical Operations squad.

"Whoa! I knew if you were on this case, I'd have fun. And you're right. It might take a few days to process this baby. I think I'll just call to get this towed into the garage right now."

Their search so far brought two things to mind for Lynch. First, they had found no such cache in Summer's car. Of course, her Audi had a trunk to conceal things and needed no fake floor. But where were her arms? He couldn't bring himself to believe she operated with only a handgun and her FFP, both of which he now possessed. He came to only one conclusion. She had stashed them at or near the motel.

Yet, alerting Sgt. Peniston to that possibility might be too late. She'd already had enough time to retrieve her belongings and head toward wherever she was going.

That's where the second idea held promise. Could her GPS system, if the car had one, tell him where she was headed by telling him where she'd been.

FORTY-FIVE

The Jacuzzi King Suite was beautifully done. That they

got a suite had surprised Amy. But then, when Lorna reserved it, they had no idea how long they might be there. Having the extra space would have served them well for a longer stay. Now, for one night, it seemed an unnecessary extravagance.

Amy filled some time by watching the news. More trouble in the Persian Gulf with small Iranian gunboats harassing the U.S. naval vessels. The details were sketchy. There was another near miss by a NEO, or near-earth object—an asteroid that sped past the planet two-plus million miles away. They called that 'near'? She decided the term was relative.

Macy climbed out of the jetted hot tub, wrapped a towel around herself, and walked toward the TV as the nylon shorts she used as a swimsuit substitute, dripped across the carpet.

"Okay. I can only take so much of looking like a prune. Anything good on? Is it time for lunch?"

Amy glanced toward her friend. "I was watching some news. It looks like a lot of the same old same old."

"Let's find a good movie. We got the premium channels for free with the room. Can't trust anything on the news anyway."

Amy tossed her the remote. "Here you go. Check the guide. And I hope you find something worthwhile. I'm bored."

Macy surfed through the on-screen channel guide. She occasionally paused for two seconds, but kept skimming.

"Nada so far. The only movies to catch my attention are ones I've already seen. Where's the room service menu?"

Amy stepped over to the desktop where the room's "Amenities" notebook sat. She tossed it to Macy, who started thumbing through it to find the menu.

"Just remember, this isn't an all-inclusive resort. We pay for what we eat."

"Uh-huh."

Amy watched her friend work all the way through to the end of the service guide, only to start again from the beginning, more slowly.

"I musta missed it." She again reached the end of the notebook. "What gives? Didn't that lady police detective say there was room service? If so, I can't detect it."

Amy took the notebook and began to peruse it. "No room service, but they offer a buffet-style breakfast between six and nine. Eleven bucks."

"Eleven dollars? For a buffet where I might like a third of what they offer. Not worth it." She shook her head. "No thanks. I'd be happy with yogurt at home."

Amy shrugged. "Find anything on TV?"

Macy sighed. "Nope."

"So, we gonna sit here and look at each other all afternoon?"

Macy's shoulders drooped. "Guess I was expecting too much, huh?"

Amy nodded. "Ready to go home? It's not like we paid for the room."

Thirty minutes later, they were back in Amy's car. She noticed a pickup truck pull out and follow them along Highway 100. *Nice truck,* she thought. *Lynch would love something like that.*

Lynch checked his phone for the time. He'd already been on scene at the warehouse for over two hours. At that point, his stomach grumbled louder than his impatience. He'd need to get some lunch soon or his mood would sour further.

After breaking away from AJ French, with the car having been towed to the county forensics garage, he was cornered by the FBI SAC who arrived on scene about the same time as the tow truck. Lynch gave the guy credit for doing his job, but he kept asking questions that Lynch wasn't about to answer. He ultimately pulled the "need-to-know" card, which prompted a call by the senior agent to Washington. Evidently he was told he had no need to know, and he then ignored Lynch.

Lynch went back to his car and climbed in to get out of the cold wind. He placed the call he'd been held up making to Sgt. Peniston.

"Lynch, it's way too soon. The guys just started processing the car. You could've given us at least a day. It's only been a few hours. We're not miracle workers here."

"Relax, Bill, that's not why I'm calling. I have another request. Could you check with your guys to see if the car has a commercial GPS system in it, like truckers use?"

"Actually, I can answer that one already. I was there when they started, and we were all surprised to see that it does have a unit like that. One of the techs is already working on it. I figured the location data stored in it might come in handy."

"Great minds think alike. Would you call me when you

have something?"

"Will do."

"Thanks, Bill. Hey, we need to go fishing again sometime this summer. Maybe we can take that grandson of yours with us. Enoch, right?"

The man laughed. "That's right. How'd you remember that? He would love it."

Lynch took one more stroll through the warehouse. The tac ops officers were long gone. The bodies had been processed and taken by the ME investigators. Half of the FBI agents had recently left as well. The SAC stood talking with his remaining agents. Lynch saw that he wasn't needed any further, so he signed out of the scene and headed toward a nearby gaggle of fast-food establishments. He made notes on the morning's events, so that he could brief the President with a complete accounting.

With the two assassins dispatched to eternal judgment, Lynch felt comfortable using his secure phone again. He replaced the battery and turned it on. A flood of messages poured through. Most were those from Amy and the President during his time as Summer's captive. He deleted them. He puzzled over how a national pizza chain had gotten the number to pitch their pizzas, and blocked that number even though he liked their pies. As per their established protocol, Lynch texted the President on the secure line. *Abdi and both assassins dead. Killed each other. Ready to give full briefing.* The man would answer at his convenience.

Lynch pondered what to do next. He could only sit on his hands until he had more information, and for that he waited on others. He moved to scratch an itch on his thigh and felt the flash drive in his pocket. How had he forgotten that?

He dialed another number by heart into his phone.

"Jurgesmeyer."

"Mike, it's Lynch. I've got a flash drive to crack open. What's your schedule look like?"

"For you my friend, *mi casa es tu casa*. Come on down."

This was one part of her plan that Summer debated. Did she truly need insurance against Lynch Cully? He had promised her protection, but at the first opportunity, she ran. Had that nullified his promise? That possibility fueled her current action.

Amy Gibbs and her friend had decided to stay at the motel. For Summer, that was a good thing because she knew where the women would be. She was prepared to spend the night in the truck, if required, in order to see them leave the following morning.

Upon leaving St. Charles, she followed the fastest route shown on the truck's map system back to the motel in Wildwood where the women stayed. She could only hope that they hadn't changed their minds and left.

Upon pulling into the parking lot, she discovered Amy's car sitting where they'd left it earlier that morning. She parked 50 feet away, pulled an RFID tracking device from her bag of goodies, and walked toward the car, trying to look as nonchalant as she could. She feigned dropping something next to the vehicle, and as she bent down, she placed the device on the back side of the car's rear license plate. She proceeded to a nearby trash can, threw something away, and sauntered back to the truck.

The RFID transmitter had a limited range, so she couldn't simply plant it and drive away, expecting to find the car later wherever it ended up. She would have to follow them as they left. That could be from a safe distance, to avoid being spotted, but it still meant staying within a quarter mile.

She had time. In some ways that was all she had. So now she waited.

FORTY-SIX

Lynch found Mike Jurgesmeyer at home. The man had established an incredible computer lab within his basement some years earlier, and while he still had to do forensic exams at the county's computer labs, as its director, he often found opportunity to work from home. He had no concerns over security; his servers, firewalls, network routers, and even the T1 line coming into his home were as secure as the Situation Room of the White House.

Mike was one man Lynch trusted explicitly. The man was a Christian first and patriot second, despite his blemish-free skin and the silky ponytail to his shoulder blades that made him look like a liberal metrosexual, an out-of-date term that still fit. Because of Lynch's trust in him, Mike was among the first to learn of Lynch's newest assignment by the President and had been instrumental in the #summersnotdead campaign.

"Coffee?" asked Mike.

"Cop coffee?"

"That's the only way I drink it."

Lynch believed that. Caffeine fueled his friend most of the day and frequently overnight. That wasn't to say the man had no regard for his health. He ate only organic foods, drank filtered water with only a rare beer on hot summer days, and worked out daily. Still, Lynch felt sorry for anyone who might be around on a day when Mike didn't get his caffeine and went into withdrawal.

With caffeine sludge in hand, they headed to the basement. As it cooled, Lynch took his first sip. The stuff was even stronger than his own. *Maybe Mike should just take to chewing coffee beans*, he thought.

"What's up?"

Lynch handed him the flash drive. "Belonged to Summer Stanton." He gave his friend a rundown on what happened, starting with the day before, when Mike had alerted him to the "Summer sightings" at the motel, and ending with his discovery that Summer took one suspect's truck and disappeared.

"She used this as leverage of sorts, hinting at all sorts of incriminating evidence against the Assembly. She said it had high-level encryption and that we couldn't access it without her. Then she ups and takes off but leaves it behind for me to find. Now I have to wonder if there's anything on it at all."

"Hah. Never met an encryption I didn't like. But you know the drill."

Lynch nodded. "Make a copy first."

"Yep." Mike set up a card reader connected to one of his workstations, inserted the drive, and with his own proprietary software, copied the drive's contents bit by bit to an SSD drive in the computer. The software then quarantined the code from the rest of the hard drive so no virus or malware could cause trouble.

"Looks like that was successful, so let's work with the copy."

Again, Lynch agreed and removed the flash drive to

prevent any accidental corruption of its files.

"It might be encrypted, but it's definitely password protected, a ten-character password. Any thoughts on what that might be?"

Lynch foresaw hours of brute force attempts to break the code, even with Mike's decrypting software. The program could run for days and might never break it. The potential combinations of ten characters—letters, lower and upper case, numbers, special characters, even foreign language characters—were astronomical.

"Well, the simple ones that come to mind are out. Her name is 13 letters. 'The Assembly' is eleven, twelve if you use an underscore or hyphen for the space. Her birthday could be ten, but that seems too simple."

"Do you have it?"

Lynch pulled up a file on his phone with a wide variety of facts on Summer Stanton. He gave Mike the birth date in mm/dd/yyyy format. No luck. They tried the European standard of dd/mm/yyyy. Again, nothing. At least they didn't see a warning that they only had X tries left.

"Is Summer her real name?"

Maybe? thought Lynch "No. Her given name was Elizabeth. Stanton is her real family name. Hey, try 'LizStanton.' That's ten and not as obvious as her birth date. She never struck me as someone who would use 'password' as her password, but I can't see her leaving this behind for me if she used some computer-generated code you could never remember."

"Good point." Mike typed in the name. Nada. He tried 'EliStanton.' Zilch. He tried both in all lowercase and all uppercase. No luck. "Let me start my decryption program while we brainstorm. We can always pause it to try something."

Lynch took another sip of stimulant to kick-start his brain. As he tried to think of possibilities, his phone rang. He glanced at the number and smiled.

"Hey, babe. How's the motel?"

"In the rearview mirror. We just left. Ends up there was no room service, no place for pampering, and Macy got tired of looking like a prune in the hot tub. So, we signed out and are heading back to her apartment. We have to stop for some groceries first, but should be there in an hour, hour and a half."

"Okay. Thanks for letting me know. I'm with Mike Jurgesmeyer trying to crack that flash drive she left behind."

"Well, then I should let you get back to work. See you later."

He disconnected and turned back to Mike. "Where are we?"

"The program is almost finished trying just numeric combinations. It'll start alphabetic combinations next, and then alphabetic and numeric combinations. Then we throw in special characters to the mix. This could take a while. How's Amy?"

"Heading back to her friend's apartment. I think she'll be celebrating the death of a certain terrorist tonight, as wrong as that sounds."

"Considering what he put her through, I see noooo problem with that, personally."

Lynch thought back to Amy's comment about seeing

the motel in the rearview mirror. While that was a common phrase, it wasn't one she typically used. In fact, he couldn't recall her ever using that phrase. Something about it struck him as something he needed to pay attention to. Why? What?

He took another sip of sludge and thought about why the reference to a rearview mirror should be important. Then it hit him. Summer's comment about mirrors in the car the day before.

"Mike, this is far out, but you'll appreciate it. The Lord works in wondrous ways. Amy just used the phrase 'in the rearview mirror' when I asked her how the motel was. They had just left the place. She never uses that phrase to refer to a place she has left. Yesterday, Summer made a weird reference to mirrors. I kept looking back in the mirror to watch her, as well as traffic. She asked me why I kept looking in the mirror and then made this cryptic comment. I'm trying to remember her exact words."

"Well?"

"Give me a sec." Lynch reflected back on the ride. "If I recall correctly, she said, 'The eyes are the mirror to the soul.' No, wait, she said, 'Funny things, mirrors. The eyes are the mirror to the soul. Keep looking, you'll never know what you'll find.' Could this be a clue?"

Lynch's phone rang again. "Uh-oh, the boss. Give me a minute."

Lynch walked upstairs as he answered. "Good afternoon, sir. Boy, do I have a lot to tell you."

"And I look forward to hearing it. Unfortunately, a bunch of troubling news coming out of the Middle East has me occupied right now. I also want Director Renzoni in on the briefing, so I need you to come to Washington. I have a plane coming for you. It will meet you on the tarmac at Spirit of St. Louis airport at three p.m., your time. You'll fly into Andrews rather than Dulles, and a car will be there to bring you to the White House. We'll make it a dinner meeting, and then I have a full evening of meetings."

"Yes, sir. I've got my go bag in the car, but I am looking a bit scruffy."

"Probably not as scruffy as I'll be after these meetings on Iran. See you in a few hours."

"Yes, sir."

Lynch wondered what was going on in the Middle East. He hadn't had time to so much as glance at the news.

"Looks like I have to go to Washington. Think you can give me something tomorrow or the next day?"

Mike smiled. "How about right now? You can give a present to the President."

"Huh?"

Mike handed him two flash drives, the original plus one. "You're the one who said it, God works in wondrous ways. What do you see in a mirror?"

"A reflection."

"Let me rephrase that. What do *you* see in a mirror?"

"Me. My reflection."

"And how many letters are in your name?"

Lynch shook his head in amazement. His name. Ten letters. He smiled. In the past 24 hours he had been truly amazed at the turn of events three times. Maybe there was some truth about things happening in threes. But then, three was God's own number.

"Did you take a look?"

"Not without permission. Shall we?"

The files on Mike's workstation were not randomly created, as if hurriedly downloaded from some computer. They were orderly. Summer had clearly spent some time on this. Why? One folder held a list and information on Adam's hits, while a second contained details on Cain's. Just in scanning the data, Lynch recognized several names on the list he had been assigned to investigate at the beginning of all this mess.

He also saw that the list started well before either man was of an age to make the hits. Clearly, Adam and Cain were call names used by several men in succession, going back to the beginning of the Assembly.

"These lists are going to clear up a bunch of cold files. I recognize some of these victims as doctors who came up with and began promoting natural cures for cancer that actually worked."

"I guess Big Pharma didn't like that." Mike clicked on a larger folder with the curious name, The Goods. "Whoa. Graham is gonna love this info. This could keep the FBI busy for years."

Lynch nodded. The folder contained documents listing all the active members of the Assembly, with special highlights on its executive council. The list included special assignments given each, with global goals, and more, detailed. One stood out—a certain software billionaire with interests in global vaccines and population control. He and his vaccine company had been kicked out of India after its polio vaccine crippled over 400,000 children. Now he was tasked with helping to fund China's development of a virus that could be used to introduce a worldwide vaccine program. The info listed a Chinese virologist in Wuhan who was working on recombinant DNA mutations in a virus from bats. That could become a real problem if such a virus were to get out.

Lynch pointed to the information. "Have you heard anything about this?"

Mike nodded. "Some vague ramblings. It's a bit scary. After that Ebola and ricin scare in northern Virginia, the U.S. banned research in this country into viral bio-warfare, something called "gain of function" research. The NIAID folks at our NIH refused to give up their work and moved their research to a new Chinese level-4 biohazard virology lab in Wuhan. The CDC gave them a $3.75 million grant to continue the work. It's a lab controlled by the Chinese military. I hear from some of my sources that their security protocols are not all that good. If anything escapes that lab, it could be really nasty."

Mike had sources that few knew existed. If he thought things were going to get bad, the odds were pretty good they would. However, Lynch had no time to dwell on these events. He sure wouldn't worry about them. God was in control.

FORTY-SEVEN

Summer parked at the far end of the lot of some grocery store. She didn't anticipate a stop, and this one dragged on. Two women's groceries . . . how could it take so long? She felt she could have shopped for the entire news staff at her old network in the time they'd already been inside. But then she acknowledged she hadn't really grocery shopped for quite a long time, even for herself. She'd had a personal assistant to take care of the mundane chores.

The store's lot was too crowded to confront Amy. She didn't need another spectacle going viral of her as a blonde. That was her main element of surprise, and she needed to keep it.

Finally, she muttered to the empty air. Their cart appeared to have enough food to last a month.

As they pulled onto the street, she remained three cars behind. She reasoned that they couldn't be too far from their destination, so she needed to stay closer than she had on the main roads.

Sure enough, a few miles away, the car turned into an apartment complex. She let them round the first corner before entering the warren of lanes and parking lots defining the layout around the buildings. Her map showed that the compound was enclosed by a wall with only two open entrances and exits. She would be able to find them wherever they stopped. And stop they did, just a tenth of a mile away by the truck's map.

She eased toward their location. Now came the most critical part.

Amy should have known better than to shop with Macy when the woman was hungry. She had offered to stop for lunch somewhere—anywhere that Macy wanted to go, but her friend insisted on grocery shopping and eating at home. She couldn't argue with Macy's claim that the meal would be healthier, but she figured Macy was just being cheap.

She developed second thoughts about that inside the store when Macy started buying everything that hit her fancy. For every selection of organic fruit or produce Amy placed in her cart, Macy matched it with prepared fruit or some other convenience product packed in high fructose corn syrup. When Amy chose hummus and whole grain crackers, Macy went for Mexican bean dip and tortilla chips. When Amy wanted free-range chicken, Macy selected 80-20 ground beef. Amy envisioned the fat dripping from the grill, if they had one. Amy picked up a six-pack of flavored seltzer water. Macy hefted a case of Coke into her cart. They did agree on avocados for homemade guacamole, as well as organic whole grain bread.

At the checkout, Amy's cart appeared to be one of someone living on a subsistence diet, while Macy must have had a family of four. Amy's two small bags barely fit into Macy's cart for the trip to the car, and all of it had to fit around Macy's case of wine in the trunk. In the end, Amy placed her groceries in the backseat with their overnight bags. She didn't want her food crushed in the trunk.

"Next time, remind me to rent a U-Haul trailer when I go shopping with you."

Macy slowly shook her head. "Girlfriend, I burn a lot of calories working the ER. After a shift there, I look forward to the comfort of home."

"You mean the comfort *foods* of home, don't you?"

"Don't you play registered dietitian with me. I know you sneak potato chips when I'm not looking."

Macy had her there.

Amy pulled into the drive that led to Macy's apartment. The parking spaces seemed empty for a Saturday midafternoon, but the warm front had finally arrived. The neighbors no doubt took advantage of the nice day to lower their winter cabin fever.

"I'll grab my overnight gear and one bag of groceries and go unlock and open the door. I'll come back to help you with all your stuff."

"Okay, thanks. That'll earn you your potato chips."

Amy did as she stated and in returning to the car, passed Macy struggling with two bags coming up the stairs. She bounced down to the ground floor, feeling light and free from worry. Her days of looking over her shoulder had ended.

As she closed in on her car, her phone buzzed with a notification. She pulled it from her coat and saw that Lynch had texted her. She stopped and opened the message. Disappointment overcame her. She hoped to celebrate that evening, but he was called to the White House and would be leaving at three. She checked the time. Ten till three already. She began to type a reply.

A voice came up behind her. "Sorry, but I'm going to need your assistance."

The electrical shock of a stun gun or Taser ripped through her torso. She lost control of her legs and began to fall, but the woman, whose voice she now recognized, caught her. The woman moved in to support her under one shoulder, with Amy's left arm held across the woman's shoulders. With little struggle, the woman moved her to a pickup truck.

"Now, help me as best you can to get into the passenger's seat, or I'll zap you again and be a lot less gentle."

Her mind was fuzzy, but she recalled having seen people stop breathing after being shocked too close in succession. That was not a risk she wanted to take. She complied, as best she could. She didn't have much, if any, control of her body. Once seated, the woman buckled her in, slammed the door, and ran to the driver's side.

Amy tried to look toward the apartment, hoping that Macy would be there, would see what was happening, and come to her aid. Or at least call for help. But her friend remained out of sight, and a moment later, the truck pulled away. What in the world did Summer need her assistance with?

* * *

Summer did not hesitate to leave the apartment complex, but she didn't want to go too far just yet. She needed to secure her passenger before getting on the road. She recalled passing an elementary school between the grocery store and apartment. She found it again and pulled into the empty lot.

She grabbed some restraints from her goody bag and walked around to the passenger door. Amy remained semiconscious and with little control over her body, as expected. She used the restraints to secure the woman's left wrist to the metal bar under the front of the seat that was used to move the seat backward and forward. She extended Amy's right arm toward the open door, closing the door just enough to secure that wrist to the handle of the door. She then closed the door and returned to her side.

As she pulled back onto the road, she said, "That's just to prevent you from trying to surprise me and attack me before we can talk."

She saw Amy move her head. That appeared to be an attempt to nod in agreement. Summer took it to mean that, whether or not it did.

By the time they crossed the Mississippi River heading east, Amy seemed fully alert and mobile, within the limits of her bonds. Summer caught her looking at her as she drove. She didn't say anything, but the look on her face told it all.

"Sorry I had to zap you. You were taking too long with the grocery shopping and all, and I needed to get on the road. I didn't have time to get into a long conversation with you."

"Why? Why did you kidnap me?" There was steel in her voice.

"Truth? I need you as insurance."

"Insurance?"

"Yeah. I left enough data behind on a flash drive for your boyfriend to do serious damage to the Assembly. But with that information on hand, he could simply turn it over to Graham and the FBI and leave me to their wiles. As it is, I don't see myself living very long. Once the Assembly learns of Adam and Cain's deaths—and they will, their tentacles run deep in the FBI—and that I had something to do with it, they won't pull any punches. It won't be two hit men sent to find and kill me cleanly and efficiently, it will be every lowlife they've ever hired with carte blanche to do whatever they want to me, as slowly as they want to do it."

"So, why me? What kind of insurance could I possibly be against that?"

"Not that. Having you will guarantee that *he* comes looking for me—Lynch. He's the only chance I have."

Summer noted Amy's tension ease and her respiratory rate decrease.

"You could have just stayed with him in St. Louis. He had promised to protect you, and when he says something like that, he will do it, even to death."

"I know. I believe that about him. I don't understand it, but I believe it." Summer paused. How much should she share? At this point, what did it matter?

"I didn't stay because I have a task to do, the very thing I set out to do by forming a partnership with the Assembly in my first years in journalism. And I have a man to pay back. When I saw that Adam and Cain were both dead, I realized I still had an opportunity to do that."

She glanced at Amy to find her scrutinizing her.

"Look, I promise I have no intention or desire to hurt you. If you cooperate with me, you'll be fine. If you put up a stink, try to run away, alert police, or anything else to try to thwart me, I'll take out Lynch, and he'll never know what hit him. But I'll let you live knowing that he died because of you."

FORTY-EIGHT

Lynch paced the pavement a few yards away from the government Gulfstream. He had texted Amy about having to go to D.C and thought she would answer. So far, nothing. Of course, often in those metal frame buildings like large groceries or Big Box stores, the signal could not penetrate. He just wished he'd heard from her before takeoff.

As he climbed aboard, the attendant asked him to put the phone on airplane mode. Now he really wished she had answered. He'd be out of touch for the next two hours.

The jet took little time to reach cruising altitude. Lynch accepted a cola to drink and sat back in his chair to think, formulate, and mentally rehearse his presentation to the President and FBI director. While relating the events of the past day and a half would be easy enough, he felt a need to offer at least an outline of the information on the flash drive.

He booted up his laptop and inserted the flash drive with the copy of the data on it. As its window came up, he saw the ten-character field appear. That his name was the passcode still surprised him. Was he expected to read something into that? He didn't know.

He entered his name and opened the folder labeled "The Goods." The name was an understatement. He found himself engrossed in what he read. There were some very, *very* prominent and powerful names in the list—judges, congressional leaders, past presidents, wealthy businessmen, foreign leaders, and more. Every facet of the economy had more than one representative. In fact, pretty much every facet of modern life seemed covered.

The one thing they appeared to have in common was the goal of a global system of governance and finance. They used their money and positions to support liberal, "progressive" ideology. Of the handful whose writings he was somewhat familiar with, they wrote of a utopia that would never materialize. Their real ideology was that of communism, with them as the ruling elite. Another thing they had in common was a denial of God. They were their own gods.

Lynch was so absorbed by the material, he felt surprise when the attendant stopped by to pick up his trash and announce that they were making their approach into Andrews Air Force Base. The flight seemed to have taken no time. He closed up shop and prepared to land.

Forty-five minutes later, with the afternoon traffic, the car cleared the security at the entrance to the White House. Lynch had expected to be ushered to the West Wing. Instead, he was shown to the elevator to the residence. He had never been to this part of the famous dwelling before.

"Lynch! It is so good to see you. Welcome, welcome."

"Mrs. Graham, it's good to see you, too. Been a long time."

She frowned. "What's this Mrs. Graham stuff? This is our temporary home. Don't get all formal on me in my own house." She laughed and stepped forward to give him a hug.

"Lyyynnnch!"

He swung around to see the Graham's 11-year-old son, Mark, running toward him. He held his palm up. "High five!" Mark slapped his hand. Lynch moved it horizontal to the floor. "Five on the side!" The boy slapped it and gained a determined look on his face. Lynch laid his hand down low with the palm facing up. "Five down low!" As the boy swung to slap it, Lynch pulled his hand away and he missed. "Too slow!"

"Grrrrrr. I'm gonna get faster one of these days."

Lynch laughed. "Yes, you are. Look at you. You've grown, what, two feet since I saw you last?"

The boy rolled his eyes. "Yeah, right. An inch maybe. Right, Mom, an inch since we got here?"

Cara Graham smiled. "That sounds about right. Now, get back to your homework. You'll have time to visit Lynch later, but only if your homework is done." The lad ran off the way he came.

Lynch looked around. "Am I early? Is the President here yet?"

She looked serious. "Not yet. This stuff in Iran has everyone worried. He might be later than he first thought. In the meantime, how about a tour? Who knows, if it gets late enough, we might have to put you up in the Lincoln Bedroom."

"Okay, sure." His phone dinged with its low battery alert. "Hey, is there someplace I can plug in my phone? It's about to die."

"Right this way." She spun around and swept her arm in the direction to head.

In the family kitchen, he plugged in the charger and

phone. Within seconds, it began to beep one notification after another. He glanced at the growing list. Amy's phone. Macy's phone. Amy's phone twice more. Then the Chesterfield Police Department. Then Amy's and Macy's phones again. In all, a mix of text messages and voice mails.

"What the—"

Cara looked concerned. "A problem?"

"I don't know." He scanned the text messages first. "Cara, excuse me. I need to make a call."

He returned the call to Macy, as it was she who had been using Amy's phone to contact him.

"Lynch, y-you need to get back here quick. Amy's d-disappeared. We just got back with groceries and she vanished. Thin air. Poof."

Lynch could tell she was rattled when she called him Lynch. She only called him by his name when she was upset or concerned. "Wait, Macy. How do you know Amy's disappeared? Start from the beginning." He saw Cara put her hand to her mouth and eyes widen.

"We got our groceries and pulled up at my place. Amy grabbed her overnight bag and one bag of groceries and preceded me to open the apartment. She headed back down to the car for more as I walked up the stairs with my first load. I unpacked my frozen foods to put in the freezer, and she didn't come back right away. I wondered what was taking her so long. I finished putting things in the freezer and went back to the car. She wasn't there. The trunk was open. A back door was still open. But she was nowhere to be seen. Then I found her phone on the ground. She had started a text message to you and never finished it."

Lynch's respiratory rate rose along with his heartbeat. Had someone from Abdi's organization decided to avenge him?

"I called the police right away. They showed up in, like, three minutes. They canvassed the area and a detective showed up. Said he knows you, but I can't recall his name right now. Got his card here somewhere. You need to stop bein' a secret agent man and hightail your butt back here."

"Macy, not that easy. Look, I'm in the White House right now. I need to brief the President, and then I'll see how fast I can get there. I have a message from the Chesterfield police waiting for me. Let me hear what they have to say, too. I'll keep you posted. Call me if anything new develops."

"Okay. Oh man, I am not gonna sleep tonight."

He reassured her twice more and finally disconnected.

"Amy's gone missing? Lynch, I'm sure Brad will understand if you need to head back there."

"Thanks, Cara. Let me call the police department there and hear what they have to say."

The voice mail simply asked him to call back. He did a dial-back to the number on the message, and it linked him to the dispatchers.

"Hi, this is Lynch Cully. Someone there called me a little while ago. It's about—"

"Yes, Agent Cully. One moment."

"Detective Kenniston. That you, Lynch?"

"Hey, Terry, returning your call. Is this about Amy?"

"Yeah. Sorry, buddy. The uni's canvassed the complex with no results, but we managed to find some security video. In a nutshell, looks like some blonde in a pickup truck nabbed her. Appears to have hit her with a stun gun, put her in the passenger seat, and drove away. No idea where they went from there. We're trying to check for any video from the surrounding area but this ain't *NCIS: Los Angeles*."

Summer Stanton! But why? And did he dare to ask for a BOLO on her? Would that stress her to a point of harming Amy? The #summersnotdead campaign had sure taken its toll on her. No, so far, he'd kept her existence out of official reports in the hope that such a move would prevent her boss or bosses from learning that she still lived while their guys didn't.

"Thanks, Terry. Look, you're not going to find her in the St. Louis metro area. I know who the blonde is, and I might have a way to find her. But, if we put out a BOLO on the truck, that could get Amy killed. Give me 24 hours. If I haven't found her by then, we'll do it the old-fashioned way."

"You mean call the FBI."

"Yes and no. I'll handle the FBI, too. I'm in Washington and about to meet with the director personally."

FORTY-NINE

Amy had been released from her bonds after giving Summer assurances that she would cooperate fully. What choice did she have? She was convinced that the woman had killed her ex-fiancé. Why shouldn't she believe she would harm Lynch if betrayed?

At the motel that night, chosen because it was Cain's usual preference and his credit card was being used, she had ample opportunities to leave, call authorities, or even call Lynch. However, she would not risk Lynch's life.

Plus, she felt at total peace in following Summer's rules, as strange as that seemed. The same sense of calm had taken hold of her in Cambodia. She had no idea how things would end, but she trusted the One who was in control.

Breakfast had been quiet. They were up before many of the other guests who slept in on Sundays. Yet, the meal was quiet for other reasons. The questions Amy wanted to ask were unlikely to be answered in a place as public as the motel's breakfast room. Also, how do you ask, "Did you kill so-and-so?" in a public space?

However, now they were in the truck, riding through central Pennsylvania. Only the two of them would hear the conversation.

"Summer, why are you doing this? You mentioned a task and payback yesterday."

The woman looked at her for a moment before returning her attention to the road. She did not respond right away.

"Why, Summer? Is that too much to ask of someone who has kidnapped me and threatened someone I care deeply about?"

Summer sighed. "No, probably not." She paused. "The Assembly destroyed my family. What do you know about Chappaquiddick and Ted Kennedy?"

Amy had no idea where this was leading. "Not a lot, other than most people thought Kennedy was responsible for a young woman's death and got away with it."

Summer nodded. "Well, my grandfather was one of those people, and he was on the Grand Jury. That Grand Jury was a sham, and he threatened to go public with the fact that they never had any real evidence presented to them. Within a week, he found himself with a broken leg and an insolvent business. There were anonymous reports of infidelity, ties to organized crime, and other malfeasance. They destroyed his reputation. He lost his home. Two of his four children wanted nothing to do with him. He left Cape Cod a ruined and bankrupt man, but at least my grandmother stuck with him. She knew the truth."

"I'm sorry. That sounds awful."

Summer went on. "My dad was the youngest child and stayed with his parents. College was not an option, so at 21, he changed his name and went off on his own. He, too, knew the truth about his father. He wanted to help, and that's when he discovered a group of people, a shadow government, that directed much of world affairs. They controlled the media, all of the liberal side of politics and some on the conservative side, much of big business, communications, pretty much everything.

"They knew that they could shape public opinion by controlling the media, and they focused on education because they needed to control the minds of children as they grew. The explosion of computer technology and the development of the Internet gave them their first real chance at global control. The advent of social media was serendipitous to them. It gave them a global reach they hadn't had, even beyond the reach of the entertainment industry.

"Do the names Illuminati, Trilateral Commission, Council on Foreign Affairs, or the Bilderbergs ring any bells?"

Amy's dad had been a proponent of some conspiracy theories. "My dad talked about stuff like that. He said the term 'conspiracy theory' was used by the CIA to belittle and cast doubt on those who were too close to the truth about JFK's assassination and the Warren Commission's report. Lynch feels that way, too. Especially after our experiences with the Assembly. The more they focus on destroying your reputation, the closer you must be to the truth."

"Well, my dad was one of *those* people, but he worked to stay under their radar. He saw what had happened to his father. A few decades or so ago, the elite decided that the best way to get these conspiracy nuts off their backs would be to reinvent themselves, and the Assembly was born. My dad was a particular thorn in their side, and one of their first troubleshooters killed him. My mom lapsed into a major depression, and it killed her three months later."

Amy didn't know what to say. The story sounded plausible, and the emotions Summer displayed in telling it were real. Yet, it didn't make sense.

"That must have been hard. And yet, you joined their ranks and ultimately became a troubleshooter yourself. I don't get it."

Summer nodded. "I did. In high school, I actually got a prestigious summer intern's slot at Senator Kennedy's office. I came to believe that Chappaquiddick changed him. In college, I became a communications major. My connections from that summer job got me established after graduation. I still had to earn my stripes, but that was part of my long-range plan. I want to finish what my father started. This time, though, there won't be any way to call it conspiracy *theory*. The only way I could do that was from the inside, and I was prepared to do whatever it took. I haven't much time, and I need to reach the finish line. I'm still prepared to do whatever it takes."

She said those last three words in such a way that Amy had no question as to what she meant.

Summer held no expectations of Amy, other than compliance. Amy had been inexplicably quiet during the previous day's drive and at the motel. Summer had anticipated, no, in some ways dreaded, being questioned.

And then it started.

"Summer, why are you doing this? You mentioned a task and payback yesterday."

Summer considered the question . . . and the

consequences of answering. That's when she realized there would be no consequences. After running out on Lynch, she figured her request for a new identity would not be considered. If she survived the day, the probability was great that she might answer for her crimes, have her day in court, and be able to tell her story. If death awaited her, someone else would need to know that tale.

". . . The Assembly destroyed my family . . ." She continued to tell Amy her family history. ". . . and I was prepared to do whatever it took." She stressed the last three words because she hoped Amy would read between the lines and not ask the one question Summer really didn't wish to answer.

Amy replied, "Oh." That was all.

Had she read what Summer hoped she read into her comment?

Another mile down the highway, Summer got her answer.

"D-did you kill Richard?"

There it was. The one question she had hoped would go unvoiced. How would she reply? At this point, as she had established with Lynch, there existed only circumstantial evidence against her for the two killings. Why would she admit to them with Amy? Still, she felt a heaviness inside, as if she had a burden to unload.

"I, um, am not admitting to anything. Let me ask you something. If you'd had a goal ever since you were a young girl, and someone, someone you actually really liked, learned enough to prevent you from reaching that lifelong goal, maybe even enough to get you killed, what would you do?"

"I sure wouldn't kill him. I couldn't kill anyone."

"Not even to avenge your parents?"

Amy had no response at first. After a moment, she said, "Vengeance is mine, says the Lord. It's not my call."

"God? What God? Where was God when my dad was killed? Where was God when my mom went into such great depression that she stopped eating?"

Amy shifted in her seat. She appeared contemplative, as if formulating an answer.

"I have no place in my life for a God who lets things happen like what happened to my parents."

"Summer, I'm no theologian, but I do know that this question has been asked a million times. No one has an easy answer. The Bible says we inherited a fallen world when the original Adam sinned. Not one of us is perfect, but God gave us a way through His Son to become part of the kingdom of God. Accepting Jesus isn't a get-out-of-jail-free card, but it is a free stay-out-of-hell card. Look at what Lynch and I have gone through. It hasn't been easy at all. My dad was a believer, and he was still murdered. But I know beyond all doubt I'm going to see him again, and this life is just a blip in the sands of time of eternity. I no longer fear death because Jesus conquered death to give me eternal life."

Summer said nothing. Death leading to eternal life? That just sounded crazy. Still, something about it resonated within her.

After a few moments, she said. "I'm done with questions. We'll be there in about three hours." That was going to be a long three hours in silence.

FIFTY

Lynch was glad that Abraham Lincoln, the tallest U.S. president, was taller than him. He had slept in some beds where his feet hung over the foot of the bed and that was never comfortable. He felt reasonably confident, however, that they didn't have Sleep Number beds in 1860.

Lynch found it hard to believe he'd spent the night in the Lincoln Bedroom. The room in the southeast corner of the second-floor residence had had many configurations. The name came not from Lincoln having slept in the room but from the fact that it had been his office. Lynch marveled to think he had slept in the room where the Emancipation Proclamation had been signed.

When Cara told him she had arranged for him to stay there, he felt humbled and honored. At first, he had protested. He knew when to give in when she told him, "Well, if being a friend isn't enough to feel that you qualify to stay there, being a British Knight certainly should." Even the First Lady could get her digs in.

As he prepared for the day, he thought back to the late-night meeting with the President and FBI Director. The discussion had gone on well after midnight. They both were astonished at the information provided by Summer Stanton, but even more so by the fact that she had given it up. Why?

Their primary concern, however, was to get Amy back.

Lynch had an idea about where Summer was heading, but no specifics. He would work on that, first thing.

After a much-needed hot shower, he had nearly finished dressing when his phone rang. All calls within the residence went through the White House security switchboard. He had no idea how they did that with his cell phone, but it was protocol.

"Sir, you have a call from St. Charles, Missouri. Patching it through."

Lynch heard no click or signal to indicate the call was his, so after a moment of dead air, he said, "Lynch Cully."

"Lynch, it's Bill Peniston. So, what, you're in the White House? How cool is that?"

"Yep, one of the perks of the job. Free room and board when I'm in D.C."

Bill laughed. "Yeah, right. Hey, I've got that GPS data you asked about. I'll send you a file, but one thing stands out. The car was parked in New York City until the day Summer Stanton supposedly died. It traveled to North Carolina and back to the same address in New York. Then it came here."

Lynch wanted to shout. That was it. That was where Summer would be going.

"What's the address, Bill?"

"The CitySpire Building on West 56th Street."

FIFTY-ONE

The Big Apple. They made good time. Churches had yet to dismiss, and the lunchtime crowds had not yet materialized.

Having left the tunnel, Summer exited the 495 onto Dyer Avenue. The traffic on 8th Avenue was typical for a late Sunday morning. Soon they turned onto 56th Street and approached the CitySpire building. If all went well, and Francois and Arikhan had not yet learned of the deaths of Adam and Cain, the truck would still have automatic access to the private parking area adjacent to the elevator.

If not, they would be denied entry, and Summer would need to switch to plan B, which was to fly by the seat of her pants. Reaching the private elevator undetected would be difficult. Even then, the codes would likely be switched. And if that was the case, they would have to hoof it up roughly 50 flights to reach the penthouse suites of the leadership. Even the business elevators serving the offices of the first 23 floors could only get them so far.

She would also need ample firepower to get past the private security which would no doubt be sent against her. The Assembly's security employed facial recognition software in all of the elevators, except its own. They had decided that no one getting that far on their home turf needed identification and clearance. That was a good thing as such software would see right past Summer's blonde hair and new look.

She held her breath as she approached the closed garage door leading to the residential and office parking. The door opened as she came within 20 feet. So far, so good. One more door to go to get into the secure parking. It, too, opened. She breathed a sigh of relief until she saw a security agent walking toward her from the elevator.

The guard waved, smiling.

The tinted windows of the truck had so far kept her identity hidden. As the man stepped near the door, she lowered the window.

"Welcome back, Cain." His smile dissolved into a scowl. "What? You?" His hand never reached his sidearm as the barbs of Summer's Taser hit him squarely in the chest. He shook violently as he fell, his head sounding a heavy thud as it hit the concrete.

Summer emerged from the pickup and turned back to Amy. "Help me." The woman sat there. "Would you prefer I shoot him in the head to keep him from waking up and alerting the others?"

Amy shook her head and climbed down from her seat. Together they dragged the man behind the truck, out of view. Summer then bound him with several zip ties on both wrists and ankles. She stuffed one of his socks in his mouth.

"He has to be able to breathe," said Amy in protest.

"Did you see him go for his gun as soon as he recognized me? He would have gladly killed us both. If he can't breathe through his nose, too bad."

Summer returned to the truck and donned what she

nicknamed her "Bat-belt." The utility belt would have served Batwoman well. She stocked it with additional zip ties, three more cartridges for the Taser, and several magazines for the 9mm Beretta she produced from under the driver's seat.

"Follow me, and stay close."

Amy shook her head. "I think I should stay here."

Summer frowned. "I don't think so. You're my insurance, remember? I need for Lynch to join us, not find you down here and stop looking. That is, of course, if he's been able to figure out where we are. I left him enough clues."

"He'll be here."

"I hope so, for both our sakes." Summer realized that commanding Amy wasn't the right approach. "Look, the Assembly takes its security *very* seriously. If you're found here, you'll be shot on sight and your body dumped far out at sea. No questions asked. Your choice."

Amy's face took on a look of resignation as she preceded Summer toward the elevator. Summer caught up, took the lead, and also made note of which vehicles were present and which weren't. Director Arikhan's car was missing. That posed a problem for her plan. He and his driver could arrive at any time and come up behind them.

Each of the troubleshooters had his, or her, own access code to the elevator, which they were supposed to use as a way for the Assembly to track their coming and going from the building. Summer had made a point of learning the access codes for both Adam and Cain, in anticipation of this day. She punched in Cain's code and the elevator door opened a few minutes later.

The ride to the 75th floor penthouse seemed to take forever. Summer prepared for another guard to greet them at the top. The man should have been alerted to Cain's return by the guard in the parking garage. The surprise would be on him.

As the door opened, she heard, "Welco—" before the startled look on the man's face turned to a grimace. After removing the Taser barbs, she bound the man as she had the guard in the garage. With Amy's help, they moved him into a service closet ten feet away.

"That should be the only other guard. They're so smug in their own superiority that they assume this place to be impenetrable and that no one would possibly want to take the risk of coming here."

Summer moved down the hallway, checking each room. The director's study, bedroom, library, and guest rooms were empty. With the man's car gone, she had anticipated as much. She found the kitchen staff working on lunch. They offered no resistance, were bound, and moved into the large walk-in pantry. Summer was able to secure that door with a large zip tie as well.

The fact that they were preparing a meal meant that at least one more person was present in the penthouse—Francois. She intended to have more than words with that man.

From the kitchen, she moved to the dining room. Empty.

She turned to Amy. "You can have a seat in here. Things might get messy from this point on." The woman complied and appeared relieved to do so.

"Chef? When will lunch be ready?"

The voice seemed to be moving toward them from the main room where the large windows overlooked Central Park. She rushed toward the arched doorway connecting the two rooms, but Francois beat her to it and entered the room.

He looked shocked upon seeing Amy sitting at the table. "What? Who are . . .?" Summer saw realization spread across his face. "Ms. Gibbs. I recognize you from the Cully file. I won't ask how—"

"Turn slowly, Francois." Summer had managed to gain a position off to his left side.

"Ah, *ma chérie.*"

"Don't *ma chérie* me, old man. You hung me out to dry. Sent Adam and Cain after me. You didn't even give me a chance."

The man shrugged. "Nothing personal."

"Huffff . . . how many times have I heard that?" During her training, that phrase had been drilled into her. Her assignments would be just business, nothing personal.

"Well, Francois, for me this whole thing, working my way up, has been personal. Does the name Isaac Feldman mean anything to you?"

The man gave a slight pursing of the lips with a subtle tilt of his head. She found it too choreographed to be realistic. Yet, his eyes darted down and to the left before he regained control of his facial expression—a telltale sign of lying.

"*Non.* I do not know this name."

Again, his eyes betrayed him. He was out of practice at

the skill of lying.

She shot him in the right knee. He screamed out in pain and buckled to the floor. Amy flinched and started to move toward the man, but apparently had second thoughts and settled back into the chair.

At that moment, a slight shaking of the entire building appeared to catch the attention of all three. It lasted but a second or two. Both Amy and Francois glanced around the room. Both had a questioning look on their face.

Summer walked closer to Francois. "That was one of the things you did to Isaac Feldman. Do you remember him now?"

He glanced up at her with disdain. She shot him in the left foot.

"How about now, old man? Isaac Feldman. One of your first assignments as an original member of The Three."

One more time, his face betrayed him. He knew the name and knew it well. And he knew she was duplicating what he had done to that target.

"What of it? Th-that was years ago, b-before you were born."

"Your memory is failing, Francois, or should I call you Adam? You were the first to use that call name, correct?"

He nodded, and his breathing began to accelerate.

"I was ten years old when you killed my father. I saw you do it from my bedroom window."

"Impossible. You aren't that old."

She laughed. "The Assembly isn't the only group with experts in creating identities and back stories. Elizabeth Stanton and her family exist only in computer databases. As for my looks, I could grow rich promoting the skin care and exercise regimen I've used for the past three decades."

Even Amy appeared shocked at that statement. Summer looked at her. "Yes, Amy, I'm actually 54, not 34. I've waited a long time for this day."

She bent down close to Francois. "Do you need more proof? What was the third injury you inflicted on my father before you killed him, you sadistic beast? He was already on the ground pleading for his life, and you did this."

She pulled a knife from her belt and stabbed him through the right hand. She pulled the knife back and repeated the attack on his left hand. The look on his face showed him to be convinced now.

Amy jumped to her feet but stayed by the chair. "Stop it! Haven't you done enough? He needs medical care."

"Sit down! Do you know how many lives this man is responsible for taking? Not just as 'Adam,' but also as 'the butler,' the power behind the throne of the Assembly. Your boyfriend has all that information now."

A look of surprise crossed Francois' face.

"Yes, Francois, I downloaded about 90% of the hard drive in the study. There was a flaw in your firewall that allowed me access from my quarters here. Your precious Assembly is going down. Cully has probably provided this to our new President by now, and he's not one who'll be bought by the likes of you."

She looked at Amy again. "Sit tight, if you know what's good for you."

Summer grabbed the man under the arms and around his chest and dragged him from the room. As he screamed in pain, she lugged him through the main room out onto the balcony.

"Remember this place, Francois? You threw Director Karling to his death here. It's time for you to experience the same. Remember my father on your way down."

He offered no resistance. He had become a pitiful old man with no fight, no strength left.

With some effort, she hoisted him up to the railing and got his arms over the top. She heard noise from inside. Someone had breached the penthouse. She quickly moved to grab his legs and with a momentous heave, she threw them up and over the rail. If he screamed, she couldn't hear it over the wind.

As she reentered the main room, she heard, "Drop the gun! Down on your knees! Hands behind your head!" The voice was a familiar one.

FIFTY-TWO

As soon as he figured out where Summer was heading, he called Director Renzoni. Within the hour, the director had a dozen handpicked agents ready to go. The Hostage Rescue Team in New York was on standby, as was one of the city's SWAT teams.

A Secret Service car, at the President's request, drove Lynch to Andrews Air Force Base, where he met up with the director and his agents. Lynch looked at their selected mode of transportation and gritted his teeth. The FBI's Tactical Helicopter Unit had two refitted UH-60 Black Hawks at the ready. The Gulfstream jet was one thing. A noisy, rattling helicopter was another. He'd had more than enough of those egg beaters in Cambodia.

The only thing urging him to climb aboard was the thought of Amy being held hostage. After donning his headset and buckling in, he grabbed onto the nearest support and cut off all blood supply to his fingers with his death grip.

To his surprise, the Black Hawk lifted off smoothly and barely vibrated, although the noise of the engine and rotors was difficult to muffle. Less than an hour later, they descended into JFK International Airport in Queens, New York, where the HRT and SWAT commanders met them on the tarmac.

"Director, welcome to New York."

Director Renzoni nodded. "What are we dealing with? We know that the building is a mix of offices and condominiums. The top four floors are owned by one corporation, while the rest of the building is owned by another. Our records searches seem to point to both being shell companies. Do you have any more info for us?"

As they walked to the awaiting vehicles, the HRT commander took the lead. "Sir, the 72nd floor appears to be more offices, with access by the regular elevators. The top three floors are residential, but curiously they have a separate private elevator leading to a private parking garage. The SWAT folks are going to secure the 72nd and ground floors and control access to the building."

The SWAT commander interjected, "We'll have additional NYPD support for that."

The HRT leader continued. "There are two emergency stairwells connecting those upper floors. They will also control those points on the 72nd floor. We believe our target is the residential areas above, so we plan to gain access to the garage and private elevator. We have no idea what, if any, resistance we might face. We'll clear the 73rd floor first and work our way up."

Lynch asked, "What if there's controlled access to the elevator? We have no codes or key cards."

The HRT commander smiled. "No, but we have New York bureaucracy to thank. All elevators require keys to give emergency personnel access. They couldn't get an occupancy permit without the appropriate elevator inspections. So, we have a representative from the fire department who'll meet us there with their key."

Lynch chuckled and grinned.

"What's funny?" asked the director.

"I bet the Assembly has spent thousands on security for this place, and yet overlooked the mundane—the fire department's elevator key. What a kick in the gut that would be."

The ride to central Manhattan took them along the 695 and 495. Even with lights and the occasional siren, the drive required 30 minutes. When they arrived, Lynch saw that SWAT and uniformed NYPD had staged a block away. Upon their arrival, the units swarmed the building. SWAT entered on the ground floor while the uniformed officers controlled the perimeter and all access points into and out of the building.

Lynch and the FBI force gained access to the main parking garage and found their way to the entrance of the private garage. A steel door—the kind that rolled up—blocked the way. They found no control panel.

"It must be radio controlled from this side, sir," said one of the agents in full tactical gear.

"Blow a hole in it."

A few minutes later, with all of the agents taking cover, a controlled explosion opened a man-sized hole in the steel. The whole building seemed to shake with the blast. The HRT filed into the opening, meeting no resistance. The other agents, along with Lynch and the director, followed them in.

As Lynch looked about, he saw the pickup truck. He pointed it out to the director.

"They're here all right. That's the truck."

One of the agents yelled out, "We have a body. He's out cold but breathing. He's also trussed up like a turkey in the oven at Thanksgiving."

"He's not going anywhere. Leave him there until cleanup. We need everyone we have until we know what we're dealing with upstairs."

Lynch nodded in agreement and followed the HRT agents to the elevator door at the end of the area. The door was controlled by a numeric keypad. There was no way they could access it easily by pressing numbers. Was it a three, four, or six-digit code? They had no way of knowing. Lynch said a quick prayer as an agent produced a key, slid it into the panel's keyhole, and turned it.

It turned with ease, but nothing appeared to happen. He reasoned that Summer and Amy were the last to use it and they would have gone to the top. How long would it take to descend 70-plus stories?

"Everyone on coms from this point on."

A few minutes later, the door opened. The box was big enough for six men. Per the plan, the HRT agents would ascend first and send the car back down. With a dozen HRT members, a dozen regular agents, and Lynch and the director, this was going to take a while.

Evidently the director did the math, too. He assigned two agents to stay behind in the garage to control access to the elevator.

Lynch began to pace. Amy was up there somewhere, and he was still in the garage. He couldn't argue against the FBI agents going first. This fell under their jurisdiction. But Amy was his primary concern, and he was stuck twiddling his thumbs waiting on a single elevator that a turtle could outrun.

Finally, the car returned for the fourth load. Lynch and Director Renzoni accompanied the final agents to the 74th floor. HRT had cleared the 73rd, connected with SWAT at the emergency stairwells to the 72nd floor, and were moving to up. The door opened, and they were greeted by an HRT agent who signaled for them to move left down the hall.

Lynch exited with the men and before the door could close stepped back into the car. They wouldn't find Amy there. If Summer had taken her anywhere, it would be the 75th floor, the penthouse. Summer's beef was with the boss.

"Lynch, don't—" The door closed on the director's words and Lynch rose one more flight.

He moved with extreme caution into the hallway. He cleared the immediate area and looked in every direction. Which way should he go? Floor plans of these upper floors had been impossible to find.

A sudden scream caught his attention. The sound was one of agony, but it wasn't that of a woman. He began to move in the direction of what had become wailing, but he couldn't run headlong into who-knows-what. The impatient run around a corner could be his last. He cleared his path as he had been trained to do.

He found his way to a massive dining room. Amy was sitting slumped over the table, her head on her forearms.

"Amy?"

She jumped up. "Lynch!" She ran to him and threw her arms around him. He used his free hand to comfort her.

"You okay?"

She nodded.

"Where's Summer?"

She pointed in the same direction as the howls. He released her and at that moment, the cries ended. He moved toward the door, examined it, and slowly moved past it into a large open living space with an incredible view of Central Park.

Summer entered the room through sliding glass doors at the far end. She hadn't seen him. She looked exhausted, and whatever she had just done had clearly not brought her any peace. Torment etched her face.

"Drop the gun! Down on your knees! Hands behind your head!"

Summer complied and looked up at him. She shook her head and said, "I wish I had your peace, Lynch. It didn't help. I paid him back, but the hole inside is that much bigger."

What didn't help? Paid back who? He didn't understand.

"Summer, my peace comes through Christ. It's not too late for you to accept Him and change your ways." He started to lower his gun.

He heard the elevator door open down the hall. Reinforcements.

She began to cry. "I want the peace that you know, Lynch. The peace in not fearing death that Amy told me about. I want to stop hurting. I want to—"

A shot rang out from Lynch's left. A hole opened in Summer's forehead and blood splattered the plate glass windows behind her.

As she fell forward, Lynch spun to his left and dropped. A middle-aged man with foreign features stood there, anger filling his face. The man raised his gun toward Lynch . . . and Lynch dealt to him what he'd just dealt to Summer.

FIFTY-THREE

Lynch reflected on the past two weeks as he drove. Amy's statement to the FBI had clarified much—Summer's motive, her real identity, what Summer had meant right before her death, and the name of the man whose body was discovered on a terrace jutting out from the 65th floor.

The name of the man who shot Summer was discovered in the documents left behind by Summer. He had been the director of the Assembly, Arieh Arikhan. However, as with Adam and Cain, the man was a ghost. Fingerprints, dental records, DNA, tax records, and all other attempts to identify the men came up with nothing.

How Arikhan had made it to the penthouse had also become clear. The two agents in the garage had been overpowered by Arikhan and a man assumed to be his bodyguard and driver. The FBI agents would live. The bodyguard hadn't fared as well. Yet, the outcome was that Arikhan gained access to the elevator and made it to the top floor without any stops below while the FBI kept busy clearing the 74th floor. They admitted fault in failing to secure the lift.

Summer's flash drive also provided the means to access the computers within the penthouse complex. Additional information had come to light from files she had not managed to download to the flash drive. The first light to shine were additional names of those murdered by the Deep State group. Over four dozen cold cases over the past forty years—including the death of Isaac Feldman—were solved through information in what were now being called "The Summer Files."

The second light flashed glaringly into the mainstream news. There was enough evidence within the files to indict four federal appeals judges on various charges, just within these past two weeks. The Assembly's mainstream media hacks were both accusing the administration over being fascist and racist and backpedaling to save their own skins. Other cases were being developed and would soon cast spotlights on their misadventures as well as those high up in government circles, both foreign and domestic.

Corruption in Washington D.C. and other venues of power was circling the drain.

Many within the DOJ and FBI had begun joking about "The Summer Files." The "Summer of Discontent," "Summer's Heat," "The Bright Light of Summer," and more were all bandied about in emails and around water coolers. No one paid homage to the benefactor of this information. Yes, she was a murderer several times over, but Lynch had seen just a glimpse of the torment that must have filled her soul and eaten away at her over the years. Even one of the thieves on the crosses next to Jesus had been shown His grace and forgiven just before his death. She had not been afforded that opportunity at the end.

Lynch arrived at the airfield, parked, and waved at Amy as she performed the preflight check on her Cessna. He patted his pocket to make sure he hadn't forgotten anything.

He walked up to her and embraced her. They kissed, but she didn't let him linger.

"Almost done. Can't wait to get in the air. It's been months now since I've flown."

He smiled but said nothing.

She stopped what she was doing and looked at him. "What? No comments? No asking me to avoid barrel rolls and loops?"

He smiled but said nothing.

"You did bring the picnic you promised, right?"

He smiled but said nothing. He did, however, hold up her wicker picnic basket that he'd borrowed the day before.

She shook her head at his silence. "Okay, buster. This was your idea in the first place." She finished her inspection and said, "Climb in. We're ready to go."

He smiled, said nothing, and climbed into the passenger seat. She looked at him again, scrunched up her brow, and shook her head. Soon they were in the air with a southwesterly bearing.

"Well?" he asked. He held his arms straight out in front of him.

"Now he speaks. Well, what?"

"Aren't you going to say anything? Did you even notice that I've not grabbed onto the handhold, the sissy bar as you call it, even once? I'm calm, collected, and enjoying the view."

She grinned and put the small plane into a quick dip, as if the bottom had fallen out. Just for a second, but Lynch instinctively grabbed onto the nearest things he could find to hold. She laughed.

"Funny. Not. Look, I'm trying. You know me and flying." Admittedly, he'd done more flying in the past few weeks than during the rest of his life. Or so it seemed. Of course, those flights were piloted by professionals, in larger aircraft. He had decided he just had to look at flying with Amy as if he was riding the fastest, steepest, scariest roller coaster in the world. He could do that.

Forty-five minutes later, Amy pointed off to her port side. "There's the farm."

She soon turned and descended onto the Bircher's grass strip. After securing the plane, they walked hand in hand toward the lake. Amy waved at Jimmy who was on a tractor in the field to their right. Lynch carried the food.

The weather was perfect for mid-March. The temperatures hovered in the upper sixties there, although the breeze off the water remained cool. As they up righted and cleaned off the picnic table left near the shore by the family, Amy zipped her hoodie up a bit more.

Lynch opened up the basket. Amy's eyes widened.

"Whoa. My man has outdone himself. Look at this spread."

He had collected as many of her favorite things as he thought appropriate for a picnic, including macarons from her favorite bakery. They talked and ate. She gazed across the water and then back at him. She sipped the wine he had provided.

"This is delicious. Thank you, Lynch, for a wonderful meal. I promise I won't push you into the water this time."

She had done just that after their last picnic here. She looked out across the water again and closed her eyes. For

Lynch, the timing was perfect.

She opened them again to find Lynch at her side, down on one knee. He pulled the ring from his pocket and extended it her way. Tears welled up in her eyes. She tried to wipe them away.

"Amy, we've had our rocky times and I know I was a real jerk early on, but I've loved you from the beginning. I just had to learn how to show it. We've been through more together than we've been through apart, and I've grown to love you more and more as time moves on. The Bible says that *He who finds a wife finds a good thing and obtains favor from the Lord.* Will you be my good thing, no, my *great* thing and do me the highest honor of becoming my wife?" He paused and gazed into her eyes. "I know that with you . . . my life will never be dull."

She smirked at him and rolled her eyes. It was a look he'd seen a thousand times, and he loved it even more today. She lifted him up and as he stood next to her, she threw her arms up in the air and screamed, "Yes!" as she jumped into his arms and kissed him with the longest, lingering kiss of his life.

FIFTY-FOUR

Amy arrived at the Bircher's home by limo that morning. Now mid-April, the weather was warm but unpredictable. They'd had rain for three of the four weeks since Lynch's proposal and the farm seemed soggy as they built a gazebo by the lake for the ceremony. And yet, for the past week the sun had dominated the skies and dried out the land. It was as if God wanted to bless them with the perfect weather for an outdoor wedding. No, Lynch would correct her. Not 'as if.' God *was* blessing them.

To have the wedding at the farm was Amy's request. Her father had always loved coming to the farm and visiting with his friends, the senior Birchers. The farm was also her brother Chad's favorite place. He often said that he wanted to farm after returning from Afghanistan. He hadn't made it back. Somehow being at the farm brought her closer to both of them. Here, they would be part of the ceremony.

Macy sat by the window sobbing. "I'm s-s-so happy. My girl's finally getting married." She sniffed. "Of course, never in my wildest dreams did I see Lynch Cully as the man who would finally snare her. Boy, was I ever wrong about *that* man. I was wrong once about my cousin Willie—"

"Macy, I could use your help. The maid of honor is supposed to be helping the bride get ready, right?"

Macy wiped her eyes and nodded. "Sorry, girlfriend."

She joined Lynch's sister, Kirsten, and Tara, one of Amy's sisters-in-law in helping Amy with her dress.

In Amy's mind she kept checking off her list. Makeup done. Check. Hair done. Check. She just hoped the breeze off the lake wouldn't undo her do. Flowers. Check. Limo ready to take her to the lake. Check.

There was a knock on the door. Jimmy's wife peeked into the room. "Oh, Amy. You look gorgeous!" She stepped inside. "I just wanted you to know that everything is ready by the lake. The rental company was a little late, but they have the chairs out and the tent is up with all the tables and chairs they need there. They pulled their truck up next to the barn and have more of each in it if we need them. Oh my, I'm as nervous as you must be. I've never hosted a wedding on the farm, much less for 200 people. Oh, and I switched out the groom on the cake like you asked."

Amy smiled. "The place looks great. You guys went out of the way to spruce up the place and get it ready." Her comments were suddenly interrupted by the growing sound of helicopters, big ones. "What in the world is that?"

The noise kept getting closer until it seemed as if it was on top of them. The windows of the house began to rattle. They *were* on top of them.

Amy risked being seen by the groom and rushed to the home's front porch. Four Army Black Hawk helicopters had just landed on the grassy field across from the house. From three of them, over two dozen men in black emerged and spread out across the property. They appeared to be securing a perimeter of some sort. Four men approached the house and nodded at Amy and the other women. One spoke into his lapel.

Amy gasped and put her hand to her mouth as two people emerged from the fourth chopper—the President and First Lady had just crashed her wedding! She hurried toward them across the gravel drive. Macy and Kirsten tried to keep up to prevent her gown's train from getting prematurely dirty. They both stopped and just looked ahead, eyes wide, when they realized who it was.

"Mr. President, Mrs. Graham, I-I don't know what to say."

"Well, first off, forget the formality. We're here as friends. I hope you don't mind our crashing your wedding."

"Are you kidding? We were disappointed when the RSVP came back as not able to attend. I, we, are so glad you came. And what an entrance."

The First Lady gave Amy a sheepish look. "Um. I hope you don't mind. We brought guests. Actually, it was their idea. Kind of encouraged us to change our plans." She gave a slight wave back toward the helicopter.

Amy stood there, stunned, as the King and Queen of England—King Arthur in full formal regalia—stepped down from the aircraft. As they approached her, she didn't know what to do. She couldn't really curtsy in her dress. The King extended his hand.

"Amy, we are so happy to see you again, especially on such an auspicious day. You remember my wife, Helen, don't you?"

The young queen extended her hand.

"I do, your Majesty. I don't know what to say, except welcome and that we're honored."

"When we heard you two were getting married, Arthur suggested we check into coming. I told Arthur that we shouldn't do it. After all, we're not supposed to upstage the bride on her big day, and I was afraid our presence would do just that. The word would get out, and the press would flood this place. We didn't want that at all. Then he suggested we crash the wedding with Brad and Cara. I thought, what a marvelous idea. They were up for it, too, so here we are."

Arthur smiled. "Yes, we do so appreciate your groom. He saved our lives and the monarchy. We will honor him in any way we can. We like Lynch . . . a lot." He winked at his wife.

She laughed. "Sorry. It's a bit of an inside joke. The children are growing up calling him Sir Lynch-a-lot. I think they would have enjoyed coming as well, but that was a bit much."

Amy started to laugh. Sir Lynch-a-lot. Oh boy, would she have fun with that one. She wondered if it was too late to alter the cake topper yet one more time.

They all turned at the sound of music coming from the direction of the lake.

Brad Graham touched Amy's arm. "It must be time. Are we holding things up?"

Amy looked at Macy and Kirsten, both still standing there dumbstruck. Kirsten finally nodded.

"I guess so." She laughed. "He can wait five more minutes."

The President's face took on a serious note. He lowered his voice and said, "Amy, we all know what happened to your dad. We know you must be really missing him on this day."

Tears welled up at his comment. She didn't need this right now. She had gotten those emotions under control. Plus, she didn't have time to redo her makeup.

"Do you have someone to walk you down the aisle?"

She sniffed. "My brothers offered. They've been wanting to give me away for years." She smiled, getting her emotions in check. "I turned them down. My dad will be at my side in spirit."

Both the President and the King leaned toward her as Arthur asked, "No bride should walk down the aisle alone. Would you do us the honor of allowing us, both of us, to escort you down the aisle?"

"Hey, you look sharp, man. You two are going to make an incredible couple."

"Thanks, Mike."

Mike Southworth, the retired colonel whom Lynch relied upon frequently for counsel, had become his spiritual father in so many ways. Lynch could think of no one more honorable to be his best man. His two brothers-in-law-to-be filled out his side of the wedding party. He and Amy had agreed to keep the wedding party small to avoid stepping on too many toes of people who expected to be asked and weren't.

Lynch's pastor from Destiny Church stepped into the room. "Hey, it's time. Do we need to hold you up, keep those wobbly knees from failing?"

"Ha. Thanks, Jim, but I'm just fine. No jitters on my

part."

Together, Lynch, Mike, and Pastor Jim left the cabin and headed to the lake. They took their place at the entrance to the gazebo. Lynch looked at Mike.

"By the way, was it you?"

Mike furrowed his brow, questioning.

"Was it me what?"

"The one who changed the cake topper groom to a knight named 'Sir Lynch' on a white horse."

Mike laughed. "Not me, but I wish I'd thought of that one. That's rich."

Lynch was determined to find out who had done that. He looked out across the crowd of people, with a few stragglers still being seated. He and Amy had invited just over 250 people, not wanting to leave anyone out, yet at the same time not expecting two-thirds of them to drive three hours, or more, to join them on their day. How wrong they'd been. A larger tent had to be ordered at the last minute for the reception.

He looked at various friends and wondered if they had been responsible. Many of them had no clue that Lynch had been knighted by the young King of England, Arthur, so he could quickly rule them out. As he scrutinized the group for the possible prankster, the noise of helicopters caught his attention. The silhouettes of four Black Hawks approaching from the east became evident. They seemed to be coming toward the farm.

And then he saw two F-35 Air Force jets zoom across the sky at a higher altitude, no doubt creating a restricted air space above the farm. Only one person in the country warranted that treatment. He smiled, knowing who was about to crash the party.

He nudged Mike and pointed up. "Looks like President Graham is about to crash a wedding."

Mike nodded. "Yeah, I saw the F-35s patrolling above."

Lynch leaned toward Pastor Jim. "You're about to meet the President of the United States."

Jim cocked his head and gave his usual quirky smile that said "No way" without needing the words.

Sure enough, the four choppers dipped down and appeared to land just over the crest of the hill. That put them near the main house. Amy was in for a surprise.

Lost in thought, Lynch came to attention with a tap on his shoulder by Jim. The music began. Amy wanted a traditional wedding but Chopin's *Nocturnes* to start the event seemed so out of place in the setting. Pachelbel's "Canon in D Major" would follow with the arrival of Amy's limo and the processional of the families and bridesmaids. Amy would come down the aisle alone to Wagner's "Wedding March." Lynch had received his lesson in wedding music. He would no longer refer to the music as "Here Comes the Bride."

Lynch felt butterflies in his gut. Not of nervousness but of eagerness. The woman of his dreams, his best friend, was about to become his wife. And then the limo arrived. The doors opened and the maid of honor, Macy, and the bridesmaids emerged along with two women whose faces he couldn't see.

The limo turned around and left. "What?" he heard Mike mutter behind him. "We didn't rehearse it this way."

Lynch realized one of the women had to be Cara Graham, but who was the other? A couple of minutes later, the limo returned. The two women turned to face the crowd, and Lynch was floored to see the identity of the second one. Murmuring rose in a crescendo among the guests. People began turning and taking photos with their phones.

Lynch leaned over to Jim as the women were escorted to front row seats. "Jim, you are not going to believe this, but you are also about to meet the King and Queen of England. Who's got the wobbly knees now?"

Jim swallowed and replied, "Guess I shouldn't do my 'mawwidge' English vicar imitation from *The Princess Bride*."

The First Lady sat on the bride's side, while Queen Helen sat right in front of him, next to his parents. She smiled, waved, and turned to introduce herself to his folks. His mom looked as if she was about to faint.

The "Wedding March" began, and Lynch stood there, stunned, as the President and the King of England assisted Amy from the limo and escorted her down the aisle. Tears welled up in his eyes at being so honored. He said a quiet prayer of thanks to his heavenly Father.

He paid no attention to the phones taking photos. The flashes of light would have made a convention of paparazzi proud. His eyes were focused on Amy. He had seen her dressed to the nines for dinner as well as wet and muddy in the tropics of southeast Asia. Today, she was absolutely, drop-dead gorgeous. He couldn't take his eyes off her.

And then he was taking her hand.

"Who gives this woman to this man?"

Jim's voice seemed far off. Lynch didn't really hear the answer. It didn't matter. Their heavenly Father now blessed them both.

Lynch's mind and actions went on autopilot. The vows, the candle lighting, and the brief session of praise and worship music to God, all seemed as if a dream. Would he even remember the details of this day? He didn't care.

And then came, "It is with great honor that I now pronounce them husband and wife. You may kiss the bride."

Lynch embraced his wife with an ardor he could not have imagined.

"I introduce to you, Mr. and Mrs. Lynch Cully."

With that, the recessional music began. Lynch couldn't recall which composer wrote this one, nor did he care. As he and Amy stepped from the gazebo, the music quickly changed. *What?* he thought. He and Amy looked at each other and started laughing. She threw her hands in the air and together they danced down the aisle to the Bee Gees singing "Stayin' Alive." He was definitely going to the find the wise guy who pulled *this* switch . . . and shake his hand!

AFTERWORD

While researching the vaccine issues for ***The Khmer Connection***, I came across an article about several doctors and holistic health practitioners who had died under mysterious circumstances within a two to three-month timespan around July 2015. All told, one website reported 13 suspicious deaths. As a premise for a thriller, that sounded quite juicy.

Of course, the reality of some of these deaths was not quite as sensational as that and other websites reported. Now, I don't trust Snopes. After all, who fact checks them? I don't trust them because of their origins and main source of funding. They definitely have an agenda. And yet, they often glean some very useful facts on controversial topics. This was one of those topics.

Snopes, in its original article on these deaths and in its follow-up to a number of these deaths, revealed that several of these deaths were from natural causes in elderly physicians. Two of the deaths still have no official explanation, and two of the three female physicians who had been murdered had been victims of domestic violence. Dr. Teresa Sievers of Bonita Springs, FL, was one of those victims. Yes, she was involved in holistic medicine, but that was irrelevant to her death. Arrests were subsequently made of two men from Hillsboro, MO, in her murder. One was a lifelong friend of her husband. Do we need three guesses as to who instigated her killing? A second, Dr. Lisa Riley, was murdered by an ex-boyfriend. The third, Dr. Marie Paas, died of an alleged suicide. Curiously, the cause of death of Dr. Nicholas Gonzalez, Susanne Sommers' physician, was never determined.

Suicide? Four of the 13 deaths were alleged suicides. All appear to have been involved in what is called "holistic medicine." However, that's a broad term covering everything from promoting vitamins to doing research on natural forms of healing.

The latter was the case of Dr. Jeffrey Bradstreet, whom I mentioned in the story and also used as the basis for the doctor killed by Summer/Hannah. His work involved GcMAF—Globulin component Macrophage Activating Factor—in patients with autism primarily. He actually testified twice before Congress on his work and reported having treated 11,000 patients with GcMAF, of which 15% showed complete resolution of their autism, 70% showed improvement, and 15% showed no change. He practiced in Florida but was found face down in the Broad River with a gunshot wound of the chest. His death was very quickly ruled a suicide, and yet, as the family asked, "Who commits suicide by shooting himself in the chest?" They quickly raised $33,000 for a private investigation of his death. I have not been able to find any report of the results of that inquiry, which in itself suggests that they, too, found it to be suicide.

Which brings up nagalase and GcMAF. Yes, these are real. The real name for nagalase is alpha-Nacetylgalactosaminidase. How's that for a mouthful? Alpha-NAGA is another nickname. And Schindler's disease is real, named after Detlev Schindler, MD who first described the disease in 1988. It's also called Kanzaki disease, after Hiro Kanzaki, MD, the Japanese physician who went on to research the disorder in 1996 and to detail what happens in it. Just like Amy, I had never heard of it. I didn't feel so bad about that when I learned it's extremely rare as a recessive genetic disorder of chromosome 22. NiMAF? Well, I made that one up for the story.

Yes, nagalase is markedly elevated with cancer and a fair number of viral infections, such as flu, HIV, herpes 1&2, and more. It breaks down the Gc protein and prevents the creation of GcMAF. As I mention in the story, that's important because macrophages are the "garbage collectors" of the body, consuming viruses, toxins, metals, and cancer cells among other things that don't belong in the body. A high nagalase level means low macrophage numbers. It makes physiologic sense that increasing GcMAF through routine injections could help fight cancer and autism (by removing metals in the brain) simply by providing the macrophages needed to do the job. Likewise, a compound that could inhibit high levels of nagalase, lowering it, could also increase macrophage numbers. (That's where I came up with the idea for NiMAF—nagalase inhibiting macrophage activating factor.)

A potential cure for cancer? Or autism? Why hasn't this been emblazoned across headlines, or given millions of dollars in research grants? Simple. It's a natural compound, and Big Pharma can't make money from it. Its promotion, in fact, could cost them billions of dollars . . . hundreds of billions, when you consider some rounds of chemotherapy cost $40,000 per dose or more. The UK company and Swiss manufacturing facility for GcMAF, as noted in the book, were indeed shut down under the premise they were making a harmful, illegal drug, even though it occurs naturally in the body. Fortunately, the Japanese continue to research it and make it, and an Israeli firm recently bought rights to the compound and continue that work. If the Israelis can create a totally effective disinfectant out of plain water (as they announced today, as I write this), I sure they'll soon have a blockbuster cure for cancer from this work. Why would they buy the rights if they didn't see potential here?

There was one other aspect of my research that I brought out in the story—the amount of effort made to discredit people whose work threatens the profits of Big Pharma and/or Big Ag. I saw this trend when researching the vaccine issue. I mentioned Dr. Stephanie Seneff, a recently retired senior research scientist at MIT, and her work on vaccines and glyphosate in the afterword of **The Khmer Connection**. In looking for information on her, I found no less than six websites, with very distinguished names, which seemed to have one purpose, smearing her reputation and denigrating her work. I found the same thing when researching Dr. Bradstreet and GcMAF for this book. True, there were also the "conspiracy theory" websites that seemed to promote GcMAF as a cure for every ailment under the sun. But for every one of those sites, I came across two or three calling the use of the compound a fraud, useless, or the work of quacks and snake oil salesmen. I also found it interesting, and concerning, that search engines delivered these latter sites on page one of your search while the others got buried further down the list. I guess we know who butters Google's and Microsoft's bread.

Another example of these tactics is the campaign against Dr. Judy Mikovits, a virologist you might have heard of during this c19 pandemic. Her story is both fascinating and troubling, but personally, I find her work compelling and valid. There are numerous websites out there working hard to dispel the truth she relays, to portray her work as irrelevant or even fraudulent, and to discredit her and smear her reputation. They all follow a set of bullet points so consistently that only the blind would be unable to see this as an orchestrated effort.

All in all, while I found the reports of these deaths interesting and having great potential for a story, the material on nagalase and GcMAF was truly intriguing. Will that research pan out as a "miracle cure" for cancer? I hope so, but only time will tell.

On a final note . . .

The book marks the end of the MedAir Series as I planned it. I hope you enjoyed the series and, while I don't expect you to agree with everything presented in the books, I also hope you found some of the topics thought-provoking. They were certainly fun to create stories around. To be honest, I'm not sure I agree with everything in some of the books. Characters take on a life of their own, and they often surprise me, too. Just when I think my story is heading one way, one of the characters decides, nope, I'm doing this instead. Or another one decides to say something you hadn't planned on her saying and it alters your story. Of course, whatever they say or do is completely in character for them. As the author, my job was to uncover that trait. If only they could write the story for me, too. Oh well, perhaps only other writers understand this.

So, where to from here? As I write this, I'm not sure. I have a couple of ideas for new series, but world events with the c19 pandemic have put those in a different perspective. Anyway, if you wish to keep abreast of my new endeavors, please sign up for my newsletter at my website.

God bless and stay safe . . . even if it's not six feet apart.

ABOUT THE AUTHOR

Braxton can't lay claim to wanting to be a writer all his life, although his mother and seventh grade English teacher were convinced he had what it would take. A bachelor's degree in Bio-Medical Engineering led to medical school and a residency in Emergency Medicine. He served for a decade in the U.S. Army Medical Corps with tours such as the Chief, Emergency Medical Services at Fort Campbell, KY, and as a research Flight Surgeon at Fort Rucker, AL. Who had time to write?

By the 1990s, as a civilian, his professional and family life had settled down, somewhat, and his mother once again took up her mantra, "Write a book. You're a good writer." In 1997, a Valentine's Day writing contest convinced him that maybe he could write fiction. He spent the next fifteen years learning the craft of writing.

Now, twenty-plus years after that first hesitant start, he has sixteen novels published, as well as non-fiction books and a children's book, and can't find enough time to write. As a Christian, he writes "true-life" Christian fiction (suspense and thrillers) that many call "cutting edge," as he's not afraid to take on such issues as human trafficking, racism, and more. His characters are real-life as well, with all the flaws and blemishes real people have. As such, his books are never likely to gain acceptance by the Christian Bookseller Association. But then, he never intended to tell stories just to the choir.

Books by Braxton DeGarmo:

Still Here Series:
The End Begins - 1
The Shaking - 2
The Beasts – 3
The Trumpets – 4
The Mark - 5

Non-fiction Study Guides:
Still Here! Surviving the End Times
Still Here! The Apocalypse is Now
Still Here! Countdown Revelation

MedAir Series:
Looks that Deceive – 1
Rescued and Remembered – 2
The Silenced Shooter – 3
Wrongfully Removed – 4
A Zealot's Destiny – 5
Kidnapped Nation - 6
The Khmer Connection - 7
Resurrected Trouble - 8

Seamus O'Connor Thrillers:
The Militant Genome
Ten Seconds 'Til

Other Books:
Indebted

<u>Children's Books:</u>
The Toucan Who Can Can-can